Bestselling author Susan Elizabeth Phillips has found fans all over the world with her warm and wonderful contemporary love stories that manage to touch hearts as well as funny bones.

She has won numerous awards for her writing, including the Romance Writers of America's Lifetime Achievement Award in 2006. In 2001 she was inducted into the Romance Writers of America Hall of Fame. She lives in the Chicago suburbs and has two grown sons.

For more information about Susan Elizabeth Phillips, visit her website: www.susanephillips.com

D0542422

And she was sick of it. Sick of being condescended to, sick of too many people getting the best of her, sick of feeling like a failure. If she backed down now, where would it end? She met those money green eyes and knew the time had come to tap deep into her Granger gene pool and play hardball.

"There was a dead body under my car." It was almost true. Mouse had been dead weight.

Unfortunately, the Python didn't look impressed, but then he'd probably been responsible for so many dead bodies that he'd grown bored with the whole concept of corpses. She took a deep breath. "All that red tape. It made me late. Otherwise, I would have been punctual. More than punctual. I'm very responsible. And professional." Just like that, she ran out of air. "Do you mind if I sit down?"

"Yes."

"Thank you." She sank into the nearest chair.

"You don't listen well, do you?"

"What?"

He gazed at her for a long moment before dismissing his receptionist. "Hold my calls for five minutes, Sylvia, unless it's Phoebe Calebow." The woman left, and he gave a resigned sigh. "I assume you're Molly's friend." Even his teeth were intimidating: strong, square, and very white.

"College buddies."

He tapped his fingers on the desk. "I don't mean to be rude, but you'll have to make this fast."

Who did he think he was kidding? He thrived on being rude. She imagined him in college dangling some poor computer geek out a dorm window or laughing in the face of a weeping, possibly pregnant, girlfriend. She sat straighter in the chair, trying to project confidence, "I'm Annabelle Granger from Perfect for You."

"The matchmaker." His fingers tapped away.

"I think of myself as a marriage facilitator."

"Do you now?" He drilled her again with those money-hard eyes. "Molly told me your company was called something like Myrna the Matchmaker."

Too late, she remembered that she'd overlooked that particular point in her conversations with Molly. "Marriages by Myrna was started by my grandmother in the seventies. She died three months ago. I've been modernizing since then, and I've also given the company a new name to reflect our philosophy of personalized service for the discriminating executive." *Forgive me, Nana, but it had to be done.*

"Exactly how large is this *company* of yours?"

One phone, one computer, Nana's dusty old file cabinet, and herself. "It's a manageable size. I believe the key to flexibility is staying lean." She hurried on. "Although this was my grandmother's company, I'm well qualified to take over." Her qualifications included a B.A. in theater from Northwestern that she'd never officially used, a short-lived stint at a dot-com that went bankrupt, partnership in a failed gift shop, and, more recently, a position at an employment agency that had fallen victim to the economy.

He leaned back in his chair. "I'm going to cut to the chase and save us both time. I'm already under contract with Portia Powers."

Annabelle was prepared for this. Portia Powers, of Power Matches, ran the most exclusive matchmaking firm in Chicago. Powers had built her business around serving the city's top executives, discriminating men too busy to find the trophy wives they desired and rich enough to pay her exorbitant fees. Powers was well connected, aggressive, and reputed to be ruthless, although that opinion came from her competitors and could be based on professional jealousy. Since Annabelle had never met her, she was withholding judgment.

"I know about your contract, but that doesn't mean you can't also use Perfect for You."

He glanced toward the flashing buttons on his phone, a

vertical slash of irritation bisecting his forehead. "Why would I bother?"

"Because I'll work harder for you than you can imagine. And because I'll introduce you to a group of women with brains and accomplishments, women who won't bore you after the newness wears off."

He lifted an eyebrow. "You know me that well, do you?"

"Mr. Champion"—*Surely that wasn't his real name?*—"you're obviously accustomed to being around beautiful women, and I'm certain you've had more opportunities than you can count to marry one of them. But you haven't. That tells me that you want something more multifaceted than simply a beautiful wife."

"And you don't think I can find that through Portia Powers."

She didn't believe in trashing the competition, even though she knew fashion models and socialites were exactly the sort of women Powers would be introducing him to. "I only know what Perfect for You has to offer, and I think you'll be impressed."

"I barely have time to deal with Power Matches, let alone adding anybody else to the mix." He uncoiled from his chair. He was tall, so it took a while.

She'd already noted the wide shoulders. Now she took in the rest of him. He had a lean-muscled athlete's body. If you liked your men swimming in testosterone and your sex life dangerous, he'd be number one on your automatic dial. Not that Annabelle was thinking about her sex life. Or at least she hadn't been until he stood up.

He stepped around the corner of his desk and extended his hand. "Good effort, Annabelle. Thanks for your time."

He wasn't going to give her a chance. He'd never intended to do more than go through the motions so he could pacify Molly. Annabelle thought of the energy she'd expended to get here, the twenty bucks it would cost to bail Sherman out of the parking garage, the effort she'd put into learning everything she could about the thirty-four-year-old overachieving country boy standing before her. She thought of her hopes for this meeting, her dreams of making Perfect for You unique and successful. Years of frustration boiled inside her, fueled by crappy judgment, bad luck, and missed opportunities.

Ignoring his hand, she shot to her feet. He was more than a head taller, and she had to tilt her neck to meet his eyes. "Do you still remember what it was like to be the underdog, Mr. Champion, or was that too long ago? Do you remember when you were so hungry to close a deal that you'd do anything to make it happen? You'd drive across the country without sleep just to meet a Heisman candidate for breakfast? You'd spend hours hanging around the parking lot outside the Bears' practice field, trying to catch the attention of one of the veterans? Or what about the time you hauled yourself out of bed with a raging fever so you could bail another agent's client out of jail?"

"You've done your homework." He cast an impatient eye at the blinking phone buttons, but he didn't throw her out, so she kept going.

"When you started in business, players like Kevin Tucker wouldn't give you the time of day. Do you remember what that was like? Do you remember when reporters weren't calling you for quotes? When you weren't on first-name terms with everybody in the NFL?"

"If I say I remember, will you leave?" He reached for the executive headset that lay next to the telephone console.

She curled her hands into fists, hoping she sounded passionate instead of loony. "All I want is a chance. The same chance you got when Kevin fired his old agent and put his faith in a fast-talking, sports-savvy guy who made his way from an armpit town in southern Illinois to Harvard Law."

He coiled back into his chair, one dark eyebrow angling upward.

"A blue-collar kid who played college football for the

scholarship, but counted on his brains to get ahead. A guy with nothing more than big dreams and a strong work ethic to recommend him. A guy who——"

"Stop before you make me cry," he said dryly.

"Just give me a chance. Let me set up one introduction. Just one. If you don't like the woman I choose, I'll never bother you again. Please. I'll do anything."

That caught his attention. He pushed aside the headset, tilted back in his chair, and rubbed the corner of his mouth with his thumb. "Anything?"

She didn't flinch from his assessing gaze. "Whatever it takes."

His eyes made a calculated journey from her rumpled russet hair to her mouth, down along her throat to her breasts. "Well . . . I haven't gotten laid for a while."

Her constricted throat muscles relaxed. The Python was toying with her. "Then why don't we do something about that on a permanent basis?" She grabbed her fake leather tote and whipped out the folder of material she'd finished preparing at five o'clock that morning. "This will tell you a little more about Perfect for You. I've included our mission statement, a timetable, and our fee structure."

Now that he'd had his fun, he was all business. "I'm interested in results, not mission statements."

"And results are what I'll give you."

"We'll see."

She drew an unsteady breath. "Does that mean . . ."

He picked up the telephone headset and hooked it around his neck, leaving the cord dangling down his shirtfront in a serpentine tail. "You've got one chance. Tomorrow night, hit me with your best candidate."

"Really!" Her knees went weak. "Yes . . . Fantastic! But . . . I need to clarify exactly what you're looking for."

"Let's see how good you are." He flipped up the headset.

"Nine o'clock at Sienna's on Clark Street. Make the introduction but don't plan on leaving. Stay at the table and keep the conversation going. I work hard at what I do. I don't intend to work hard at this, too."

"You want me to stay?"

"Twenty minutes exactly. Then take her away."

"Twenty minutes? Don't you think she'll find that a little . . . demeaning?"

"Not if she's the right woman." He gave her his country boy's smile. "And do you know why, Miss Granger? Because the right woman will be too damned *sweet* to take offense. Now get the hell out of here while you're ahead."

She did.

By the time she slipped into the McDonald's restroom, Annabelle had stopped shaking. She changed into capris, a tank, and sandals. Today's experience had justified her lifelong phobia of snakes. But other women wouldn't see Heath Champion like that. He was rich, successful, and gorgeous, which made him a dream match, assuming he didn't scare his dates to death, which was a distinct possibility. All she needed to do was find the right woman.

She pulled her wild hair back from her face with a pair of barrettes. She'd always worn her hair short to keep it under control, but her curly pixie had made her look more like a college freshman than a serious professional, so she was biting the bullet and letting it grow out. Not for the first time did she wish she had a spare five hundred dollars to have it professionally straightened, but she couldn't even pay her utility bill.

She stowed Nana's pearl earrings in an empty Altoids box and took a swig of lukewarm water from one of the bottles she'd dug out of Sherman's backseat. She kept the car well stocked: snacks and water bottles; a change of clothes; Tampax and toiletries; her new brochures and business cards; workout gear in case the mood struck her, which it hardly ever did; and, just recently, a box of condoms in the event one of her new clients developed a sudden, desperate need, although she couldn't see men like Ernie Marks or John Nager being that impulsive. Ernie was an elementary school principal, good with kids, but nervous with grown women, and John the hypochondriac wouldn't have sex without running his partner through the Mayo Clinic.

One thing was certain. She'd never have to pass out emergency condoms to Heath Champion. A man like that always came prepared.

She wrinkled her nose. Time to rise above her dislike. So what if he was overbearing and dictatorial, not to mention too rich and too successful for his own good? He was the key to her economic future. If she wanted Perfect for You to be successful as a specialized, high-end matchmaking service, she had to find him a wife. Once that happened, the word would spread, and Perfect for You would become the hottest service in Chicago. Which it definitely wasn't now, because inheriting her grandmother's business had also meant inheriting her remaining clients. Although Annabelle was doing her best to honor Nana's memory, it was time to move forward.

She squirted soap on her hands and considered her place in the business world. Matchmaking services came in mind-boggling varieties, and the rise of inexpensive online dating services had forced a lot of brick-and-mortar companies like hers to shut down while others scrambled to find a niche. They offered speed dates, lunch dates, and adventure outings. Some staged singles dinner parties, others served only graduates of prestigious universities or members of specific religious denominations. A lucky few, like Power Matches, were holding their own as "millionaire services," accepting only male clients and charging them staggering fees for introductions to beautiful women.

Annabelle intended to set Perfect for You apart from all of them. She wanted to make her name the first one that upscale Chicago singles, male and female, thought of when they were ready for a committed relationship and realized that old-fashioned personalized service was the best way to get it. She already had a few clients—Ernie and John her most recent—but not nearly enough to turn a profit. And until she'd established her credentials, she couldn't charge higher fees. Finding a match for Heath Champion would make those select clients and bigger fees possible. Except why hadn't he been able to find a wife on his own?

She'd have to speculate on that later because it was time to get to work. She'd intended to spend the afternoon patrolling Loop-area coffeehouses, fertile ground for finding both prospective clients and possible matches for the ones she had, but that was before she'd known how quickly she needed to come up with a candidate who'd knock Heath Champion off his feet.

Heat shimmered from the asphalt as she made her way across the parking lot to her car. The air smelled of fried food and exhaust. Chicago had declared its first Ozone Action Day of the summer, and it was barely June. She tossed the hopelessly wrinkled yellow suit in a trash bin so she never had to look at it again.

As she climbed inside the stifling car, her cell rang. She propped the door open to get some air. "This is Annabelle."

"Annabelle, I have wonderful news."

She sighed and dropped her forehead against the hot steering wheel. Just when she'd thought the worst of her day was behind her. "Hi, Mom."

"Your father talked to Doug an hour ago. Your brother is officially a vice president. They announced it this morning."

"Ohmygod! That's great!"

Annabelle exuded enthusiasm, bubbled over with bliss, radiated relish, but her mother's ESP kicked in anyway. "Of course it's great," she snapped. "Honestly, Annabelle, I don't know why you have to be so begrudging. Doug has worked hard to get where he is. No one handed him a thing."

Except adoring parents, a first-rate college education, and a generous postgraduation cash gift to tide him over.

Exactly the same things Annabelle had been given.

"Only thirty-five," Kate Granger went on, "and vice president of one of the most important accounting firms in Southern California."

"He's amazing." Annabelle lifted her forehead from the burning hot steering wheel before it branded her with the mark of Cain.

"Candace is giving a pool party next weekend to celebrate Doug's promotion. They're expecting Johnny Depp."

Somehow Annabelle couldn't imagine Johnny Depp showing up at one of her sister-in-law's pool parties, but she wasn't stupid enough to express her skepticism. "Wow! That's impressive."

"Candace is trying to decide between a South Pacific theme or going with the western thing."

"She entertains so well, I'm sure whatever she decides will be perfect."

Kate Granger's psychic abilities were worthy of her own 800 line. "Annabelle, you have to try harder to get over your hostility toward Candace. Nothing is more important than family. Doug adores her. We all do. And she's a wonderful mother."

Beads of perspiration were forming at her hairline. "How's Jamison's potty training coming along?" Not Jimmy, Jamie, Jim, or any variation thereof. Just Jamison.

"He's so bright. It's only a matter of time. I'll admit I was skeptical about all those learning tapes, but here he is, only three, and what an amazing vocabulary."

"Is he still saying *asshole*?"

"That's not funny."

In the old days, when her mother had a sense of humor, it would have been funny, but, at sixty-two, Kate Granger wasn't taking well to retirement. Even though she and Annabelle's father had bought a spectacular oceanside home in Naples, Florida, Kate missed St. Louis. Restless and bored, she'd turned all the energy she'd once directed toward a successful banking career onto her three grown children. Especially Annabelle, her only failure.

"How's Dad?" Annabelle said, hoping to postpone the inevitable.

"How do you think he is? He plays eighteen holes in the morning and watches the Golf Channel all afternoon. He hasn't opened a medical journal in months. You'd think after forty years as a surgeon, he'd be a little curious, but the only time he shows any interest in medicine is when he's talking to your brother."

On to chapter 2 in the amazing saga of *The Granger Wonder Twins,* this chapter featuring the dazzling life of that prominent St. Louis heart surgeon, Dr. Adam Granger. Annabelle reached for her water bottle, wishing she'd had the foresight to fill it with a nice peach-flavored vodka. "There's a lot of traffic, Mom. I don't think I can stay on my cell much longer."

"Your father's so proud of Adam. He just had another article published in the *Journal of Thoracic and Cardiovascular Surgery.* Yesterday, when we met the Andersons for Caribbean Night at the club, I had to kick him under the table to get him to shut up about it. The Andersons' children are a terrible disappointment."

Just like Annabelle.

Her mother swooped in for the kill. "Did you get the applications I sent?"

Since Kate had sent the applications FedEx and undoubtedly tracked their arrival on her computer, the question was rhetorical. Annabelle's head started to pound. "Mother . . ."

"You can't keep drifting like this—jobs, relationships—I won't even mention that awful business with Rob. We should have cut you off financially in college when you insisted on majoring in theater. And hasn't that been a gold mine of job opportunities? You're thirty-one. And you're a Granger. It's long past time you settled down and applied yourself."

Annabelle had told herself she wouldn't rise to the bait regardless of the provocation, but between Mouse, Heath Champion, the mention of Rob, and a fear that her mother was right, she broke. "Applying myself in the Granger family only means two things, right? Medicine or finance?"

"Don't start. You know exactly what I mean. That awful matchmaking business hasn't turned a profit in years. Mother only opened it so she could nib into other people's lives. You're not getting any younger, Annabelle, and I won't stand by and watch you waste more of your life when you could be going back to school and preparing for the future."

"I don't want—"

"You've always been good with numbers. You'd make a wonderful accountant. And I've told you we'll pay your tuition."

"I don't want to be an accountant! And I don't need my parents supporting me."

"Living in Nana's house doesn't count, then?"

It was a knockout punch. Annabelle's cheeks burned. Her mother had inherited Nana's Wicker Park house. Annabelle was living in it, ostensibly to keep it from being vandalized, but really because Kate didn't want Annabelle staying in some "dangerous urban neighborhood." Annabelle lashed back. "Fine! Do you want me to move out? Is that what you want?"

Oh, God, she sounded like she was fifteen again. Why did she always let Kate do this to her? Before she could retrench, her mother went on, speaking in the same overly patient maternal voice she'd used when Annabelle was eight and had announced that she'd run away from home if her brothers didn't stop calling her Spud.

"What I want you to do is go back to school and get your accounting degree. You know Doug will help you get a job."

"I'm not going to be an accountant!"

"Then what are you going to be, Annabelle? Tell me. Do you think I enjoy nagging? If you could just once explain it to me . . ."

"I want to run my own business," Annabelle said, sounding whiny even to herself.

"You tried that, remember? The gift shop? Then there was that awful dot-com. Doug and I both warned you. Then that tacky employment agency. You can't stick with anything."

"That's not fair! The employment agency folded."

"So did the gift shop and the dot-com. Did you ever think it's more than coincidental that whatever business you attach yourself to goes bottom up? It's because you deal in daydreams not in reality. Like that whole fantasy you had about being an actress."

Annabelle sank lower in her seat. She'd been a decent actress, taking solid supporting roles in a couple of university productions and directing some studio plays. But by her junior year, she'd realized theater wasn't her passion, just an escape into a world where she didn't have to be Doug and Adam Granger's incompetent little sister.

"And look what happened with Rob," Kate went on. "Of all the— Well, never mind about that. The point is, you've bought into this New Age nonsense that all you have to do is want something badly enough, and you can get it. But life doesn't work that way. It takes more than desire. Successful people are pragmatic. They make plans that are rooted in reality."

"I don't want to be an accountant!"

A long, disapproving silence followed this outburst. Annabelle knew exactly what her mother was thinking. That Annabelle was being Annabelle again, high-strung, overly dramatic, and impractical, the family's lone failure. But no one could upset her like her mother.

Except her father.

And her brothers.

"Stop screwing around with your life, Spud, and settle on something practical," Adam, the big-shot doctor, had written in his last e-mail, which he'd thoughtfully copied to the rest of the family plus two aunts and three cousins.

"You're thirty-one," Doug, the big-shot accountant, had noted on her recent birthday card. *"I was making two hundred grand a year when I was thirty-one."*

Her father, the ex-big-shot surgeon, took a different approach. *"Birdied number four yesterday. My putting game's finally come together. And, Annabelle . . . It's long past time you found yourself."*

Only Nana Myrna had offered support. *"You'll find yourself when the time is right, sweetheart."*

Annabelle missed Nana Myrna. She'd been a failure, too.

"The accounting field is wide open," her mother said. "It's growing by leaps and bounds."

"So is my business," Annabelle retorted in a mad act of self-destruction. "I've landed a very important client."

"Who?"

"You know I can't give you his name."

"Is he under seventy?"

Annabelle told herself not to take the bait, but there was a reason she'd earned her reputation as the family screwup. "He's thirty-four, a high-profile multimillionaire."

"Why on earth has he hired you?"

Annabelle gritted her teeth. "Because I'm the best, that's why."

"We'll see." Her mother's voice softened, driving the point of her maternal knife home. "I know I aggravate you, baby, but it's only because I love you, and I want you to fulfill your potential."

Annabelle sighed. "I know you do. I love you, too."

The conversation finally ground to an end. Annabelle stowed her cell, slammed the door, and jabbed the key into the

ignition. Maybe if there wasn't so much truth behind her
mother's words, they wouldn't sting so badly.

As she backed out of the parking place, she gazed into
the rearview mirror and uttered little Jamison's favorite word.
Twice.

Chapter Two

Dean Robillard entered the club like a frigging movie star, a linen sports coat draped over his shoulders, diamond studs glittering in his earlobes, and a pair of Oakleys shading his Malibu blue eyes. With his sun-bronzed skin, rakish stubble, and blond, surfer-boy hair all shiny and gel-rumpled, he was L.A.'s gift to the city of Chicago. Heath grinned, glad for the distraction. The boy had style, and the Windy City had missed him.

"Do you know Dean?" The blonde trying to drape herself over Heath's right arm watched as Robillard flashed the crowd his red carpet smile. She had to raise her voice to be heard over the crap music coming from the dance floor of Waterworks, the site of tonight's private party. Although the Sox were playing in Cleveland and the Bulls hadn't drifted back to town yet, the city's other teams were well represented at the party, mainly players from the Stars and Bears, but also most of the Cubs out-field a couple of Blackhawks, and a goalie for the Chicago Fire.

the blonde a condescending look. "Heath knows every football player in town, doncha, lover?" As she spoke, she surreptitiously slid her hand around his inner thigh, but Heath ignored his hard-on, just as he'd been ignoring all his hard-ons since he'd gone into training for marriage.

Going into training for marriage was hell.

He reminded himself that he'd gotten where he was by sticking to a plan, and being married before he hit thirty-five was the next step. His wife would be the ultimate symbol of his accomplishments, the final proof that he'd left the Beau Vista Trailer Park behind him forever.

"I know him," he said. He didn't add that he hoped to know him a whole lot better.

As Robillard moved deeper into the room, the Waterworks crowd parted, making way for the former Southern Cal player who'd been tapped by the Stars to take over as the team's first-string quarterback when Kevin Tucker hung up his spikes at the end of the upcoming season. A hint of mystery surrounded Dean Robillard's family background, and the quarterback typically gave vague answers when anyone tried to pry. Heath had done a little digging on his own and unearthed some interesting rumors, but he kept them to himself. The Zagorski brothers, slobbering over a pair of brunettes at the other end of the bar, finally became aware of what was happening and shot to attention. Within seconds, they were stumbling over all four of their Prada loafers trying to be the first to get to him.

Heath took another sip of beer and left them to it. The Zagorskis' interest in Robillard didn't surprise him. The quarterback's agent had died in a rock-climbing incident five days earlier, leaving him without representation, something the Zagor retaliated by taking Rocco Jefferson from them, which hadn't been all that hard to do. The Zagorskis were good at making big promises to their clients but not as good at delivering them.

Heath had no illusions about his profession. In the past ten years, the business of being a sports agent had grown more corrupt than a cockfight. In most states licensing was a joke. Any two-bit hustler could print up a business card, call himself a sports agent, and prey on gullible college athletes, especially the guys who'd grown up with nothing. These sleazeballs slipped them money under the table, promised cars and jewelry, hired hookers, and paid "bounties" to anybody who could deliver the signature of a high-profile athlete on a management contract. Some reputable agents had left the business because they didn't believe they could be both honest and competitive, but Heath wouldn't be driven away. Despite the sleaze factor, he loved what he did. He loved the adrenaline rush of signing a client, of making the deal. He loved seeing how far he could push the rules. That's what he did best. He pushed the rules . . . but he didn't break them. And he never cheated a client.

He watched Robillard bend his head to hear what the Zagorski boys were saying. Heath wasn't worried. Robillard might be an L.A. glamour boy, but he wasn't stupid. He knew every agent in the country was after him, and he wouldn't be making any decisions tonight.

A sex kitten Heath had slept with a couple of times in his pre-training camp days zeroed in on him, hair swaying, nipples puckered like overripe cherries beneath her slinky top. "I'm taking a poll. If you could only have one kind of sex for the rest of your life, what would it be? So far the vote's running three to one in favor of oral."

"How about I just vote for heterosexual."

All three of the women laughed uproariously, as if they'd never heard anything funnier. He was the king of stand-up comics, all right.

The party began to heat up, and a few of the women on the

dance floor started running through the jets of water that gave
Waterworks its name. Their clothes melted to their bodies, out-
lining every curve and hollow. He'd loved the club scene when
he'd first come to town, the music and booze, the beautiful
women and free sex, but by the time he'd hit thirty, he'd grown
jaded. Still, making the scene, bullshit or not, was an important
part of his business, and he couldn't remember the last time
he'd been in bed alone at a decent hour.

"Heath, my man."

He grinned as Sean Palmer approached. The Chicago Bears
rookie was a great-looking kid, tall and muscular with a square
jaw and mischievous brown eyes. The two of them executed
one of a dozen or so tricky handshakes Heath had mastered over
the years.

"How's the Python doin' tonight?" Sean asked.

"No complaints." Heath had worked hard to recruit the
Ohio State fullback, and when Sean had gone ninth to the
Bears in the first round of last April's draft, it had been one of
those perfect moments that made up for all the crap. Sean was
a hard worker, and he came from a great family. Heath intended
to do everything he could to keep him out of trouble.

He signaled the women that he wanted some privacy, and
Sean looked only momentarily disappointed as they faded away.
Like everyone else in the club, he wanted to talk about Robillard. "Why aren't you over there kissing Dean's skinny white
ass like everybody else?"

"I do my ass kissing in private."

"Robillard's one smart dude. He's gonna take his time
findin' a new agent."

"Can't blame him. He's got a great future."

"You want me to put in a word with him?"

"Sure." Heath hid a grin. Robillard wouldn't give a damn
about the recommendation of a rookie. The only person's opinion Dean Robillard might care about would be Kevin Tucker's,

and even that wasn't certain. Dean alternated between idolizing Kevin and resenting him because Kevin had stayed healthy last season, which kept Dean on the bench for one more year.

"So what's this I been hearing about you givin' up women? All the ladies tonight are talkin' about it. They're feeling neglected, you know what I'm sayin'?"

No use trying to explain to a twenty-two-year-old kid with freshly minted hundred-dollar bills stuffed into every pocket that the chase had gotten old. "I've been busy."

"Too busy for *pussy*?"

Sean looked so honestly dumbfounded that Heath laughed. And, face it, the kid had a point. Everywhere Heath looked, ripe breasts spilled from plunging necklines, and tiny skirts cupped soft, sweet asses. But he wanted more than sex. He wanted the ultimate prize. Someone polished, beautiful, and sweet. He imagined his silver spoon wife, lithe and lovely, the calm in the center of his storm. She'd always have his back, keep his rough edges smoothed down. She'd be the woman who'd finally make him feel as though he'd achieved everything he'd dreamed of. Except playing for the Dallas Cowboys.

He smiled at his boyhood fantasy. That one he'd had to let go of, right along with his teenage plan to nail a different porn star every night. He'd gone to the University of Illinois on a football scholarship and played first team all four years. But as a senior, he'd accepted the fact that he'd never be good enough to be more than a third-stringer for the pros. Even then he'd known he couldn't dedicate his life to being anything but the best, so he'd turned his dreams in another direction. He'd gotten top marks on his LSATs, and an influential U of I alum had pulled the political strings that got him into Harvard. Heath had learned to utilize his brains, his street smarts, and his ability to camouflage himself so that he could fit in anywhere: a tenement, a locker room, the deck of a private yacht.

Although he made no secret of his country boy roots—flaunted them when he needed to—he didn't let anybody see how much dirt still clung to those roots. He wore the best clothes, drove the best cars, lived at the best address. He knew wine, even if he seldom drank it; understood the fine arts academically, if not aesthetically; and didn't need a reference book to identify a fish fork.

"I know what your problem is," Sean said, mischief in his eyes. "Chicks here don't have enough class for Mister Ivy League. You rich guys like your ladies with big fancy monograms tattooed on their asses."

"Yeah, so they match up with that big, fancy Harvard *H* I've got tattooed on mine."

Sean started laughing, and the women drifted back to see what was so funny. A few years ago, Heath would have enjoyed their predatory sexuality. From the time he was a kid, women had been attracted to him. When he was thirteen, he'd been worked over by one of his father's girlfriends. Now he knew it had been sexual abuse, but at the time he hadn't understood, and he'd been so panicky and guilt stricken that he'd thrown up for fear of the old man finding out. One more sordid episode in a childhood filled with them.

He'd put most of the remnants of that childhood behind him, and the rest would disappear when he found the right woman. Or when Portia Powers found her for him. After spending the past year looking on his own, he'd realized the woman of his dreams wouldn't be hanging out in the clubs and sports bars where he spent his so-called leisure time. Still he'd never have thought of hiring a matchmaker if he hadn't seen a glowing article about Powers in *Chicago* magazine. Her impressive connections and formidable track record were exactly what he needed.

Annabelle Granger, on the other hand, wasn't. As a professional hard-ass, he didn't usually let himself get suckered in, but all that desperate earnestness had gotten to him. He remembered her awful yellow suit, her big honey-colored eyes, those flushed round cheeks, and flyaway red hair. She'd looked as though she'd tumbled out of Santa's bag after a bad sleigh ride.

He should have kept his mouth shut about his wife hunt around Kevin, but how could he have known his star client's wife, Molly, would have a friend in the matchmaking business? As soon as Heath sat through the introduction he'd promised, Annabelle Granger and her screwball operation were history.

A little after one in the morning, Dean Robillard finally made his way to Heath's side. Despite the club's dim lighting, the boy still wore his Oakleys, but he'd ditched his sports coat, and his sleeveless white silk T-shirt showed off the Holy Grail of football shoulders—big, strong, and unmarred by arthroscopic surgery. Dean propped one hip on the empty bar stool that opened up next to Heath. As he extended his leg for balance, he revealed a tan leather cap-toe boot Heath had heard one of the women say was from Dolce & Gabbana.

"Okay, Champion, your turn to suck up."

Heath set his elbow on the bar. "My condolences on your loss. McGruder was a good agent."

"He hated your guts."

"I hated his, too, but he was still a good agent, and there aren't a whole lot of us left." He studied the quarterback more closely. "Shit, Robillard, you been bleaching your hair?"

"Highlights. You like 'em?"

"If you were any prettier, I'd want to date you."

Robillard grinned. "You'd have to stand in line."

Both of them knew they weren't talking about dating.

"I like you, Champion," Robillard said, "so I'm going to tell you up front. You're out of the running. I'd be stupid to sign with the agent who's at the top of Phoebe Calebow's shit list."

"The only reason I'm on that list is because Phoebe's

cheap." Not entirely true, but this wasn't the time to go into the complexities of his relationship with the owner of the Chicago Stars. "Phoebe doesn't like the fact that I won't roll over and play dead for her like everybody else. Why don't you ask Kevin if he has any complaints?"

"Yeah, well, Kevin happens to be married to Phoebe's sister and I don't, so the situation isn't exactly the same. The truth is, I already piss Mrs. Calebow off without even trying, and I'm not going to make it worse by hiring you."

Once again, Heath's dysfunctional relationship with Phoebe Calebow was getting in the way of what he wanted. No matter how hard he tried to fix things with her, his early mistakes kept coming back to bite him in the ass. He never let the pressure show and only shrugged. "You gotta do what you gotta do."

"You guys are all bloodsuckers," Dean said bitterly. "You take two, three percent off the top, and for doing what? For pushing a few papers around. Big fucking deal. How many two-a-days have you sweated through?"

"Not as many as you, that's for damn sure. I was too busy getting As in my classes on contract law."

Robillard smiled.

Heath smiled back. "And just so we're straight . . . When it comes to those big endorsements I've been landing for my clients, I take a hell of a lot more than three percent off the top."

Robillard didn't blink. "The Zagorskis are guaranteeing me Nike. Can you do that?"

"I never guarantee what I don't have in my pocket." He took a sip of beer. "I don't bullshit my clients, at least about anything important. I also don't steal from them, lie to them, or disrespect them behind their backs. There's no agent in the business who works harder than I do. Not a one. And that's all I've got to offer." He rose, pulled out his money clip, and slapped a hundred-dollar bill on the bar. "If you want to talk about it, you know where to find me."

• • •

W hen Heath got home that night, he pulled the smudged invitation from his dresser drawer. He kept it lying around as a reminder of the gut-wrenching pain he'd felt when he'd first opened it. He'd been twenty-three.

You are cordially invited to attend the marriage of
JULIE AMES SHELTON
and
HEATH D. CAMPIONE
The Silver Anniversary Celebration of
VICTORIA AND DOUGLAS PIERCE SHELTON III
and
The Golden Anniversary Celebration of
MILDRED AND DOUGLAS PIERCE SHELTON II

Valentine's Day
6:00 P.M.
The Manor
East Hampton, New York

The wedding planner had sent him the invitation by mistake, not realizing he was the groom, which spoke volumes all by itself. For the first time he'd discovered his marriage to Julie was just one cog of a well-oiled family production. All his securities came crashing in. He'd known it was too good to be true, Julie Shelton falling in love with a guy who was grubbing his way through law school by cleaning out septic tanks.

"*I don't see why you're so upset about this,*" Julie had said when he'd confronted her. "*The dates just worked out that way. You should be happy we're keeping up the tradition. Getting married on Valentine's Day is good luck in my family.*"

"This isn't just any Valentine's Day," he retorted. *"Golden anniversary, silver anniversary . . . What would you have done for a husband if I hadn't come along on schedule?"*

"But you did, so I don't see the problem."

He'd pleaded with her to change the date, but she'd refused. *"If you love me, you'll do this my way,"* she'd said.

He had loved her, but after a week of sleepless nights, he'd realized she only loved him as a convenience.

The wedding had gone on with one of Julie's childhood friends standing in as the third-generation Valentine's Day groom. It had taken Heath months to recover. Two years later, the couple had divorced, putting a permanent end to Shelton family tradition, but he'd felt no satisfaction.

Julie wasn't the first person he'd given his heart to. As a kid, he'd given it away to everybody, beginning with his drunken father and continuing through the never-ending stream of transient women the old man had brought home. As each woman entered that beat-up trailer, Heath had prayed she'd be the one who'd make up for his mother's death.

When the women didn't work out—and they never did— he'd given his love to the stray dogs that ended up as roadkill on the nearby highway, to the old biddy in the next trailer who screamed at him if his ball landed near her tractor tire garden, to classroom teachers who had children of their own and didn't want another. But it had taken his experience with Julie before he'd finally learned the lesson he never let himself forget. His emotional survival depended on not falling in love.

Someday he hoped that would change. He'd love his kids, that was for damn sure. He'd never let them grow up as he had. As for his wife . . . That would take a while. But once he was sure she'd stick, he'd give it a try. For now, he intended to treat his search for her like he'd treat any other part of his business, which was why he'd hired the best matchmaker in the city. And why he had to get rid of Annabelle Granger . . .

• • •

L ess than twenty-four hours later, Heath entered Sienna's, his favorite restaurant, to do the job. Annabelle had *screwup* stamped all over her, and this was a big waste of time he didn't have to spare. As he headed to his regular table in the far corner of the well-lit bar, he called out a greeting in Italian to Carlo, the owner. Heath had learned the language in college instead of from his Italian father, who'd only spoken Drunk. The old man had died from a combination of emphysema and cirrhosis of the liver when Heath was twenty. He had yet to shed a tear.

He made a quick call to Caleb Crenshaw, the Stars' running back, and another to Phil Tyree in New Orleans. The alarm on his watch buzzed just as he finished. Nine o'clock. He looked up, and sure enough, Annabelle Granger was heading toward him. But it was the blond knockout at her side who claimed his attention. Whoa . . . Where had this one come from? Her short, straight hair fell in a trendy cut to her jaw. She had perfectly balanced features and a long, leggy figure. So, Tinker Bell hadn't been all talk.

His matchmaker was half a head shorter than the woman she'd brought to meet him. Her tangle of reddish gold hair gleamed around her small head. The short white jacket she wore with a lime green sundress was a definite improvement over yesterday's ensemble, but she still looked like a scatter-brained tree fairy. He rose as she performed the introductions.

"Gwen, I'd like you to meet Heath Champion. Heath, this is Gwen Phelps."

Gwen Phelps looked him over with a pair of intelligent brown eyes that tilted attractively down at the corners. "A pleasure," she said in a deep, low voice. "Annabelle's told me all about you."

"I'm glad to hear it. That means we can talk about you, which I can see right away will be a lot more interesting." It was a corny line, and he thought he heard a snort, but when he shot a quick glance at Annabelle, he saw in her expression only eagerness to please.

"Somehow I doubt that." Gwen slipped gracefully into the chair he held out for her. The woman oozed class. Annabelle tugged on the opposite chair, but it caught on the table leg. Concealing his annoyance, he reached over to free it. She was a walking disaster, and he regretted ordering her to sit with them, but it had seemed like a good idea at the time. When he'd decided to hire a matchmaker, he'd also promised he'd make the process efficient. He'd already sat through a couple of Power Matches introductions. Even before the drinks had arrived, he'd known neither woman was right for him, but he'd wasted a couple of hours getting rid of them. This one, however, showed definite promise.

Ramon came over from the bar to take their orders. Gwen asked for club soda, Annabelle for something terrifying called a green phantom. She regarded him with the bright, too-eager expression of a dog owner waiting for her prized pooch to perform his tricks. So much for expecting her to lead the conversation. "Are you a native Chicagoan, Gwen?" he asked.

"I grew up in Rockford, but I've been in the city for years. Bucktown."

Bucktown was a near north neighborhood popular with the younger crowd. He'd lived there for a while himself, and they exchanged general Bucktown chat, which was exactly the sort of getting nowhere bullshit he'd wanted to avoid. He shot Miss Matchmaker a look. She wasn't stupid, and she took the hint.

"You'll be interested to know that Gwen's a psychologist. She's one of the country's leading authorities on sex surrogates."

That got his attention. He suppressed every locker room comment that sprang into his head. "An unusual field of study."

"Sex surrogacy is very misunderstood," the beautiful psychologist replied. "When it's properly used, it can be a wonderful therapeutic tool. I've made it my mission to bring it out from the shadows."

She began giving him an overview of her profession. She was good-humored, sharp, and sexy. God, was she sexy. He'd way underestimated Annabelle Granger's matchmaking skills. Just as he began to relax into the conversation, however, Annabelle glanced at her watch and rose. "Time's up," she announced, in a chipper voice that set his teeth on edge.

The sexy psychologist came to her feet with a smile. "It's been lovely meeting you, Heath."

"My pleasure." Since he was the one who'd set the time limit, he concealed his irritation. He'd never expected a goof-ball like Annabelle to produce a stunner like this first time up at bat. Gwen gave Annabelle a quick hug, smiled at him again, and made her way out of the restaurant. Annabelle settled back into her chair, took a sip from her green phantom, then dug into her tote, this one turquoise blue with sequined palm trees. Seconds later, he was gazing at a contract identical to the one she'd left on his desk yesterday.

"I guarantee a minimum of two introductions a month." A springy lock of red gold hair fell over her forehead. "I charge t-ten thousand dollars for six months." He didn't miss either the stammer or the high color rising in those chipmunk cheeks. Tinker Bell was going for the gusto. "Normally, the fee would include a session with an image consultant, but . . ." Her gaze took in his haircut, touched up every two weeks at eighty bucks a pop, his black Versace dress shirt, and pale gray Joseph Abboud slacks. "I, uh, think we can dispense with that."

Damn right they could. Heath had crap taste when it came to clothes, but image was everything in his profession, and just because he didn't give a damn what he wore didn't mean his clients felt the same way. A very gay, very discriminating wardrobe consultant purchased everything Heath wore, and he'd forbidden Heath to match up any shirts, pants, or ties that weren't already coordinated on the charts hanging in his closet.

"Ten thousand is steep for someone with no track record," he said.

"Like you, I believe in charging what I'm worth." Her eyes hung up on his mouth.

He suppressed a smile. Tinker Bell needed to practice her poker face. "I've already paid through the nose for my contract with Portia Powers."

The small cupid's bow at the center of her top lip grew a little pale, but she had game. "And how many women has she introduced you to like Gwen?"

She had him there, and this time he didn't hide his smile. Instead, he picked up the contract and started to read. The ten thousand dollars was a bluff, nothing more than wishful thinking on her part. Still, there was Gwen Phelps. He scanned the two pages. He could lowball her, but how far did he want to go? The art of the deal required that everybody come out feeling like a winner. Otherwise, resentment got in the way of performance.

He pulled out his Mont Blanc and began making modifications, scratching through a clause here and there, amending another, adding one of his own. Finally, he slid the papers back to her. "Five thousand up front. I only fork over the balance if you've found the right woman."

The flecks of gold in her brown eyes flashed like the glitter embedded in a kid's yo-yo. "That's unacceptable. You're practically asking me to work for free."

"Five thousand dollars isn't exactly chicken feed. You have no track record with someone like me."

"And yet I brought you Gwen."

"How do I know she's not all you've got? There's a big difference between talking a good game and playing one." He flicked his thumb toward the contract. "The ball's yours."

She snatched up the pages and glowered as she scanned the changes he'd made, but finally she signed, as he'd known she would. He did the same, then kicked back in his chair and studied her. "Hand over Gwen Phelps's phone number. I'll set up the next date myself."

She tugged on her bottom lip, revealing small, white teeth.

"I have to check with her first. It's an agreement I make with all the women I introduce."

"Sensible. But I'm not too worried."

As she reached for her cell, he glanced at his watch. He was tired. He'd spent the day in Cleveland, and he still needed to make a quick stop at Waterworks to see if he could pick up any new scuttlebutt on Dean Robillard. Tomorrow he was scheduled from breakfast straight through until midnight. Friday, he had an early morning flight to Phoenix and, the following week, trips to Tampa and Baltimore. If he had a wife, his overnight case would be packed when he needed it, and he'd be able to find something other than beer in the refrigerator after a late-night flight. He'd also have somebody to talk over his day with, a chance to let down his guard without worrying about the country twang that crept into his speech when he was tired, or inadvertently dropping an elbow on the table while he was eating a sandwich, or any of the other crap he always had to be aware of. Most of all, he'd have somebody who'd *stick*.

"Gwen, it's Annabelle. Thanks again for agreeing to meet Heath on such *short* notice." She shot him a pointed look. Tinker Bell was chastising him. "He's asked for your phone number. I happen to know he's planning a dinner date at"—another pointed look tossed his way—"Charlie Trotter's."

He wanted to laugh, but he deadpanned her so she didn't get too full of herself.

She paused, listened, and nodded. He pulled out his cell and paged through the list of calls that had come in while he was talking to Gwen. It wasn't quite nine o'clock in Denver. He still had time to check in with Jamal to see how his hamstring was coming along.

"Yes," she said. "Yes, I'll pass it on. Thanks." She flipped her cell closed, slipped it into her tote, then gazed at him across the table. "Gwen liked you. But only as a friend."

For one of the few times in his life, he was struck speechless.

"I was afraid that might happen," she said briskly. "The

twenty-minute time frame didn't exactly give you a chance to put your best foot forward."

He stared at her, not quite able to believe what he was hearing.

"Gwen asked me to pass on her best wishes. She thinks you're very good-looking, and she's sure you won't have any trouble finding someone more suitable."

Gwen Phelps had rejected him?

"We might . . . ," Annabelle said thoughtfully, ". . . need to start looking a little lower on the female totem pole."

Chapter Three

The midnight blue Jaguar crept around the corner of Hoyne onto the narrow Wicker Park street. The woman behind the wheel peered at the house numbers through a pair of rimless Chanel sunglasses with tiny interlocking rhinestone Cs at the hinges. Strictly speaking, they were fashion sunglasses, which meant they barely had enough UV protection for even a cloudy day, but they looked incredible against her pale skin and cloud of dark hair, and Portia Powers didn't believe in sacrificing style for function. Not even her approaching birthday—her thirty-seventh to close acquaintances, her forty second as her mother remembered it—would let her consider trading in her Christian Louboutin stilettos for Easy Spirits. Her ex-husband had said that Portia's inky hair, winter white complexion, startling blue eyes, and whippet-thin body made her look like Snow White after a few months on the South Beach diet.

She slowed as she found what she was looking for on the tree-lined street. She'd never seen a more likely candidate for a teardown than this tiny frame house, which was painted a fading robin's egg blue with peeling periwinkle trim. A blistered black wrought-iron fence surrounded a patch of yard the size of her bathroom. The place looked like a gardening shed for one of the elegant two-story brick rehabs rising on each side of it. How had it managed to escape the wrecking ball that had already claimed most of Wicker Park's shabbier homes?

Portia had spotted the Perfect for You folder on Heath Champion's desk when she'd stopped by yesterday, and her formidable competitive instincts had gone into hyperdrive. In the past year, she'd lost two big clients to new agencies, and one husband to a twenty-three-year-old event planner. Failure had a smell to it, and she'd work herself to the bone before she ever let that smell cling to her. A few hours' research had unearthed the information that Perfect for You was simply a new name for Marriages by Myrna, a small-time operation that had been little more than a curiosity. The granddaughter had taken it over after Myrna Reichman's death. A little more digging had revealed that this same granddaughter had gone to college with Kevin Tucker's wife, Molly. Portia had let herself relax a little. Naturally Heath would feel obligated to give the girl a courtesy interview if his client's wife requested it, but he was too demanding to work with an amateur. She'd gone to bed with an easy mind . . . and had a painfully erotic dream about her prized client. Not that she'd ever consider acting on it. A fling with Champion would be exciting, but she never let her personal life interfere with business.

Unfortunately, this morning's phone call had reignited her anxiety. Ramon, the bartender at Sienna's, was one of many well-placed service people who received lavish gifts from her in return for useful information, and he'd reported that a matchmaker named Annabelle had shown up last night with a beautiful woman in tow whom she'd introduced to Heath. Portia had set off for Wicker Park as soon as she could get away. She needed to see how big a threat the woman posed, but this derelict house proved that Perfect for You was a business only in Ms. Granger's imagination. Champion was simply making nice to please Kevin Tucker's wife.

Feeling marginally reassured, she headed south toward the Loop for her monthly dermabrasion. She spent vast amounts of money keeping her complexion unlined and her body reed thin. Age might add to a man's power, but it stole from a woman's, and an hour later, makeup reapplied, complexion glowing, she entered the Power Matches offices on the first floor of a white-painted brick Victorian not far from the Newberry Library.

Inez, her receptionist-secretary, looked guilty and quickly got off the phone. More child care problems. How could women ever get ahead when the burden of child care always fell on them? Portia took in the calm elegance of the open office area with its cool green walls and low, Asian-inspired black couches. Her three assistants were at their desks, which were set apart with stylish parchment screens set in black lacquer frames. Ranging in age from twenty-two to twenty-nine, her assistants scouted the city's trendiest clubs and handled all the initial interviews. Portia had hired them for their connections, brains, and looks. They were required to wear black on the job: simple, elegant dresses; slacks with classic tops; and well-fitting jackets. She had more latitude, and today she'd chosen pearl gray Ralph Lauren: a summer-weight cardigan, tailored blouse, pencil skirt, and pearls, all set off with lavender stilettos that had a girly bow across the vamp.

There were no clients in the office, so she made the dreaded announcement. "It's that day of the week, everybody. Chop, chop. Let's get the agony over with."

SuSu Kaplan groaned. "I'm getting my period."

"You were getting your period last week," Portia replied. "No excuses." Only her controller and the computer guru who ran the Power Matches Web site were exempt from this weekly ritual, since they didn't deal directly with clients. Besides, they were men, and didn't that just say it all?

Portia walked toward her private office. "You, too, Inez."

"I'm the receptionist," Inez protested. "I don't have to be in the clubs at night."

Portia ignored her. They all wanted the prestige of working for Power Matches, but nobody wanted the hard work and the discipline that went along with it. *Discipline turns the dream into reality.* How many times had she said those words to the women she mentored at the Community Small Business Initiative? And how many times had they chosen to ignore her?

Kiki Ono had a chipper smile on her face, and Briana didn't seem too worried, but if SuSu Kaplan kept frowning that way she'd need Botox before she hit thirty. Inside Portia's office, half a dozen curry-colored ceramic pieces provided the only decorative accessories in a space dominated by glass, straight lines, and hard surfaces. Her personal preferences ran toward softer, more feminine interiors, but she believed a woman's office should project authority. Men could surround themselves with all the bowling trophies and family photos they wanted, but female executives didn't have that luxury.

As she made her way into her private bathroom, she heard the rustle of shoes and jackets being removed, the chink of discarded belts and bracelets. She slid the glass-and-chrome precision scale from beneath the pedestal sink with the pointed toe of her lavender Christian Louboutins, then picked it up and carried it out to the black marble office floor. By the time she extracted the chart she needed from her desk, SuSu had stripped down to a navy bra and panty set.

"Who's brave enough to go first?"

"I will." Briana Olsen, a willowy Scandinavian beauty, mounted the scale.

"One hundred and twenty." Portia noted the weight on her chart. "You've picked up a pound since last month, but with your height, that's not a problem. Your manicure, though . . ." She gestured toward the chipped mocha polish on Briana's index finger. "Honestly, Briana, how many times do I have to tell you? Appearances are everything. Get it fixed. Inez, you're next."

Inez's extra pounds were a foregone conclusion, but she had fabulous skin, a marvelous touch with makeup, and a way of putting clients at ease. Besides, the reception desk was high enough to cover the worst of her chub. "If you ever want to get another husband . . ."

"I know, I know," Inez said. "One of these days I'll get serious."

Kiki, always a team player, took the heat off her. "My turn," she chirped. Flipping her silky black hair over one shoulder, she stepped on the scale.

"One hundred and two pounds," Portia noted. "Excellent."

"It's a lot easier when you're Asian," SuSu said sullenly. "Asian women are small-boned. I'm Jewish."

As she reminded them at every weigh-in. But SuSu had a degree from Brown and connections to some of the wealthiest families on the North Shore. With her great hair—incredible caramel highlights—and her infallible eye for fashion, she radiated a Jennifer Aniston kind of sex appeal. Unfortunately, she didn't have Aniston's body. Portia gestured toward the scale. "Let's put you out of your misery."

SuSu balked. "I want to go on record. I find this demeaning and insulting."

"Possibly. But it's also for your own good, so up you go."

She reluctantly climbed on. Portia noted the number with a sigh. "One hundred and twenty-seven pounds." Unlike Inez, SuSu had no desk to hide behind. She was out in the clubs representing Power Matches. "Everybody else, back to work. SuSu, we have to talk."

SuSu hooked a lock of that gleaming hair behind her ear and looked sullen. Kiki shot her a sympathetic glance then filed out with the others. SuSu picked up her black Banana Republic sheath and held it in front of her. "This is discriminatory and illegal."

"My lawyer disagrees, and the employment contract you signed is clear. We talked about this before I hired you, remember? Personal appearance is paramount in this business, and I put my money where my standards are. No one offers the bonuses and benefits that I do. In my mind that means I deserve to be a little demanding."

"But I'm the best associate you have. I want to be judged by my work, not by how much I weigh."

"Then grow a penis." SuSu still didn't understand that Portia had their best interests at heart. "Did you even try?"

"Yes, but—"

"How tall are you?" Portia knew the answer, but she wanted SuSu to come to terms with this herself.

"Five feet four."

"Five feet four and one hundred twenty-seven pounds." She leaned against the hard glass ridge of her desktop. "I'm four inches taller. Let's see how much I weigh." Ignoring the resentment in SuSu's eyes, she slipped off her shoes and sweater, dropped the pearls on her desk, and stepped on the scale. "One hundred and twenty-two. I'm up a bit. Oh, well. No carbs for me tonight." She stepped back into her shoes. "Do you see how easy it is? If I don't like what I see on the scale, I cut back."

SuSu collapsed on the couch, her eyes filling with tears. "I'm not you."

Women who cried on the job reinforced every negative stereotype about females and the workplace, but SuSu hadn't developed the hard shell of experience, and Portia knelt at her side, trying to make her understand. "You're a terrific worker, SuSu, and you have a great future. Don't let obesity stand in your way. Studies show that overweight women receive fewer job promotions and make less money. It's one more way the business world is stacked against us. But at least our weight is something we can control."

SuSu regarded her mulishly. "One twenty-seven isn't obese."

"No, but it's not perfect, is it? And perfection is what we all need to strive for. Now go into my bathroom and take a few minutes to pull yourself together. Then get back to work."

"No!" Red-faced, SuSu leaped to her feet. "No! I do a good job for you, and I don't have to put up with this. I'm quitting."

"Now, SuSu—"

"I hate working for you! Nobody can ever live up to your expectations. Well, I don't care anymore. You might be rich and successful, but you don't have a life. Everybody knows that, and I feel sorry for you."

The words stung, but Portia didn't flinch. "I have a very good life," she said coolly. "And I won't apologize for demanding excellence. Obviously, you're not prepared to give it, so clear out your desk." She walked to the door and held it open.

SuSu was crying and furious, but she didn't have the nerve to say more. Clutching her dress in front of her, she rushed from the office. Portia closed the door carefully, making sure it didn't slam, then leaned back and shut her eyes. SuSu's angry words had struck home. By the age of forty-two, Portia had expected to have everything she wanted, but despite all the money she'd made and the accolades she'd received, the pride of accomplishment eluded her. She had dozens of friends, but no soul-deep friendships, and she had a failed marriage. How could that have happened when she'd waited so long and chosen so carefully?

Carleton had been her perfect match—a power match—urbane, wealthy, and successful. They'd been one of Chicago's A-list couples, invited to all the best parties, chairing an important benefit. The marriage should have worked, but it had barely lasted a year. Portia would never forget what he'd said when he'd left. "I'm exhausted, Portia . . . I'm too worried about having my dick cut off to get a good night's sleep."

Too bad she hadn't done just that because, three weeks later, he'd moved in with a bubble-headed twenty-three-year-old event planner who had breast implants and a giggle.

Portia splashed half a bottle of Pellegrino into one of the Villeroy & Boch goblets Inez kept by her desk. Maybe someday SuSu would understand what a mistake she'd made by not taking advantage of Portia's willingness to mentor her. Or maybe not. Portia wasn't exactly drowning in thank-you notes from either former employees or the women she tried to mentor.

Heath Champion's file lay on her desk, and she sat down to study it. But as she gazed at the folder, she saw the gold teapot wallpaper in the kitchen of the Terre Haute house where she'd grown up. Her working-class parents had been content with their lives—the discount store clothes, the imitation wood end tables, the mass-produced oil paintings bought in a famous artists' sale at the Holiday Inn. But Portia had always craved more. She'd used her allowance to buy magazines like *Vogue* and *Town & Country*. She'd posted photographs of beautiful houses and elegant furniture on her bedroom bulletin board. In junior high school, she'd terrified her parents with the crying jags she'd thrown if she didn't get an A on a test. Throughout her childhood, she'd ignored the fact that she'd inherited her father's eyes and coloring and pretended she was a victim of one of those freakish hospital mix-ups.

Straightening in her chair, she took another sip of Pellegrino and turned her attention back to where it belonged, finding Heath Champion the perfect wife. She might have lost two prominent clients and an equally prominent husband, but she wouldn't fail again. Nothing and no one would keep her from making this match.

Chapter Four

The deep male voice rumbled its displeasure into the phone. "I've got a call coming in. You have thirty seconds."

"Not enough time," Annabelle replied. "We need to sit down together so I can get a more specific idea of what you're looking for." She didn't waste her breath asking him to complete the questionnaire she'd spent so many hours perfecting. The only way she'd get the information she needed was to pull it out of him.

"Let's put it this way," he retorted. "My future wife's idea of a good time is sitting in Soldier Field in January with the wind blowing in off the lake at thirty knots. She can feed half a dozen college athletes a spaghetti dinner with no warning and play eighteen holes of golf from the men's tees without embarrassing herself. She's sexy as hell, knows how to dress, and thinks fart jokes are funny. Anything else?"

"It's just so darned hard to find women who've had lobotomies these days. Still, if that's what you want . . ."

A muffled snort. Whether it was displeasure or laughter, she couldn't tell. "Would tomorrow morning be convenient?" she asked, chirpy as one of the cheerleaders he'd undoubtedly dated by the gross in his college playing days.

"No."

"Then name the time and place."

She heard a combined sigh of resignation and exasperation. "I have to see a client in Elmhurst in an hour. You can ride out there with me. Meet me in front of my office at two. And if you're not on time, I'm leaving without you."

"I'll be there."

She hung up and grinned at the woman sitting across the green metal bistro table from her. "Bingo."

Gwen Phelps Bingham set down her iced tea glass. "You talked him into filling out the questionnaire?"

"Sort of," Annabelle replied. "I'll have to interview him in his car, but it's better than nothing. I can't go any further until I get a more specific idea of what he wants."

"Boobs and blond hair. Be sure and give him my best." Gwen smiled and gazed toward the collection of weedy day-lilies that formed a border between her yard and the alley behind her Wrigleyville duplex. "I've got to admit, he's quite a hottie . . . if you like your men rough and tumble, but oh so rich and successful."

"I heard that." Gwen's husband, Ian, poked his head through the open patio door. "Annabelle, that big fruit basket doesn't even come close to making up for what you put me through last week."

"How about the year of free babysitting I promised?"

Gwen patted her nearly flat tummy. "You've got to admit, Ian, it was worth it just for that."

He wandered outside. "I'm not admitting anything. I've seen pictures of that guy, and he's still got hair."

Ian was more sensitive about his thinning hair than he should be, and Gwen regarded him affectionately. "I married you for your brain, not your hair."

"Heath Champion graduated at the top of his law class,"

Annabelle said, just to make trouble. "So he's definitely got a brain, too. Which is why he was so captivated by our Gwennie."

Ian refused to bite. "Not to mention the minor fact that you told him she was a sex surrogate."

"Wrong. I told him she was an *authority* on sex surrogates. And I read her master's thesis, so I know it's true."

"Funny you neglected to mention she's now an elementary school psychologist."

"Considering everything else I neglected to mention, it seemed a minor point."

Annabelle had met Gwen and Ian right after college when they'd lived in the same apartment building. Despite his thinning hair, Ian was a great-looking guy, and Gwen adored him. If they weren't so much in love, Annabelle would never have considered asking to borrow Gwen for the evening, but Heath had backed her into a corner, and she'd been desperate. Although she had several women in mind for him to meet, she hadn't been certain any of them would score the knockout punch she needed to ensure that he'd sign her contract. Then she'd thought of Gwen, a woman who'd been born with that mysterious gene that made men whimper just from looking at her.

Ian was still feeling put-upon. "The guy's rich, successful, and good-looking."

"So are you," Gwen said loyally, "except for being rich, but we'll get there someday."

Ian's home-based software company had finally begun to show a profit, which was why they were about to move into their first house. Annabelle experienced one of those pangs of envy that hit her every other minute when she was with them. She wanted a relationship like this. Once she'd thought she had it with Rob, which proved the folly of believing in following her heart.

She rose, patted Gwen's stomach, and gave Ian an extra hug. Not only had he lent her his wife, but he was also designing

Annabelle's Web site. Annabelle knew she needed a presence on the Web, but she didn't intend to turn Perfect for You into an Internet dating service. Nana had been vehement on the subject. *"Three-quarters of the people who sign up for those things are already married, sex deviants, or in prison."* Nana had exaggerated. Annabelle knew couples who'd found love online, but she also didn't believe any computer in the world could beat the personal touch.

She freshened up her makeup in Gwen's bathroom, checked her short khaki skirt and mint green blouse for stains, and set off downtown. She reached Heath's office building a few minutes early, so she ducked into the Starbucks across the street and ordered an overpriced mocha Frappuccino. As she came back outside, she saw him emerge with a cell phone pressed to his ear. He wore aviators, a light gray polo shirt, and slacks. An expensive-looking sports coat dangled over one shoulder from his thumb. Men like him should be required by law to carry a heart defibrillator.

He headed toward the curb, where a shiny black Cadillac Escalade with darkened windows sat with its motor idling. As he reached for the passenger-door handle, he didn't even glance around for her, and she realized he'd forgotten she existed. The story of her life.

"Wait!" She made a dash across the street, dodging a taxi and a red Subaru. Horns blared, brakes squealed, and Champion looked up. He flipped his cell shut as she finally stepped up on the curb.

"I haven't seen anybody run a pattern like that since Bobby Tom Denton retired from the Stars."

"You were going to leave without me."

"I didn't see you."

"You didn't look!"

"Things on my mind." At least he held the back door of the rapmobile open for her, then climbed in at her side. The driver moved up the passenger seat for more legroom before he turned to check her out.

The driver was big and terrifyingly buff. Tattoos decorated a massive set of arms and the wrist he'd draped over the steering wheel. With his shaved head, wise-guy eyes, and crooked smile, he had a Bruce Willis's evil twin thing going that was sexy in a very scary sort of way. "Where we off to?" he asked.

"Elmhurst," Heath said. "Crenshaw wants me to see his new house."

As a Stars fan, Annabelle recognized the name of the team's running back.

"The Sox are up two–one," the driver said. "You want to listen in the back?"

"Yeah, but unfortunately I have some business I promised to take care of. Annabelle, this is Bodie Gray, the best linebacker who never played for Kansas City."

"Second-round draft pick out of Arizona State," Bodie said as he pulled the SUV into the traffic. "Played two years for the Steelers. My right leg was crushed in a motorcycle accident the day I got traded to the Chiefs."

"That must have been terrible."

"You win some, you lose some, right, boss?"

"He calls me that to piss me off."

Bodie studied her in the rearview mirror. "So you're the matchmaker?"

"Marriage facilitator." Heath swiped her mocha Frappuccino.

"Hey!"

He took a drag on the straw, and Bodie chuckled. "Marriage facilitator, huh? You got your work cut out for you with the boss, Annabelle. He has a long history of lovin' and leavin'." He made a left on LaSalle. "But here's what's ironic . . . The last woman he was interested in—some pooh-bah in the mayor's office—dumped him. How's that for a laugh?"

Heath yawned and stretched his legs. Despite his pricey wardrobe, she could easily imagine him in jeans, a ratty T-shirt, and scuffed-up work boots.

Bodie turned onto Congress. "She dumped him because of the way he screwed around on her."

Annabelle's stomach sank. "He was unfaithful?"

"Big-time." Bodie made a lane change. "He kept humpin' his cell phone."

Heath took another swig of the Frappuccino. "He's bitter because I'm successful, and he's screwed up for life."

No response from the front seat. What sort of weird relationship was this?

A cell rang. Not the same cell Heath had been talking on a few minutes earlier. This one came from the pocket of his sports coat. Apparently, he was ambi-phonorous.

"Champion."

Annabelle took advantage of the distraction to reclaim her Frappuccino. As she closed her lips around the straw, she had the depressing thought that this would probably be as close as she'd get to swapping spit with a multimillionaire hunk.

"The restaurant business is littered with the dead bodies of great athletes, Rafe. It's your money, so I can only advise you, but . . ."

The downside of being a matchmaker meant that she might never have another date. When she met attractive single men, she had to turn them into clients, and she couldn't let her personal life complicate that. Not a problem in this particular case . . . She gazed at Heath. Just being near so much unbridled macho made her want to break out in hives. He even smelled sexy, like expensive sheets, good soap, and musky pheromones. The Frappuccino sliding down her throat didn't do much to cool her hot thoughts, and she faced the sad truth that she was sex starved. Two miserable years since she'd broken her engagement to Rob . . . Way too long to sleep alone.

The opening bars of the *William Tell Overture* intruded. Heath had the gall to frown as she retrieved her phone. "Hello."

"Annabelle, it's your mother."

She sank back into the seat, cursing herself for not remembering to turn the thing off.

Heath took advantage of her distraction to reclaim the Frappuccino while he continued his own conversation. ". . . it's all a matter of setting financial priorities. Once your family's secure, you can afford to take a flyer on a restaurant."

"I tracked the application through FedEx," Kate said, "so I know you got it. Have you filled it out yet?"

"Interesting question," Annabelle chirped. "Let me call you back later so we can discuss it."

"Let's discuss it now."

"You're a prince, Raoul. And thanks for last night. You were the best." She disconnected, then turned off her phone. There'd be hell to pay, but she'd worry about that later.

Heath ended his own call and regarded her through those money green, country boy's eyes. "If you're going to program your cell to play music, at least make it original."

"Thanks for the advice." She gestured toward the Frappuccino. "Luckily for you, there's only a slight chance I have diphtheria. Let me tell you, those skin lesions are a bitch."

The corner of his mouth kicked up. "Put the drink on my bill."

"You don't have a bill." She thought of the parking garage where she'd once again been forced to leave Sherman since she hadn't known how long they'd be gone. "Although I'm starting one today." She retrieved the questionnaire from her tropical print Target tote.

He eyed the papers with distaste. "I told you what I'm looking for."

"I know. Soldier Field, fart jokes, yada yada. But I need a

little more than that. For example, what age group are you thinking of? And please don't say nineteen, blond, and busty."

"He's been there and done that, right, boss?" Bodie chimed in from the front seat. "For the last ten years."

Heath ignored him. "I've outgrown my interest in nineteen-year-olds. Let's say twenty-two to thirty. Nothing older. I want kids, but not for a while."

Which made Annabelle, at thirty-one, feel ancient. "What if she's divorced and already has children?"

"I haven't thought about it."

"Have you considered religious preference?"

"No fruitcakes. Other than that, I'm open-minded."

Annabelle made a note. "Would you date a woman who doesn't have a college degree?"

"Sure. What I don't want is a woman without a personality."

"If you had to describe your physical type in three words, what words would you choose?"

"Thin, toned, and hot," Bodie said from the front seat. "He's doesn't like a whole lot of booty."

Annabelle shifted her own booty deeper into the seat.

Heath ran his thumb over the metal band of his watch, a TAG Heuer, she noticed, similar to the one her brother Adam had bought for himself when he'd been named St. Louis's top heart surgeon. "Gwen Phelps isn't in the phone book."

"Yes, I know. What are your turnoffs?"

"I'm going to find her."

"Why would you want to?" Annabelle said a little too hastily. "She's not interested."

"You really don't think I can be put off that easily, do you?"

She made a business of clicking her pen and perusing the questionnaire. "Your turnoffs?"

"Flakes. Gigglers. Too much perfume. Cubs fans."

Her head shot up. "I love the Cubbies."

"Surprise, surprise."

She decided to let that one pass.

"You never dated a redhead," Bodie offered.

A lock of Annabelle's own red hair chose that moment to fall over her cheek.

Heath eyed the back of Bodie's neck where a Maori warrior's tattoo curled into his shirt collar. "Maybe I should let my faithful manservant answer the rest of your questions, since he seems to have all the answers."

"I'm saving her time," Bodie replied. "She brings you a redhead, you'll give her grief. Look for women with class, Annabelle. That's most important. The sophisticated types who went to boarding schools and speak French. She has to be the real thing because he can spot a phony a mile away. And he likes them athletic."

"Of course he does," she said dryly. "Athletic, domestic, gorgeous, brilliant, socially connected, and pathologically submissive. It'll be a snap."

"You forgot hot." Heath smiled. "And defeatist thinking is for losers. If you want to be a success in this world, Annabelle, you need a positive attitude. Whatever the client wants, you get it for him. First rule of a successful business."

"Uh-huh. What about career women?"

"I don't see how that would work."

"The kind of potential mate you're describing isn't going to be sitting around waiting for her prince to show up. She's heading a major corporation. In between those Victoria's Secret modeling gigs."

He lifted an eyebrow. "Attitude, Annabelle. Attitude."

"Right."

"A career woman can't fly across the country with me on two hours' notice to entertain a client's wife," he said.

"Two on, no outs." Bodie flipped up the volume.

As the men listened to the game, Annabelle contemplated her notes with a sinking heart. How was she going to find a woman who met all these criteria? She couldn't. But then neither could Portia Powers, because a woman like this didn't exist.

What if Annabelle took a different path? What if she found the woman Heath Champion really needed instead of the woman he thought he needed? She doodled in the margin of the questionnaire. What made this guy tick besides money and conquest? Who was the real man behind the multiple cell phones? On the surface, he was all polish, but she knew from Molly that he'd grown up with an abusive father. Apparently, he'd started rooting around in the neighbors' garbage looking for things to sell before he could read, and he'd been working ever since.

"What's your real name?" Annabelle asked as they got off the East West Tollway at York Road.

"What makes you think Heath Champion isn't my real name."

"Too convenient."

"*Campione.* Italian for *champion.*"

She nodded, but something in the way he avoided looking at her told her there was more to the story.

They headed north toward the prosperous suburb of Elmhurst. Heath consulted his BlackBerry. "I'll be at Sienna's tomorrow night at six. Bring on your next candidate."

She turned her doodle into a stop sign. "Why now?"

"Because I just rearranged my schedule."

"No, I mean why have you decided now that you want to get married?"

"Because it's time."

Before she could ask what that meant, he was back on his cell. "I know you're nearly capped out, Ron, but I also know you don't want to lose a great running back. Tell Phoebe she's going to have to make some adjustments."

And so, apparently, was Annabelle.

Bodie sent her back to the city in a cab paid for by Heath. By the time she'd retrieved Sherman and driven home, it was after five. She let herself in through the back door and tossed her things down on the kitchen table, a pine drop leaf Nana had bought in the 1980s when she'd gone big on country-style decorating. The appliances were vintage but still serviceable, just like the farm-table chairs with their faded mattress-ticking pillows. Although Annabelle had lived in the house for three months, she'd always think of it as Nana's, and tossing out the dusty grapevine wreath along with the ruffled cranberry curtain at the kitchen window were about as much as she'd done to update the eating area.

Some of her happiest childhood memories had taken place in this kitchen, especially during the summers when she'd come for a week to visit. She and Nana used to sit at this very table, talking about everything. Her grandmother had never laughed at her daydreams, not even when Annabelle had turned eighteen and announced that she intended to study theater and become a famous actress. Nana dealt only in possibility. It hadn't occurred to her to point out that Annabelle possessed neither the beauty nor the talent to hit it big on Broadway.

The doorbell rang, and she went to answer it. Years earlier, Nana had converted the living and dining rooms into the reception and office areas for Marriages by Myrna. Like her grandmother, Annabelle lived in the rooms upstairs. Since Nana's death, Annabelle had repainted and modernized the dining room office space with a computer and a more efficient desk arrangement.

The old front door had a center oval of frosted glass, but the beveled border allowed her to see the distorted figure of Mr. Bronicki. She wished she could pretend she wasn't home, but he lived across the alley, so he'd seen her pull up in Sherman. Although Wicker Park had lost many of its elderly to gentrification, a few holdouts still lived in the houses where they'd raised their families. Others had moved into a nearby senior living facility, and still others lived on the less expensive fringe streets. Every one of them had known her grandmother

"Hello, Mr. Bronicki."

"Annabelle." He had a lean, wiry build and gray caterpillar eyebrows with a Mephistophelean slant. The hair missing from his head sprouted copiously from his ears, but he was a natty dresser, wearing long-sleeved checked sports shirts and polished oxfords even on the warmest days.

He glared at her from beneath his satanic eyebrows. "You was supposed to call me. I left three messages."

"You were next on my list," she lied. "I've been out all day."

"And don't I know it. Running around like a chicken with your head cut off. Myrna used to stay put so people could find her." He had the accent of a born-and-bred Chicagoan and the aggression of a man who'd spent his life driving a truck for the gas company. He bulldozed past her into the house. "What are you going to do about my situation?"

"Mr. Bronicki, your agreement was with my grandmother."

"My agreement was with Marriages by Myrna, 'Seniors Are My Specialty,' or have you forgotten your grammie's slogan?"

How could she forget, when it was plastered over every one of the dozens of yellowed notepads Nana had scattered around the house? "That business no longer exists."

"Bull pippy." He made a sharp gesture around the reception area, where Annabelle had exchanged Nana's wooden geese, silk flower arrangements, and milk-can end tables for a few pieces of Mediterranean-style pottery. Since she couldn't afford to replace the ruffled chairs and couches, she'd added pillows in a cheery red, cobalt, and yellow Provençal print that complemented the creamy new buttercup paint.

"Addin' some doodads don't change a thing," he said. "This is still a matchmaker business, and me and your grammie had a contract. With a guarantee."

"You signed that contract in 1989," she pointed out, not for the first time.

"I paid her two hundred dollars. In *cash*."

"Since you and Mrs. Bronicki were together for almost fifteen years, I'd say you got your money's worth."

He whipped a dog-eared paper from his pants pocket and waved it at her. "'Satisfaction guaranteed.' That's what this contract says. And I'm not satisfied. She went loony on me."

"I know you had a difficult time of it, and I'm sorry about Mrs. Bronicki passing."

"Sorry don't cut the mustard. I didn't have satisfaction even when she was alive."

Annabelle couldn't believe she was arguing with an eighty-year-old about a two-hundred-dollar contract signed when Reagan was president. "You married Mrs. Bronicki of your own free will," she said as patiently as she could manage.

"Kids like you, they don't understand about customer satisfaction."

"That's not true, Mr. Bronicki."

"My nephew's a lawyer. I could sue."

She started to tell him to go ahead and try, but he was just cranky enough to do it. "Mr. Bronicki, how about this? I promise I'll keep my eyes open."

"I want a blonde."

She bit the inside of her cheek. "Gotcha."

"And not too young. None of them twenty-year-olds. I got a granddaughter twenty-two. Wouldn't look right."

"You're thinking . . . ?"

"Thirty'd be good. With a little meat on her bones."

"Anything else?"

"Catholic."

"Of course."

"And nice." A wistful expression softened the slant of those ferocious eyebrows. "Somebody nice."

She smiled despite herself. "I'll see what I can do."

When she finally managed to close the door behind him, she remembered there was a good reason she'd earned her reputation as the family's screwup. She had *sucker* written all over her.

And way too many clients living on Social Security.

Chapter Five

B odie readjusted the treadmill speed, slowing the pace. "Tell me more about Portia Powers."

A bead of sweat trickled into the already damp neckband of Heath's faded Dolphins T-shirt as he set the barbell he'd been lifting back on the rack. "You met Annabelle. Do a one-eighty, and you've got Powers."

"Annabelle's interesting. Kinda hard to get a bead on her."

"She's a flake." Heath stretched out his arms. "I'd never have hired her if she hadn't struck it lucky with Gwen Phelps."

Bodie chuckled. "You still can't believe you got rejected."

"I finally meet somebody intriguing, and she's not interested."

"Life's a bitch." The treadmill slowed to a stop. Bodie climbed off and picked up a towel from the uncarpeted living room floor.

Heath's Lincoln Park house still smelled like new construction, probably because it was. A sleek wedge of glass and stone, it jutted toward the shady street like the prow of a ship. Through the sweeping V of floor-to-ceiling living room windows, he could see sky, trees, a pair of restored nineteenth-century town houses across the way, and a well-maintained neighborhood park surrounded by an old iron fence. His rooftop deck—which, admittedly, he'd only visited twice—afforded a distant view of the Lincoln Park Lagoon.

Once he found a wife, he'd let her furnish the place. For now, he'd set up a gym in the otherwise empty living room, bought a state-of-the-art sound system, a bed with a Tempur-Pedic mattress, and a big-screen plasma TV for the media room downstairs. All of that, combined with hardwood and tumbled marble floors, custom-built cabinets, limestone bathrooms, and a kitchen outfitted with the latest in European-designed appliances made this the house he'd dreamed about since he was a kid.

He just wished he liked it more. Maybe he should have hired a decorator instead of waiting, but he'd done that with his old place—cost a fortune, too—and he hadn't liked the results. The interior might have been impressive, but he'd felt weird there, like a visitor in somebody else's house. He'd sold everything when he moved here so he could start new, but now he wished he'd held on to enough furniture to keep the place from echoing.

Bodie picked up a water bottle. "Word is, she's a ballbuster."

"Gwen?" Heath stepped on the treadmill.

"Powers. High employee turnover rate."

"Seems like a good businesswoman to me. She also does some volunteer work mentoring other women."

"If she's so good, why aren't you letting her sit through any of her introductions like you made Annabelle do last week?"

"I tried once, but it didn't work. She's pretty wired, a little hard to take in big doses. But she's sent along some decent candidates, and she knows how to get the job done."

"That explains all those second dates you haven't asked anybody out on."

"Sooner or later I will."

Bodie wandered into the kitchen. He had a condo in

Wrigleyville, but sometimes came over here so they could work out together.

Heath turned up the treadmill speed. He and Bodie had been together almost six years now. After his motorcycle injury, Bodie had lost himself in drugs and self-pity, but Heath had admired him as a player, and he'd hired him to be a runner. Good runners tended to be former athletes, men the college players knew by reputation and trusted. Agents used them to bring potential clients to the table. Although Heath hadn't spelled it out, Bodie had known he had to get sober first, and that's what he'd done. Before long, his no-bullshit style had turned him into one of the best.

Bodie had started driving for him accidentally. Heath spent a lot of hours on Chicago's tollways, heading up to Halas Hall, out to Stars headquarters, or making endless trips to and from O'Hare. He hated wasting time stuck in traffic jams, and Bodie liked being behind the wheel, so Bodie'd started taking over when it was convenient for both of them. With Bodie driving, Heath could make phone calls, answer e-mail, and handle paperwork, although, just as frequently, they used their time to strategize, and this was where Bodie earned the six-figure income Heath paid him. Bodie's intimidating appearance hid a highly analytical mind—cool, focused, and unsentimental. He'd become Heath's closest friend, and the only person Heath completely trusted.

Bodie returned from the kitchen with a beer. "Your matchmaker doesn't like you."

"I care."

"I think you amuse her, though."

"Amuse her?" Heath lost his rhythm. "What the hell does that mean?"

"Ask her, not me."

"I'm not asking her a damn thing."

"It'll be interesting to see who she comes up with next.

You sure didn't like that brunette Powers introduced you to last week."

"Too much perfume, and she was hard to get rid of." He punched at the display, raising the treadmill's incline. "I guess I should make Powers sit in on the introductions the same way I did with Annabelle, but Powers takes over so much it's tough to get a good read."

"You should make Annabelle sit in on all of them. She doesn't seem to get on your nerves."

"What are you talking about? She sure as hell got on my nerves this afternoon—her and her questionnaire." His cell rang. Bodie tossed it to him. Heath checked the caller ID and hit the button. "Rocco . . . Exactly the man I want to talk to . . ."

H ow rich do you think he is?" Barrie Delshire's long brown hair swung around the perfect oval of her face, unlike Annabelle's hair, which continued to defy the new straightening product she'd obviously paid too much for.

"He's rich enough." Annabelle poked a curl behind her ear.

"That's cool. My last boyfriend still owes me fifty bucks, but he says he'll pay me back."

Barrie wasn't the brightest bulb in the Pottery Barn chandelier, but she was sweet, exquisitely beautiful, and her bustline alone should catch Heath's attention. Barrie didn't want to walk into the restaurant alone, so Annabelle had met up with her at a nearby convenience store. As they drew nearer to Sienna's, a stylish, rail-thin woman with pale skin and inky hair turned from the window where she was perusing the menu to watch them approach. She wore a silky blue halter top that tied behind her neck, white slacks, and backless navy-and-white kitten-heeled slides. She gazed at Annabelle with an odd intensity, then turned her attention back to the menu.

Barrie flicked her hair. "Thanks again for arranging this. I'm so sick of dating losers."

"Heath definitely isn't a loser." Annabelle had been too nervous about tonight to eat, and as they entered the restaurant, the fragrant smells of garlic and fresh-baked bread made her mouth water. Heath sat at the same table he'd occupied when she'd introduced him to Gwen. Tonight, he wore an open-collar knit shirt a shade lighter than his thick, barely rumpled hair. As they got closer, she saw him pocket his BlackBerry.

He rose in an unconscious display of athletic grace—no fumbling with the chair or bumping against the table for this dude. Annabelle made the introductions. He wasn't easy to read, but as she watched him take in Barrie's long hair and amazing breasts, she could tell he was interested.

He held out the chair next to him for her, leaving Annabelle to fend for herself. Barrie gave him an alluring, moist-lipped smile. "You're just as amazing-looking as Annabelle said you were."

Heath shot Annabelle an amused glance. "Did she now?"

Annabelle ordered herself not to flush. She'd been doing her job, and that was all.

The conversation unfolded without much effort on Annabelle's part, other than steering Barrie away from discussing her horoscope. Fortunately, Barrie was a big Stars fan, so they had plenty to talk about, and Heath gave her his full attention. Annabelle wished somebody would listen to her with so much interest. His cell rang. He pulled it out to check the number but didn't answer, which Annabelle took as a positive sign, or maybe a negative one, because she was growing increasingly convinced that Barrie was completely wrong for him.

"Did you play football?" Barrie said with breathless intensity.

"I played college ball, but I wasn't good enough to be more than a benchwarmer for the pros, so I passed."

"You turned down a chance to play for the pros?"

"I don't do anything where I can't be the best."

What about doing something just for fun? Annabelle wondered. Again, she thought of her work-obsessed brothers.

Barrie pushed her shampoo-model hair back over one shoulder. "Where did you go to college?"

"I got my undergraduate degree at the University of Illinois, then grabbed a chance to go to Harvard Law."

"You went to Harvard?" Barrie exclaimed. "Oh my God, I'm so impressed. I always wanted to go to a big West Coast school, but my parents couldn't afford it."

Heath blinked.

Annabelle grabbed her green phantom and calculated how quickly she could set up his next date.

Your friend sure won't be bringing the cheese dip to the next MENSA potluck," Heath said, after Barrie left the restaurant.

Annabelle resisted the urge to drain her green phantom. "Maybe not, but you've got to admit that she's gorgeous."

"Sweet, too. But I expected better from you, especially after answering all those stupid questions yesterday."

"They weren't stupid. And there's a big difference between what men say they want in a woman and what they really want."

"So this was a test?"

"Sort of. Maybe."

"Don't do it again." He leveled his roughneck's gaze at her. "I'm crystal clear about what I want, and Barrie—while admittedly hot—isn't it."

Annabelle gazed wistfully toward the doorway. "If I could put my brain in her body, the world would be mine for the taking."

"Ease up, Dr. Evil. The next candidate is due in five minutes, and I have a call to make. Keep her entertained till I get back, will you?"

"The next—? I didn't—"

But he'd already disappeared into a back room. She shot up, ready to go after him, only to see a stylishly dressed blonde enter. With her Escada suit and Chanel bag, she had the stamp of Power Matches all over her. Was he serious? Did he really expect her to entertain a competitor's candidate?

The woman glanced around the bar. Despite her designer duds, she seemed unsure of herself, and Annabelle's Good Samaritan instinct reared its namby-pamby head. She fought it for almost thirty seconds, but the woman looked so uncomfortable that she finally gave in and made her way to her side. "Are you looking for Heath Champion?"

"Yes, I am."

"He got called away for a few minutes. He asked me to keep an eye out for you. I'm Annabelle Granger, his . . ." She hesitated. Saying she was his backup matchmaker was out of the question, and she couldn't stomach saying she was his assistant, so she settled on the next best thing. "I'm Heath's boss."

"Melanie Richter." The woman took in Annabelle's khaki skirt and fitted persimmon jacket—which, next to all the Escada, wasn't too impressive. Still, she didn't seem judgmental, and she had a friendly smile. "Being a woman in such a male-dominated field must be challenging."

"You have no idea."

Melanie followed her back to the table. Since Annabelle wasn't anxious to discuss her career as a sports mogul, she asked Melanie about herself and learned that she was divorced with one child. She had a background in fashion, along with a creepy ex who used to yell at her if she didn't disinfect their doorknobs every day. Heath finally joined them. Annabelle introduced him and began to rise only to have his hand settle hard on her bare thigh.

She didn't know which was more annoying, the jolt of sexual electricity that shot through her or the realization that he expected her to stay, but the pressure on her thigh didn't ease.

Melanie fiddled with her purse, looking uncomfortable again. This wasn't her fault, and Annabelle retrenched.

"Melanie has such an interesting background." In the spirit of fair play, she emphasized Melanie's Junior League charity work and fashion training. Although she mentioned Melanie's son, she said nothing about the creepy ex. She'd barely finished, however, before Heath's cell rang. He glanced at it, apologized with all kinds of sincerity, and excused himself.

Annabelle glared at his back. "My hardest-working employee. Incredibly conscientious."

"I can see that."

Annabelle decided to take advantage of Melanie's fashion expertise by soliciting her opinion about the best jeans for short women with a tendency toward full hips. Melanie replied graciously—medium low rise, boot cut to the ankle. Then she complimented Annabelle on her hair. "The color is so unusual. There's a lot of gold in it. I'd kill for hair like yours."

Annabelle's hair had always attracted a lot of attention, but she took the compliments she received with a grain of salt, suspecting that people were so startled by the mess they felt they had to say something. Heath returned, apologized again, and got down to business with Melanie. He leaned in when she spoke, smiled in all the right places, asked good questions, and seemed genuinely interested in everything she said. Finally, his hand settled on Annabelle's thigh, but this time she didn't let herself get worked up about it. He was signaling that Melanie's time was over.

After she left, he shot a look at his watch. "Terrific woman, but disappointing."

"How can she be terrific and disappointing? She's *nice*."

"Very nice. I enjoyed talking with her. But we had no chemistry, and I don't want to marry her."

"Chemistry takes more than twenty minutes to develop. She's smart, and she's a heck of a lot more courteous than you and your cell deserve. She also has that class thing going you say you want. Give her another chance."

"Just a suggestion. I'll bet you could get further in your business by pushing your own candidates instead of somebody else's."

"I know, but I like her." She frowned at him. "Although I couldn't help but notice that she seemed to blame me for breaking up the evening, which is so unfair."

"You'll also go further if you at least pretend to suck up to me."

"Here's what's sad. I have been sucking up."

That country boy mouth crooked at the corner. "The best you can do, huh?"

"I know. Depressing, isn't it."

His amusement turned to suspicion. "What did Melanie mean when she said you should give me a raise?"

"No idea." Her stomach rumbled. "I don't suppose you'd consider feeding me?"

"We don't have time. The next one will be here in ten minutes. I'll buy you another drink instead."

"The *next* one?"

He pulled out his BlackBerry in a blatant attempt to ignore her, but she wasn't having it. "Portia Powers can babysit her own introductions. I'm not doing it."

"Yet only six days ago, you were in my office on your knees telling me you'd do anything to land me as a client."

"I was young and stupid."

"Here's the difference between us . . . The reason I'm running a multimillion-dollar business and you're not. I give my clients what they want. You give your clients grief."

"Not all of them. Just you. Okay, and sometimes Mr. Bronicki, but you can't imagine what I'm up against there."

"Let me give you an example of what I'm talking about."

"I'd settle for a breadstick."

"Last week I was on the phone with a client who plays for the Bills. He just bought his first house, and he mentioned that he liked my taste and wished I could help him pick out some furniture. Now I'm his agent, not his interior decorator. Hell, I don't know jack about decorating; I haven't even furnished my own place. But the guy broke up with his girlfriend, he's lonely, and two hours later, I was on a plane to Buffalo. I didn't blow him off. I didn't send a lackey. I went myself. And do you know why?"

"A newly discovered passion for country French?"

He arched an eyebrow. "No. Because I want my clients to understand I'm always there for them. When they sign a contract with me, they sign with someone who cares about every aspect of their lives. Not just when times are good, but when things get rough, too."

"What if you don't like them?" She'd intended the question as a small dig—implying she didn't like him—but he took her seriously, which was just as well. This weird compulsion to put him in his place had to stop. Her future depended on making him happy, not alienating him.

"I'd never sign a client I didn't like," he said.

"You like them *all*? Every single one of those demanding, egotistical, overpaid, self-indulgent jocks? I don't believe you."

"I love them like they're my brothers," he replied, with unflinching sincerity.

"You are such a bullshitter."

"Am I?" He gave her an inscrutable smile then rose to his feet as Portia Powers's second socialite of the evening made her appearance.

"D on't you have it memorized yet?"

Portia jumped at the sound of a deep and very threatening male voice. She spun around from her spot on the sidewalk in front of Sienna's window and took in the man who'd come up next to her. It was only a little after ten, and people still strolled the sidewalk, but she felt as though she'd been sucked into a dark alley at midnight. He was a goon, huge and menacing, with a shaved head and a serial killer's translucent blue eyes. An intimidating display of tribal tattoos decorated the ropy muscles visible beneath the sleeves of his tightly fitted black T-shirt, and his thick, muscular neck belonged to a man who'd done hard time.

"Didn't anybody tell you spying on people isn't nice?" he said.

For the past hour, she'd been circling the block, stopping each time she passed the restaurant to pretend to study the menu. If she looked over the top, she could see the table where Heath was sitting, along with Annabelle Granger and the two women Portia had arranged for him to meet tonight. Normally Portia wouldn't have thought of being present during an initial introduction—only a few clients had ever requested it—except she'd learned he wanted Granger there, and Portia couldn't tolerate that.

"Who are you?" she said, pretending a bravado she didn't feel.

"Bodie Gray, Champion's bodyguard. And he sure will be interested to hear what you've been up to tonight."

The muscles in the small of her back cramped. This was beyond humiliating. "I haven't been up to a thing."

"That's not what it looks like to me."

"But then you're hardly an authority on matchmaking, are you?" She regarded him coldly, doing her best to stare him down. "How about minding your own business and letting me mind mine?"

Her assistants would have dived for cover, but he didn't even blink. "Champion's business is my business."

"My, my . . . Quite the dedicated gofer."

"Everybody should have one." He grabbed her arm and pulled her toward the curb.

She gave a hiss of dismay. "What are you doing?" She tried to wrench away, but he didn't let go.

"I'm going to buy you a beer so Mr. Champion can finish his business in private."

"It's my business, too, and I'm not—"

"Yeah, you really are." He steered her between two parked cars. "But if you make nice, you might be able to convince me to keep my mouth shut."

She stopped struggling and gazed at Mr. Bodyguard through the corner of her eyes. So . . . he was willing to sell out his boss. Heath should have known better than to hire a thug, but since he hadn't, she'd take advantage of his naïveté because she did not want him to find out about this. If he did, he'd see it for exactly what it was, a sign of weakness.

The bar they entered was smoky and sour, with a cracked linoleum floor and a dying philodendron sitting on a dusty shelf between a couple of fly-specked trophies and a faded photograph of Mel Torme.

"Hey, Bodie, how's it hanging?" the bartender called out.

"No complaints."

Bodie steered her toward a barstool. On the way, one of her shoes stuck to something on the floor. As she freed it, she wondered how such a seedy establishment could exist so close to Clark Street's best restaurants.

"Two beers," Mr. Bodyguard said as she perched gingerly on the stool next to him.

"Club soda," she interjected. "With a sliver of lime."

"No limes," the bartender said, "but I got a can of fruit cocktail in the back room."

Muscle Man found this hilarious, and a few moments later she was staring at the faint outline of a leftover lipstick imprint on the rim of a beer mug. She pushed it aside. "How did you know who I was?"

"You match Champion's description."

She didn't ask how Heath had described her. She tried not to ask any question where she wasn't certain of the answer, and something had gone seriously haywire in her relationship with Heath the moment Annabelle Granger had entered the picture.

"I won't apologize for doing my job," she said. "Heath is paying me a lot of money to help him, but I can't do that properly if he cuts me out."

"So it's okay if I tell him about the spying?"

"What you call spying, I call earning my paycheck," she said carefully.

"I doubt he'll see it that way."

She doubted it, too, but she wouldn't let him intimidate her. "Tell me what you want."

She watched as he thought it over. Reading people was an important part of her business, but her clients were wealthy and well educated, so how could she tell what was going on behind those ice pick blue eyes? She hated uncertainty. "Well?"

"I'm thinking."

She opened her purse, extracted two fifty-dollar bills, and set them in front of him. "Maybe this will help that difficult process along."

He looked down at the money, shrugged, and shifted his weight to stuff the bills in his pocket. His hips were much narrower than his shoulders, she noticed, his thighs long boned and solid.

"Now," she said. "We can just forget all about tonight."

"I don't know. It's a lot to forget . . . even for someone like me."

She gazed at him more closely, trying to decide if he was putting her on, but she couldn't read him.

"I'll tell you what," he said. "Why don't we talk the situation over next weekend? Let's say a week from Friday. See how things are coming along by then."

She hadn't expected this. "Why don't we not."

"I'd do it this weekend, but I gotta be out of town."

"What do you want?"

He studied her openly. His mouth was finely chiseled, almost delicate, which made the rest of his features seem all the more sinister. "I'll let you know when I decide."

"Forget it. I'm not going to allow you to string me along." She tried to stare him down, but he refused to play. Instead, his mouth quirked in a gangster's cocky grin.

"Are you sure? If you are, I can always talk to Mr. Champion tonight."

She gritted her teeth. "Fine. Next Friday." She slid off the stool and pulled open her purse. "Here's my card. Don't try to screw me, or you'll regret it."

"Probably." His eyes slid over her like hot caramel on ice cream. "Still, it might be interesting."

Something heady and unexpected shot through her. She snapped her purse shut and left the bar to the sound of a wicked chuckle.

The next Power Matches candidate proved to be beautiful but self-centered, and Annabelle led the conversation to showcase her flaws. She needn't have bothered. Heath had the woman's number from the start. At the same time, he treated her with the utmost respect, and Annabelle realized that Heath wasn't quite the egomaniac she'd first thought. He seemed to find the human condition in all its forms interesting. Knowing that made it tough for her to hold on to her dislike. Not that she'd been holding on to it very hard.

"Entertaining," he said after she left, "but not in a good way. This evening's been a time sink."

"Your next match won't be. I've got someone special lined up." Nana's senior client base was turning out to be a rich source of referrals. Rachel Gorny, the granddaughter of one of Nana's oldest friends, didn't have Barrie's extravagant beauty, but she was intelligent, accomplished, and strong-minded enough to hold her own against him. She also had the social polish Heath seemed to require. Annabelle had considered introducing them tonight, but she'd wanted to see how he'd react to Barrie first.

She toyed with her swizzle stick to keep herself from studying Heath's profile and made a mental note to look for a sweet, hunky, not-too-bright guy who'd treat Barrie well.

"You'll need to do a better job, Annabelle. No more dates like the first one tonight."

"Agreed. And no more making me sit through your Power Matches introductions, either. As you so wisely pointed out, helping Portia Powers isn't in my best interests."

"Then why are you still trying to talk me into seeing Melanie again?"

"Hunger makes me weird."

"You got rid of the last one in fourteen minutes. Well done. I'm rewarding you by letting you sit in on all the introductions from now on."

She nearly choked on an ice cube. "What are you talking about?"

"Exactly what I said."

"By *all*, you don't mean—"

"As a matter of fact, I do." He drew out a big gold money clip stuffed with bills, tossed a few on the table, and pulled her from her chair. "Let's get you fed."

"But— I'm not— I won't—" She sputtered her way across the bar, trying to tell him that she had no intention of hanging around with Powers's candidates and that he'd obviously lost what was left of his mind, but he ignored her to greet the owner, a wiry terrier of a man. They conversed in Italian, which surprised her, although why anything about Heath should surprise her at this point, she had no idea.

They'd barely been seated in the dining room's prime booth before the waiter took their drink orders and Mama greeted Heath with a breadbasket and antipasto platter. More Italian flew. Annabelle couldn't resist the yeasty smell of the warm bread, so she tore off a chunk and dredged it through a rosemary-flavored puddle of olive oil.

Like the bar, the dining room had roughly plastered gold walls and heavy purple moldings, but the lighting was brighter here, showcasing the salmon tablecloths and grape-colored napkins. Small earthenware pots at each table held simple arrangements of country flowers and herbs. The restaurant had a homey, comfortable feel, yet still projected an air of elegance.

Heath knew more about wine that she did, and he ordered a cabernet for her, but he drank Sam Adams himself. The antipasto platter overflowed with meats, stuffed mushrooms, sprigs of fried sage, and matchstick skewers of pecorino cheese and plump red cherries. "Eat first," he said. "Then we'll talk."

She was more than happy to comply, and he didn't bother her until the entrées appeared—pale islands of sea scallops floating in a choppy sea of porcini and cremini mushrooms for her, pasta drenched in a spicy *pomodoro* sauce chunky with sausage and goat cheese for him.

He took a few bites, sipped his beer, then turned the same razor-sharp focus on her he'd directed at his dates all evening. "I want you around for all the introductions from now on, doing exactly what you did tonight."

"If you ruin the best meal I've eaten in forever, I'll never forgive you."

"You're intuitive, and you kept the conversations going. Despite your opinion about Melanie, you seem to know what's working for me and what's not. I'd be stupid not to make use of that, and I'm definitely not stupid."

She loaded up her fork with a scoop of golden, garlicky polenta. "Remind me how it's to my advantage to help Portia Powers make this match because I've forgotten that part."

He picked up his knife. "We're cutting a new deal." With one efficient motion, he split a chunk of sausage in half. "That ten thousand dollars you wanted to charge me was nothing more than a fishing expedition, and we both know it."

"It wasn't a—"

"I paid you five thousand instead and promised the balance only if you made the match. As it turns out, this is your lucky day because I've decided to write you the full check, whether the match comes from you or from Portia. As long as I have a wife and you've been part of the process, you'll get your money." He toasted her with his beer mug. "Congratulations."

She put down her fork. "Why would you do that?"

"Because it's efficient."

"Not as efficient as having Powers handle her own introductions. You're paying her a fortune to do exactly that."

"I'd rather have you."

Her pulse kicked. "Why?"

He gave her the melty smile he must have been practicing since the cradle, one that made her feel as though she was the only woman in the world. "Because you're easier to bully. Do we have a deal or not?"

"You don't want a matchmaker. You want a lackey."

"Semantics. My hours are erratic, and my schedule changes without warning. It'll be your job to cope with all that. You'll soothe ruffled feathers when I need to cancel at the last minute. You'll keep my dates company when I'm going to be late, entertain them if I have to take a call. If things are going well, you'll disappear. If not, you'll make the woman disappear. I told you before. I work hard at my job. I don't want to have to work hard at this, too."

"Basically, you expect me to find your bride, court her, and hand her over at the altar. Or do I have to come on the honeymoon, too?"

"Definitely not." He gave her a lazy smile. "I can take care of that all by myself."

Something sizzled in the air between them, something that

felt heady and seductive, at least in her sex-starved imagination. She took a sip of water and absorbed the dismaying realization that she was attracted to him, even though she wanted to hit him in the head with that beer bottle. Well, so what? He was a natural charmer, and she was only human. This wouldn't be a problem unless she let it be.

She took her time thinking it over. Although she hated the idea of being at his beck and call, this arrangement would give her more control, as well as potentially doubling her money. Power Matches only signed contracts with men, but Perfect for You signed both men and women, so she might be able to pick up some great female clients out of Heath's rejects. Melanie, for example, could be a match for Shirley Miller's godson, Jerry. He was nice looking, moderately successful, and they had children about the same age. Just because Jerry wasn't currently a client didn't mean Annabelle couldn't land him as one.

"Portia Powers will never agree to this," she said.

"She won't have a choice."

Just like I don't, Annabelle thought. But that wasn't entirely true. She had a choice, all right. Unfortunately, making it would be self-defeating. "You should cancel your contract with her and let me take care of everything."

"She has access to women you don't," he replied. "Odds are, she'll find the one I end up choosing."

"Tonight being a sterling example of her good judgment?"

"Tonight being a sterling example of yours?"

He had her there. She toyed with a mushroom. "You understand, don't you, that it's in my best interest to sabotage her candidates. As much as I need the money, I need to build the reputation of Perfect for You even more."

"I stand warned, Mata Hari."

"You're not taking me seriously."

He cocked an eyebrow. "You told me to see Melanie again."

"Only because my blood glucose was out of whack. Now that I've eaten it's clear to me that she's way too decent for you."

"Give it a rest, Annabelle." He offered up his snake's smile. "You're one of those people who was cursed with personal integrity. And I'm one of those people who's smart enough to take advantage of it."

There wasn't much she could say to that, so she returned her attention to the scallops.

It had been a long time since Heath had enjoyed watching a woman eat, but Annabelle knew how to appreciate a good meal. A blissful expression came over her face as she slipped another mushroom into her mouth. The tip of her tongue picked up a dab of leftover sauce at the bow of her lip. His eyes drifted along her throat to her collarbone and down to those small, guinea-fowl breasts . . .

"What?" Her fork hung in midair, and tiny frown lines creased her forehead.

He quickly rearranged his expression. "I was wondering about your next candidate. Do you really have one lined up?"

She smiled and propped an elbow on the table. "Yes. And she's special. Sharp, attractive, fun to be with."

"At the risk of incurring your wrath, there are thousands of women who meet that description. I'm looking for someone extraordinary."

Her honey-colored eyes announced an amber alert. "Extraordinary women tend to fall in love with men who put them first. Which pretty much rules out a guy who excuses himself in the middle of a conversation to take a phone call like you did tonight."

"It was an emergency."

"With you, I suspect they all are. No offense."

He ran his thumb around the rim of his mug. "I don't usually feel the need to defend myself, but I'm going to make an exception now, and you can apologize when I'm done."

"We'll see."

"A player I recruited a couple of years ago wrapped his Maserati around a telephone pole tonight. That was his mother on the phone. He's not even my client—he signed with another agent—but I got to know his folks a little. Nice people. He's in intensive care . . ." He nudged his plate back from the edge of the table with his thumb. "She called to let me know they don't expect him to last until morning." He gazed at her. "You tell me which was most important. Making small talk or comforting that mother?"

She stared at him. Then she laughed. "You just made that up."

He was seldom taken by surprise, but Annabelle Granger had done it. He gave her his iciest glare. "Interesting that you find someone's tragedy so amusing."

Her eyes crinkled at the corners, golden flecks dancing in the irises. "You *totally* made it up."

He tried to stare her down—he was superb at stare-downs—but she looked so pleased with herself that he lost it and laughed.

She regarded him smugly. "I have two brothers who are also overachieving workaholics, so I'm intimately acquainted with the tricks performed by men of your ilk."

"I have an ilk?"

"A definite ilk."

"It finally becomes clear . . ." He propped his elbow on the table, rubbed the corner of his mouth, and studied her over the back of his hand. "Poor, pathetic Annabelle. All the inappropriate put-downs you've subjected me to, the snide comments . . . A simple case of transfer. The result of growing up overshadowed by those magnificent brothers. Was it very painful to feel so neglected? Do the scars still ache when it rains?"

She snorted, a surprisingly loud sound coming from such a small woman. "I prayed to be neglected. Ballet, piano, horseback riding. Fencing, for Pete's sake. Who makes their kid take fencing lessons? Girl Scouts, orchestra, tutors if I slipped below a B, monetary incentives to join every club with a special bonus if I ran for office. And yet somehow I survived, although the torture continues."

She'd just described his dream childhood. Fragments of memory swept over him. His father's drunken voice . . . *Pull your head out of that goddamned book and go buy me some cigarettes.* Cockroaches scrambling under the refrigerator, leaky pipes dripping rusty water on the linoleum. The scent of Lysol—a good memory—when one of the old man's girlfriends tried to clean up the place, and then the inevitable bang of that warped metal door when she'd storm out.

Annabelle chased her remaining scallop to the edge of the plate and looked up at him. "I really think you'll like Rachel."

"I like Gwen."

"That's because she refused you. The two of you had no chemistry."

"You're so wrong. There was definite chemistry."

"I don't get why you need a wife right now. You have Bodie, you have assistants, and you can hire a housekeeper to handle all those impromptu dinner parties. As for having kids . . . It's hard to raise them with a cell phone super glued to your ear."

It was long past time to put Tinker Bell in her place. He settled back in his chair and let his eyes drift to her breasts. "You left out sex."

She took a few seconds too long to respond. "You can hire that, too."

"Honey," he drawled, "I've never had to pay for sex in my life."

She flushed, and he thought he finally had her where he wanted her, only to watch that small nose shoot into the air. "Which merely points out how desperate some women can be."

"Speaking personally?"

"Raoul's opinion. My lover. He's very insightful."

He grinned, and right then it occurred to him that he hadn't enjoyed himself so much with a woman in a very long time. If Annabelle Granger were a few inches taller, a hell of a lot more sophisticated, better organized, less bossy, and more inclined to worship at his feet, she'd have made a perfect wife.

Chapter Six

‹❤›

S omeone took the seat next to Heath in the first-class cabin, but he was too preoccupied with the spreadsheet he'd pulled up on his laptop to pay attention. It wasn't until the flight attendant called for electronic devices to be shut off that he grew conscious of a dark, subtle perfume. He lifted his head and found himself looking into a set of intelligent blue eyes. "Portia?"

"Good morning, Heath." She leaned against the headrest. "How in the world do you cope with these early morning flights?"

"You get used to it."

"I'll pretend to believe you."

She was wearing some kind of a silky lilac wrap dress, slim and sleeveless, with a purple cardigan knotted around her shoulders and a silver chain at her neck studded with three bezel-set diamonds. She was a beautiful woman, cultured and accomplished, and he liked doing business with her, but he didn't find her sexy. She was too carefully put together, too aggressive. Pretty much a female version of himself. "What takes you to Tampa?" he asked, already knowing the answer.

"Not the weather, that's for sure. It's going to be ninety-three degrees there today."

"Is it?" Heath paid no attention to any weather that didn't affect the outcome of a game.

She gave him a smile designed to charm. It might have worked if he didn't own a similar smile that he used for exactly the same purpose. "After your phone call last night, I decided we needed to evaluate where we are and see what adjustments we should make. I promise I won't talk your head off the entire flight. Nothing is more annoying than being trapped on a plane with someone who won't shut up."

If he had to be cooped up on a plane with one of his match-makers, he would have preferred Tinker Bell. He could have bullied her into leaving him alone. Portia's appearance this morning had nothing to do with a sudden urge to visit Tampa. He'd explained the new arrangement to her over the phone last night then hung up while she was still in shock. Obviously, she'd recovered.

She contented herself with general chitchat until they were in the air, but once the breakfast service started she began working her way to the point. "Melanie really enjoyed meeting you. More than enjoyed. I do believe she has a bit of a crush on you."

"I hope not. Nice person, but I didn't feel any real connection with her."

"You were only together for twenty minutes." She gave him the identical sympathetic smile he used when a client was being difficult. "I understand exactly where you're coming from, but the time limit you've set is a bit of a problem. I've been in this business long enough to recognize when two people need to give themselves a second chance, and I think you and Melanie qualify."

"Sorry, but it's not going to happen."

Her forehead remained smooth, her expression composed. "This won't work, you know." She toyed with the yogurt carton on her fruit plate. "I never put down the competition, especially when it's a tiny operation like Marriages by Myrna. It smacks too much of bullying. But—"

"Perfect for You."

"What?"

"She calls it Perfect for You, not Marriages by Myrna." He couldn't imagine why he felt the need to clarify this, but somehow it seemed necessary.

"A wise decision," Portia replied, with only a whiff of condescension. "But let me just say this. I resent the way people think a trip to Kinko's to get business cards printed up is all it takes to be a matchmaker. But then, as a sports agent, you know exactly what I mean."

She'd scored a field goal with that one. Annabelle had no depth of experience, only enthusiasm.

Portia pushed aside her tray, although she'd only nibbled at the corner of a honeydew cube. "Is there something we're not providing that makes you feel the need to expose my candidates to an outsider? I'd be lying if I said I wasn't the tiniest bit threatened, especially since I offered to sit in on these initial interviews myself."

"Don't worry about it. Annabelle lacks the killer instinct. She liked Melanie better than she liked her own candidate. She tried to talk me into seeing her again."

That caught her by surprise. "Really? Well . . . Ms. Granger is an odd little duck, isn't she?"

It must have been the engine noise because, for a moment, he thought she said "odd little fuck," and he was hit with a vision of Annabelle naked. The notion took him aback. Annabelle amused him, but she didn't turn him on. Not really. Maybe he'd thought about her sexually a couple of times, and he'd made a couple of smarmy references to fluster her. But nothing serious. Just messing around.

The plane hit an air pocket, and he pulled his mind from the bedroom back to business. "I don't expect you to be comfortable with this, but as I said last night, the process will go smoother if Annabelle's there for all the introductions."

The fire in her eyes told him exactly what she was thinking, but she was too much of a pro to lose her cool. "That's a matter of opinion."

"She's a tadpole, Portia, not a shark. The women relax with her, and I can get a clearer picture of who they are in a shorter period of time."

"I see. Well, I've been doing this for a lot more years than she has. I'm sure I could expedite these interviews better than—"

"Portia, you couldn't be nonthreatening if you tried, and I mean that as the highest form of compliment. I told you from the beginning that I intended to make this easy on myself. It turns out that Annabelle's the key, and nobody's more surprised about that than I am."

She retrenched, but she wasn't happy about it. He didn't entirely blame her. If somebody poached on his territory, he'd have come out swinging, too. "All right, Heath," she said. "If this is what you need, then I'll make sure it works."

"Exactly what I want to hear."

The flight attendant took their trays, and he pulled out his copy of the *Sports Lawyers Journal*. But the article on tort liability and fan violence didn't hold his attention. Despite his best efforts to keep it simple, his hunt for a wife was growing more complicated by the day.

I like her," Heath said to Annabelle on the following Monday evening as Rachel left Sienna's. "She's fun. I had a good time."

"Me, too," Annabelle said, even though that was hardly the point. But the introduction had gone better than she'd dared hope, with lots of laughter and lively conversation. The three of them had shared their food prejudices (Heath wouldn't touch an organ meat, Rachel hated olives, and Annabelle couldn't stomach anchovies). They told embarrassing stories from their high school years and debated the merits of the Coen brothers' movies. (Thumbs-up from Heath, thumbs-down from Rachel and Annabelle.) Heath didn't seem to mind that Rachel wasn't a knockout on the order of Gwen Phelps. She had both the polish and the brains he was looking for, and there were no cell phone interruptions. Annabelle allowed the twenty minutes to expand to forty.

"Good work, Tinker Bell." He drew out his BlackBerry and typed a memo to himself. "I'll call her tomorrow and ask her out."

"Really? That's great." She felt a little queasy.

He looked up from the BlackBerry. "What's wrong?"

"Nothing. Why?"

"You have a funny expression."

She pulled herself back together. She was a professional now, and she could handle this. "I'm just imagining the newspaper interviews I'll give after Perfect for You hits the Fortune Five Hundred."

"Nothing's more inspiring than a girl with a dream." He returned the BlackBerry to his pocket and withdrew his well-stuffed money clip. She frowned. He frowned back. "Now what?"

"Don't you have a nice, discreet credit card tucked away somewhere?"

"In my business, it's all about the flash." He flashed a hundred-dollar bill and tossed it on the table.

"I'm only mentioning it because, as I think I told you, image consultation is part of my business." She hesitated, knowing she had to tread carefully. "For some women . . . women of a certain upbringing . . . obvious displays of wealth can be a little off-putting."

"Believe me, they're not off-putting to twenty-one-year-old kids who've grown up with food stamps."

"I see your point, but—"

"Got it. Money clip for business, credit card for courtship." He slipped the object under discussion back into his pocket.

She'd basically accused him of vulgarity, but instead of being offended, he seemed to have filed the information away as dispassionately as if she'd given him tomorrow's weather report. She considered his flawless table manners, the way he dressed, his knowledge of food and wine. Clearly these things had all been part of his curriculum, right along with torts and constitutional law. Exactly who was Heath Champion, and why was she beginning to like him so much?

She pleated her cocktail napkin. "So . . . about your real name . . . ?"

"I already told you. Campione."

"I did some research. Your middle initial is *D*."

"Which stands for none of your damned business."

"Something bad then."

"Horrifying," he said dryly. "Look, Annabelle, I grew up in a trailer park. Not a nice mobile home park—that would have been paradise. These heaps weren't good enough for scrap. The neighbors were addicts, thieves, people who'd gotten lost in the system. My bedroom looked out over a junkyard. I lost my mother in a car accident when I was four. My old man was a decent guy when he wasn't drunk, but that wasn't very often. I earned everything I have, and I'm proud of that. I don't hide where I came from. That dented metal sign on my office wall, the one that says BEAU VISTA, used to hang on a post not far from our door. I keep it as a reminder of how far I've come. But beyond that, my business is mine, and yours is doing what I tell you. Got it?"

"Jeez, all I did was ask your middle name."

"Don't ask again."

"Desdemona?"

But he refused to entertain her, and she ended up staring at his back as he headed for the kitchen to pay his respects to Mama.

• • •

I want you in the clubs every night," Portia announced to her staff the next morning. Ramon, Sienna's bartender, had awakened her at midnight with the disturbing news about Annabelle Granger's success with her latest match, and she hadn't been able to fall back to sleep. She couldn't get past the feeling that another important client was slipping away from her. "Pass out your business cards," she told Kiki and Briana, along with Diana, the girl she'd hired to replace SuSu. "Pick up phone numbers. You know the routine."

"We've done that," Briana said.

"But apparently not well enough or Heath Champion wouldn't have made plans with Granger's prospect last night instead of ours. And what about Hendricks and Mccall? We haven't shown them anybody new in two weeks? What about the rest of our clients? Kiki, I want you to spend the rest of the week staking out the modeling agencies. I'll hit the charity luncheons and the Oak Street boutiques. Briana and Diana, work the hair salons and the big department stores. All of you—clubs at night. By this time next week, we're going to be screening a fresh batch of candidates."

"A lot of good it'll do with Heath," Briana muttered. "He doesn't like anybody."

They didn't get it, Portia thought as she returned to her office and flipped through her calendar. They didn't understand how hard you had to work to stay on top. She gazed down at Friday's calendar entry. In a short, terse phone conversation, Bodie Gray had set up their date for this weekend. She'd done her best not to think about it since. Just the possibility that someone might see them together gave her nightmares. But at least he didn't seem to have told Heath about her spying episode.

A helicopter flew overhead. She rubbed her temples and considered setting up a spa day. She needed something to lift her spirits, something to make her feel like her old self again. But as she turned toward her computer, a traitorous voice whispered there weren't enough massages, ayurvedic facials, or hot stone pedicures in the world to fix whatever wanted to stop working inside her.

A nnabelle couldn't afford to pin all her hopes on Rachel's date with Heath, so she spent the rest of the week hanging out at two of Chicago's top universities. At the University of Chicago in Hyde Park, she alternated between haunting the hallways of the Graduate School of Business and lingering by the steps of the Harris School of Public Policy. She also made her way to Lincoln Park, where she spent most of her time with the music majors at the De Paul Concert Hall. At both schools, she kept her eyes open for comely graduate students and beautiful faculty members. When she found them, she approached them directly, explained who she was and what she was looking for. Some were married or engaged, one was a lesbian, but the world loves a matchmaker, and most of the women were interested in helping her. By the end of the week, she had two great candidates ready to go if she needed them, as well as half a dozen women who weren't right for Heath, but who were interested in signing on as clients themselves. Since they couldn't afford the kinds of fees she wanted to charge, she established an academic discount.

Heath was out of town for the week, and he didn't call. Not that she expected him to. Still, for someone who spent all his time on the phone, she would have thought he could have spared a few minutes to check in with her. Instead of stewing about it, she slipped on her sneakers, jogged to Dunkin' Donuts, and distracted herself with an apple Danish.

H eath spent the first four days of the week traveling between Dallas, Atlanta, and St. Louis, but even as he met with clients and player personnel directors, he found himself thinking ahead to his Friday afternoon powwow at Stars head-quarters. When it came to the Stars, he tried to do as much business as possible with Ron McDermitt, the team's top-notch general manager, but once again Phoebe Calebow had insisted on seeing him instead. Not a good sign.

Heath prided himself on having a good relationship with all the team owners. Phoebe was the glaring exception. It was his fault they'd gotten off to a bad start. One of his first clients had been a Green Bay veteran unhappy with the contract his for-mer agent had negotiated. Heath wanted to prove how tough he was, so when the Stars expressed interest in the guy, Heath had unfairly strung Phoebe along, letting her believe she had a good chance at signing him even though he knew otherwise. He'd then taken her interest in the player to the Packers' bar-gaining table and used it to gain the leverage he needed to get his client a better deal. Phoebe was furious and, in a blistering phone call, warned him never to use her like that again.

Instead of taking her words to heart, he'd gotten into an-other battle with her a few months later over a second client, this one a Stars player. Heath had decided he needed to sweeten the third year of an existing three-year contract, again negoti-ated by a former agent, but Phoebe refused to budge. After a few weeks, Heath threatened to hold the player out of training camp. The guy was her best tight end, and since Heath had her over a barrel, she came through with a respectable counteroffer. Still, it wasn't the splashy new deal Heath thought he needed to establish his reputation as an agent on the move. He dug in and sent the player deep-sea fishing the day training camp started.

Phoebe was enraged, and the media had a field day playing up the feud between the Stars' tight-fisted owner and the city's brash new agent. Heath capitalized on the player's popularity with the fans by giving interviews at the drop of a hat and dra-matically berating Phoebe for treating one of her best men so shabbily. As the first week of training camp came to end, Heath kept on showboating, staying cozy with the sports columnists and working the sound bites on the ten o'clock news. A back swell built against Phoebe. Still, she wouldn't budge.

Just as he'd begun to have second thoughts about the wisdom of his strategy, a stroke of luck occurred. The Stars' backup tight end broke his ankle in practice, and Phoebe was forced to cave. Heath got the extravagant deal he wanted, but in the process, he'd made her look bad, and she'd never forgiven him. The experiences taught him two hard lessons: In a good negotiation, everybody comes out feeling like a winner. And a successful agent doesn't build his reputation by humiliating the people he has to work with.

The Stars' receptionist directed him to the practice field, and as he approached, he saw Dean Robillard cozying up to Phoebe on the sidelines bench. He swore under his breath. The last thing he wanted Robillard to witness was Phoebe Calebow cutting him to shreds. Dean looked like he'd stepped out of *Surfer Magazine:* beard stubble, gel-rumpled blond hair, tropical print shorts, a T-shirt, and athletic sandals. Hoping to minimize the collateral damage, Heath made a quick decision and concentrated on him first. "Is that a new Porsche I saw sitting in your parking space?"

Dean gazed at him through the yellow iridium lenses of a pair of high-tech Oakleys. "That ol' junker? Heck, no. I bought it at least three weeks ago."

Heath found a laugh, even though the hair had begun to stand up on the back of his neck. And not from being around Robillard. He slipped on his own sunglasses, not so much to protect his eyes, but to even out the playing field.

"Well, well, well . . . ," Phoebe Somerville Calebow cooed in the husky, bimbo voice she used to conceal her razor-sharp mind. "Look who's joined us. And I thought our exterminator had gotten rid of all the rats around here."

"Nope. The meanest and strongest somehow manage to survive." Heath grinned, doing his best to hit the balance between not pissing her off any more than he had to and letting Dean see she couldn't intimidate him.

The Stars' owner and chief operating officer was in her forties now, and nobody wore the years better. She looked like a more intellectual version of Marilyn Monroe, with the same cloud of pale blond hair and a powerhouse body, today clad in a clingy aqua shell and pencil-slim canary yellow skirt slit up the side. Busty, leggy, and delectable, she should have been a centerfold instead of the most powerful woman in the NFL.

Dean rose. "I think I'll get out of here before the two of you accidentally hurt my passing arm."

Heath couldn't back down now. "Shoot, Dean, we haven't even started having fun yet. Stick around and watch me make Phoebe cry."

Robillard gazed down at his beautiful boss. "I've never seen this crazy man before in my life."

She smiled. "Run along, Dean honey. Your sex life will be screwed up forever if you're forced to watch all the ways a woman can chop up a snake."

Retreat wouldn't win Heath the quarterback's heart, and as Robillard began to walk away, Heath called out after him. "Hey, Dean . . . Sometime ask Phoebe to show you where she buries the bones of all the agents who don't have the balls to stand up to her."

Dean waved good-bye without turning around. "I didn't hear that, Mrs. Calebow. I'm just a sweet mama's boy from California who wants to play a little football for you and go to church in my spare time."

Phoebe laughed and stretched her long bare legs as Dean disappeared through the fence. "I like that boy. I like him so much I'm going to make sure you never get your grubby hands on him."

"I doubt it was too hard to lure him out here today so he could witness our little meeting."

"Not hard at all."

"It's been seven years, Phoebe. Don't you think it's time we bury the hatchet?"

"As long as the blade ends up in the back of your neck, I'm game."

He slipped his fingers in his pockets and smiled. "The best day of my career was the day your brother-in-law signed on as my client. I still savor every minute of it."

Phoebe scowled. She loved Kevin Tucker as though they were blood relatives instead of being related by marriage, and the fact that he'd ignored her entreaty and signed with Heath was a bitter pill she'd never quite been able to swallow. Heath's first negotiations with her over Kevin's contract had been brutal. Just because family was involved didn't mean Phoebe believed in loosening her iron grip on the Stars' finances, and he still remembered the way she'd methodically x-ed out an admittedly outrageous bonus package Heath had stuck in to test the waters.

"Family is family, and business is business. I love the boy, but not that much."

"Who are you kidding?" Heath had said. *"You'd walk over coals for him."*

"Yes, but I'd leave my checkbook behind while I was doing it."

Heath gazed toward the practice field. Although training camp wouldn't start for more than a month, a few players were running drills with the team's trainer. He nodded toward a fourth-year player, one of the Zagorskis' clients. "Keman's looking good."

"He'd look a lot better if he spent more time in the weight room and less time selling used cars on TV. But Dan likes him."

Dan Calebow was the Stars' president and Phoebe's husband. They'd met when Phoebe had inherited the Stars from her father. At the time, Dan had been the head coach and Phoebe had known nothing about football, something that was

hard to believe now. Their early battles were nearly as leg-
endary as their ensuing love story. Last year one of the cable
channels had made a cheesy movie about them, and Dan was
still getting ribbed because he'd been portrayed by a former
boy band singer.

"I want a three-year contract," Phoebe said, getting down
to the business of Caleb Crenshaw.

"Yeah, I'd want one, too, if I were you, but Caleb's only
signing for two years."

"Three. It's not negotiable." She stated her case without
consulting notes, reeling off complex statistics in her breathy,
sex-kitten's voice. They both had excellent memories, and he
didn't write anything down, either.

"You know I can't advise Caleb to take that offer." He
propped his foot on the bench next to her. "By the third year,
he'll be worth millions more than you'll be paying him."
Which was exactly why she wanted the three-year deal.

"Only if he stays healthy," she retorted, as he'd known she
would. "I'm the one taking all the risk. If he blows out his knee
that third year, I'll still have to pay him." She went on from
there, emphasizing her altruism and the unending gratitude a
player should feel for simply being allowed to wear the uniform
of football legends like Bobby Tom Denton, Cal Bonner, Darnell Pruitt, and, yes, Kevin Tucker.

Heath threatened a holdout, even though he had no intention of carrying it through. What he'd once seen as a canny
bargaining tool he now regarded as a desperate measure guaranteed to do more harm than good.

Phoebe bore down, hitting him with more breathy statistics, peppered with allusions to ungrateful players and blood-
sucking agents.

He countered with statistics of his own, all of them pointing toward the fact that tightwad owners ended up with resent-
ful players and a losing season.

In the end, they arrived at the place they'd both pretty much known they'd reach. Phoebe got her three-year contract, and Caleb Crenshaw got a one-and-a-half-million-dollar signing bonus for the insult. Win. Win. Except it was an agreement they could have reached three months ago if Phoebe hadn't gone out of her way to make things as hard for him as she could.

"Hey, Heath."

He turned to see Molly Somerville Tucker approaching. Kevin's wife couldn't have been more different from the standard-issue knockout blond NFL spouse. Her body was trim and compact, but hardly memorable. Except for a pair of blue-gray eyes that tilted up at the corners, she and Phoebe bore little physical resemblance. He definitely liked Molly a lot more than he liked her sister. Kevin's wife was smart, funny, and easy to talk to. In some ways, she reminded him of Annabelle, although Annabelle was smaller, and her shock of russet curls bore no resemblance to Molly's straight brown bob. Still, they were both feisty smart-asses, and he wasn't letting down his guard in front of either of them.

Molly had a baby in her arms, one Daniel John Tucker, aged nine months. She held a curly-haired little girl by the opposite hand. Heath was glad to see Molly, neutral about seeing the baby boy, and less than pleased to be in the presence of the three-year-old girl. Thankfully, Victoria Phoebe Tucker had a more important target in sight.

"Aunt Phoebe!" She dropped her mother's hand and made her way toward the Stars' owner as fast as her small feet, clad in bright red rubber boots, could carry her. The boots looked weird with her purple polka-dot shorts and top. It also hadn't rained in two weeks, but he had personal experience with Pippi Tucker's single-mindedness, and he didn't blame Molly for choosing her battles.

In a case of like attracting like, Phoebe hopped up from the bench to greet the little curly-haired larcenist. "Hey, punkin'."

"Guess what, Aunt Phoebe . . ."

Heath tuned the kid out as Molly came over to him. She touched the side of his neck. "I don't see any puncture marks, so your meeting must have gone well."

"I'm still alive."

She shifted the baby from one arm to the other. "So have you found Mrs. Champion yet? Annabelle's got this weird— and totally unnecessary—thing going about confidentiality."

He smiled. "I'm still looking." He grabbed the baby's drooly fist as a distraction. "Hey, pal, how's that throwing arm coming along?"

He wasn't great with kids, and the little boy buried his face in his mother's shoulder.

"No football," Molly said. "This one's going to be a writer like me. Aren't you, Danny?" Molly kissed the top of the baby's head, then frowned. "Have you talked to Annabelle today?"

"No, why?" Out of the corner of his eye he saw Phoebe smile fondly at Pippi. He wished just once she'd give him a smile half that genuine.

"I've been trying to get hold of her all day," Molly said, "but her phones aren't working. If she happens to call you, tell her I want to talk to her about the grand soirée tomorrow afternoon."

"One o'clock." Phoebe spoke over the top of Pippi's curly blond head. "Does she know we changed the time?"

Heath went still. A party? This was exactly the chance he'd been waiting for.

"I wish I could remember," Molly said. "But I'm on dead-line, and I've been distracted."

The Tuckers and Calebows got together all the time, but Heath never received an invitation, no matter how many times he explained to Kevin that he needed one. Heath wanted a chance to be with Phoebe when they weren't doing battle, and an informal social gathering was the perfect opportunity. Maybe if they weren't wrangling over a contract, she'd see he was generally a decent guy. Over the years, he'd tried to set up a dozen lunches and dinners, but she always ducked, generally with cracks about food poisoning. Now Molly was throwing a party, and she'd invited Annabelle. The person she hadn't invited was him.

Maybe it was a female-only affair. Or maybe not.

There was only one way to find out.

Chapter Seven

❧

"That woman doesn't know a damn thing about running a business," Heath grumbled as Bodie shot through an I-Pass lane at the York Road toll plaza heading east for the Eisenhower Expressway. "Neither of her numbers are working. We'll have to find her."

"Suits me," Bodie said. "I've got plenty of time before my date tonight."

Heath placed a call to his office, got Annabelle's Wicker Park address, and forty-five minutes later, they drew up in front of a tiny blue-and-lavender gingerbread house stuck between two very expensive-looking town houses. "Looks like Bo Peep's love nest," he said as Bodie pulled to the curb.

"The front door's open, so she's home." Bodie peered toward the house. "I'm going to run up to Earwax and grab some coffee while you fight with her. You want me to bring you back something?"

Heath shook his head. Earwax was a funky Milwaukee Avenue coffeehouse that had become a Wicker Park institution. Bodie, with his shaved head and tattoos, fit right in there, but then so did everybody else. Bodie drove off, and Heath made his way through an old iron gate leading to a doormat-size lawn containing neatly mowed crabgrass. He heard Annabelle's voice even before he reached the door.

"I'm doing my best, Mr. Bronicki."

"That last one was too old," a wheezy voice replied.

"She's nearly ten years younger than you are."

"Seventy-one. That's too old."

Stopping at the open door, Heath saw Annabelle standing in the middle of a cheery blue-and-yellow room that seemed to serve as her reception area. She wore a short white T-shirt, a pair of low-slung jeans, and rainbow flip-flops. She'd caught her hair up on top of her head in a curly little whale spout that made her look like Pebbles Flintstone, except with a better body.

A bald, elderly man with bushy eyebrows glowered down at her. "I told you I wanted a lady in her thirties."

"Mr. Bronicki, most women in their thirties are looking for a man who's a little closer to their own age."

"That shows what you know. Women like older men. They know that's where the money is."

Heath smiled, enjoying himself for the first time all day. As he stepped over the threshold, Annabelle spotted him. Her honey-colored eyes widened as if a big bad dinosaur had shown up at the door of the Flintstones' cave. "Heath? What are you doing here?"

"You don't seem to be answering your phone."

"That's because she's been trying to dodge me," the elderly man interjected.

Annabelle's whale spout hairdo twitched indignantly. "I wasn't trying to dodge you. Look, Mr. Bronicki, I need to talk with Mr. Champion. You and I can discuss this some other time."

"Oh, no you don't." Mr. Bronicki crossed his arms over his chest. "You're just trying to weasel out of that contract."

Heath made an open-handed, accommodating gesture. "Don't mind me. I'll just stand here and watch."

She shot him an exasperated look. He drew in the corners of

his mouth and moved closer to the couch, which improved his view of her clingy white T-shirt. His eyes drifted down a trim pair of legs to her feet and then her toes, which were painted a sparkly grape with white polka dots. Pebbles had her own sense of style.

She returned her attention to her elderly visitor. "I don't weasel," she said hotly. "Mrs. Valerio happens to be a lovely woman, and you two have a lot in common."

"She's too old," the man shot back. "Satisfaction guaranteed, remember? That's what the contract said, and my nephew's a lawyer."

"So you've mentioned before."

"A good one, too. He went to a real good law school."

The steely glint that appeared in Annabelle's eyes didn't bode well for poor Mr. Bronicki. "As good as *Harvard*?" she said triumphantly. "Because that's where Mr. Champion went to school, and"—she zeroed in on him—"he's *my* lawyer."

Heath lifted an eyebrow.

The old man studied him suspiciously, and Annabelle's cheeks plumped in a kitten-ate-the-cream smile. "Mr. Bronicki, this is Heath Champion, otherwise known as the *Python*, but don't let that worry you. He hardly ever sends seniors to prison. Heath, Mr. Bronicki is one of my grandmother's former clients."

"Uh-huh."

Mr. Bronicki blinked but quickly recovered. "If you're her lawyer, maybe you'd better tell her how a contract works."

Annabelle bristled all over again. "Mr. Bronicki is under the impression that a contract he signed with my grandmother in 1986 is still valid and that I should honor it."

"It said satisfaction guaranteed," Mr. Bronicki retorted. "And I wasn't satisfied."

"You were married to Mrs. Bronicki for fifteen years!" Annabelle exclaimed. "I'd say you got your two hundred dollars' worth."

"I told you. She went loony on me. Now I want another one."

Heath didn't know which was more amusing, Mr. Bronicki's jiggling eyebrows, or the indignant twitching of Pebbles's whale spout. "I'm not running a supermarket!" She spun on Heath. "Tell him!"

Ah, well. All good things had to come to an end. He went into lawyer mode. "Mr. Bronicki, apparently your contract was with Ms. Granger's grandmother. And since the original terms seemed to have been fulfilled, I'm afraid you don't have grounds for complaint."

"What do you mean I don't have grounds? I got grounds, all right." Eyebrows hopping, he started hammering Annabelle with one grievance after another, none of which had anything to do with her. The more he ranted, the more Heath's amusement faded. He didn't like anybody but himself browbeating her.

"That's enough," he finally said.

The old guy must have realized Heath meant business because he stopped in midsentence. Heath moved closer, putting himself between Bronicki and Annabelle. "If you think you have a case, talk to your nephew. And while you're talking to him, ask him to fill you in on the laws against harassment."

The bushy eyebrows drooped like dying caterpillars, and the old guy's aggression instantly dissolved. "I never harassed nobody."

"That's not what it looks like to me," Heath said.

"I didn't mean to harass her." He wilted even more. "I was just trying to make a point."

"You've made it," Heath replied. "Now maybe you'd better leave."

His shoulders dipped, his head dropped. "Sorry, Annabelle." He made his way out the door.

A loose lock of Annabelle's hair whipped her cheek as she spun on Heath. "You didn't have to be so mean!"

"*Mean?*"

She hurried out on the porch, her flip-flops slapping the wooden boards. "Mr. Bronicki! Mr. Bronicki, stop! If you don't ask Mrs. Valerio out again, you're going to hurt her feelings. I know you don't want to do that."

His reply was subdued. "You're just trying to make me do what you want."

The flip-flops thumped more softly down the steps, and her voice grew wheedling. "Would that be so bad? Pretty please. She's a nice lady, and she likes you so much. Ask her out again. As a favor to me."

There was a long pause.

"All right," he replied with some of his former spunk. "But I'm not asking her out for Saturday night. That's when *Iron Chef*'s on."

"Fair enough."

Annabelle returned, a satisfied smile on her face. Heath regarded her with amusement. "I sure hope I never have to go head to head with you in the wrestling ring."

A furrow formed along the bridge of her small nose. "You were mean. He's lonesome, and arguing with me gives him something to look forward to." She eyed him suspiciously. "What are you doing here?"

"Your phones aren't working."

"Sure they are." Her hand flew to her mouth. "Oh, jeez . . ."

"Forgot to pay your bill?"

"Just for my cell. I know my other phone's working." She disappeared through the archway. He followed her into her office. Quality art posters filled the long wall behind her computer desk. He recognized a Chagall and one of Jasper Johns's white-on-white American flags.

She lifted the receiver and, when she didn't hear a dial tone, looked mystified. Heath picked up the cord dangling next to the ancient black answering machine. "It works better when it's plugged in."

Annabelle shoved it back in. "I was trying to fix it last night."

"Good job. You've never heard of voice mail?"

"This is cheaper."

"When it comes to keeping in touch with your clients, never cut corners."

"You're right. I know better."

The fact that she didn't try to argue took him aback. Most people went on the defensive when they screwed up.

"I don't make a habit of not paying my bills," she said. "I think what happened with my cell was subconscious. We're not getting along."

"Maybe counseling would help."

"In what universe did I ever think it was a good idea to let my mother find me whenever she wanted?" She sank down in the chair, her expression an entertaining combination of indignation and woe. "Tell me you're not here because you canceled your date with Rachel tonight."

"No. We're on."

"Then what's up?"

"A goodwill mission. I saw Molly today at Stars headquarters, and she asked me to remind you about tomorrow. One o'clock."

"The party . . . I almost forgot." She cocked her head, suspicion back in those melted butterscotch eyes. "You drove all the way up here just to remind me about Phoebe's party?"

"Phoebe's party? I thought it was Molly's."

"No."

This was even better. He picked up the small, pink Beanie Baby rabbit she kept on her computer monitor and examined it. "Do you go to a lot of parties at the Calebows?"

"A few," she said slowly. "Why?"

"I was thinking about tagging along." He turned the rabbit bottoms up and checked out its tail. "Or do you already have a date?"

"No, it's not—" She sank back into her desk chair, her eyes widening. "Wow. This is truly pathetic. You're using me to get to Phoebe. You can't get an invitation to her parties on your own, and now you're using me."

"Pretty much." He returned the rabbit to its perch.

"You're not even embarrassed."

"It's hard to embarrass an agent."

"I don't get it. Phoebe and Dan invite everybody to their parties."

"She and I are going through a bumpy period, that's all. I need to smooth things out."

"And you think you can do that at a party?"

"I figure she'll be more relaxed in a social situation."

"How long has this bumpy period been going on?"

"About seven years."

"Ouch."

He studied the Jasper Johns poster. "I was overly aggressive when I started out, and I made her look bad. I've apologized, but she can't seem to get past it."

"I'm not sure this is the best way to fix your problem with her."

"Look, Annabelle, do you want to help me or not?"

"It's just that—"

"Right," he said abruptly. "I keep forgetting we have different philosophies about running a business. I like to please my clients, and you don't care. But then maybe you enjoy limiting yourself to senior citizens."

She shot up from her chair, whale spout quivering. "Fine. You want to go to the party with me tomorrow, go ahead."

"Great. I'll pick you up at noon. What's the dress code?"

"I'm so tempted to tell you black tie."

"Casual then." Through the window, he spotted Bodie pulling up to the curb. He propped a hip on the corner of her desk. "Let's not mention to Phoebe that I asked you to bring me along. Just tell her you think I've been working too hard, and I need a little relaxation before I meet any more of those women you have lined up."

"Phoebe's not stupid. You don't really think she'll believe that?"

"If you're convincing she will." He straightened and headed for the door. "Successful people create their own reality, Annabelle. Grab the ball and get in the game."

Before she could tell him that she was already playing as hard as she knew how, he was on his way down her sidewalk. She walked over to the door and shut it behind him. Once again, he'd seen her at her worst: no makeup, phones out of order, and wrangling with Mr. Bronicki. On the positive side, Rachel was going to look really good to him this evening by comparison.

Annabelle wondered if they'd sleep together. The idea depressed her way too much. She headed for the kitchen and poured herself a glass of iced tea, then carried it back to her office, where she called John Nager to check on the lunch date she'd arranged.

"She had a cold, Annabelle. Noticeable congestion."

"John, women come with germs."

"It's a question of degree."

She wondered how Heath would deal with a hypochondriacal client. "She wants to see you again," she said, "but if you're not interested, I have other clients who will be."

"Well . . . She's very pretty."

"And germy, like every other woman I've fixed you up with. Can you handle that?"

John eventually decided he'd give it a go. She dragged out the vacuum and made a few desultory swipes at the downstairs, then filled a pitcher to water Nana's African violet collection. As she added a few drops of fertilizer, she contemplated arranging a date between Mrs. Porter and Mr. Clemens. They were both widowers in their seventies, two more of Nana's clients she couldn't quite shake. Mrs. Porter was black and Mr. Clemens white, which might give their families trouble, but Annabelle had sensed a lot of interest when she'd run into them at the grocery store, and they both loved to bowl. She carried the pitcher into her office. Would she ever get rid of these seniors? No matter how many times she explained to them that Marriages by Myrna had closed its doors, they kept on showing up. Even worse, they expected her to continue charging Nana's fees.

When she finished with the African violets, she sat down to pay bills. Thanks to Heath's check, she'd settled the worst of them. Yesterday she'd called Melanie to see if she'd be interested in signing on as a client, which had meant coming clean about her real occupation. Fortunately, Melanie had a sense of humor, and she'd seemed interested. Things were looking up.

The Little Mermaid clock on her desk ticked away. Heath would be picking up Rachel about now. They were going to Tru, where caviar appeared at the table in a miniature glass staircase and dinner for two could easily run four hundred dollars. Not that she'd ever been there herself, but she'd read about it.

She considered visiting a couple of local coffee shops to pass out her business card, but she didn't have enough energy to change clothes. Friday night. No hot date. No prospects for a hot date. The matchmaker needed a matchmaker. She wanted to get married, wanted a family, a job she loved . . . Was that too much to ask out of life? But how would she ever find a man of her own if she had to keep giving the best ones away? Not that Heath was the best. He was husband material only in his own mind. No, that wasn't entirely fair. Whatever he did, he did well, and he'd give marriage his best effort. Whether or not that would prove good enough remained to be seen. Fortunately, not her problem.

She pulled out a DVD of *Waiting for Guffman,* then remembered it belonged to Rob and chose *Freaky Friday* instead. She'd just gotten to the part where Jamie Lee Curtis and her daughter switch bodies when the phone rang.

"Annabelle, it's Rachel."

She hit the Stop button. "How's it going?"

"I'm out of my league."

"What do you mean? Where are you calling from?"

"The ladies' room at Tru. The date's not working. I can't understand it. Heath and I had so much fun together the night you introduced us—you remember—but now everything feels flat."

"I knew he'd do this. He's been on his cell all night, hasn't he?"

"He hasn't taken a single call. In fact, he's been a perfect gentleman. But we're both working too hard to keep the conversation going."

"He's been traveling all week. He might be tired."

"I don't think it's that. It's just— Nothing's happening. I'm really disappointed. I felt sparks that first time. Didn't you?"

"Definitely. Ask him about his work. Or about baseball. He's a Sox fan. Just keep trying."

Rachel said she would, but she didn't seem optimistic, and when Annabelle hung up, she felt deflated . . . and relieved.

One more reason to be depressed.

Chapter Eight

Moths swarmed in the caged lights over the doors. The bar, located in a former warehouse just off North Avenue, was named Suey, and the sign featured a giant red pig wearing a trucker's cap. "Charming," Portia drawled.

Bodie gave her a dumb, cocky grin, which went right along with his menacing shaved head, intimidating tattoos, and hit man's muscles. "I knew you'd like it."

"I was being sarcastic."

"Why?"

"Because this is a sports bar."

"You don't like sports bars? That's weird." He held the door open for her.

She rolled her eyes and followed him in. The place was huge and noisy, smelling of stale beer, french fries, and aftershave, all topped off with eau de gym. The bar opened into a bigger room with tables, games, and cinder-block walls displaying the logos of the Chicago teams. She glimpsed an even larger area in the back holding metal lockers and a sand volleyball court surrounded by orange plastic fencing. Blow-up sex dolls, beer signs, and *Star*

Wars light sabers hung from the open rafters. Boys would be boys. Thankfully, not the sort of place her friends would be prone to hang out.

She'd dressed down for the evening, digging out an old pair of magenta cotton slacks, a clingy navy top with a built-in bra, and flat sandals. She'd even traded in her diamond studs for simple silver hoops. She followed Bodie past a rowdy group of twenty-somethings who were ignoring the overhead televisions to do tequila shots at the bar. As the crowd parted, she grew conscious of the women's eyes on Bodie. A few greeted him by name. Muscle-bound men always tended to look sloppy, but his espresso brown polo shirt and chinos couldn't have fit him better, and every woman in the place noticed.

She slipped into his wake, which was large enough to keep people from bumping against her, and let him lead her to a table that afforded a view of a mechanical bull and the volleyball game in the next room. Ordering either wine or a mixed drink struck her as high risk, so she settled on a lite beer, but asked that it be served in the bottle. Easier to guard against roofies.

He kicked back with his own beer and openly studied her. "How old are you?"

"Old enough to know this is the worst date of my life."

"Women like you are hard to figure. Your skin is great, but you've got old eyes."

"Anything else?" she asked coldly.

"I figure forty-three, forty-four."

"I'm thirty-seven," she snapped.

"No, *I'm* thirty-seven. You're forty-two. I did some research."

"Then why did you ask?"

"I wanted to see if you give yourself away when you lie." Amusement danced in his pale eyes. "Now I know."

She resisted taking the bait. "Is this date over yet?"

"Just getting started. I think we should wait till after we play to eat, don't you?"

"Play?"

He jerked his head toward the volleyball court. "We've got a game in forty minutes."

"Oh, right. And that would be just after I walk out, right?"

"I already signed us up. You have to play."

"Wrongo."

"I should have told you to bring shorts."

"You probably had too many other weighty matters on your mind."

He smiled. "You are one beautiful bitch."

"Thank you."

His smile grew broader, and her skin prickled. Once again, she considered the possibility that he wasn't as dumb as he seemed to be.

"Definitely a ballbuster," he said. "This is my lucky day." She flinched as he reached toward her, but when he touched the base of her throat with the tip of his finger, a tiny shock zipped along her skin. "You and me are going to be great together . . . as long as I keep that dog collar snapped good and tight around your neck."

Another jolt zapped her nerve endings, and she jerked away. Fortunately, three of the men who'd been hanging out at the bar chose that moment to approach. They were all young and respectful. Bodie introduced her, but they were only interested in him. She learned he'd played pro football, and as the men talked sports, she experienced the unusual, and not unwelcome, feeling of being invisible. She let herself relax a little. When the young-sters drifted away, however, she knew it was time to take control. "Tell me about yourself, Bodie. Where are you from?"

He studied her, almost as if he were making up his mind how much he wanted to reveal. "A dot on the map in southern Illinois."

"Small-town boy."

"You might say. I grew up in a trailer park, the only kid in the place." He took a sip of beer. "My bedroom looked out over a junkyard."

His rough background was written all over him, so she wasn't surprised. "What about your parents?"

"My mother died when I was four, and my father was a good-looking drunk who had a way with the ladies. Believe me, there were a lot of them around while I was growing up."

It was all so sordid that Portia wished she hadn't asked. She thought of her ex-husband, with his impeccable pedigree, of the dozens of other men she'd dated over the years, some of them self-made, but all polished and well mannered. Yet here she was in a sports bar with a man who looked like he made his living stuffing dead bodies in car trunks. One more sign that her life was veering away from her.

Bodie excused himself, and she checked her cell. A message had come in from Juanita Brooks, the director of the Community Small Business Initiative. Portia immediately returned it. Volunteering with the CSBI had helped fill the hole left in her life by her divorce. Although she'd never confess it to anyone, she wanted validation—proof that she was the best—and mentoring these new businesswomen was giving her that. She had so much hard-earned wisdom to offer. If only they would listen to her.

"Portia, I've spoken with Mary Churso," Juanita said. "I know you were excited about advising her, but . . . she's asked to be assigned to someone else."

"Someone else? But that's not possible. I've spent so much time with her. I've worked so hard. How could she do that?"

"I think she was a little intimidated," Juanita said. "Just like the others." She hesitated for a moment. "I appreciate your commitment, Portia. Truly I do. But most of the women who come to us need to be nurtured a bit more gently." Portia listened incredulously as Juanita explained that she had no one else currently in mind for her to work with, but that she'd let her know if someone "special" came along. Then she hung up.

Portia couldn't believe it. She felt as if a giant fist had squeezed all the air from her lungs. How could Juanita steal this from her? She fought off her panic with anger. The woman was a terrible administrator. The absolute worst. She'd effectively fired Portia for expecting the best from these women instead of patronizing them.

Just then Bodie reappeared. He was exactly the distraction she needed, and she shoved her cell in her purse to watch him approach. A white T-shirt molded to his chest, and black athletic shorts displayed the powerful musculature of his legs, one of which had a long, puckered scar. She was shocked to feel her senses quickening.

"Showtime." He pulled her to her feet.

Juanita had unhinged her so much that she'd forgotten about the game. "I'm not doing this."

"Sure you are." He ignored her protests as he steered her toward the volleyball court. "Hey, guys, this is Portia. She's a volleyball pro from the West Coast."

"Hey, Portia."

All but two of the players were male. One of the women wore shorts and looked like she meant business. The other was dressed in street clothes and also seemed to have been dragged into the game. Portia hated doing things she wasn't good at. She hadn't played volleyball since her freshman year in college, and the only part of her game that had ever amounted to anything was her serve.

Bodie slipped his fingers around the back of her neck and squeezed just firmly enough to remind her of his dog collar remark. "Kick off those sandals and show us what you've got."

He didn't believe she'd do it. This was a test, and he expected her to fail. Well, she wouldn't fail. Not again. Not after what had just happened with Juanita. She kicked off her sandals and stepped into the sand. He inclined his head—a mark of respect?—and turned away to address another player.

The ball didn't come close to her until several minutes into the game when it shot right at her chest. She couldn't get under it, and she pushed it into the net. As it came out, Bodie dove for it, sending up a spray of sand and somehow managing to get it up and over. He was an amazing athlete, intensely physical, quick, and intimidating. He was also a team player, setting up shots for the others instead of hogging the ball. Portia played hard, but other than scoring a point on a serve, she was a liability. Still, with Bodie taking up the slack next to her, their team won both games, and as she celebrated with them, she felt an odd exhilaration. She wanted Juanita Brooks—everybody at the Community Small Business Initiative—to see her now.

She cleaned up as well as she could in the restroom, but only a shower would remove the grit that had made its way into her hair and between her toes. She returned to the table just as Bodie reappeared in his street clothes. The bar didn't have showers, so he shouldn't have smelled so good, of agreeable male exertion, piney soap, and clean clothes. As he took his seat, the sleeve of his knit shirt rode up on his biceps, revealing more of the intricate tribal tattoo that encircled it. He grinned. "You sucked."

No one else was getting the best of her tonight. "Now you've gone and hurt my feelings," she cooed.

"God, I can't wait to get you into bed."

Another of those unnerving shocks skittered through her. She snatched up the beer he'd ordered for her and took a sip, but it was too warm to cool her off. "You're assuming a lot."

"Not so much." He leaned in. "How else can you make sure I'll keep my mouth shut around Heath? It's the damnedest thing, but I can't seem to forget that little spying episode."

"You're blackmailing me with sex?"

"Why not?" He settled back in his chair with a crooked

grin. "It'll give you a good excuse to do what you want to anyway."

If another man had delivered a line like that, she would have laughed in his face, but the pit of her stomach dipped. She had the oddest feeling Bodie knew something about her that other people didn't understand, maybe something she'd missed herself. "You're delusional."

He rubbed his knuckles. "There's nothing I love more than sexually dominating a strong woman."

Her fingers tightened around the bottle, not because she felt threatened—he was enjoying himself too much—but because his words aroused her. "Maybe you should talk to a shrink."

"And spoil all our fun? I don't think so."

No one ever played sexual games with her. She crossed her legs and gave him a withering smile. "You deluded little man."

He leaned forward and whispered against her earlobe. "One of these nights I'm going to make you pay for that." And then he bit.

She nearly groaned, not with pain—he wasn't hurting her—but with an unsettling excitement. Fortunately, one of the men from the volleyball game came up to the table, so Bodie backed off, giving her a chance to regain her balance.

Their food arrived shortly afterward. Bodie had ordered without consulting her, then had the nerve to chastise her for not eating. "You don't really bite into anything. You just lick. No wonder you're scrawny."

"You silver-tongued devil."

"As long as your mouth's open . . ." He slipped in a french fry. She savored the shock of the grease and the salt but turned away when he offered another. More volleyball players stopped by the table. As Bodie chatted with them, she automatically surveyed the women in the bar. Several were quite beautiful, and she itched to give them her card, but she couldn't motivate herself to get up. Bodie's presence had sucked the oxygen out of the room, leaving the air too thin for her to breathe.

By the time they left the sports bar and entered the lobby of her building, she'd grown almost giddy with desire. She mentally rehearsed how she'd handle him. He knew exactly the effect he was having on her, so of course he expected her to invite him up. She wouldn't, but he'd get in the elevator anyway, and she'd respond with cool amusement. Perfect.

But Bodie Gray had one more surprise up his sleeve. "Good night, slugger." With nothing more than a kiss on the forehead, he walked away.

Saturday morning Annabelle got up early and headed for Roscoe Village, a former haven for drug dealers that had been gentrified in the 1990s. Now it was a pretty urban neighborhood with refurbished houses and charming shops that projected a small-town feel. She was meeting the daughter of one of Nana's former neighbors in her storefront architectural office on Roscoe Street. She'd heard the woman was exceptionally pretty, and she wanted to meet her in person to see if she'd be a match for Heath.

As it turned out, the woman was lovely but nearly as hyperactive as he was, a surefire recipe for disaster. Annabelle considered her a good prospect for a match though, and she decided to keep her eyes open.

A hunger pang reminded her that she hadn't taken time for breakfast. Since Heath wasn't picking her up until noon, she made her way across the street to Victory's Banner, a cheery, pocket-size vegetarian café operated by the followers of one of the Indian spiritual masters. Instead of a musty, incense-scented interior, Victory's Banner had powder blue walls, sunny yellow banquettes, and chalk white tables that matched the tieback curtains at the windows. She took an empty table and began to order one of her favorites, homemade French toast with peach butter and real maple syrup, only to be distracted by a platter of golden-brown Belgian waffles passing by. She finally settled on apple pecan pancakes.

As she took her first sip of coffee, the door to the restroom at the back opened and a familiar figure emerged. Annabelle's heart sank. The woman would have been tall even without her high-heeled woven slides. She was broad shouldered and well dressed in crisp white slacks and a short-sleeved coral blouse that complemented her shoulder-length light brown hair. Her makeup was well applied with subtle eye shadow that emphasized her familiar dark eyes.

The café was too small to hide in, and Rosemary Kimble spotted Annabelle right away. She clutched her straw purse more tightly. Her big, broad hands had long, toffee-painted nails and a trio of gold bracelets encircling one wrist. It had been nearly six months since Annabelle had last seen her. Rosemary's face was thinner, her hips rounder. She approached the table, and Annabelle experienced an all-too-familiar barrage of emotions: anger and betrayal, compassion and repulsion . . . a painful tenderness.

Rosemary shifted her purse from one hand to the other and spoke in her low, melodious voice. "I just finished breakfast, but . . . Would you mind some company?"

Yes, I'd mind, Annabelle wanted to say, but she'd only feel guilty afterward, so she tilted her head in the general direction of the opposite chair. Rosemary tucked her purse in her lap and ordered an iced chai, then began fiddling with a bracelet. "I hear through the grapevine that you landed a big client."

"Grapevine Molly."

Rosemary gave her a wry smile. "You don't call, you don't write. Molly's my only source of information. She's been a good friend."

Unlike Annabelle, who hadn't. She concentrated on her coffee. Rosemary finally broke the awkward silence. "So how's Hurricane Kate these days?"

"Her usual interfering self. She wants me to get an accounting degree."

"She worries about you."

Annabelle set her cup down too hard, and coffee sloshed over the brim. "I can't imagine why."

"Don't try to blame all your troubles with Kate on me. She's always driven you crazy."

"Yes, well, our situation sure didn't help."

"No, it didn't," Rosemary said.

Annabelle had waited nearly a week after her world had crashed to call her mother, hoping by then she could manage her announcement without crying.

"Rob and I've called off our engagement, Mom."

She still remembered Kate's screech. *"What are you talking about?"*

"We're not getting married."

"But the wedding's only two months away. And we love Rob. Everybody does. He's the only man you've dated who has a head on his shoulders. You complement each other perfectly."

"Turns out too perfectly. Get ready to laugh." Her voice had caught on a snag. *"Turns out Rob is a woman trapped in a man's body."*

"Annabelle, have you been drinking?"

Annabelle had explained it to her mother just as Rob had explained it to her—how he'd felt wrong in his body for as long as he could remember; the nervous breakdown he'd suffered the year before they'd met but never quite gotten around to mentioning; his belief that loving her would cure him; and his final realization that he couldn't keep on living if he had to do it as a man.

Kate had started to cry and Annabelle had cried right along with her.

She'd felt so stupid for not suspecting the truth, but Rob had been a decent lover, and they'd had an okay sex life. He was nice looking, funny, and sensitive, but she hadn't considered him effeminate. She never caught him trying on her clothes or using her makeup, and until that awful night when he'd started to cry and told her he couldn't go on any longer trying to be someone he wasn't, she'd assumed he was the love of her life.

Looking back, there'd been hints: his moodiness, frequent references to an unhappy childhood, odd questions about Annabelle's experiences growing up as a girl. She'd been flattered by the attention he'd paid to her opinions, and she'd told her friends how lucky she was to have a fiancé who was so interested in her as a person. Never once had she suspected he was gathering information, weighing her experiences against his own so he could make his final decision. After he'd broken the devastating news, he'd told her he still loved her as much as ever. She'd cried and asked him exactly what he expected her to do about that?

Her broken dreams had been painful enough, but she'd also had to face the humiliation of telling her friends and relatives.

"You remember my ex-fiancé Rob. Funniest thing . . ."

Try as she might, she couldn't get past what she'd come to think of as the "ick factor." She'd made love with a man who wanted to be a woman. She found no comfort in his explanation that gender identity and sexuality were two different issues. He'd known this monster hung over them when they'd fallen in love, but he hadn't said a word about it until the afternoon she'd had her bridal gown fitted. That evening, he'd taken his first dose of estrogen and begun his transition from Rob into Rosemary.

Nearly two years had passed since then, and Annabelle still hadn't overcome her sense of betrayal. At the same time, she couldn't pretend not to care. "How's the job?" Rosemary was the longtime marketing director at Molly's publishing company, Birdcage Press. She and Molly had worked closely together to grow the market for Molly's award-winning *Daphne the Bunny* children's books.

"People are finally getting used to me."

"I'm sure it wasn't easy." For a while Annabelle had wanted it to be hard, wanted her old lover to suffer, but she didn't feel that way now. Now she simply wanted to forget.

The woman who'd once been her fiancé gazed at her across the table. "I just wish that . . ."

"Don't say it."

"You were my best friend, Annabelle. I want that back."

The old bitterness resurfaced. "I know you do, but you can't have it."

"Would it help if I told you I'm not sexually attracted to you anymore? Apparently the hormones have done a job on me. For the first time in my life, I've started to look at men. Very strange."

"Tell me about it."

Rosemary laughed, and Annabelle managed a smile in return, but as much as she wished Rosemary well, she couldn't be her confidante. Their relationship had robbed her of too much. Not only had she lost trust in her ability to judge people, but she'd also lost her sexual confidence. What kind of loser could be in an intimate relationship for so long without suspecting that something was seriously askew?

Her pancakes arrived. Rosemary rose and regarded her sadly. "I'll let you eat in peace. It's been good seeing you."

The most Annabelle could manage in return was a quiet "Good luck."

Do you get invited to many of Phoebe and Dan's parties?" Heath asked a few hours later as he steered his BMW into the long, wooded drive that led to the Calebow home. A hawk circled in the afternoon sun above the old orchard to their right, where the apples were just beginning to turn red.

"A few," she replied. "But, then, Phoebe likes me."

"Go ahead and laugh, but it's not funny to me. I've lost some great clients because of this."

"I'd be lying if I didn't tell you it's nice having you at my mercy for a change."

"Don't enjoy it too much. I'm trusting you not to screw this up."

She was afraid she already had. She should have been up front with him about today's affair, but she always got pig-headed when workaholics started ordering her around, another legacy from her childhood.

The tires clattered on a narrow wooden bridge. They rounded a bend, and an old stone farmhouse came into sight. Build in the 1880s, the Calebow property was a rustic gem in an area of affluent suburban sprawl. Dan had bought the house in his bachelor days, and as their family had grown, he and Phoebe had added wings, raised the roof, and expanded the grounds. The end result was a charming ramble of a house perfect for a family with four growing children.

Heath parked in the drive next to Molly's SUV, which had Tigger sunshades suction-cupped to the glass. He shifted his weight and tucked his keys in the hip pocket of his khaki slacks. He wore them with a designer polo and another of his TAG Heuer watches, this one with a brown crocodile strap. Annabelle felt a little underdressed in gray knit drawstring shorts, aqua tank top, and J. Crew flip-flops.

She saw the exact moment when he spotted the multitude of pink balloons tied to the spindled railing that surrounded the old-fashioned front porch.

He turned to her slowly, a python uncoiling for the strike. "Exactly what kind of party is this?"

She caught her bottom lip between her teeth and tried to look adorable. "Uh, funny you should ask . . ."

His grim green eyes belatedly reminded Annabelle that he had no sense of humor when it came to business. Not that she'd exactly forgotten it.

"No bullshit, Annabelle. Tell me right now what's going on."

He'd trample her if she tried to stage a retreat, so she

attempted a chipper sort of savoir faire. "Relax and enjoy yourself. It'll be fun." She didn't sound convincing, but before he could crush the life out of her, Molly appeared on the front porch with Pippi at her side. Both of them sported glittery pink tiaras, Pippi's accessorized with a strawberry pink princess gown, Molly's with bright yellow capris and a *Daphne the Bunny* T-shirt. Heath's already grim expression grew even more forbidding.

Molly looked startled, then laughed as she spotted Heath. He shot Annabelle a life-threatening glare, plastered a smile on his face for Molly, and stepped out of the car. Annabelle grabbed her tote and followed. Unfortunately, the knot that had begun to form in her stomach came right along with her.

"Heath? I don't believe it," Molly said. "I couldn't even talk Kevin into helping out today."

"Is that so?" he replied slowly. "Annabelle invited me."

Molly gave her a thumbs-up. "Cool."

Annabelle forced a smile.

Heath walked toward Molly, projecting an air of amusement Annabelle knew he didn't feel. "Annabelle neglected, however, to tell me exactly what she was inviting me to."

"Oops." Molly's eyes sparkled.

"I would have if you'd asked." Annabelle's words sounded lame even to herself, and he ignored her.

Molly leaned down to her daughter. "Pippi, tell Mr. Heath about our party."

The three-year-old's tiara wobbled as she jumped and gave an ear-splitting shriek. "*Princess party!*"

"Ya don't say," Heath drawled. Slowly, he turned to face Annabelle. She pretended to examine the climbing rose next to the front porch.

"It was Julie and Tess's idea," Molly said. "Annabelle volunteered to help out."

Annabelle thought about explaining that Julie and Tess

were the Calebows' oldest children, fifteen-year-old twins, then realized Heath wouldn't need an explanation. He'd have made it his business to know all about Dan and Phoebe's four children: the twins, twelve-year-old Hannah, and nine-year-old Andrew. He probably knew their favorite foods and when they'd had their last dental checkups.

"The twins are volunteering at a summer day care center that serves low-income families," Molly went on. "They work with the four- and five-year-old girls, supervising activities to jump-start them in math and science. They wanted to throw a party just for fun."

"*Princess party!*" Pippi shrieked again, hopping up and down.

"I can't tell you how glad I am you're here," Molly said. "Tess and Julie woke up with fevers this morning, so we've been a little frantic. Hannah's going to help, but she gets emotionally involved, so she's not entirely reliable. I tried to call Kevin and beg him to reconsider, but he and Dan have taken the boys somewhere and they're not picking up. Wait till they hear who saved them."

"My pleasure." Heath projected such sincerity that Annabelle would have believed him if she hadn't known better. No wonder he was so good at what he did.

They heard the sound of an engine and saw a yellow minibus approaching. Molly turned to the door. "Hannah, the girls are here!"

Seconds later, twelve-year-old Hannah Calebow emerged. Thin and awkward, she resembled her Aunt Molly more than her mother, Phoebe. Her light brown hair, expressive eyes and slightly asymmetrical features bore the promise of something more interesting than conventional prettiness when she grew older, although at this point it was hard to tell exactly what. "Hi, Annabelle," she said as she came forward.

Annabelle returned the greeting, and Molly introduced Heath as the minibus stopped in front of the house. "Annabelle, why don't you and Heath help Phoebe in the backyard while Hannah and I get the girls unloaded?"

"Maybe you should be a little careful around Mom," Hannah said in a soft, anxious-to-please voice. "She's in a bad mood because Andrew got into the cake this morning."

"It just keeps getting better and better," Heath muttered. And then he headed for the flagstone path that led around the side of the house. He walked so quickly that Annabelle had to trot to catch up with him.

"I guess I should apologize," she said. "I'm afraid I might have let my—"

"Not one word," he said on a single ominous note. "You screwed me over, and we don't have a thing to say to each other."

She hurried to his side. "I wasn't trying to screw you over. I thought—"

"Save your breath. You wanted me to look stupid."

She hoped that wasn't true but suspected it might be. Not stupid, exactly. Just not so together. "You're totally over-reacting."

That was when the Python struck.

"You're fired."

She stumbled on one of the flagstones. There was no emotion in his voice, no expression of regret for good times and shared laughs, only a stony declaration.

"You can't mean that."

"Oh, I mean it, all right."

"It's a kids' party! It's no big deal."

He walked away without another word.

She stood chilled and silent in the shadow of an old elm. She'd done it again. Once more, she'd let her impulsiveness lead her into disaster. She knew him well enough by now to understand how much he hated being put at a disadvantage. How could she have believed he'd find this amusing? Maybe she hadn't. Maybe the person she'd really intended to sabotage was herself.

Her mother was right. It couldn't be entirely coincidental that everything Annabelle attached herself to failed. Did she believe she didn't deserve success? Was that why all her ventures ended in disaster?

She leaned against the trunk of the elm and tried not to cry.

Chapter Nine

Heath was furious. He didn't like looking foolish under any circumstances, but especially not in front of Phoebe Calebow. Yet here he was, completely out of his element. If the party had involved teenagers, he'd have been fine. He liked teenagers. He knew how to talk to them. But little kids—little female kids—were a mystery to him.

His anger against Annabelle grew. She thought putting one over on him was funny, but nothing involving Phoebe amused him. Where business was concerned, he didn't play games. Annabelle knew that, but she'd decided to test him, and he'd had to cut her off at the knees. He wouldn't let it bother him, either. Sentiment and second-guessing were for losers.

He focused on the Calebows' backyard with its swimming pool, climbing trees, and open stretch of well-used yard, all of it designed for a large family. This afternoon, pink filmy crap hung from the trees, around the flagstone patio, and over the jungle gym. It also festooned tiny tables where pink balloons bobbed in the breeze above the back of each small chair. Glittery dresses like the one Pippi Tucker wore spilled from pink cardboard cartons, and a battered pink wagon held a pile of plastic slippers. Fake pink jewels decorated a throne-shaped chair sitting in the middle of the patio. Only the green dragon piñata dangling from the branch of a maple tree had escaped the pink plague.

He'd always been comfortable in his body, but now he felt awkward and out of place. He glanced toward the swimming pool and experienced a flicker of hope. In a pool, he'd be right at home. Unfortunately, the iron gate was padlocked. Apparently Molly and Phoebe had decided supervising so many little kids around water was too dangerous, but he'd have supervised the damn kids. He liked danger. If he'd gotten lucky, one of the little buggers would have gone under for a while, and he could have saved her from drowning. That would have caught Phoebe's attention.

The Stars' owner stood behind the farthest of the little tables, setting out some kind of cardboard whoogees. Like everybody else, she had one of those frickin' pink crowns on her head, and he regarded her with a profound sense of personal insult. Team owners should wear Stetsons or go bareheaded. No other options.

Phoebe chose that moment to look up. Her eyes widened in surprise, and she dropped one of the cardboard whoogees. "Heath?"

"Hey, Phoebe."

"Well. And isn't this special?" She snatched up the—whatever-the-hell they were. "As much as I'd love to climb into the trenches with you for another round of mud wrestling, I'm a little busy now."

"Annabelle thought you could use some help."

"And you're it? I don't think so."

He arranged his mouth in his most disarming smile. "I'll admit I'm a little out of my element, but if you point me in the right direction, I'll give it my best."

Instead of charming her, he'd made her suspicious, and her face assumed its customary distrustful expression. Before she could interrogate him, however, an army of little girls charged around the corner. Some of them held hands, others walked by themselves. They came in different shapes, different colors, and one of them was crying.

"New places can be scary," he heard Hannah say, "but everybody here is very, very nice. And if you get really scared, come and tell me. I'll take you for a walk. Also, if you need to go to the potty, I'll show you where it is. Our doggie is all locked up so she can't jump on anybody. And if you see a bee, tell one of the grown-ups."

This must be what Molly had meant when she'd said that Hannah got emotionally involved.

Molly stepped toward the pink cardboard boxes. "Every princess needs a beautiful gown, and here are yours." A few of the bolder girls rushed forward.

Phoebe thrust the whoogees in his hand. "Put one of these at each place. And you'd better not charge me for it." She hurried away to help.

Annabelle was nowhere to be seen. He'd come down on her hard, and he wasn't surprised that she needed time to recover. He ignored an unpleasant twinge in his gut. She'd brought this on herself when she'd crossed the line. He studied the whoogees, pink cardboard starbursts glued to the ends of wooden dowels. His mood grew gloomier. They must be magic wands. What the hell did magic wands have to do with helping girls learn math and science? He'd been good at both. He could have helped them with math and science. Weren't these girls supposed to be building skills? Screw magic wands. He'd have handed out some fucking calculators.

He tossed the wands on the table and looked around for Annabelle, but she still hadn't appeared, which was starting to bother him. Even though he'd needed to sack her, he didn't want to destroy her. High-pitched screams emerged from the gown boxes. Although the girls looked like an army, there were only fifteen or so of them. Something brushed his leg, and he gazed down into the face of Pippi Tucker. The theme from *Jaws* raced through his head.

The three-year-old's gown was the color of Pepto-Bismol, her eyes green gumballs of innocence. Only the rakish tilt of the pink tiara in her blond curls hinted at a desperado's heart. She held out a tiara she was clutching in her grubby little fist. "You gotta wear a crown."

"Not in this lifetime." He gave her a ministare, enough to get his point across without making her scream for her mother.

Her small, pale eyebrows shot together just like her father's when he spotted a safety blitz.

"Heath!" Molly's voice emerged from a pool of gowns, sequins, and little girls. "Keep your eye on Pippi till we get everybody dressed, will you?"

"My pleasure." He looked down at the kid.

The kid looked up at him.

He studied her gumball eyes and pink tiara.

She scratched her arm.

He searched his brain and finally came up with something. "Anybody ever teach you how to use a calculator?"

The squeals emanating from the direction of the gown box grew louder. Pippi tipped her chin to get a better view of him, and her tiara scooted farther back on her head. "You got some bubbles?"

"What?"

"I like bubbles."

"Uh-huh."

Her eyes darted to his pockets. "Where's your phone?"

"Let's go see how your mother's doing."

"I wanna see your phone."

"Give me back my old one first, and then we'll talk."

She grinned. "I luvvvv phones."

"Tell me about it."

Last month when he'd dropped by the Tucker house, he'd been left alone with their little adorable for a few minutes. She'd demanded to see his cell. It was a brand-new state-of-the-art five hundred-dollar Motorola equipped with enough peripherals so he could basically run his business from it, but he hadn't seen the harm. Just as he'd handed it over, however, Kevin had called from the other room asking Heath to look at a piece of game film, and that was the last he'd seen of it.

He'd managed to get her alone before he'd left and tried to cross-examine her, but all of a sudden the kid no *hablo*-ed the *in-glés*. As a result, he'd lost a couple of dozen important e-mails and the final notes on a new contract. Later, Bodie had said Heath should have just told Kevin what had happened, but Kevin and Molly were starry-eyed when it came to their kids, and Heath couldn't imagine saying anything they could interpret as criticism of their little darling.

She stomped a foot in the grass. "Wanna see phone *now*."

"Forget it."

She screwed up her face. Oh, shit, she was going to cry. He knew from past experience that the tiniest sound of dismay coming from her moppet's mouth sent Molly's head spinning. Where the hell was Annabelle? He whipped his hand into his pocket and pulled out his newest cell. "*I'll* hold it while you look." He knelt at her side.

She made a grab. "I wanna hold it."

Heath would never for a moment have let it go—he wasn't that stupid—but Annabelle chose that particular instant to make her appearance, and he was so surprised by what he saw that he lost track.

A queen of England–size crown nestled in her wild tumble of curls, and she wore a long silvery gown. Shimmering rhinestones sprinkled the fluffy skirt, and a wisp of silver netting framed her bare shoulders. As she walked onto the grass, the sun struck her from every direction, setting her hair on fire and striking sparks in the rhinestones. No wonder the shrieking little girls fell silent. He was fairly awestruck himself.

For a moment, he forgot how pissed he was with her. Although the gown was a costume and the tiara fake, she seemed almost magical, and something inside him didn't want to look away. Most of the girls were dressed by now, their tiny pink gowns pulled on over shorts and T-shirts. As Annabelle approached them, he spotted her flip-flops peeking from under the hem of her gown. For some weird reason, they seemed just right.

"Greetings, my little beauties," she trilled, sounding like the good witch in *The Wizard of Oz*. "I'm Annabelle, your fairy godmother. I'm going to ask each of you your name and then cast a magic spell that will turn you into an official princess. Are you ready?"

Their shrill squeals seemed to indicate they were.

"After I do that," she went on, "I'll help you make your own magic wand to take home."

Heath snatched up the wands he'd dumped in a heap and began tossing them among the pots of pink glitter and plastic jewels on the tables. Annabelle moved along the row of little girls, leaned down to ask each child her name, then waved her own wand over the child's head. "I dub thee Princess Keesha . . . I dub thee Princess Rose . . . I dub thee Princess Dominga . . . I dub thee Princess Victoria Phoebe."

Damn it! Heath whirled around, remembering too late that the kid had his phone. He searched the grass where they'd been standing and checked his pockets, but his cell was nowhere to be seen. He turned toward the girls, and there she stood, a pint-size phone felon with empty hands and a crooked pink tiara on her head.

The kid was only three, and hardly any time had passed. How far could she have gone with it? As he considered his next move, Phoebe popped up at his side with a Polaroid camera. "We want a picture of each of the girls sitting on the throne in her costume. Will you take them for free," she cooed, "or are you going to put a lien on their tooth fairy money?"

"Phoebe, I'm wounded."

"Not to worry. I doubt you'll bleed." She plopped the camera in his hand, and off she went, pink tiara aglitter, ill will oozing from every pore. Great. So far, he'd managed to fire his

matchmaker and lose another cell without getting one step closer
to repairing his relationship with the Stars' owner. And the party
was just getting started.

Annabelle finished the naming ceremony, then she and
Molly guided some of the girls to the tables to decorate their
wands while Phoebe and Hannah led the others toward a tray
of lipsticks and eye shadows. He had a few minutes before he
needed to set up his photo shop, enough time to figure out
where a three-year-old could have hidden a phone.

A trill of laughter coming from Glinda the Good Witch
drifted his way, but he refused to be distracted. Unfortunately,
Pippi had hunkered down with her mother. Her hands were
occupied, one with a glue stick, the other attached to the thumb
she'd popped in her mouth, so she must have stashed it somewhere. Maybe she'd slipped it into her shorts pocket under her
gown. He remembered he'd programmed it to vibrate, and he
set the camera down, then cut around the house to grab his
BlackBerry with its built-in phone from his car. When he returned, he entered the number of the lost cell and stood off to
the side to see if she'd react.

She didn't. Not in her pockets then.

Damn. He needed Annabelle. Except he'd cut her out of his
life.

All of the little girls were clamoring for her attention, but
instead of being rattled, she seemed to like it. He made himself
turn away. So what if she looked as innocent as a Disney cartoon? He didn't forgive and he didn't forget.

He slipped deeper into the shade of the patio. None of the
girls were ready for their photos, and he had time to make a few
calls, but as sure as anything, she'd catch him at it and make
some withering remark. Once again, the theme from *Jaws* blared
in his head. He looked down.

Pippi wore bright blue eye shadow and sported a rosebud
mouth slick with red lipstick. He quickly shoved his Black-
Berry in his pocket.

"See my wand?"

"Hey, that's a wand, all right." He crouched, pretending to check out her artwork, but really getting down to business. "Pippi, show Uncle Heath where you put his phone."

She gave him a killer smile, front teeth the tiniest bit crooked, probably from that thumb. "Want phone," she said.

"That's great. Me, too. Let's go find it together."

She pointed to his pocket. "Want that phone!"

"Oh, no, you don't." He shot to his feet and strode away so that, if Pippi started to cry, he wasn't anywhere in the vicinity. "Who's ready for a picture?" he called out, hearty as all hell.

"Princess Rosa, you're ready," Molly said. "Go sit on the throne and let Prince Heath take your picture."

A snort came from the general direction of Glinda the Good Witch.

"I'm scared," the little girl whispered to Molly.

"As well you should be," Glinda muttered.

Her comment should have aggravated him, but he hadn't wanted to crush her spirit, just to teach her a lesson about business that was ultimately for her own good. "Do you want me to go with you?" Molly asked the child. But the little girl was gazing adoringly at Annabelle.

"I want my pitcher with her," she said.

Molly grinned at Annabelle. "Fairy Godmother, you seem to have a photo call."

"Sure." Annabelle took the child's hand and headed toward the throne. As she reached his side, she stuck her nose in the air and swept past him. The nose, he couldn't help but notice, had a pink glitter smudge at the tip.

After that, it seemed as though every princess in the land wanted her photo taken with the good fairy godmother, who, not coincidentally, acted as if the royal photographer didn't exist. He knew how to play that game, and he confined his comments to the girls. "Give me a smile, princess. That's good."

Annabelle might be ignoring him, but she giggled with the

children, cast magic spells, arbitrated disputes, and let Princess
Pilar see what fairy godmothers wore under their gowns. He
was more than a little interested himself. Unfortunately, this
particular fairy godmother wore gray drawstring shorts instead
of the bright red thong that would have been his choice. But,
hey, that was just him.

Before long, he forgot about the phone calls he needed to
make and concentrated on getting good pictures of the girls. He
had to admit they were cute. Some of them were shy and needed
encouragement. Others were big talkers. A couple of the four-
year-olds wanted Annabelle to sit on the throne so they could
perch in her lap. A few had her stand next to them. She made
them laugh—made him smile—and by the time they'd gotten to
the end of the photos, he'd decided to forgive her. What the hell.
Everybody deserved a second chance. First he'd give her the lecture of her life, then he'd take her back on probation.

Photos done, she set off to help Hannah, who was supervising a game of pin the kiss on the frog. Since Hannah wasn't
making anyone wear a blindfold, it didn't look like much of a
game to him, but maybe he was missing something. Phoebe
and Molly, in the meantime, had started a treasure hunt.

Pippi popped up at his side and tried to frisk him for his
backup phone, but he distracted her with an open pot of green
eye shadow.

"Pippi! How did you get into that?" Molly shrieked a few
minutes later.

He busied himself with the camera and pretended not to
see the hard, suspicious look Phoebe shot at him.

Molly gathered the girls under a shady tree and entertained them with a story she seemed to be making up on the
spot called *Daphne and the Princess Party*. She incorporated all
the girls' names and even added a frog named Prince Heath
who specialized in taking magical pictures. Now that he'd
decided to forgive Annabelle, he relaxed enough to enjoy
watching her. She sat cross-legged in the grass, her billowing

skirts enveloping the children around her. She laughed when they did, clapped her hands, and, in general, acted pretty much like a kid herself.

While the tables were set up for refreshments, he was put in charge of the dragon piñata. "Don't make them wear blindfolds," Hannah whispered. "It scares them."

So he didn't. He let them whack away to their hearts' content, and when the piñata refused to break, took a swing at the sucker himself and finished it off. Goodies flew. He supervised the distribution and did a damn good job of it, too. Nobody got hurt, nobody cried, so maybe he wasn't entirely clueless about kids.

The refreshments arrived in a sea of pink. Pink punch. Sandwiches made with pink bread, a castle cake complete with pink-frosted ice-cream-cone turrets and a chunk conspicuously missing from the pink drawbridge, undoubtedly the work of young Andrew Calebow. Molly slipped him a beer.

"You're an angel of mercy," he said.

"I don't know what we'd have done without you."

"It was fun." Well, the last twenty minutes anyway, when there'd been some action with the piñata and at least a faint potential for bloodshed.

"Princesses!" Phoebe called from the cake table. "I know we all want to thank our fairy godmother for taking time out of her busy schedule to be with us today. Princess Molly, we loved your story so much, and Princess Hannah, everyone appreciated all the hugs you gave out." Her voice dropped to that coo he'd come to dread. "As for Prince Heath . . . We're so glad he could help us with the piñata. Who knew his talent for battering things would come in so handy?"

"Brother . . . ," Molly muttered. "She really does hate your guts."

Half an hour later, a group of tired princesses headed home with giant goody bags stuffed full of treats for themselves, as well as for their brothers and sisters.

"It was a very nice party," Hannah said from the front step as the bus disappeared. "I was worried."

Phoebe looped her arm around her daughter's shoulders and kissed the top of her head, just behind her tiara. "You made everybody feel right at home."

And what about me? Heath wanted to say. He couldn't see that he'd gained an inch of ground with her, even though he'd cleared tables, taken photos, and dealt with the piñata, all without making a single phone call *or* catching one lousy inning of the Sox game.

Annabelle braced her hand on the porch railing and wiggled out of her fairy godmother dress. "I'm afraid it has some grass stains and a punch spill, so I don't know if you'll be able to use it again."

"One Halloween was enough," Molly replied.

"Thanks so much, Annabelle." Phoebe gave her the genuine smile she didn't offer him. "You were a perfect fairy godmother."

"I loved every minute. How are the twins feeling?"

"Sulky. I checked on them half an hour ago. They're upset about missing the party."

"I don't blame them. It was quite a party."

A cell rang. He automatically reached into his pocket, forgetting for an instant that he'd turned off his phone. He came up empty. *What . . . ?*

"Hey, babe . . . ," Molly spoke into her own cell. "Yes, we survived, no thanks to you and Dan. Luckily, your valiant agent came to our rescue . . . Yes, really."

He slapped his pockets. Where the hell was his BlackBerry?

"Wanna talk to Daddy!" Pippi squealed, reaching for Molly's phone.

"Hold on a minute. Pip wants to say hi."

Molly lowered the phone to her daughter's ear. Heath headed for the backyard. Damn it! She couldn't possibly have stolen two of them in one afternoon. It must have fallen out of his pocket when he was running around with the piñata.

He looked under the tree, in the grass, everywhere he could think of, and came up empty. She'd picked his pocket when he'd crouched down to talk to her.

"Are you missing something?" Phoebe cooed, coming up behind him. "A heart, perhaps?"

"My BlackBerry."

"I haven't seen it. But if I find it, I'll be sure to let you know right away." She spoke with all kinds of sincerity, but he suspected if she found it she'd toss it in her swimming pool.

"Much appreciated," he said.

Annabelle and Molly had returned to the backyard, but Pippi seemed to have gone off with Hannah. "I'm exhausted," Molly said, "and I'm used to being around kids. Poor Annabelle."

"I wouldn't have missed it for the world." Studiously ignoring him, Annabelle began gathering up the paper plates.

Phoebe waved her off. "Leave everything. My cleaning service is coming by soon. While they work, I'm going to put my feet up and recover. I haven't started the new book for the book club, and I have to make up for not finishing the last one."

"That book was a stinker," Annabelle said. "I don't know what Krystal was thinking of when she chose it."

Heath's ears pricked up. Annabelle and Phoebe were in a book club together? What other interesting secrets was she hiding from him?

Molly yawned and stretched. "I like Sharon's idea of giving the guys a book of their own to read when we go on our retreat. Last year, whenever they weren't in the lake or with us, they were rehashing old games. I don't care what they say. That's just got to get boring after a while."

Every cell in Heath's body went on full alert.

"Don't let Darnell choose," Phoebe said. "He's hung up on

Márquez now, and I can't see the rest of the men getting too excited about *One Hundred Years of Solitude*."

There was only one Darnell they could be talking about, and that was Darnell Pruitt, the Stars' All Pro former offensive tackle. Heath's mind raced. What kind of book club had Annabelle gotten herself involved in?

Even more important . . . Exactly how was he going to use this to his advantage?

Chapter Ten

Annabelle collected a few more paper plates, even though Phoebe had told her not to bother. She dreaded the idea of being closed up in the car with Heath for the ride home. Phoebe scooped a dab of pink icing from the mangled castle cake and popped it in her mouth. "Dan and I are both looking forward to the retreat at the campground. We love any excuse to go to Wind Lake. Molly definitely lucked out when she married a man with his own resort."

"With training camp coming up, it'll be the last break any of us have for a long time." Molly turned to Annabelle. "I almost forgot. We had a cancellation on one of the cottages. You and Janine can share it, since you're both singles, or would you rather keep your room at the B&B?"

Annabelle thought it over. Although she'd never been to the Wind Lake Campground, she knew it had both a Victorian bed-and-breakfast and a number of small cottages. "I guess I'd—"

"The cottage for sure," Heath said. "Apparently Annabelle hasn't gotten around to mentioning that she ordered me to go with her."

Annabelle turned to stare at him.

Phoebe's finger froze in the cake icing. "You're coming on the retreat?"

Annabelle spotted a small pulse beating at the base of his neck. He loved this. She could expose him with only a few words, but he was an adrenaline junky, and he'd thrown the dice. "I've never been able to turn down a bet," he said. "She thinks I can't go an entire weekend without my cell."

"You can barely make it through dinner," Molly muttered.

"I'll expect an apology from both of you after I've proved exactly how wrong you are."

Molly's and Phoebe's expressions were equally quizzical as they turned to Annabelle. Her wounded pride demanded she punish him. Right now. She deserved her pound of flesh for the cold-blooded way he'd fired her.

An awkward pause fell. He watched her, waited, the pulse at the base of his neck marking the passing seconds.

"He'll fold." She forced a smile. "Everybody knows it but him."

"Interesting." Molly refrained from saying more, although Annabelle knew she wanted to.

Twenty minutes later, she and Heath were heading back toward the city, the silence in the car as thick as the castle cake's pink frosting, but not nearly as sweet. He'd done better than she'd expected with the girls. He'd listened respectfully to Hannah's concerns, and Pippi adored him. Annabelle had been surprised how many times she'd looked over to see him crouched down talking to her.

Heath finally broke the silence. "I'd already made up my mind to rehire you before I heard about the retreat."

"Oh, I believe you," she said, using sarcasm to hide her hurt.

"I mean it."

"Whatever lets you sleep at night."

"Okay, Annabelle. Unload. Get it all out. Everything you've been saving up all afternoon."

"Unloading is the prerogative of equals. Lowly employees like myself pucker their lips and kiss the sweet spot."

"You were out of line, and you know it. This thing with Phoebe never gets any better. I thought I might be able to change that."

"Whatever."

He shot into the left lane. "Do you want me to bow out? I can call Molly in the morning and tell her that something's come up. Is that what you want me to do?"

"Like I have any choice if I want to keep you as a client."

"Okay, let me make it easy for you. Regardless of what you decide, you're rehired. One way or another, our contract still holds."

She let him see she wasn't impressed with his offer. "And I can just imagine how cooperative you'd be if I refused to take you on the retreat."

"What do you want from me?"

"I want you to be honest. Look me in the eye and admit that you didn't have the slightest intention of rehiring me until you heard about the retreat."

"Yeah, you're right." He didn't look her in the eye, but at least he was being honest. "I wasn't going to forgive you. And you know why? Because I'm a ruthless son of a bitch."

"Fine. You can come with me."

Annabelle spent the next few days feeling pissy. She tried to chalk her mood up to getting her period, but she wasn't as good at self-deception as she used to be. Heath's cold-blooded behavior had left her feeling bruised, betrayed, and just plain mad. One mistake, and he'd written her off. If it weren't for the Wind Lake retreat, she'd never have seen him again. She was totally expendable, another one of his worker bees.

On Tuesday he left a terse voice message. "Portia has someone she wants me to meet at eight-thirty on Thursday evening. Set me up with one of your introductions at eight so we can kill two birds with one stone."

Finally, she put the anger where it belonged, on her own shoulders. He wasn't to blame for those sexual images that wanted to burn themselves into her brain when her guard was down. To him, this was business. She was the one who'd let it become personal, and if she forgot that again, she deserved the consequences.

On Thursday evening before she headed to Sienna's for the next round of introductions, she met her newest client at Earwax. Ray Fiedler had been referred by a relative of one of Nana's oldest friends, and Annabelle had sent him on his first date the night before with a Loyola faculty member she'd met during her campus cruising. "We had a nice time and everything," Ray said after they'd settled around one of Earwax's wooden tables, which was painted like the wheel of a circus wagon, "but Carole's not really my physical type."

"How do you mean?" Annabelle drew her eyes away from the ominous beginnings of his comb-over. She knew the answer, but she wanted to make him say it.

"She's . . . I mean, she's a really nice woman. A lot of people don't get my jokes. It's just that I like women who are . . . more fit."

"I'm not sure I understand."

"Carole's a little overweight."

She took a sip of her cappuccino and studied the red-and-gold wooden dragon on the wall rather than the extra twenty pounds that hung around what used to be Ray Fiedler's waistline.

He wasn't stupid. "I know I'm not exactly Mr. Buff myself, but I work out."

Annabelle fought the urge to reach across the table and

smack him in the head. Still, this type of challenge was part of what she liked about being a matchmaker. "You usually date thin women, then?"

"They don't have to be beauty queens, but the women I've dated have been pretty nice looking."

Annabelle pretended to look thoughtful. "I'm a little confused. When we first talked, you gave me the impression that you hadn't dated in a long time."

"Well, I haven't, but . . ."

She let him squirm for a few moments. A kid with multiple piercings passed their table followed by a pair of soccer moms. "So this weight thing is really important to you? More important than personality or intelligence?"

He looked as if she'd asked a trick question. "I just had somebody a little . . . different in mind."

And don't we all? Annabelle thought. The Fourth of July weekend was coming up, and she had no date, no prospects for a date, and no plans beyond starting her exercise program again and trying not to brood about the Wind Lake book club retreat. Ray fiddled with his spoon, and her annoyance with him faded. He was a decent guy, just clueless.

"Maybe you're not a love match," she said, "but I'll tell you the same thing I told Carole last night when she expressed a few misgivings. You have a common background, and you enjoyed each other's company. I think that justifies another date, regardless of your current lack of physical attraction. If nothing else, you could end up with a friend."

A few beats passed before he got it. "What do you mean misgivings? She doesn't want to see me again?"

"She has a few doubts, just like you do."

His hand flew to his head. "It's because of my hair, isn't it? That's all women care about. They see a guy who's losing his hair, and they don't want to give him the time of day."

"Women are less influenced by a receding hairline or a few

extra pounds than men assume. Do you know what's most important to women as far as male physical appearance goes?"

"Height? Hey, I'm almost five-ten."

"Not height. Studies show that good grooming is most important to women. They value cleanliness and neatness more than anything else." She paused. "And good haircuts are very important to women."

"She didn't like my haircut?"

Annabelle gave him a wide smile. "Isn't that cool? A haircut can be fixed so easily. Here's the name of a stylist who gives great men's cuts." She slid the business card across the table. "You've got everything else together, so this will be easy."

It hadn't occurred to him that he might be the one getting rejected, and his competitive instincts came into play. By the time they left the coffee shop, he'd begrudgingly agreed to both the haircut and to meeting Carole again. Annabelle told herself she was getting good at this, and she shouldn't let her mother or her troubles with Heath Champion plant all those seeds of doubt.

She entered Sienna's in a better mood, but things went to hell quickly. Heath hadn't arrived, and the De Paul harpist she'd arranged for him to meet called to say she'd cut her leg and was heading for the emergency room. She'd barely hung up before Heath called. "The plane's late," he said. "I'm on the ground at O'Hare, but we're waiting for a gate to open up."

She told him about the harpist and then, because he sounded tired, suggested he postpone his Power Matches date.

"Tempting, but I'd better not," he said. "Portia's really high on this one. A gate's opening up now, so I shouldn't be too late. Hold the fort till I get there."

"All right."

Annabelle chatted with the bartender until Portia's candidate arrived. Her eyes widened. No wonder Powers had been enthusiastic. She was the most beautiful woman Annabelle had ever seen . . .

• • •

The next morning Annabelle returned from her semiannual morning run to see Portia Powers standing on her porch. They'd never met, but Annabelle recognized her from her Web site photograph. Only as she came closer, however, did she realize this was the same woman she'd seen standing in front of Sienna's the night she'd introduced Heath to Barrie. Powers wore a silky black blouse crisscrossed at her small waist, shocking pink slacks, and retro black patent leather heels. Her inky hair was beautifully cut, the kind of hair that moved with the slightest toss of the head, and her skin flawless. As for her body . . . She obviously only ate on government holidays.

"Don't you dare pull another trick like you did last night," Portia said the minute Annabelle's running shoes hit the porch steps. She oozed the brittle sort of beauty that always made Annabelle feel dumpy, but especially this morning in her baggy shorts and a sweaty orange T-shirt that said BILL'S HEATING AND COOLING.

"Good morning to you, too." Annabelle pulled the key from her shorts pocket, unlocked the door, and stepped aside to let Powers enter.

Portia took in the reception area and Annabelle's office with a single disdainful glance. "Do not ever . . . *ever* . . . take it upon yourself to get rid of one of my candidates before Heath has had a chance to meet her."

Annabelle closed the door. "You sent a bad candidate."

Powers pointed one manicured finger in the direction of Annabelle's sweat-beaded forehead. "That was for him to decide, not you."

Annabelle ignored the fingernail pistol. "I'm sure you know how he feels about wasting time."

Portia threw up her hand. "Can you really be this incompetent? Claudia Reeshman is the top model in Chicago. She's beautiful. She's intelligent. There are a million men who'd like a shot at her."

"That may be true, but she seems to have some serious emotional problems." A fairly obvious drug habit topped the list, although Annabelle wouldn't make any accusations she couldn't prove. "She started crying before her first drink arrived."

"Everyone has a bad day now and then." Powers draped a hand on her hip, a feminine pose, but she made it look as aggressive as a karate chop. "I've worked all month trying to talk her into meeting Heath. I finally get her to agree, and what do you do? You decide he's not going to *like* her, and you send her home."

"Claudia was going through more than a bad day," Annabelle countered. "She's an emotional train wreck."

"I don't care if she was rolling on the floor barking like a dog. What you did was stupid and underhanded."

Annabelle had dealt with strong personalities all her life, and she wasn't going to back down from this one, even with sweat dripping in her eyes and BILL'S HEATING AND COOLING sticking to her chest. "Heath's been clear about what he expects."

"I'd say the sexiest, most sought after woman in Chicago exceeds his expectations."

"He wants more than beauty in a wife."

"Oh, please. When it comes to men like Heath, cup size wins over IQ any time."

They were getting nowhere, so Annabelle did her best to sound professional instead of pissed off. "This whole process would be easier for both of us if we could work together."

Portia looked as if Annabelle had offered her a big bag of fatty junk food. "I have strict qualifications for my trainees, Ms. Granger. You don't fit any of them."

"Now that's just bitchy." Annabelle stalked to the door. "From now on, take your grievances right to Heath."

"Oh, believe me, I will. And I can't wait to hear what he has to say about this one."

W hat the hell were you thinking?" Heath bellowed into the phone a few hours later, not exactly yelling, but coming close. "I just found out you blew off Claudia Reeshman?"

"And?" Annabelle took a vicious jab at the notepad next to her kitchen phone with a lollipop pen.

"I obviously gave you way too much power."

"When I called you back last night and told you I'd canceled the introduction because she wasn't what you wanted, you thanked me."

"You neglected to mention her name. I've never had a thing for models, but Claudia Reeshman . . . Jesus, Annabelle . . ."

"Maybe you'd like to fire me again."

"Will you let it go?"

"How's this going to work?" She took another stab at the notepad. "Do you trust me or not?"

Through the phone, she heard a car horn, followed by a long silence. "I trust you," he finally said.

She almost choked. "Really?"

"Really."

Just like that, she got a lump in her throat the size of the Sears Tower. She cleared it away and tried to sound as though this was exactly what she'd expected him to say. "Good. I hear horns. Are you on the road?"

"I told you I was driving to Indianapolis."

"That's right. It's Friday." For the next two nights, he'd be in Indiana with a client who played for the Colts. He'd originally planned the trip for the following weekend, but he'd rescheduled because of the book club retreat she didn't want to think about. "The way you keep going out of town on weekends makes scheduling these introductions challenging."

"Business comes first. You sure did piss off Powers. She wants your head on a platter."

"Along with a knife and some fat-free sour cream to help wash it down."

"I didn't know Reeshman was still in Chicago. I thought she'd gone to New York for good."

Annabelle suspected Claudia didn't want to be that far from her drug dealer.

"Do me a favor," he said. "If Powers sets up a date for me with anybody else who's posed for *SI*'s swimsuit edition, at least tell me her name before you get rid of her."

"All right."

"And thanks for agreeing to help me out tomorrow."

She drew a daisy on her notepad. "What's not to like about spending the day running around town with your credit card and no spending limit?"

"Plus Bodie and Sean Palmer's mother. Don't forget that part. If Mrs. Palmer wasn't so afraid of him, Bodie could have done this by himself."

"She's not the only one who's afraid of him. You're sure we'll be safe?"

"As long as you don't mention politics, Taco Bell, or the color red."

"Thanks for the warning."

"And don't let him get too close to anybody wearing a hat."

"I'm going now."

As she hung up, she realized she was smiling, which wasn't a good idea at all. Pythons could strike at will, and they seldom gave any warning.

Sean Palmer's mother, Arté, had salt-and-pepper dreadlocks, a tall, full-figured body, and a hearty laugh. Annabelle liked her immediately. With Bodie as their travel guide, they saw the sights, beginning with an early morning architectural boat tour followed by a sweep through the Impressionists collection at the Art Institute. Although Bodie handled all the arrangements, he stayed in the background. He was a strange guy, full of intriguing contradictions that made Annabelle want to know more about him.

After a late lunch, they headed for Millennium Park, the glorious new lakefront park Chicagoans believed finally put them ahead of San Francisco as America's most beautiful city. Annabelle had visited the park many times, and she enjoyed showing off the terraced gardens, the fifty-foot-high Crown Fountain with its changing video images, and the shiny, mirrorlike Cloud Gate sculpture affectionately known as The Bean.

As they walked through the futuristic music pavilion, where the bandshell's curling stainless-steel ribbons blended so exquisitely with the skyscrapers behind it, their conversation returned to Arté's son, who'd soon be playing fullback for the Bears. "Sean had agents all over him," his mother said. "It was a happy day for me when he signed with Heath. I stopped worrying so much about people taking advantage of him. I know Heath's going to look out for him."

"He definitely cares about his clients," Annabelle said.

The July sunlight flirted with the waves on the lake as the two women followed Bodie over the snaking steel pedestrian bridge that meandered above the traffic on Columbus Drive. When they reached the other side, they wandered toward the jogging trail. As they stopped to admire the view, a biker called out to Bodie, then pulled up beside him.

Annabelle and Arté fell still, both of them gazing at the man's skintight black biker shorts. "Time to praise God for the glory of his creation," Arté said.

"Amen."

They moved closer, checking out the biker's sweat-slicked calves and the blue-and-white mesh T-shirt clinging to his perfectly developed chest. He was in his mid-to-late twenties, and he wore a high-tech red helmet that hid the top of his damp blond hair, but not his Adonis profile.

"I need a plunge in the lake to cool off," Annabelle whispered.

"If I were twenty years younger . . ."

Bodie gestured toward them. "Ladies, I've got somebody for you to meet."

"Come to mama," Arté murmured, which made Annabelle giggle.

Just before they reached the men, Annabelle recognized the biker. "Wow. I know who that is."

"Mrs. Palmer, Annabelle," Bodie said. "This is the famous Dean Robillard, the Stars' next great quarterback."

Although Annabelle had never met Kevin's backup in person, she'd seen him play, and she knew him by reputation. Arté shook his hand. "It's nice to meet you, Dean. You tell your friends to take it easy on my boy Sean this season."

Dean gave her his ladykiller smile. *And didn't he know exactly the effect he had on women?* Annabelle thought.

"We'll do just that for you, ma'am." Oozing sex appeal like an oil slick, he turned his charm on her. His openly assessing eyes slid down her body with a confidence that said he could have her—or any woman he wanted—whenever and however he liked. *Oh, no, you can't, you naughty, sexy little boy.*

"Annabelle is it?"

"I'd better check my driver's license to make sure," she said. "I'm all out of breath here."

Bodie choked, then laughed.

Apparently Robillard wasn't used to women calling his visual bluffs because he looked momentarily taken aback. Then he ratcheted up the old charm-o-meter. "Maybe it's the heat."

"Oh, it's hot all right." Normally, gorgeous men intimidated her, but he was so full of himself she was merely amused.

He laughed, this time genuinely, and she found herself liking him in spite of his cockiness. "I do admire a feisty red-haired woman," he said.

She slipped her sunglasses lower on her nose and gazed at him over the top. "I'll just bet, Mr. Robillard, that you admire women in general."

"And they admire you right back." Arté chuckled.

Dean turned to Bodie. "Where did you find these two?"

"Cook County Jail."

Arté snorted. "You behave yourself, Bodie."

Dean returned his attention to Annabelle. "Something about your name rings a bell. Wait a minute. Aren't you Heath's matchmaker?"

"How did you know about that?"

"Word gets around." A Rollerblader whizzed by, brunette hair flying. He took his time enjoying the view. "I never met a matchmaker," he finally said. "Maybe I should hire you?"

"You do know my business doesn't have anything to do with lighting campfires, right?"

He folded his arms over his chest. "Hey, everybody wants to meet somebody special."

She smiled. "Not when they're having so much fun meeting all those un-specials."

Dean turned to Bodie. "I don't think she likes me."

"She likes you," Bodie said, "but she thinks you're immature."

"I'm sure you'll grow out of it," Annabelle said.

Bodie slapped him on the back. "I know it doesn't happen very often, but it looks like Annabelle's immune to your movie star face."

"Then somebody better get her to the eye doctor," Arté muttered, which made them all laugh.

Dean wheeled his bike off the path and leaned it against a tree while the four of them chatted. Dean asked Arté about Sean, and they talked about the Bears for a while. Then Bodie brought up Dean's search for an agent. "I hear you've been meeting with Jack Riley at IMG."

"I'm meeting with a lot of people," Dean replied.

"You should at least hear what Heath has to say. He's a smart guy."

"Heath Champion is number one on my do–not–call list. I've got enough ways of making Phoebe unhappy." Dean turned to Annabelle. "How'd you like to come to the beach with me to-morrow?"

She hadn't seen this coming, and she was stunned. Also suspicious. "Why?"

"Can I be honest?"

"I don't know. Can you?"

"I need protection."

"From overtanning?"

"Nope." He flashed his glamour boy smile. "I love the beach, but so many people recognize me that it's hard to chill. Usually, if I'm with a woman, people give me a little more space."

"And I'm the only woman you can find to go with you? I doubt that."

His eyes twinkled. "Don't take this the wrong way, but it'll be more relaxing if I invite somebody I'm not planning to sleep with."

Annabelle burst out laughing.

"Poor Dean needs a friend, not a lover." Bodie chuckled.

"You're invited, too, Mrs. Palmer," Dean said politely.

"Honey, not even a hottie like you could get me out in public wearing a bathing suit."

"What do you think, Annabelle?" Dean cocked his head toward the lakefront. "We'll go to the Oak Street Beach. I'll bring a cooler. We can hang out, swim, listen to music. It'll be fun. You can lower your standards for a couple of hours, can't you?"

Her life had gotten so weird since she'd met Heath Champion. Chicago's hottest young jock had just asked her to spend Sunday afternoon lying on the beach with him when, only two days ago, she'd been feeling sorry for herself because she didn't have any plans for the Fourth of July weekend. "As long as you promise not to ogle younger women while I'm with you."

"I'd never do that!" he declared, apparently forgetting the brunette Rollerblader.

"Just so we're clear."

And he didn't.

He didn't talk on his cell, either, or whip out a BlackBerry. It was a hot, cloudless day, and he even provided a beach umbrella to protect her redhead's skin. They lay on towels listening to music, talking when they felt like it, and gazing out at the water when they didn't. She wore her two-piece white suit, which was cut high enough at the thigh to make her legs look longer, but not so high that she needed a Brazilian wax. Some of his fans interrupted, but not too many. Still, everyone seemed to want a piece of Dean Robillard. Maybe that was why she sensed an odd sort of loneliness beneath his oversize ego. He dodged questions about his family, and she didn't press him.

She had four voice mails waiting when she got home, all from Heath, demanding she call him right away. Instead, she took a shower. She was toweling her hair dry when she heard the doorbell ring. She fastened her yellow terry robe at the waist and headed downstairs, running one hand through her mop as she padded to the door.

A tall hunk of a man gazed back at her through the wavy glass. The Python was paying his second house call.

Chapter Eleven

O nly two boxes of thin mint cookies this year, girls," Annabelle said as she pulled the door open. "I'm on a diet."

Heath pushed past her. "Do you *ever* check your phone messages?"

She gazed down at her bare feet. "Once again, you've caught me looking my best."

He was in hyper mode, and he barely glanced at her, exactly as it should be. "You look beautiful. So there I am, stuck in a *Bible* study class in Indianapolis, when I hear the news that my matchmaker is sunning herself on the beach with Dean Robillard."

"You took a phone call in the middle of Bible study?"

"I was bored."

"And you were in the class because . . . ? Never mind. Your client wanted you to go." She shut the door.

"Why the hell did Robillard ask you out?"

"He's smitten. It happens all the time. Raoul says I can't help the effect I have on men."

"Uh-huh. Bodie told me Dean wanted to go to the beach, and he needed a decoy."

"Then why did you ask?"

"So I could get Raoul's take on it."

She grinned and padded after him into her reception room. "Your scary henchman knew about this yesterday. Why did he wait until today to tell you?"

"My question exactly. You got anything to eat?"

"Some leftover pad thai, but it's starting to grow hair, so I can't recommend it."

"I'm ordering a pizza. How do you like it?"

Maybe it was because she was practically naked and didn't like his attitude, or maybe she was just an idiot because she settled a hand on her hip, slid her eyes over him, and let the words slide off her tongue. "I like it hot . . . and . . . spicy."

His eyelids dropped to the V of her robe. "Exactly what Raoul told me."

She beat a hasty retreat for the stairs. His low chuckle accompanied her all the way to the top.

She took her time changing into her last pair of clean shorts and a vintage blue camie top with a lacy insert that nestled in what passed for her cleavage. Just because she had to be on guard didn't mean she couldn't look good. She dusted bronzing powder over her cheeks, dabbed on lip gloss, then ran a big-tooth comb through her hair, where a few rebellious corkscrews had already begun framing her face like Christmas curling ribbon.

When she got downstairs, Heath was in her office tilted back in her chair, his crossed ankles propped on her desk, and her receiver tucked under his chin. His eyes took in her lacy cleavage, then her bare legs, and he smiled. He was messing with her again, and she didn't let herself make anything out of it.

"I know, Rocco, but she's only got ten fingers. How many diamonds can she wear?" As he listened to the response at the other end of the line, he frowned. "Listen to the people who care about you. I'm not saying she isn't for real, but give it a couple more months, okay? We'll talk next week." He slammed down the phone and dropped his feet to the floor. "Bloodsuckers. They see these guys coming and take them for all they're worth."

"These would be the same guys who stand in hotel lobbies pointing their finger at the bloodsuckers and going *you, you,* and *you*? Then ten minutes later they're explaining all the reasons they won't wear a condom."

"Yeah, well, there's definitely that." He picked up the beer he'd swiped from her refrigerator. "But some of these women are unbelievable. The guys might be tough while they're on the field, but once the game's over, it's a different story. Especially the younger ones. Suddenly all these beautiful women are coming on to them and saying they're in love. The next thing you know, the boys are giving out sports cars and diamond rings for one-month anniversary presents. And don't get me started on the bottom feeders who get pregnant so they can squeeze out hush money."

"Again, nothing a condom wouldn't take care of." She picked up a blue plastic watering can and carried it over to Nana's African violets.

"The guys are young. They think they're invincible. I know in Annabelle Land everybody's nice and sweet, but there are more avaricious women in the world than you can imagine."

Annabelle stopped watering to gaze at him. "Did one of those avaricious women find her way into your pockets? Is that why you're so picky?"

"By the time I'd earned enough to be a target, I'd learned how to watch out for myself."

"Just out of curiosity . . . Have you ever been in love? With a woman," she said hastily, so he didn't start throwing the names of his clients at her.

"I was engaged in law school. It didn't work out."

"Why not?"

"The pain's too fresh for me to revisit," he drawled.

She made a face at him, and he smiled. His cell rang. As he answered, she realized he looked more at home sitting at her desk than she did. How did he manage it? Somehow, he found a way to mark whatever space he occupied. He might as well lift his leg when he walked into a room.

She finished watering the African violets and headed for the kitchen, where she unloaded Nana's cranky dishwasher. The doorbell rang, and a few moments later Heath appeared with the pizza. She gathered up plates and napkins. He retrieved another beer for himself and one for her and carried them over to the table.

As he sat, he gazed at the blue enameled cupboards and Hello Kitty cookie jar. "I like this place. It's homey."

"Tactfully phrased. I know I should update, but I haven't gotten around to it." She could barely afford paint, let alone a major remodeling.

They began to eat, and the silence that settled over them was surprisingly comfortable. She wondered what he was doing for the Fourth tomorrow. He polished off his first slice and took another. "How is it, Annabelle, that you've managed to get close to the two people who are most important to me right now? What is it with you?"

"Natural charm coupled with the fact that I have a life, and you don't." Not much of a life. On Wednesday night, Mr. Bronicki had bullied her into attending the seniors' potluck at the rec center. She'd only agreed after he'd promised to take Mrs. Valerio out again.

Heath swiped the corner of his mouth with his napkin. "What did Robillard say about me?"

She nibbled on her crust. This, she reminded herself, was the reason he'd suggested their cozy dinner party. "He said you're numero uno on his do-not-call list. Pretty much a direct quote. But you probably already know that."

"And what did you tell him?"

"Nothing. I was too busy drooling. God, he's gorgeous."

He frowned. "Dean Robillard isn't one of those naive kids I was talking about. You watch yourself with him. He goes through women like potato chips."

"Well, baby, he can snack on me anytime he wants."

To her surprise, he took her seriously. "No way you're falling for him."

Now this was interesting. "Can I get back to you on that?"

"Look, Annabelle, Dean's not a bad guy, but when it comes to women, all he cares about is racking up notches."

"Like I don't?"

"God, you're a wiseass."

He'd handed her a golden opportunity to delve a little deeper into the life and times of Heath Champion. "Just out of curiosity, how many notches did you rack up? When you were racking them up, that is. And how long ago was that, by the way?"

"Too many notches. I'm not proud of it, either, so no lectures."

"You really think your notching days are behind you?"

"If I didn't, I wouldn't be getting married."

"You're not getting married. You haven't even gone out on a second date."

"Only because I've hired two semi-incompetent matchmakers."

She hadn't told him about Portia's visit, but what could she say? That Portia Powers was a bitch. He probably already knew that. Besides, she had something else she needed to tell him, and she dreaded doing it. "I got a call from Claudia Reeshman this morning. She still wants to meet you."

"No kidding?" He kicked back in his chair, a crooked grin on his face. "Why'd she call you instead of Powers?"

"I guess we sort of connected on Thursday."

"Amazing."

"I thought I'd convinced her you were unworthy, but apparently not." She picked up her pizza, even though she'd lost her appetite. "So I suppose you want me to add her to Wednesday night's agenda?"

"No."

A glob of cheese slid into her lap. "You don't?"

"Didn't you say she wasn't right for me?"

"She's not, but . . ."

"Then no."

Something warm and sweet unfurled inside her. "Thanks." Embarrassed, she scrubbed at her lap.

"You're welcome."

She took her time wiping off her fingers. "The woman I'm introducing you to on Wednesday isn't as beautiful."

"Not many are. Reeslman's last *SI* cover was incredible."

"She's a harpist finishing up a master's in music performance. Twenty-eight, an undergraduate degree from Vassar. You were supposed to meet her last Thursday."

"Is she ugly?"

"Of course she's not ugly." She snatched up her plate and carried it to the sink.

Heath didn't say anything for a few minutes. Finally, he picked up his own plate and brought it to her. "On the off chance Dean calls you again, be careful what you say about me."

"What makes you think there's only an off chance?"

He nodded toward the table. "You want another slice?"

"No." She shoved his plate in the dishwasher. "No, I want to hear this. Why are you so sure he won't call?"

"Calm down. I only meant that you've got a few years on him."

"So?" She slammed the dishwasher closed and told herself to shut up, but the words kept coming. "Older women and younger men are all the fashion these days. Don't you read *People*?"

"Dean only dates party girls."

She knew what he really meant, and a streak of masochism made her push him to say it aloud. "Spit it out. You don't think I'm hot enough for him."

"Stop putting words in my mouth. All I'm saying is that the two of you aren't going to make a love connection."

"True. But we might make a sex connection."

She'd flung the last remnants of caution to the winds, and a long, lean finger came right at her. "You're not having sex with him. I know these guys, and you don't. I'm trusting you about Claudia Reeshman. You need to trust me about Dean Robillard."

She wouldn't let him off that easily. "You're looking for a wife. Maybe I'm just looking for a little fun."

"If you need fun," he shot back, "I'll give you fun."

She was stunned.

A car raced by in the street outside, its radio blaring. They stared at each other. He looked surprised, too. Or maybe not. Slowly, deliberately, the corner of his mouth curled, and she realized the Python was toying with her again.

"Gotta go, Tinker Bell. I have some work I need to catch up on. Thanks for dinner."

Only after the front door closed behind him did she manage a weak "You're welcome."

Y es . . . Yes, all right. Send him up." Portia's hands trembled as she set down the phone. Bodie was in the lobby.

He hadn't called once since their date at the sports bar ten days ago, and now he'd shown up at her condo at nine o'clock on the night of the Fourth of July, expecting her to be waiting for him. She should have told the doorman to send him away, but she hadn't.

She moved automatically toward her bedroom, stepping out of her cotton shift on the way. The Jensons had invited her out on their boat tonight to watch the fireworks, but fireworks depressed her, like most holiday rituals, and she'd declined. It had been a terrible week. First the Claudia Reeshman debacle, then the assistant she'd hired to replace SuSu Kaplan had quit, saying the job was "too stressful." Portia desperately missed the mentoring program. She'd even tried to set up a lunch with Juanita to discuss the situation, but the director was dodging her calls.

She tried to imagine how Bodie would react to the condo she'd bought after her divorce. Because she used her home to host monthly cocktail parties for her most important clients, she'd chosen a spacious unit on the top floor of an excruciatingly expensive prewar limestone just off Lakeshore Drive. She wanted to project old-world elegance, so she'd borrowed from the color palate of the Dutch masters: rich shades of brown, antique gold, muted olive, along with subtle touches of bittersweet. In the living room, a pair of masculine, deep-seated couches and a big leather club chair bordered the tea-stained oriental rug. A similar oriental rug complemented the heavy teak dining room table with its lushly upholstered side chairs. It was important for men to feel comfortable here, so she kept the tables free of bric-a-brac and the liquor cabinet well stocked. Only in her bedroom did she indulge her passion for over-the-top femininity. Her bed was a confection of ivory and ecru satin, with lace pillows and beribboned shams. Chunky silver candleholders sat on delicate chests, and a small crystal froth of a chandelier dangled in the corner near a powder puff reading chair piled with fashion magazines, several literary novels, and a self-help book that purported to help women find their inner happiness.

Maybe Bodie was drunk. Maybe that's why he'd shown up tonight. Still, who knew what motivated a man like him? She pulled on a scoop-necked sundress printed with antique roses and slipped into a pair of rose-colored ankle-strap stilettos embellished with tiny leather butterflies. The buzzer sounded. She forced herself to walk slowly to the door.

He wore a silky long-sleeved taupe shirt and matching trousers in one of those pricey microfabrics that moved against his legs. From the shoulders down, he looked muscular, but respectable, even elegant. But from the shoulders up, all respectability vanished. His sinewy tattooed neck, ice pick blue eyes, and ominous shaved head made him appear even more dangerous than she remembered.

He gazed around the living room without speaking, then walked toward the French doors that led to her small balcony. Each summer she vowed to start a container garden there, but gardening took patience she didn't possess, and she never followed through. A cloud of humidity blew into the climate-controlled interior as he opened one of the doors and stepped outside. She considered for a few moments then wandered over to the wet bar. She ignored the assortment of imported beers he'd prefer, choosing instead a bottle of champagne and two frail tulip goblets. She carried them over to the French doors and flicked on the exterior light before she went outside.

The air was thick and woolly, with high, dark clouds swirling over the roof of the apartment building on the opposite corner. She approached the concrete railing, which had a wide, flat top supported by chubby, urn-shaped balusters. She set the champagne bottle down, along with the delicate glasses.

He still hadn't spoken. On the street ten stories below, a car pulled out of a parking space and turned the corner. A group of stragglers headed toward the lake to view the city's fireworks display, which would be starting any minute. Bodie uncorked the bottle and poured. The fragile glasses didn't look nearly as ridiculous in his big hands as she'd hoped they would. The silence between them lengthened. She wished she'd spoken when he'd first come in, because now it felt like a competition to see who could hold out the longest.

A car horn blared, and the muscles in her shoulders knotted with tension. She slipped one of her feet onto the bottom rail. The concrete baluster scraped her bare ankle bone. He set his glass on the rail next to the bottle and turned toward her. She didn't mean to look up, but she couldn't help herself. Dark clouds swirled behind his head in a devil's halo. He was going to kiss her, she could feel it. But he didn't. Instead, he took the tulip glass from her fingers and set it next to his. Then he lifted his arm and ran his thumb across her lips with just enough pressure to smear her lipstick onto her cheek.

The tiny hairs at the back of her neck prickled. She told herself to move away, but she couldn't. Instead, he was the one who moved . . . over to the French doors, where he reached inside and flicked off the light, plunging the balcony into darkness. A thrill of panic shot through her. Her heart began to pound. She turned away and curled her damp palms around the railing. She felt him come up behind her, and she trembled as his big hands settled around her hips. The heat of his palms penetrated the silky rose-garden fabric of her dress. Beneath, she wore only a pair of silk tap pants in palest cream. Her skin quivered, and heat licked at her insides. He traced the narrow band at the top of the tap pants through her dress, the exploration more erotic than if he'd touched bare flesh.

A diadem of strobes erupted in the sky, crystal white spheres of noise and light exploding over the lake to announce the beginning of the fireworks display. His breath fell hot on her damp neck, and his teeth settled around the tendon that marked the place where her neck and shoulder joined. He restrained her that way—not hurting, but holding her still like an animal. His hands slipped under the hem of her skirt.

She didn't try to get away, didn't move. He kneaded her bottom through her tap pants. He ran his thumbs down the crack, then up, then down again, taking his time. A light flicked on in the window across the street, and golden palms opened like umbrellas in the sky. She caught her breath as his thumbs slid between her thighs.

Just when her legs felt as though they were giving out, he eased his mouth from her neck and glazed his tongue over the place where he'd held her prisoner. He knelt behind her. She stayed where she was, gripping the rail, staring out as orange and silver serpents uncoiled against the clouds. He touched her calves, then slid his hands up beneath her skirt to skim her outer thighs, then her tap pants. He hooked his thumbs over the waistband and drew them down to her ankles. He lifted one foot and pulled the panties over her shoe. They pooled around her opposite ankle where he left them. He rose.

A forest of blue and green willows dripped from the sky. She felt his hand against the center of her back. He pressed, but it took her a moment to understand what he wanted her to do. Slowly, he bent her over the rail. Below, a taxi slid along the street. He pushed her floaty skirt up to her waist. From the front, the fabric covered her modestly so that anyone glancing out an opposite window would only see a woman leaning over the balcony rail with a man standing behind her. But from the back, she was fully exposed to him.

Now when he traced her, no silky barrier lay between her flesh and the pads of his thumb. He opened her like the segments of an orange. Played in the juice. Her breath came shallow and fast. She moaned. He stepped back. She heard a rustle as he dealt with his clothes, dealt with a condom that told her he'd planned this from the beginning. And then he dealt with her.

She caught her breath against the thrilling indignity of his fingers. Comets shot into the sky then raced to their death in the water. She gripped the rail tighter and gasped as he spread her with his thumbs, toyed, then thrust deep inside her. He drove from behind, gripping her hips, holding her where he wanted her to be, where she wanted to be. He stroked . . . stretching her, filling her. She soared with the comets . . . bloomed with the willows . . . exploded with the rockets. And in the end, she tumbled to the earth in a shower of sparks.

Afterward, he smoothed her skirt back in place then disappeared into her bathroom with its antique vanity, Italian mirror, and Colefax & Fowler wallpaper. When he came out, he looked cool and unruffled. She wanted to weep. Instead, she gave him her iciest glare, strode to the door, and yanked it open.

The corner of his mouth twitched with amusement. He

made his way to her side and traced the lipstick smear on her cheek with his finger. She refused to flinch. With another smile, he stepped into the hallway and walked toward the ornate brass elevator. Before he got there, he turned back and spoke for the first time.

"Are we clear now?"

Chapter Twelve

A nnabelle and Heath left Chicago Friday afternoon. The Wind Lake Campground was located in north-eastern Michigan about an hour from the pretty town of Grayling. Kevin and Molly had been there all week and the other book club members were driving up, but Mr. Super Agent couldn't spare that much time, so he'd snagged a ride for them on a friend's corporate jet. While he made phone calls, Annabelle, who'd never been on a private jet, gazed out the window and tried to talk herself into relaxing. So what if she and Heath were sharing a cottage for the weekend? Most of the time he'd either be hanging out with the men or trying to impress Phoebe, so she'd hardly see him, which was definitely for the best, because all those male pheromones he emitted were getting to her. Fortunately, she understood the difference between biological attraction and lasting affection. She might be horny, but she wasn't entirely self-destructive.

A gray rental SUV waited for them at the small airstrip. They were only about eighty miles from Mackinac Island, and the warm afternoon air carried the crisp, piney scent of the north woods. Heath grabbed her bag along with his own and carried them to the car, then went back for his golf clubs. She'd strained her budget to buy a few new things for the trip, including her buff slacks, which had thin brown stripes that made her legs look longer. A flirty bronze top set off tiny amber eardrops, a Christmas gift from Kate. She'd gotten her split ends trimmed, and for once her hair wasn't giving her trouble. Heath wore another of his expensive polo shirts, this one moss green, along with stone-colored chinos and loafers.

He set the suitcases in the back then tossed her the keys. "You drive."

She repressed a smile as she climbed behind the wheel. "With each passing day, your reasons for wanting a wife become clearer."

He shoved his laptop in the back and settled into the passenger seat. She consulted Molly's directions, then pulled out onto a winding two-lane highway. She wondered how he'd spent the Fourth. She hadn't seen him since Wednesday, when she'd introduced him to the De Paul harpist, whom he found intelligent, attractive, but too serious. After the date, he'd pressed her for more information about Gwen. Someday very soon she'd have to tell him the truth about that. Not a pleasant thought.

As he made another call, she concentrated on the pleasure of driving a car that wasn't Sherman. Molly hadn't exaggerated when she'd described how beautiful it was up here. Woods stretched on each side of the road, stands of pine, oak, and maple. Last year, Annabelle had been forced to cancel her plans to attend the retreat after Kate had shown up in Chicago unannounced, but she'd heard all about it: the walks they'd taken through the campground, how they'd gone swimming in the lake and held their book discussion in the new gazebo Molly and Kevin had build near their private living area, which was attached to the B&B. It had sounded so relaxing. But she didn't feel relaxed now. She had too much at stake, and she had to get her head together.

Heath made a second call before he put his phone away and occupied himself with criticizing her driving. "You have plenty of room to pass that truck."

"As long as I ignore the double yellow line."

"You'll be fine if you step on it."

"Right. Why worry about a silly thing like a head-on collision?"

"The speed limit's fifty-five. You're barely doing sixty."

"Don't make me stop this car, young man."

He chuckled, and for a few moments, his tension eased. Soon, however, he was back at it: sighing, tapping his foot, fiddling with the radio. She shot him a dark look. "You're never going to be able to manage three whole days away from work."

"Sure I can."

"Not without your cell."

"Definitely not. You'll win our bet."

"We don't have a bet!"

"Good. I hate losing. And it's not really three days. I've already put in eight hours today, and I'm taking off for Detroit on Sunday morning. You made plans to get back to the city, right?"

She nodded. She was riding back with Janine, the group's other unmarried member. He peered over at the speedometer. "You must have spoken to Molly since the party, and I'm guessing she grilled you about this weekend. How did you explain why I was coming with you?"

"I said that someone was at my door, and I'd get back to her. Is that a wild turkey?"

"I don't know. Did you call her back?"

"No."

"You should have. Now she'll be suspicious."

"What was I supposed to say? That you're obsessed with sucking up to her sister?"

"No, you were supposed to say that I've been working too hard, and it's made me so tense I can't appreciate all the great women you're introducing me to."

"That's for sure. You should give Zoe another chance. The harpist," she added, in case he'd already forgotten.

"I remember."

"Just because she thinks Adam Sandler is moronic doesn't mean she has no sense of humor."

"You think Adam Sandler's funny," he pointed out.

"Yes, but I'm immature."

He smiled. "Admit it. You know she wasn't right for me. I don't even think she liked me that much. Although she did have great legs." He leaned against the headrest, his mouth curling like a Python's tail. "Tell Molly you can't find me a wife when all I think about is work. Say you need to get me away from the city this weekend so you can have a serious talk with me about my screwed-up priorities."

"Which they are."

"See? You've already made progress."

"Molly's sharp. She won't buy that for a minute." She didn't add that Molly had already started asking Annabelle probing questions about how she and Heath were getting along.

"You can handle whatever she throws at you. And do you know why, Ace? Because you're not afraid of a challenge. Because you, my friend, live for challenges, the tougher the better."

"That's me, all right. A real shark."

"Now you're talking." They flew past a sign pointing toward the town of Wind Lake. "Do you know where you're going?"

"The campground's on the other end of the lake."

"Let me see."

As he reached for the crumpled page of directions lying in her lap, his thumb brushed the inside of her thigh, and she got goose bumps. She distracted herself with a little passive aggression. "I'm surprised this is your first trip to the campground. Kevin and Molly come up here all the time. I can't believe he hasn't invited you."

"I never said I hadn't been invited." He glanced from the directions to a road marker. "Kevin's a solid guy. He doesn't need the same amount of hand holding my younger clients do."

"You're weaseling. Kevin's never invited you up here, and do you know why? Because nobody can *relax* around you."

"Exactly what you're trying to change." A green-and-white sign with gilt-edged letters came into view on their left.

WIND LAKE COTTAGES
BED AND BREAKFAST
ESTABLISHED 1894

She turned into a narrow lane that tunneled through a dense stand of trees. "I know this might be hard to process, but I think you should be honest. Everybody knows you and Phoebe are at loggerheads, so why don't you just admit that you saw an opportunity to improve your relationship and took advantage of it?"

"And put Phoebe on guard? I don't think so."

"I'm guessing she already will be."

Another lazy smile. "Not if I play my cards right."

Fresh gravel pinged against the undercarriage of the car, and a few minutes later, the campground came into sight. She took in the shady commons, where a group of kids were playing softball. Gingerbread cottages with tiny eaves that dripped wooden lace surrounded the grassy rectangle. Each house looked as though it had been painted with brushes dipped in sherbet cartons: one lime green with root beer and cantaloupe trim, another raspberry with touches of lemon and almond. Through the trees she glimpsed a slice of sandy beach and the bright blue water of Wind Lake.

"No wonder Kevin likes it here so much," Heath said.

"It's exactly like Nightingale Woods in Molly's *Daphne* books. I'm so glad she talked Kevin out of selling it." The campground had been in Kevin's family since his great-grandfather, an itinerant Methodist minister, had founded it for summer religious revivals. Eventually, it had passed to Kevin's father, then Kevin's aunt, and finally to Kevin.

"The upkeep on the place is unbelievable," Heath said. "I've always wondered why he kept it."

"Now you know."

"Now I know." He slipped off his sunglasses. "I miss not being outdoors more. I grew up banging around in the woods."

"Huntin' and trappin'?"

"Not too much. I never got into killing things."

"Preferring slow torture."

"You know me so well."

They followed the road that looped around the common. Each cottage bore a neatly painted sign over the door: GREEN PASTURES, MILK AND HONEY, LAMB OF GOD, JACOB'S LADDER. She slowed to admire the bed-and-breakfast, a stately, turreted Queen Anne with sweeping porches; lush, hanging ferns; and wooden rockers where two women sat chatting. Heath checked the directions and pointed toward a narrow lane that ran parallel to the lake. "Take a left."

She did as he said. They passed an elderly woman with binoculars and a walking stick, then two teenagers on bikes. Finally, they reached the end of the lane, and she pulled up in front of the last of the cottages, a doll's house with a sign above the door that read LILIES OF THE FIELD. Painted a creamy yellow with dusty pink and pale blue accents, the house looked as though it had tumbled out of a child's nursery tale. Annabelle was captivated. At the same time, she found herself wishing it weren't quite so isolated from the other cottages.

Heath bounded from the car and unloaded their suitcases. The screen door squeaked as she followed him into the cottage's main living area. Everything was worn, chipped, and homey, authentic shabby chic instead of the overpriced decorator variety. Off-white walls, a cozy couch with a faded floral print, battered brass lamps, a scrubbed pine chest . . . She poked her head into a tiny kitchen with an old-fashioned gas stove. A door next to the refrigerator led to a shady, screened-in porch. She walked outside and saw a glider, bent willow chairs, and an ancient drop-leaf table with two painted wooden chairs.

Heath came up behind her. "No sirens, no garbage trucks, no car alarms. I've forgotten what real quiet sounds like."

She drew in the damp, cool smell of vegetation. "It's so private. It feels like a nest."

"It's nice."

This was too much coziness for her, and she slipped back inside. The rest of the cottage consisted of an old-fashioned bathroom along with two bedrooms, the largest of which held a double bed with an iron headboard. And two suitcases . . .

"Heath?"

He poked his head through the door. "Yeah?"

She gestured toward his suitcase. "You left something in here."

"Just until we flip for the big bed."

"Nice try. It's my party. You get the kiddy bedroom."

"I'm the client, and this one looks more comfortable."

"I know. Which is why I'm taking it."

"Fine," he said with a surprising display of good humor. "I'll drag that other mattress onto the porch. I can't remember the last time I slept outside." He tossed her suitcase up on the bed then handed her an envelope with her name on it in Molly's handwriting. "I found this in the kitchen."

She pulled out a note written on Molly's new line of Nightingale Woods stationery. "Molly says this is one of her favorite cottages and she hopes we like it. The refrigerator's stocked with necessities, and there's a cookout on the beach at six o'clock." The P.S. Annabelle kept to herself.

Do not do anything stupid!

"Fill me in on this book club." He moved his suitcase out of the way and set a shoulder against the doorjamb as she slipped the note inside the pocket of her slacks. "How did you get involved?"

"Through Molly." She unzipped her suitcase. "We've been meeting once a month for the past two years. Last year Phoebe said she thought it would be fun if we all went away for a weekend. I think she had a spa in mind, but Janine and I couldn't afford it—Janine writes young adult books—so Molly jumped in and said we should all come to the campground. Before long, the men were involved."

Annabelle and Janine were two of only three book club members not directly associated with the Stars. The other was Heath's dream woman, Gwen. Fortunately, she and Ian were closing on their new house this weekend and couldn't come.

Heath gave a soft whistle. "This is one hell of a book club. Phoebe and Molly. Didn't you mention Ron McDermitt's wife?"

She nodded and flipped open her suitcase. "Sharon used to teach nursery school. She keeps us in line."

"And now she's married to the Stars' general manager. I've met her." He gazed directly at the bras and panties lying on top, but his mind was on business, not underwear. "At the party, Phoebe mentioned Darnell. That can only be Darnell Pruitt."

"His wife's name is Charmaine." She surreptitiously slipped a T-shirt over her lingerie pile

"The greatest D.T. the Stars ever had."

"Charmaine played football?"

But he was a John Deere on his way to a tractor-pulling contest, and she couldn't distract him. "Who else?"

"Krystal Greer." She pulled out her toiletry case and set it on the dresser's cracked white marble top.

"Webster Greer's wife. Unbelievable. He went to the Pro Bowl nine years in a row."

"It's the women who are members, not the men. Try not to embarrass me."

He snorted and picked up his suitcase but paused at the door. "Did anybody bring their kids?"

"Adults only."

He smiled. "Excellent."

"Except for Pippi and Danny. They're too young to leave behind."

"Shit."

She frowned at him. "What's wrong with you? They're adorable children."

"One of them's adorable. I'd sign him right now if I could."

"The road trips might be a challenge, since he's still nursing. And Pippi's just as cute as Danny. That little girl is precious."

"She'll be in prison before she makes it to first grade."

"What are you talking about?"

"Just rambling." He headed out the door only to poke his head back in. "Good taste in panties, Tinker Bell." Then he was gone.

She sank down on the side of the bed. The man didn't miss anything. What else about her might he notice that she didn't want him to see? With a sense of foreboding, she traded in her new slacks for biscuit-colored shorts but left the flirty bronze top on. After running her fingers through her hair, she headed for the porch. Heath was already there. He'd also changed into shorts, along with a light gray T-shirt that curled like pipe smoke around the contours of his chest. A blade of light angling through the screen caught one cheekbone, etching its tough, uncompromising contour. "Are you going to sabotage me this weekend?" he asked quietly.

He had grounds for being suspicious, so she shouldn't have been offended, but she was. "Is that what you think of me?"

"Just making sure we're on the same page."

"*Your* page."

"All I'm asking is that you don't undermine me. I'll take care of everything else."

"Oh, I'm sure you will," she said, sarcastic as all hell.

"What's your beef, anyway? You've been marginally bitchy all afternoon."

She was pleased that he'd noticed. "I have no idea what you're talking about."

"And not just this afternoon. You're taking potshots at me whenever you see the opportunity. Is it personal or symbolic of your feelings toward men in general? It's not my fault your last boyfriend decided to play for the same team you're on."

Okay. Now she was mad. "Who told you that?"

"I didn't know it was a secret."

"It's not exactly." Molly wouldn't have said anything, but Kevin still had trouble accepting what Rob had done, which made him the likely culprit. She shoved one of the chairs back under the table. She wouldn't talk about Rob to Heath. "I'm sorry if I've been testy," she said, still sounding testy, "but I have a hard time understanding people who make work the center of their lives to the exclusion of personal relationships."

"Which is exactly why you brought me here. To fix that."

He had her there.

"Shall we?" He gestured toward the porch door.

"Why not?" She tossed her hair and marched past him. "Time to get Operation Suck Up off and running."

"Now, that's the kind of can-do attitude I like to hear."

The fire popped and sparks shot into the sky. Only the platter of chocolate brownies Molly had baked for them in the B&B's kitchen that afternoon remained on the picnic table. A young couple took care of the everyday operation of the campground, but Molly and Kevin always pitched in when they were here. The meal had been delicious: grilled steaks, baked potatoes with plenty of toppings, sweet onions perfectly charred at the edges, and a salad laced with juicy slices of ripe pear. Kevin and Molly had left their children with the couple who ran the campground, nobody had to drive home, and the wine and beer flowed. Heath was in his element, friendly and charming with the women, perfectly at home with the men. He was a chameleon, Annabelle thought, subtly adjusting his behavior to suit his audience. Tonight, everyone except Phoebe was enjoying his company, and even she hadn't done much worse than shoot him a few poisonous glares.

As the music from the boom box began to crank up, Annabelle wandered out onto the deserted dock, but just as she'd begun to enjoy the solitude, she heard the purposeful tap of a pair of sandals coming her way and turned to see Molly approaching. With the exception of the more generous bust-line that nursing Danny had given her, she looked like the same studious girl Annabelle had first met more than a decade ago in a comparative lit class. Tonight she'd pulled her straight brown hair back from her face with a barrette, and a tiny pair of silver sea turtles bobbed at her earlobes. She wore purple capris with a matching top and a necklace made out of elbow macaroni.

"Why haven't you returned my calls?" she demanded.

"Sorry. Things got totally crazy." Maybe she could distract her. "Remember I told you I have a client who's a hypochondriac? I set him up with a woman who's—"

"Never mind that. What's going on with you and Heath?"

Annabelle pulled a little wide-eyed innocence out of her rusty bag of college acting skills. "What do you mean? Business."

"Don't give me that. We've been friends too long."

She switched to a furrowed brow. "He's my most important client. You know how much this means to me."

Molly wasn't buying it. "I've seen the way you look at him. Like he was a slot machine with triple sevens tattooed on his forehead. If you fall in love with him, I swear I'll never speak to you again."

Annabelle nearly choked. She'd known Molly would be suspicious, but she hadn't expected an outright confrontation. "Are you nuts? Setting aside the fact that he treats me like a flunky, I'd never fall for a workaholic after what I've had to go through with my family." Falling in lust, however, was an entirely different matter.

"He has a calculator for a heart," Molly said.

"I thought you liked him."

"I love him. He handled Kevin's negotiations brilliantly, and, believe me, my sister can be a real cheapo. Heath's smart, I've never met anybody who works so hard, he'll do anything for his clients, and he's as ethical as any agent's ever going to get. But he's the worst candidate for a love match I've ever met."

"You think I don't know that? This weekend is business. He's rejected everybody Powers and I set him up with. There's something we're both missing, and I can't figure out what that is during those stingy slivers of time he gives me." She was speaking the truth. This was exactly where she needed to concentrate her attention this weekend, looking into his psyche instead of noticing how good he smelled or how gorgeous his stupid green eyes were.

Molly still looked worried. "I'd like to believe you, but I've got a weird feeling that—"

What kind of feeling she had was lost as more footsteps sounded on the dock. They turned to see Krystal Greer and Charmaine Pruitt joining them. Krystal looked like a younger Diana Ross. Tonight, she'd tied her long, curly hair up with a red ribbon that matched her bandanna top. She was tiny, but she carried herself like a queen, and entering her forties hadn't altered either her model's cheekbones or her take-no-prisoners attitude.

Despite their diametrical personalities, she and Charmaine had been best friends for years. Charmaine, conservatively dressed in a cranberry cotton twin set and twill walking shorts, was curvy, sweet, and serious. A former librarian and current church organist, she centered her life around her husband and two little boys. The first time Annabelle had met Charmaine's husband, Darnell, she'd been struck speechless by what seemed the mismatch of the century. Although Annabelle knew Darnell had once played for the Stars, she hadn't paid much attention to football in those days, and she'd imagined someone as conservative as Charmaine. Instead, Darnell had a diamond-embedded gold front tooth, a seemingly endless collection of dark glasses, and a penchant for bling-bling that rivaled a hip-hop headliner. Appearances, however, were deceiving. Over half their book club selections were based on his recommendations.

"I can't get over the way the sky looks up here." Charmaine wrapped her arms around herself and gazed at the stars. "Living in the city, you forget."

"You're going to have a bigger surprise this weekend than a sky full of pretty stars," Krystal said smugly.

"Either spill your big secret or keep quiet about it," Charmaine retorted. She turned to Annabelle and Molly. "Krystal keeps dropping hints about some big surprise she has planned. Do either of you know what it is?"

Annabelle and Molly shook their heads.

Krystal slipped her thumbs in the front pockets of her shorts and stuck out a set of still perky breasts. "I'll just say this . . . Our Miss Charmaine might need a little therapy after I'm done with her. As for the rest of you . . . Just be prepared."

"For what?" Janine approached with Sharon McDermitt and Phoebe, who'd pulled on a pink zippered hoodie with matching sweatpants and held a glass of chardonnay. Janine, with her prematurely gray pixie, artisan's jewelry, and ankle-length block-print sundress, was coming off a bad year: the death of her mother, breast cancer, and a bad bout of writer's block. The friendship of the book club meant everything to her. When she'd been sick, Annabelle and Charmaine had brought her meals and run errands, Phoebe had arranged for regular massages and called her daily, Krystal tended her garden, and Molly nagged her into starting to write again. Sharon McDermitt, the best listener in the group, had been her confidante. Next to Molly, Sharon was Phoebe's best friend, and she headed the Stars' charity foundation.

"Apparently Krystal has a secret," Molly said, "which, as usual, she'll reveal when she's good and ready."

While the rest of them speculated over what Krystal's secret might be, Annabelle tried to figure out the best way to broach a perilous subject. Although she'd been lucky so far, she couldn't count on her luck lasting forever, and when there was a lull in the conversation, she plunged in. "I might need a little help this weekend."

She knew by their expectant expressions that they wanted her to explain why she'd shown up with Heath, but she wasn't volunteering any more than she already had. She toyed with the yellow band of her Swatch daisy watch. "All of you know how much Perfect for You means to me. If I don't make a success of this, it'll basically prove my mother's right about everything. And I really don't want to be an accountant."

"Kate puts too much pressure on you," Sharon said, not for the first time.

Annabelle shot her a grateful smile. "Thanks to Molly, I had an interview with Heath. But the thing is, I needed to engage in a small act of subterfuge to get his name on my contract."

"What kind of subterfuge?" Janine asked.

She took a deep breath and told them how she'd fixed him up with Gwen.

Molly gasped. "He's going to *kill* you. I mean it, Annabelle. When he finds out you deceived him—*and he will find out*—he'll go ballistic."

"He boxed me into a corner." Annabelle hunched her shoulders and rubbed her arm. "I admit it was a crappy thing to do, but I only had twenty-four hours to come up with a knockout candidate, or I was going to lose him."

"That is not a man to mess with," Sharon said. "You wouldn't believe some of the stories I've heard from Ron."

Annabelle gnawed her bottom lip. "I know I have to tell him the truth. I just need to find the right moment."

Krystal cocked her hip. "Girl, there is no right moment to die."

Charmaine clucked her tongue. "You are going straight to the top on my prayer list."

Only Phoebe looked pleased, and her amber eyes glowed like a cat's. "I love this. Not the fact that you'll end up in a shallow grave—I'm really sorry about that, and I'll make sure he's prosecuted to the fullest extent of the law. But I love knowing that a mere slip of a female put one over on the great Python."

Molly glared at her sister. "This is the exact reason why Christine Jeffreys won't let her daughter have a sleepover with the twins. You frighten people." And then, to Annabelle, "What do you want us to do?"

"Just don't mention Gwen's name around him, that's all. I can't see any reason the guys would mention her, so I'll have to hope for the best with them. Unless any of you can find a way to clue them in without actually telling them what I did."

"I vote we tell them the truth," Phoebe said. "They'll laugh at him behind his back for months."

"You don't get a vote," Krystal said. "Not on anything that involves the Python."

"That is *so* unfair." Phoebe sniffed.

Charmaine patted her arm. "You're a little irrational on the subject."

The sound of male laughter drifted toward them from the beach. "We'd better get back," Molly said. "We've got all day tomorrow to talk about Annabelle's problems, including why she brought Heath in the first place."

Sharon looked worried. "I think that's fairly obvious. Annabelle, really, what were you thinking?"

"It's business!" she exclaimed.

"Monkey business," Krystal muttered.

"Heath needed to get away for a while, and I need a chance to figure out why the matches aren't working. There's nothing more to it than that."

Charmaine exchanged a loaded glance with Phoebe, ready to say more, but Molly came to Annabelle's rescue. "We'd better get back before they start running plays."

All of them turned toward the end of the dock.

And came to a dead stop.

Phoebe was the first to break the long silence. In her soft, husky voice, she said what all of them were thinking. "Welcome to the Garden of the Gods, ladies."

Sharon spoke quietly over the lapping water. "When you're standing right next to them, you don't get the full impact."

Krystal's voice had a dreamy edge. "We're getting it now."

The men stood by the campfire . . . all six of them . . . one more gorgeous than the other. Phoebe licked her bottom lip and pointed to the oldest, a big blond giant with a hand cocked at his hip. On a never-to-be-forgotten day in the Midwest Sports Dome, Dan Calebow had saved her life with a perfectly thrown spiral. "I pick him," she said softly. "Forever and ever."

Molly slipped her arm through her sister's and said, just as softly. "I'll take the golden boy right next to him. Forever and ever." Kevin Tucker, tan and fit, had hazel eyes and a star-kissed talent that had earned him two Super Bowl rings, but he still told people the night he'd mistaken Molly for a burglar was the luckiest night of his life.

"I'll take that righteous brother with the soulful eyes and smile that melts my heart." Krystal pointed toward Webster Greer, the second largest of the men standing by the flames. "As mad as he makes me, I'd marry him again tomorrow."

Charmaine gazed toward the largest and most menacing of the gods. Darnell Pruitt had left his silk shirt unbuttoned to the waist, revealing a brawny chest and a trio of gold chains. As the firelight turned his skin to polished ebony, he looked like an ancient African king. She pressed her fingertips to the base of her throat. "I still don't quite understand it. He should terrify me."

"Instead, it's the other way around." Janine's smile held a

trace of longing. "Somebody lend me one of them. Just for the night."

"Not mine," Sharon said. The fact that Ron McDermitt was the smallest man around the fire and a self-proclaimed geek didn't dim his sexual megawattage one bit, not when the right pair of sunglasses turned him into a ringer for Tom Cruise.

One by one, the women's gazes fell on Heath. Lithe, square-jawed, his crisp brown hair dusted with gold from the fire, he stood in the exact center of this elite group of warriors, both one of them and somehow set apart. He was younger, and his battle-hardened edges had been honed at the negotiating table instead of on the gridiron, but that didn't make him any less commanding. This was a man to be reckoned with.

"Spooky how he fits right in," Molly observed.

"It's the favorite trick of the undead," Phoebe said tartly. "Shape-shifters transform themselves into whatever people want to see."

Annabelle suppressed a powerful urge to defend him.

"Harvard brains, GQ polish, and country boy charm," Charmaine said. "That's why the young guys want to sign with him."

Phoebe tapped the toe of her sneaker against the dock. "There's only one good use for a man like Heath Champion."

"Here we go again," Molly muttered.

Phoebe's lip curled. "Target practice."

"Stop it!" Annabelle rounded on her.

They all stared. Annabelle unclenched her hands and tried to retrench. "What I mean is . . . I mean . . . If a man said something like that about a woman, people would throw him in jail. So, I don't . . . you know . . . think maybe a woman should say it about a man."

Phoebe seemed fascinated by Annabelle's rebuke. "The Python has a champion."

"I'm just saying," Annabelle murmured.

"She has a point." Krystal began walking toward the beach.

"It's hard to raise male children with good self-esteem. That kind of thing doesn't help."

"You're right." Phoebe slipped her arm around Annabelle's waist. "I'm the mother of a son, and I should know better. I'm just . . . a little uneasy. I've had so much more experience with Heath than you."

Her concern was genuine, and Annabelle couldn't stay upset. "You really don't have to worry."

"It's hard not to. I feel guilty."

"About what?"

Phoebe's steps slowed just enough so they fell behind the others. She patted Annabelle the same way she patted her children when she was worried. "I'm trying to figure out a tactful way to say this, but I can't. You know, don't you, that he's manipulating you to get to me?"

"You can't blame him for trying," Annabelle said quietly. "He's a good agent. Everybody says so. Maybe it's time to let bygones be bygones." She regretted her words the moment she spoke them. She knew nothing about the inner workings of the NFL, and she shouldn't presume to tell Phoebe how to run her empire.

But Phoebe merely sighed and dropped her hand from Annabelle's waist. "There are no good agents. But at least some of them don't go out of their way to stab you in the back."

Heath had scented danger, and he came striding toward her. "Ron had his eye on the last brownie, Annabelle, but I snagged it first. I've seen how cranky you get if you go too long without chocolate."

She was more of a caramel person, but she wouldn't contradict him in front of his archenemy, and she took the brownie he extended. "Phoebe, do you want to split this?"

"I'll save my calories for another glass of wine." Without even glancing at Heath, she walked away to join the others.

"So how's your plan working so far?" Annabelle said, studying Phoebe's back.

"She'll come around."

"Not anytime soon."

"Attitude, Annabelle. It's all about attitude."

"So you've mentioned." She handed him the brownie. "You can work this off easier than me."

He took a bite. From the beach, she heard Janine say she needed to finish the book before tomorrow. As everybody told her good night, Webster slipped another CD in the boom box, and a Marc Anthony song came on. Ron and Sharon began to salsa in the sand. Kevin grabbed Molly, and they joined in, executing the steps more gracefully than the McDermitts. Phoebe and Dan looked into each other's eyes, laughed, and began to dance, too.

Heath's fingers tightened around Annabelle's elbow. "Let's take a walk."

"No. They're suspicious enough as it is. And Phoebe knows exactly what you're up to."

"Does she now?" He tossed the rest of the brownie in the trash. "If you don't want to walk, let's dance."

"Okay, but dance with the other women, too, so nobody gets suspicious."

"Of what?"

"Molly thinks . . . Oh, never mind. Just spread your dubious charm around, okay?"

"Will you relax?" He grabbed her hand and led her back to the others.

It didn't take long for her to kick off her sandals and get into the spirit of the evening. After all the classes Kate had forced her to take, Annabelle was a good dancer. Either Heath had taken a few classes himself or he was a natural because he stayed right with her. When it came to mastering the social graces, he didn't seem to have missed a trick. The song came to an end, and Annabelle waited for the next one. With the water lapping the shore, a crackling fire, a star-spangled sky, and a frighteningly tempting man at her side, this was a romantic cliché of a night.

She couldn't handle a ballad—that would be too cruel. To her relief, the music stayed upbeat.

She danced with Darnell and Kevin, Heath with their wives. After a while, the couples drifted back together, and they stayed that way for the rest of the evening. Eventually, Kevin and Molly disappeared to check on their kids. Phoebe and Dan wandered away, hand in hand, for a stroll along the beach. The rest of them kept dancing, shedding their sweatshirts, mopping their brows, refreshing themselves with a cold beer or a glass of wine while the music urged them on. Annabelle's hair whipped her cheeks. Heath pulled a Travolta move that made them both laugh. They drank more wine, came together, slipped apart. Their hips touched, their legs rubbed, the blood surged through her veins. Krystal ground her bottom against her husband like a freak-dancing teenager. Darnell took his wife by the hips, gazed into her eyes, and Charmaine no longer looked prim at all.

Sparks shot into the sky. Outkast launched into "Hey Yah!" Annabelle's breasts brushed Heath's chest. She gazed up into a pair of half-lidded deep green eyes and thought about how being drunk could give a woman the perfect excuse to do something she normally wouldn't. The next morning, she could always say, "God, I was so hammered. Remind me never to drink again."

It would be like having a free pass.

Somewhere between Marc Anthony and James Brown, Heath started forgetting that Annabelle was his matchmaker. As they headed back to the cottage, he blamed the night, the music, too many beers, and that wild auburn rumpus dancing around her head. He blamed the impish amber sparks in her eyes as she'd dared him to keep up with her. He blamed the feisty curve of her mouth as her small bare feet kicked up the sand. But most of all, he blamed his training regimen for marital fidelity, which he now realized had been way too strict or he'd be able to remember this was Annabelle, his matchmaker, his—sort of—buddy.

She fell silent as they approached the darkened cottage. Granted, tonight wasn't the first time his thoughts toward her had turned in a sexual direction, but that had been a normal male reaction to an intriguing female. Annabelle as a potential bed partner had no place in his life, and he needed to get a grip.

He held the cottage door open for her. All evening, her laughter had chimed like bells in his head, and, as she brushed his shoulder, an unwelcome surge of blood shot straight to his loins. He smelled wood smoke, along with a light, floral shampoo, and fought the urge to bury his face in her hair. His cell sat on the end table, where he'd left it before the cookout so he wouldn't be tempted to use it. Normally, he'd have checked for messages first thing, but he didn't feel like it tonight. Annabelle, however, was busy as a bee. She slipped past him to turn on a lamp, knocking the shade askew in the process. She opened a window, fanned herself, picked up the purse she'd left on the couch, set it back down. When she finally gazed at him, he saw the damp spot on her top where she'd spilled her third glass of wine. Bastard that he was, he'd refilled it right away.

"I'd better get to bed." She nibbled on her bottom lip.

He couldn't look away from those small, straight teeth sinking into that rosy flesh. "Not yet," he heard himself say. "I'm too wired. I want somebody to talk to." *Somebody to touch.*

Being Annabelle, she read his mind, and she confronted the situation head-on. "How sober are you?"

"Almost."

"Good. Because I'm not."

His eyes settled on that moist blossom of a mouth. Her lips parted like flower petals. He tried to come up with a smarmy comment that was sure to offend her, which would snap them both out of this, but he couldn't think of a thing. "And if I weren't almost sober?" he said.

"You are. Almost." Those melted caramel eyes didn't leave

his face. "You're a very self-disciplined person. I respect that about you."

"Because one of us needs to be self-disciplined, right?"

Her hands twisted at her waist. She looked adorable—rumpled clothes, sandy ankles, that hullabaloo of shiny hair. "Exactly."

"Or maybe not." To hell with it. They were both adults. They knew what they were doing, and he took a step toward her.

She threw up her hands. "I'm drunk. Really, really drunk."

"Got it." He moved closer.

"I'm *totally* wasted." She took a quick, awkward step backward. "Hammered *out of* my mind."

"Okay." He stopped where he was and waited.

The toe of her sandal eased forward. "I am *not* responsible!"

"I'm readin' you loud and clear."

"Any man would look good to me right now." Another step toward him. "If Dan walked in, Darnell, Ron—*any* man!—I'd think about jumping him." The bridge of her nose crinkled with indignation. "Even Kevin! My best friend's husband, can you imagine? That's exactly how drunk I am. I mean . . ." A gulp of air. "*You!* Can you believe it? I'm so wasted, I couldn't tell one man from another."

"You'll take whatever you can get, right?" *Oh, this was too easy.* He closed the remaining distance between them.

The muscles in her throat worked as she swallowed. "I have to be honest."

"You'd even take me."

Her narrow shoulders rose, then fell. "Unfortunately, you're the only man in the room. If somebody else was here, I'd—"

"I know. Jump him." He ran the tip of his finger over the curve of her cheek. She leaned into his hand. He rubbed his thumb over her chin. "Could you be quiet now so I can kiss you?"

She blinked, thick lashes sweeping her pixie's eyes. "Really?"

"Oh, yes."

"Because, if you do, I'll kiss you back, so you need to remember that I'm—"

"Drunk. I'll remember." He slipped his hands into the hair he'd been aching to touch for weeks. "You're not responsible for your actions."

She gazed up at him. "Just so you understand."

"I understand," he said softly. And then he kissed her.

She arched against him, her body pliant, her lips hot and Annabelle-spicy. Her hair curled around his fingers, ribbons of silk. He freed one hand and found her breast. Through her clothes, the nipple pebbled under his palm. She wound her arms around his neck, pressed her hips to his. Their tongues played an erotic game. He was hard, mindless. He needed more, and he reached under her top to feel her skin.

A muffled little whimper penetrated his fog. She shuddered, and the heels of her hands pressed against his chest.

He drew back. "Annabelle?"

She gazed up at him through watery eyes and sniffed, the corners of her soft, rosy mouth drooping. "If only I were drunk," she whispered.

Chapter Thirteen

nnabelle heard Heath's sigh. That kiss . . . She'd known he'd be a wonderful kisser: domineering in the best possible way, master and commander, lord of the realm, leader of the pack. No need to worry about this one slipping into high heels when she wasn't paying attention. But none of that justified her foolishness. "I—I guess I have more self-discipline than I thought," she said, her voice unsteady.

"So gosh darned thrilled you figured that out now."

"I can't throw everything away for a couple of minutes of heavy breathing."

"A couple of minutes?" he exclaimed indignantly. "If you think I'm not good for longer than—"

"Don't." Pain shot through her. All she wanted to do now was climb into bed and pull the covers over her head. She hadn't cared about her business, her life, her self-respect. All she'd cared about was giving in to the moment.

"Let's go, Tinker Bell." He snagged her arm and steered her toward the kitchen. "We're taking a walk to cool down."

"I don't want to walk," she cried.

"Fine. Let's go back to what we were doing."

Even as she pulled away, she knew he was right. If she intended to get her footing back, this couldn't wait till morning. She had to do it now. "All right."

He grabbed the flashlight hanging by the refrigerator, and she followed him outside. They set off down a path soft with pine needles. Neither of them said a word, not even when the path opened into a small, moonlit cove where limestone boulders edged the water. Heath turned off the flashlight and set it on the lone picnic table. He stuffed his hands in the rear pockets of his shorts and walked toward the water. "I know you want to make a big deal out of this, but don't."

"Out of what? I've already forgotten." She kept her distance, wandering toward the water but stopping a good ten feet from him. The air smelled warm and marshy, and the lights from the town of Wind Lake twinkled off to her left.

"We were dancing," he said. "We got turned on. So what?"

She dug her fingernails into her palms. "As far as I'm concerned, it never happened."

"It happened all right." He turned toward her, and the tough note in his voice told her the Python had uncoiled. "I know the way you think, and that wasn't some big, unforgivable sin."

Her composure dissolved. "I'm your matchmaker!"

"Right. A matchmaker. You didn't have to swear a Hippocratic oath to get your business card."

"You know exactly what I mean."

"You're single; I'm single. It wouldn't have been the end of the world if we'd seen this through."

She couldn't believe she'd heard him right. "It would have been the end of my world."

"I was afraid of this."

His mildly exasperated air pushed her over the edge, and she stomped toward him. "I should never have let you come with me this weekend! I knew it was a bad idea from the beginning."

"It was a great idea, and no harm's been done. We're two

healthy, unattached, reasonably sane adults. We have fun together, and don't even try to deny that."

"Yeah, I'm a great buddy, all right."

"Believe me, tonight I wasn't thinking of you as a buddy."

That threw her totally off stride, but she recovered quickly. "If another woman had been around, this would never have happened."

"Whatever you're trying to say, just spit it out."

"Come on, Heath. I'm not blond, leggy, or stacked. I was the default setting. Even my ex-fiancé never said I was sexy."

"Your ex-fiancé wears lipstick, so I wouldn't take that to heart. I promise, Annabelle, you're very sexy. That hair . . ."

"Do *not* start in on my hair. I was born with it, okay. It's like making fun of someone with a birth defect."

She heard him sigh. "We're talking about simple physical attraction brought on by some moonlight, a little dancing, and too much liquor," he said. "Do you agree that's what this is?"

"I guess."

"Basic physical attraction."

"I suppose."

"I don't know about you," he said, "but it's been a long time since I've had such a good time."

"Okay, I'll admit it was fun. The dancing," she added hastily.

"Damned right it was. So we got a little carried away. Nothing more than circumstances, right?"

Pride and self-respect dictated that she agree. "Of course."

"Circumstances . . . and a little animal instinct." His huskier pitch began to sound almost seductive. "Nothing to get worked up about. Are you with me?"

He was throwing her off stride, but she nodded.

He moved closer, his gravelly whisper a rasp over her skin. "Perfectly understandable, right?"

"Right." She was still nodding, almost as if he'd mesmerized her.

"Are you sure?" he whispered.

She kept nodding, no longer remembering exactly what the question was.

His eyes gleamed in the moonlight. "Because that's the only way . . . you can explain something like this. Pure animal attraction."

"Uh-huh," she managed, beginning to feel like a bedazzled, bobble-headed doll.

"Which sets us free"—he touched her chin, the barest brush—"to do exactly what neither of us can stop thinking about, right?" He dropped his head to kiss her.

The night wind hummed; her heart pounded. Just before his lips touched hers, his eyelids flickered, and she glimpsed the faintest hint of cunning loitering in those green irises. That's when it hit her.

"You snake!" She pushed against his chest.

He stepped back, all wounded innocence. "I don't deserve that."

"Ohmygod! You've just put me through Sales 101. I bow to the master."

"You've had way too much to drink."

"The Great Salesman asks just the right questions to get his mark agreeing with everything he says. He makes her nod her stupid head until it feels like it's coming off her neck. Then he dives in for the kill. You just tried to make a sale!"

"Have you always been this suspicious?"

"This is so *you*." She stomped toward the path, then spun back because she had so much more to say. "You want something you know is totally outrageous, and then you try to sell it with a combination of leading questions and fake sincerity. I just watched the Python in action, didn't I?"

He knew she had his number, but he didn't believe in conceding defeat. "My sincerity's never fake. I was stating the facts. Two single people, a warm summer night, a hot kiss . . . We're only human."

"One of us, anyway. The other's a reptile."

"Harsh, Annabelle. Very harsh."

She advanced on him again. "Let me ask you a question, one business owner to another." She planted her fingernail in his chest. "Have you ever had sex with a client? Is that acceptable professional behavior in your book?"

"My clients are men."

"Stop weaseling. What if I were a world champion figure skater on my way to the Olympics? Let's say I'm a favorite for the gold medal, and I just signed you as my agent last week. Are you going to have sex with me or not?"

"We only signed last week? That seems a little—"

"Fast-forward, then, to the Olympics," she said with exaggerated patience. "I've won the stupid medal. Only the silver, since I couldn't land my triple axel, but nobody cares because I'm a charmer, and they still want my face on their breakfast cereal. You and I have a contract. Are you sleeping with me?"

"It's apples and oranges. In the case you describe, millions of dollars would be at stake."

She made a rude buzzer noise. "Wrong answer."

"True answer."

"Because your megabusiness is so much more important than my silly little matchmaking agency? Well, it might be to you, Mr. Python, but it's not to me."

"I understand how important your business is to you."

"You don't have a clue." Pinning the blame on him felt so much better than assuming her rightful share, and she stomped back to the picnic table to grab the flashlight. "You're just like my brothers. Worse! You can't stand having anybody say no to you about anything." She thrust the flashlight toward him. "Well, listen up, Mr. Champion. I am not somebody you can pass the time with while you wait for your spectacular future wife to show up. I won't be your sexual entertainment."

"You're insulting yourself," he said calmly. "I may not be crazy about all of your business practices, but I have nothing except respect for you as a person."

"Great. Watch me build on that."

She turned on her heel and stalked off.

Heath gazed after her as she disappeared into the trees. When he could no longer see her, he picked up a stone, skipped it over the dark water, and smiled. She couldn't have been more right. He was a snake. And he was ashamed of himself. Okay, maybe not at this exact instant, but by tomorrow for sure. His only excuse was that he liked her so damned much, and he hadn't done anything just for fun in longer than he could remember.

Still, trying to nail a friend was a rotten thing to do. Even a sexy friend, although she didn't seem too clear about that, which made the effect of those mischievous eyes and the swirl of that amazing hair all the more enticing. Still, if he was going to blow his training for marital fidelity, he should have done it with one of the women at Waterworks, not with Annabelle, because she was right. How could she sleep with him then introduce him to other women? She couldn't, they both knew it, and since he never wasted his time supporting an unsupportable position, he couldn't imagine why he'd done it tonight. Or maybe he could.

Because he wanted his matchmaker naked . . . and that definitely wasn't part of his plan.

Heath slept on the porch that night and awakened the next morning to the sound of the front door closing. He rolled over and squinted at his watch. It was a few minutes before eight, which meant Annabelle was heading off to meet the book club for breakfast. He rose from the mattress he'd dragged out to the porch for the best night's sleep he'd experienced in weeks, a hell of a lot better than tossing and turning in his empty house.

The men had a round of golf scheduled. As he showered and dressed, he went over the events of the previous night and reminded himself to mind the manners he'd worked so hard to acquire. Annabelle was his friend, and he didn't screw over friends, figuratively or literally.

He drove to the public course with Kevin but ended up sharing a golf cart with Dan Calebow. Dan kept himself in great shape for a man in his forties. With the exception of a few character lines, he didn't look all that different from his playing days when his steely eyes and cold-blooded determination on the field had earned him the nickname Ice. Dan and Heath had always gotten along well, but whenever Heath mentioned Phoebe, as he did that morning, Dan always said pretty much the same thing.

"When two hardheaded people get married, they learn to pick their battles." Dan spoke softly so he didn't distract Darnell, who was lining up his tee shot. "This one's all yours, pal."

Darnell hooked his ball into the left rough, and the discussion returned to golf, but later, as they were riding down the fairway, Heath asked Dan if he missed his head coaching job, which he'd left for the front office.

"Sometimes." As Dan checked the scorecard, Heath spotted one of those rub-on tattoos on the side of his neck. A baby blue unicorn. Pippi Tucker's handiwork. "But I have a great consolation prize," Dan went on. "I get to watch my kids grow up."

"A lot of coaches have kids."

"Yeah, and their wives are raising them. Being president of the Stars is a big job, but I can still get the kids off to school in the mornings and be at the dinner table most nights."

Right now, Heath couldn't see anything too exciting about either activity, but he took it on faith that someday he might.

He finished the round only three shots behind Kevin, which wasn't bad, considering his own twelve handicap. They turned in their carts, and then the six of them headed into the clubhouse's private room for lunch. It was a dingy space with cheap paneling, battered tables, and what Kevin insisted were the best cheeseburgers in the county. After a couple of bites, Heath found himself agreeing.

They were enjoying replaying their round when, out of nowhere, Darnell decided he had to spoil it. "It's time to talk about our book," he said. "Did everybody read it like you was supposed to?"

Heath nodded along with the rest of them. Last week Annabelle had left him a message with the title of the novel all the men were supposed to read, the story of a group of mountain climbers. Heath didn't get to read for pleasure much anymore, and he'd enjoyed having an excuse. When he'd been a kid, the public library had been his refuge, but once he'd hit high school, he'd gotten wrapped up in the demands of working two jobs, playing football, and studying for the straight As that would put the Beau Vista Trailer Park behind him forever. Reading for fun had gone by the wayside, along with a lot of other simple pleasures.

Darnell rested an arm on the table. "Anybody want to start the ball rolling?"

There was a long silence.

"I liked it," Dan finally said.

"Me, too," Kevin offered.

Webster held up his hand to order another Coke. "It was pretty interesting."

They stared at one another.

"Good plot," Ron said.

An even longer silence fell.

Kevin made some accordion folds in a straw wrapper. Ron messed with the saltshaker. Webster looked around for his Coke. Darnell tried again. "What did you think about the way the men reacted to their first night on the mountain?"

"Pretty interesting."

"It was okay."

Darnell took his literature seriously, and storm clouds were gathering in his eyes. He shot Heath a menacing look. "You got anything to say?"

Heath set down his burger. "Combining adventure, irony,

and unabashed sentimentality is always tricky to pull off, especially in a novel with such a strong central conceit. We ask ourselves, where is the conflict? Man v. nature, man v. man, man versus himself? A fairly complex exploration of our modern sense of disconnection. Bleak undertones, comic high notes. It worked for me."

That cracked 'em all up. Even Darnell.

Finally, they quieted down. Webster got his Coke, Dan found a fresh bottle of ketchup, and the discussion turned right back to where everybody except Darnell wanted it to be.

Football.

A fter lunch, the book club took a walk around the campground and continued their discussion of the biographies of the famous women they'd read. Annabelle had dug into both Katharine Graham's and Mary Kay Ash's books. Phoebe had concentrated on Eleanor Roosevelt, Charmaine on Josephine Baker, Krystal on Coco Chanel. Janine had read several biographies of cancer survivors, and Sharon had explored the life of Frida Kahlo. Molly, predictably, had chosen Beatrix Potter. As they talked, they related the women's lives to their own, looked for common themes, and examined each woman's survival skills.

After their walk, they returned to Kevin and Molly's private gazebo. Janine began setting out an assortment of old magazines, catalogs, and art supplies. "We did this in my cancer support group," she said. "It was pretty revealing. We're going to cut out words and pictures that appeal to us and assemble them into individual collages. When we're done, we'll talk about them."

Annabelle knew a land mine when she saw one, and she was very careful what she chose. Unfortunately, not careful enough.

"That man looks a lot like Heath." Molly pointed to a hunky model in a Van Heusen shirt Annabelle had pasted in the upper left corner of her poster.

"He does not," Annabelle protested. "He represents the kind of male clients I want Perfect for You to attract."

"What about that bedroom furniture?" Charmaine pointed out a Crate & Barrel sleigh bed. "And the little girl and the dog?"

"They're on the other side of the paper. Professional life. Personal life. Totally separate."

Luckily, the dessert tray arrived just then, so they stopped interrogating her, but even a slab of lemon cake didn't stop her from lambasting herself for last night. Had she been born stupid or was this a skill she'd worked to acquire? And one more night stretching in front of her . . .

T winz!"

Heath winced as he spotted the pint-size demon from the blue lagoon clomping toward him through the sand in a polka-dot bathing suit, her red rubber boots, and a baseball cap that came down so far over her ears only the curly ends of her blond hair peeked out from beneath. He grabbed the newspaper from under his beach chair and pretended not to see her.

The guys had played a couple of games of pickup basketball after lunch, then Heath had gone back to the cottage to make some phone calls. Afterward, he'd pulled on his trunks and headed for the beach, where they were supposed to meet the women later for a swim before they all headed to town for dinner. Despite the time he'd spent on the phone, he'd started to feel as though this really was a vacation.

"Twinz?"

He pulled the newspaper closer to his face, hoping Pippi would go away if he ignored her. She was unpredictable, and that made him uncomfortable. Who knew what she'd come up with next? Off to his left, Webster and Kevin tossed a Frisbee with some of the kids who were staying at the campground. Darnell lay on a Mickey Mouse beach towel, engrossed in a book. Small, sandy fingers tapped Heath's arm. He turned a page.

"Twinz?"

He kept his eyes on the headlines. "No twins here."

She tugged on the leg of his swim trunks and said it for the fourth time, except this time it sounded like *pwinz,* and that's when he got it. *Prince.* She was calling him Prince. And wasn't that just cuter than crap?

He peered at her around the side of the paper. "I didn't bring my phone."

She beamed at him and patted her little round stomach. "I got a baby."

He dropped the paper and looked frantically around for her father, but Kevin was showing a skinny kid with a bad haircut how to get more mileage from the Frisbee.

"Hey, Pip."

He whipped around to the sound of a familiar female voice and saw the cavalry walking toward him in the form of his sexy little matchmaker, delectably dressed in a modestly cut white bikini. A rainbow-colored plastic heart gathered the material between her breasts into pleats, and a second heart, this one larger and printed directly on the fabric, nested next to her hip. He couldn't see a hard edge or sharp angle anywhere. She was all pliant curves and soft contours: narrow shoulders, nipped waist, round hips, and thighs that she, being a woman, undoubtedly thought were too fat, but he, being a man, judged extremely nuzzle-able.

"Belle!" Pippi squealed.

He swallowed. "I've never been happier to see a person in my life."

"Why's that?" Annabelle stopped next to his chair but refused to look directly at him. She hadn't forgotten about last night, which was fine with him. He didn't want her to forget, proving her point that he was a snake, but not an unredeemable one. As much as he'd enjoyed himself—and he'd definitely enjoyed himself—there'd be no repeat performance. He was bad, but not that bad.

"Guess what?" Pippi went through the stomach-rubbing routine again. "I got a baby in my tummy."

Annabelle looked interested. "No kidding? What's its name?"

"Daddy."

Heath winced. "That's why."

Annabelle laughed. Pippi sprawled in the sand and picked at a dab of blue polish on her big toe. "Pwinz don't have his phone."

Annabelle sat in the sand next to her, looking puzzled. "I don't understand."

Pippi patted Heath's calf with a sandy hand. "Pwinz. He don't have his phone."

Annabelle gazed up at him. "I understand about the phone part, but what's that other thing she's saying?"

Heath gritted his teeth. "Prince. That's me."

Annabelle grinned and hugged the little troublemaker, who launched into a monologue about how Daphne the Bunny used to come into her bedroom and play but wouldn't come anymore because Pippi was too big. As Annabelle tilted her head to listen, her hair brushed his thigh, and he nearly jumped out of his chair.

Pippi finally ran off to join her father and demand he go in the water with her. He was agreeable, although they had a small dispute about the boots, which he eventually won.

"I love that kid." Annabelle's expression held a trace of longing. "She's got a lot of spirit."

"Which is bound to get her into trouble when she's incarcerated."

"Will you stop it?"

Her hair brushed his thigh again. He could only handle so much stimulation, and he shot up. "I'm going swimming. Want to join me?"

She sent a longing glance toward the lake. "I think I'll stay here."

"Come on, girly-girl." He grabbed her arm and pulled her to her feet. "Unless you're afraid to get your hair wet?"

Quick as a flash, she jerked free and raced for the water. "Last one to the raft is an obsessive-compulsive fathead." She plunged in and set off. He was right after her. Although she was a good swimmer, he had her on endurance. Still, he made himself back off when they got close so she could win.

As she touched the ladder, she rewarded him with one of those Annabelle grins that took over her whole face. "Sissy boy got beat."

That was too much, and he dunked her.

They horsed around like that for a while, climbing up on the raft, diving in, and attacking each other. Growing up with older brothers had taught her more than a few dirty tricks, and her expression of glee when she got the best of him was priceless. Once again, she tried to make him tell her what the *D* in his middle name stood for. He refused and got a face full of water. The horseplay gave him a good excuse to get his hands on her, but he finally lingered too long, and she pulled back.

"I've had enough. I'm going back to the cottage to rest up before dinner."

"I understand. You're not as young as you used to be."

But he couldn't bait her, and she swam away. He watched as she waded toward the beach. Her bathing suit rode up, revealing two round, water-slicked cheeks. She reached around and slipped her finger under the leg openings to tug it back into place. He groaned and dove under, but the water wasn't nearly cold enough, and it took awhile before he settled down.

When he got back to the beach, he spent some time shooting the bull with Charmaine and Darnell, but all the while he was conscious of Phoebe lazing on a chaise a few yards away. She wore a big straw hat, a low-cut one-piece black suit with a tropical print sarong wrapped around her waist, and an invisible

DO NOT DISTURB sign. He decided it was time to make his move and excused himself from the Pruitts to wander over. "Mind if I pull up some sand so we can talk?"

Her lids dropped behind a pair of sunglasses with pink lenses. "And my day was going so well until now."

"All good things have to come to an end." Instead of taking the empty chaise next to her, he gave her the advantage of the superior position and sat on an abandoned towel in the sand. "I've been curious about something ever since that party for the kids."

"Oh?"

"How did a dragon lady like you end up with a sweetheart like Hannah?"

For once, she laughed. "Dan's gene pool."

"Did you hear Hannah talking to the girls about the balloons?"

She finally looked at him. "I guess I missed that conversation."

"She said that if their balloons broke, they could cry if they really wanted to, but all it meant was that a grumpy fairy had stuck a pin in them. Where does she come up with stuff like that?"

She smiled. "Hannah has quite an imagination."

"I'll say. She's a special kid."

Even the toughest moguls were pushovers when it came to their children, and the ice cracked a little more. "We worry about her more than the others. She's so sensitive."

"Considering who her parents are, I'm guessing she's a lot tougher than you think." He should have been ashamed of himself for laying it on so thick, but Hannah really was a great kid, and he didn't feel too bad about it.

"I don't know. She feels things pretty deeply."

"What you call sensitive, I call having people smarts. Once she graduates from ninth grade, send her to me and I'll give her a job. I need somebody to put me in touch with my feminine side."

Phoebe laughed, a sound of genuine amusement. "I'll think about it. Might be useful to have a spy in the enemy camp."

"Come on, Phoebe. I was a cocky kid trying to show everybody how tough I was. I blew it, and we both know it. But I haven't screwed you over once since then."

A shadow fell over her face. "Now, you've moved on to Annabelle."

Just like that, their fragile camaraderie evaporated. He spoke carefully. "Is that what you think I'm doing?"

"You're using her to get to me, and I don't like it."

"It's hard to use Annabelle. She's pretty sharp."

Phoebe shot him her no-nonsense look. "She's special, Heath, and she's my friend. Perfect for You means everything to her. You're making things messy."

A fairly accurate assessment, but a knot of anger still formed under his breastbone. "You don't give her enough credit."

"She doesn't give herself enough credit. That's what makes her vulnerable. Her family's convinced her she's a failure because she's not earning six figures. She needs to be concentrating on making her business work, and I'm getting the feeling you deliberately turned yourself into a bad distraction."

He forgot that he never let himself get defensive. "Exactly what do you mean by that?"

"I saw how you were looking at her last night."

The insinuation that he might deliberately hurt Annabelle stuck in his craw. He wasn't his father. He didn't use women, and he especially didn't use a woman he liked. But he was dealing with Phoebe Calebow, and he couldn't afford to lose his temper, so he dug into his always reliable supply of self-control . . . and came up empty. "Annabelle's my friend, and I don't make it a habit of hurting my friends." He pushed to his feet. "But then you don't know me well enough to figure that out, do you?"

As he stalked away, he called himself every name in the book. He never lost it. He absolutely never fucking lost it. Yet he'd basically just told Phoebe Calebow to go to hell. And for what? Because enough truth lurked in what she'd said to hurt. The fact was, he'd committed a foul, and Phoebe had dropped a penalty flag on him.

A nnabelle waited for Heath on the front porch at the B&B along with Janine, whom she'd invited to ride into town with them for dinner. Annabelle had stayed in her bedroom at the cottage until she'd heard Heath come in. As soon as the shower started running, she'd jotted a quick note, left it on the table, and slipped out. The less time she spent alone with him the better.

"Any ideas about Krystal's mysterious surprise?" Janine straightened the clasp on her silver necklace as they sat in the porch rockers.

"No, but I hope it's fattening." Annabelle didn't really care what the surprise was, as long as it kept her away from Heath after dinner.

He pulled up in the car, and Annabelle insisted Janine sit with him in the front. On their way into town, he asked about her books. He'd never read a word she'd written, but by the time they reached the inn, he'd convinced her she had everything it took to be the next J. K. Rowling. The weird thing was, he seemed to believe it. No question that the Python was a powerful motivator.

The Wind Lake Inn's rustic north woods decor complemented a varied menu of beef, fish, and game. Conversation was lively, and Annabelle limited her alcohol consumption to a single glass of wine. As they dug into their entrées, Phoebe asked the men how their book discussion had gone. Darnell opened his mouth to respond, his gold tooth flashing, only to have Dan cut in. "So much came up, I don't even know where to start. Ron?"

"It was intense, all right," the Stars' general manager said. Kevin looked thoughtful. "A lot of sharing."

"Intense?" Darnell scowled. "It was—"

"Heath could probably summarize better than any of us," Webster interjected.

The others nodded solemnly and turned their heads toward Heath, who set down his fork. "I doubt I could do it justice. Who figured we could have so many different opinions about postmodern nihilism?"

Molly looked at Phoebe. "They didn't talk about the book at all."

"I told you they wouldn't," her sister replied.

Charmaine reached over to rub her husband's back. "I'm sorry, honey. You know I tried to talk the women into letting you join our group, but they said you'd upset our dynamics."

"Besides trying to bully us into reading *One Hundred Years of Solitude*," Janine added.

"That is a great book!" Darnell exclaimed. "Y'all don't want to challenge your minds."

Kevin had heard Darnell's lecture on people's reading tastes before and quickly moved to deflect it. "We know you're right. And we're all ashamed of ourselves, aren't we, guys?"

"I am."

"Me, too."

"Can't hardly stand to look in the mirror."

Kevin seized on Annabelle as the next distraction to keep Darnell from getting worked up. "So what's this I hear about you dating Dean Robillard?"

Everyone at the table stopped eating. Heath set down his knife. The women's heads swiveled. Molly gazed into her husband's not-so-innocent green eyes. "Annabelle's not dating Dean. She would have told us."

"I'm really not," Annabelle said.

Kevin Tucker, the wiliest quarterback in the NFL, scratched the back of his head like a gorgeous doofus. "I'm confused. I talked to Dean on Friday, and he mentioned that the two of you went out last week and that he'd had a real good time."

"Well, we went to the beach . . ."

"You went to the beach with Dean Robillard, and you didn't think to mention it?" Krystal shrieked.

"It was . . . a last-minute thing."

The women started buzzing. Kevin had more mischief on his mind and didn't wait for them to calm down. "So Dean's planning to ask you out again?"

"No, of course not. No. I mean . . . is he? Why? Did he say something?"

"I kind of got that idea. Maybe I misunderstood."

"I'm sure you did."

Heath sat stony-faced, a fact that caught Phoebe's interest. "Your little matchmaker certainly is getting around."

"I'm glad," Sharon said. "It's time she came out of her shell."

Heath regarded Annabelle dubiously. "You were in a shell?"

"Kind of."

Charmaine gazed at her across the table. "Are we allowed to talk about your unfortunate engagement?"

Annabelle sighed. "Why not? We seem to be examining every other part of my life."

"Shocked the hell out of me," Kevin said. "Rob and I played golf together a couple of times. He had an ugly duck hook, but still . . ."

Molly covered his hand with her own. "It's been two years, and Kevin's still not reconciled."

Kevin shook his head. "I feel like I should invite him . . . her . . . to play again, just to show I'm broad-minded, which I am under ordinary circumstances, but I like Annabelle, and Rob knew from the beginning he had a problem. He should never have asked her to marry him."

"I remember Rob's duck hook," Webster said.

"Yeah, I remember it, too." Dan shook his head in disgust.

A short silence fell. Kevin gazed at his brother-in-law. "Are you thinking the same thing I am?"

"Yep."

"Me, too," Webster said.

Ron nodded. So did the others. Heath smiled, and they all returned their attention to their dinner plates.

"What?" Molly shrieked.

Kevin shook his head. "No sex-change operation in the world is going to fix a duck hook like that."

The women left the men at the inn and returned to the B&B, where Krystal locked them into the cozy back parlor, drew the shades, and turned down the lights. "Tonight," she announced, "we're going to celebrate our sexuality."

"I read that book," Molly said. "And if anybody starts taking off her clothes and grabbing a mirror, I'm out of here."

"We're not celebrating that way," Krystal said. "All of us have some issues we need to face. For example . . . Charmaine's too uptight."

"Me?"

"You undressed in the closet for the first two years of your marriage."

"That was a long time ago, and I don't undress there anymore."

"Only because Darnell threatened to take the door off. But you're not the only one with sexual hang-ups. Annabelle doesn't say much about it, but we all know she hasn't slept with anybody since Rob traumatized her. Unless last night . . . ?"

They all turned to gaze at her.

"I'm his matchmaker! We're not having sex!"

"Which is a good thing," Molly said. "But Dean Robillard's a whole different matter. Talk about the ultimate boy toy."

"We're straying," Krystal said. "Three of us have been married for a long time, and no matter how much we love our husbands, things can get a little stale."

"Or not," Phoebe drawled with her cat's smile.

They all snickered, but Krystal wouldn't be distracted. "Molly and Kevin have young kids, and we know what a crimp that can put in your sex life."

"Or not." Molly offered up her own cat's smile.

"The point is . . . It's time we get more in touch with our sexuality."

"I'm way too much in touch with mine," Janine said. "I just wish somebody else would touch it, too."

More snickers.

"Go ahead and make jokes," Krystal said. "We're still going to watch this film. We'll be better women for it."

Charmaine went on full alert. "What kind of film?"

"An erotic movie made especially for women."

"You're kidding. Really, Krystal."

"The one I selected—a personal favorite—involves actors of various races, ages, and degrees of hotness, so nobody'll feel excluded."

"This is your big mystery?" Phoebe said. "That we're going to watch porn together?"

"Erotica. Made just for women. And until you've seen some of these movies, you shouldn't judge."

Annabelle suspected more than a few of them already had, but no one wanted to put too much of a damper on Krystal's enthusiasm.

"Here's what I really like about this particular film," Krystal said. "The men are all gorgeous, but the women are fairly ordinary. No silicone."

"That sets it apart from porn for men, all right," Sharon said. "At least from what I've heard."

Krystal began fussing with the DVD player. "There's also

a story, and real foreplay. A lot of it. Kissing, slow undressing, lots of caressing . . ."

Janine buried her face in her hands. "This is pathetic. I'm already getting turned on."

"I'm not," Charmaine said in a huff. "I'm a Christian, and I refuse to—"

"Good Christians—good Christian *women*—are supposed to please their husbands." Krystal smiled and hit the remote. "And believe me, this'll please the hell out of Darnell."

Chapter Fourteen

When Annabelle returned to the cottage shortly after midnight, her cheeks were still flushed from watching the film, and her sundress clung to hot, damp . . . *very* damp flesh. Seeing the light shining through the front window filled her with dismay. Maybe he'd left it on as a courtesy. *Please don't still be waiting up.* She absolutely could not face him tonight. Even without watching a dirty movie, she could barely keep her hands off him, but after what she'd just seen . . .

She tiptoed up to the porch, slipped off her sandals, and let herself in as silently as the squeaky screen door and wobbly doorknob would allow.

"Hey."

She gasped and dropped her sandals. "Don't scare me like that!"

"Sorry." He lay sprawled on the couch, a sheaf of papers in one hand. He wasn't wearing a shirt, just a pair of faded black athletic shorts. His feet were bare, his ankles crossed on the arm of the couch, where light from the floor lamp turned the hair on his calves golden. Her eyes returned to the gym shorts. After what she'd seen on the screen, he was criminally overdressed.

As she tried to get her breath back, he lifted his head and shoulders, which, *of course,* contracted his abs into the gold standard of six-packs. "Why's your face so red?" he said.

"S-sunburn." She knew how vulnerable she was, and she should have thrown herself in the lake to cool off before she came back here.

"That's not sunburn." He swung his feet to the floor, and she noticed his hair was damp. "What's wrong with you?"

"Nothing!" She began inching away. It meant taking the long route around, but she wasn't turning her back on him. "You took another shower."

"So?"

"You showered after you swam. What are you, some kind of clean freak?"

"Ron and I went for a run after dinner. Why do you care?" Oh, God, that chest, that mouth . . . those green eyes that saw everything. Except her naked. They'd never seen that. "I'm . . . going to bed now."

"Was it something I said?"

"Don't be cute. Please."

"I'll do my best." He gave her a crooked smile. "But me being me . . ."

"Stop it!" She didn't intend to quit moving, but her feet went on some kind of labor strike.

"You need warm milk or something?"

"No, I definitely don't need anything hot."

"I said warm. I didn't say anything about hot." He set down his papers.

"I—I know that."

She might be standing still, but he wasn't, and he took in her damp, rumpled dress as he approached. "What's going on?"

She couldn't take her eyes off his mouth. It brought to mind all the mouths she'd seen on that small television screen so recently and exactly what they'd been doing. Damn Krystal and her movie. "I'm just tired," she managed.

"You don't look tired. Your lips are sort of puffy, like you've been chewing on them, and you're breathing hard. Frankly, you look turned on. Or is that my one-track mind taking over again?"

"Let it go, okay?" He had a small scar on one rib, probably a knife wound from a spurned girlfriend.

"What the hell did you women do tonight?"

"It wasn't my idea!" She sounded guilty, and her flush deepened.

"I'll find out. One of the guys will tell me, so you might as well fill me in now."

"I don't think the men will be talking about this. Or maybe they will. I don't know. I have no idea how much you men talk."

"Not as much as you women do, that's for damn sure." He inclined his head toward the kitchen. "Do you want something to drink? There's a bottle of wine in the refrigerator."

"Oh, yeah . . . Wine's exactly what I *don't* need right now."

"A mystery just waiting to be solved . . ." He'd clearly begun to enjoy himself.

"Leave it alone, will you?"

"Exactly what a nice guy would do." He leaned down and picked up his cell. "Janine'll tell me what happened. She seems like an up-front lady."

"She's at the B&B. She doesn't have a phone in her room."

"Right. I'll ask Krystal. I talked to Webster not half an hour ago."

Annabelle had a pretty good idea what Krystal and Webster were doing about now, and they wouldn't appreciate being interrupted. "It's midnight."

"Your powwow just broke up. She won't have gone to bed yet."

Don't bet on it.

He rubbed his thumb over the number pad. "I've always liked Krystal. She's straightforward." He pressed the first button.

Annabelle sucked in air. "We watched porn, okay?"

He grinned and tossed the phone down. "Now we're getting somewhere."

"Believe me, it wasn't my idea. And it's not funny. Besides, it wasn't really porn. It was erotica. For women."

"There's a difference?"

"That's exactly the kind of thing I'd expect a man to say. Do you think most of us get off watching a bunch of women with collagen lips and soccer-ball implants go at each other?"

"From your expression, I'm guessing not."

She needed something cold to drink, and she headed for the kitchen, still talking because she had a point to make. "Like seduction. Does your average porn film even think about showing a little seduction?"

He followed her. "To be fair, there's not usually much need. The women are pretty aggressive."

"Exactly. Well, I'm not." As soon as the words were out, she could have kicked herself. The last thing she'd wanted to do was bring the subject back to the personal.

He didn't pounce on her misstep, not the wily Python. He liked to play with his prey before he struck. "So did the film have a plot?"

"Rural New England, virginal artist, studly stranger, 'nuff said." She pulled open the refrigerator door and stared inside without seeing a thing.

"Only two people. That's disappointing."

"There were a couple of subplots."

"Ah."

She turned on him, her damp palm still curled around the refrigerator door handle. "You think this is funny, don't you?"

"Yeah, but I'm ashamed of myself."

She wanted to smell him. His hair was nearly dry, his

skin freshly showered. She wanted to press her face against his chest and inhale, to burrow in, maybe find an errant tuft of silky hair and let it tickle her nose. She nearly whimpered. "Please go away."

He cocked his head. "I'm sorry. Did you say something?"

She grabbed the first cold thing she touched and pushed the door shut. "You know the way I feel about this. About . . . us."

"You were pretty clear last night."

"I'm right, too."

"I know you are."

"So why did you argue with me?"

"Jerk syndrome. I can't help it. I'm a guy." His lips curved in a lazy smile. "And you're not."

Enough bolts of sexual electricity charged the air to light up the planet. He stood between her and the bedroom, and if she passed too close, she'd be tempted to lick, so she headed for the porch and nearly stumbled over the mattress he'd dragged out there last night. He'd tidied the sheets, stacked the pillows, and folded the blanket in half, doing a better job of it than she'd done with the double bed.

He ambled out. "Do you want a sandwich with that?"

She couldn't figure out what he was talking about until she followed his gaze to her hand and saw a jar of French's mustard there instead of a can of Coke. She'd stared at it. "Mustard happens to be a natural sleep aid."

"Never heard that."

"You don't know everything do you?"

"Apparently not." A few beats of silence ticked by. "Do you eat it or apply it?"

"I'm going to bed."

"Because if you apply it . . . I could probably help with that."

Her redhead's temper ignited, and she slammed the jar down on the farmhouse table. "Why don't I just hand you my panties and be done with it?"

"That'll work." His teeth glinted like a shark's. "So if I kiss you right now, will you turn into a big sissy again?"

Her anger faded, leaving trepidation in its wake. "I don't know."

"I've got a good-size ego—you know that. But the way you rejected me last night still bordered on the traumatic." He slipped a thumb into the top of his shorts, causing the elastic waistband to dip in a deep, mouthwatering V. "Now I'm wondering, what if I've lost my touch? What do I do then?" He moved his thumb closer to the blade of his hip bone, revealing even more skin. "You can see why I'm a little concerned."

As she gazed at the wedge of taut abdomen, she had to fight the urge to roll the cold mustard jar over her forehead. "Uh . . . I wouldn't lose too much sleep over it." Summoning her last ounce of willpower, she began to slide past him, and she might have made it if he hadn't reached out and touched her arm. It was the merest brush of his finger—a simple parting gesture—but he'd found bare skin, and that was enough to make her stop in her tracks.

He went as still as she. As he gazed down at her, his green eyes were an invitation to disaster overlaid with faint apology. "Damn it," he whispered. "Sometimes I'm too much of a smart-ass for my own good."

He pulled her against him, feasted on her mouth, ran his hands down the contours of her back. And she let him, just as she had last night, ignoring the fact that this was the Super Bowl of bad ideas, ignoring all the reasons why she shouldn't live every moment of this one night and deal with the consequences tomorrow.

"No patience." His dusky murmur fell like a caress over her cheek as he lowered the zipper on her dress in one effortless motion.

"This is going to ruin everything," she whispered against his mouth, needing to say the words even though she didn't do one thing to stop him.

"Let's do it anyway," he said in a husky rasp. "We'll sort it out afterward."

Exactly what she wanted to hear. She lost herself in their kiss—limp, spellbound, stupid . . . a little bit in love.

Moments later, her dress lay in a puddle around her feet along with her bra, a pair of panties, and everything he'd been wearing—one pair of black athletic shorts. They were on the porch, but it was dark, the trees thick, and who cared? He gazed down at her breasts, not touching them, simply looking. With one hand he cupped her shoulder. With the other, he ran the tips of his fingers down her spine and dabbled with her coccyx. She shivered and pressed her cheek to his chest, then turned her lips against his skin only to have him spring back and catch his breath in a long hiss.

"Do *not* move."

He broke away and dashed toward the kitchen, giving her an all-too-brief glimpse of a spectacularly tight male butt. It flashed through her mind that he might be retrieving his cell so he could multitask, but he turned off the overhead fixture in the kitchen, leaving only the stove light on, then disappeared into the living area and shut off more lights. Moments later he reappeared. The dim golden light from the kitchen played along his long-muscled body as he came toward her. He was fully erect. When he reached her side, he held up a trio of condoms and said softly, "Consider these a token of my affection."

"Noted and appreciated," she replied, just as softly.

He pressed her onto the mattress. She remembered how goal driven he was and realized that Girls Night at the Movies might have raised her expectations for lingering foreplay too high. Sure enough, in much too short a time he rolled above her, his mouth at her breast. She sank her fingers into his hair. "You're going to rush me, aren't you?"

"No doubt about it." He slipped his hand to her belly, already zeroing in on command central.

"I want more kissing."

"No problem." He took her nipple between his lips.

She sucked in her breath. "On the mouth."

He teased the tiny, turgid nub, his breath growing shallow. "Let's negotiate."

She dug her fingers into his back, which was already damp from whatever small amount of restraint he might be practicing. Her thighs automatically parted. "I should have expected this."

He trailed his thumb over the thatch of curly hair at the base of her stomach and played in the fiery threads. "I'll go too fast for you. That's a given, and I apologize in advance." She gave a soft gasp of pleasure when he touched warm, wet flesh. "But it's been a long time for me, and what might, in reality, only take minutes—"

"If that." Her toes curled.

"—will seem like years to me." His voice grew ragged. "So here's what I'm going to suggest." She gripped his hips as he played with her. "Let's accept the fact that I can't satisfy you the first time. That takes the pressure off both of us."

She bent her knees and said, in a strangled gasp, "Off you, anyway."

"But once I've released that first burst of . . . steam . . ."— he sucked in his breath, his words coming fast and choppy— "I'll have all the time in the world"—her head thrashed as his wily fingers teased her in the most intimate way—"to do the job right." He nudged her thighs wider. "And you, Tinker Bell . . ." She took his weight. "You'll have a night you'll never forget."

He entered her with a groan, and even though she was slick and oh-so-ready, it wasn't an easy fit. She drew up her knees and arched her back. He closed his mouth over hers, took her hips in his palms, and tilted her to the angle they both wanted.

Feverish, demented images shimmered behind her eyelids. The long, thick body of a python pushing into her, uncoiling . . . stretching . . . going deeper . . . deeper still. His back grew rigid beneath her palms. The sweet attack . . . The plunge. Again and again. And then the final climb. He began to shudder. She swallowed his low, guttural moan. Light shimmered behind her eyes. She took his weight, threw back her head, and gave herself up.

Long minutes passed. He brushed his lips against her temple, then rolled to his side, barely staying on the narrow mattress. She slid over to give him room. They readjusted. He drew her against his damp skin and began playing with her hair. She was dazed, surfeited, determined not to think. Not yet.

"It . . . it didn't happen for me," she said.

He propped himself up on one elbow and gazed into her lying eyes. "I hate to say this, but I told you so."

"You were right, as usual."

Crinkles formed at the corners of his eyes, and he pressed a quick kiss to her lips. "Let this be a lesson." He pulled himself up. "I'm going to need a few minutes."

"I'll do some word scrambles in my head."

"Good idea." As she listened to the night sounds that surrounded their nest in the woods, he disappeared inside. He returned a few minutes later with a beer, sat on the side of the mattress, and held the bottle out for her. She took a swig and gave it back. He set the bottle on the floor, then lay down and pulled her to his shoulder, where he began playing with a lock of her hair again. The tender intimacy made her want to cry, so she rolled on top of him and began her own sensuous exploration.

Before long, his breath quickened. "I guess . . ." he said in a strangled voice, "it's not going to take me quite as long to recover as I thought."

She brushed her lips over his abdomen. "I suppose you can't be right about everything."

And that was the last thing either of them said for a very long time.

Finally, he fell asleep, and she could slip away to her bedroom. As she curled into her pillow, she could no longer repress the reality of what she'd done. He'd attacked lovemaking with the same workaholic zeal he did everything else, and, in the process, she'd fallen a little more in love with him.

Tears trickled from the corners of her eyes, but she didn't wipe them away. Instead, she let them fall while she readjusted, re-created, reframed. By the time she drifted off to sleep, she knew exactly what she had to do.

Heath heard Annabelle go into her bedroom, but he didn't stir. Now that the hunger in his body had been satisfied, the despicability of what he'd done hit him hard. She cared about him. A whole world of emotions he didn't want to acknowledge had been looking back at him from those honey sweet eyes tonight. Now he felt like the biggest jerk in the world.

She'd told him that this was a disaster in the making, but he'd built his life around crashing through roadblocks, so he'd ignored the obvious and charged ahead. Even though he'd known she was right, he wanted her, so he'd taken, and the consequences be damned. Now that it was too late, he absorbed exactly how big a disaster this was for her, professionally and personally. Her emotions were engaged—he'd seen it in her face—and that meant she couldn't ever go back to the business of being his matchmaker.

He rolled over and punched his pillow. What the hell had he been thinking? He hadn't been thinking, that was the whole problem. He'd only been reacting, and in the process of getting what he wanted, he'd blown her dreams right out of the water. Now he had to make it up to her.

He began drawing up a plan in his head. He'd talk up her business and find some decent clients to throw her way. He'd use his PR people and media contacts to get her press. It was a good story—a second-generation matchmaker brings her grandmother's old-fashioned business into the twenty-first century. Annabelle should have come up with it herself, but she didn't think big enough.

One thing he couldn't do was let her keep introducing him to other women. That would break her heart. Selfishly, he didn't like the idea of her not working for him anymore. He liked having her around. She made things easier for him . . . something he'd repaid by screwing her over, literally and figuratively.

Like father. Like son.

The despair that settled over him felt old and familiar, like the sound of a rusty trailer door slamming in the night.

He didn't remember falling asleep, but he must have because it was daylight when the earth moved. He eased one eye open, saw a face he wasn't ready to face, and turned his head into the pillow. Another small earthquake rattled the mattress. He peeled open his lids and blinked as a blade of sunlight hit him between the eyes.

"Wake up, you gorgeous gift to womankind," a voice chirped.

She sat on the porch floor next to him, a coffee mug cradled in her hand, one bare leg extended so she could nudge the mattress with her foot. She wore bright yellow shorts and a purple T-shirt printed with a grotesque cartoon troll and a caption that said WE'RE PEOPLE, TOO. Her hair curled in a crazy fracas around her imp's face, her lips were rosy, and her eyes a lot clearer than his. She sure as hell didn't look devastated. Shit. She thought last night had changed things. He felt sick. "Later," he managed.

"Can't wait. We're meeting everyone for breakfast in the gazebo, and I have to talk to you." She picked up a second mug from the floor and held it out. "Something to ease the pain of reentry."

He needed to be alert for this, but he felt like the bottom of a dirty ashtray, and all he wanted was to avoid this discussion by rolling over and going back to sleep. But he owed her better than that, so he propped himself on one elbow, took the coffee, and tried to will the cobwebs from his brain.

Her eyes followed the sheet as it slipped to his waist, and he wanted her all over again. He moved his arm to conceal the evidence. How was he going to break the news that she was a friend, not a candidate for a long-term relationship, without tearing her apart?

"First," she said, "last night meant more to me than you can imagine."

Exactly what he didn't want to hear. She looked so damned sweet. It took a real shithead to hurt someone like this. If only Annabelle were the woman he'd always dreamed about—sophisticated, elegant, with impeccable taste and a family that traced its roots back to a nineteenth-century robber baron. He needed someone worldly enough to survive life's bumps, a woman who saw life as he did—a competition to be won, not a perpetual invitation to come out and play.

"At the same time . . ." Her voice shifted to a lower, more serious note. "We can't ever do that again. It was a serious breach of professional conduct on my part, although not quite the problem I'd imagined." A smile he could only describe as impish broke through. "Now I can recommend you with *complete* enthusiasm." The smile faded. "No, the bigger problem is how manipulative I was."

Coffee slopped over the edge of the mug. *What the hell was this?*

She dashed into the kitchen for a paper towel and handed it over so he could mop up. "Back to business," she said. "You have to understand I'm truly grateful for what you did. The whole thing with Rob really messed with my head. Ever since we broke up, well . . . I've been running from sex. The brutal truth is, I've been pretty screwed up about it." She dabbed at some drips he'd missed. "Thanks to you, I'm past that."

He took a cautious sip and waited, no longer sure where any of this was heading. She touched his arm in a gesture that felt annoyingly maternal. "I feel healthy again, and I owe that

to you. Well, and to Krystal's movie. But, Heath . . ." The tiny
scatter of freckles on her forehead met as she frowned. "I can't
stand this feeling that I—I sort of used you."

His coffee mug stalled midair. "Used me?"

"That's what we need to talk about. I consider you a
friend, in addition to being a client, and I don't use my friends.
At least I haven't until now. I know it's different with men—
maybe you don't feel taken advantage of. Maybe I'm making
too big a deal out of this. But my conscience tells me I need to
be totally honest about my motivations."

He tensed. "By all means."

"I needed someone safe who could help me reconnect with
my body, someone I wasn't emotionally involved with. So, of
course, you were perfect."

Not emotionally involved?

She nibbled at her bottom lip, beginning to look as though
she'd rather be anywhere but here. "Tell me you're not mad,"
she said. "Oh, crap . . . I'm not going to let myself cry. But I
feel so bad. You heard Kevin last night. I . . ." She gulped.
"That whole other complication. What a mess, right?"

She'd thrown one more curveball. "Other complication?"

"You know."

"Refresh my memory."

"Don't make me say it. It's too embarrassing."

"What's a little embarrassment between friends?" he said
tightly. "Since we're being so honest."

She gazed up at the ceiling, rolled her shoulders, looked
down at the floor. Her voice grew small, almost timid. "You
know . . . The tiny crush I have on Dean Robillard."

The floor shifted beneath him.

She pressed her hands to her face. "Oh, God, I'm blushing.
I'm awful, aren't I, talking to you about this?"

"No, please." He ground out the words. "Feel free."

She dropped her hands and regarded him with all kinds of
earnestness. "I know it probably won't come to anything—this

thing with Dean—but before last night, I didn't even have the nerve to give it a chance. He's obviously an experienced guy, and what was I going to do if the connection I felt wasn't just in my imagination? What would I do if he was interested in me, too? I couldn't cope with the sexual ramifications. But after what you did for me last night, I finally have the courage to at least give it a shot. If nothing comes of it, well, that's life, but at least I'll know it wasn't my neurosis that held me back."

"Are you saying . . . I was your *icebreaker*?"

Those honey-colored eyes darkened with concern. "Tell me that's okay with you. I know your emotions weren't involved, but, still, nobody likes to think they've been taken advantage of."

He unclenched his teeth. "And that's what you did? You took advantage of me?"

"I wasn't, you know, picturing him in my mind last night when I was with you or anything. Well, maybe for a couple of seconds, but that's all, I swear."

He narrowed his eyes.

"So are we okay?" she asked.

He didn't understand the smoldering mass of resentment growing in his chest, especially since she'd handed him a free pass. "I don't know. Are we?"

She had the nerve to grin. "I think so. You look a little grouchy, but you don't look like a man whose honor's been violated. I shouldn't have been so worried. For you, it was just sex, but for me it was this huge emancipation. Thanks, pal."

She stuck out her hand, forcing him to set down his coffee mug to shake it or look like a dick. Then she hopped to her feet, threw her arms over her head, and uncurled her small body in a cat's satisfied stretch that pulled up her T-shirt and displayed the small oval belly button he'd dipped the tip of his tongue into last night. "I'll meet you at the gazebo." Her expression clouded with earnestness. "And, Heath, I promise, if you have even the tiniest leftover resentment toward me, it'll disappear by next week. This makes me even more determined to find you the perfect woman. Now, it's not just business. It's personal."

Shooting him a blazing smile, she bounced away into the kitchen, only to pop her head back out. "Thanks. I mean it. I owe you one."

Moments later the cottage door closed. He fell back on the pillow, set his coffee mug on his chest, and tried to take it in.

Annabelle had used him as a warm-up act for Robillard?

Chapter Fifteen

❤

As Annabelle approached the gazebo, she saw Ron and Sharon ahead of her on the path, their arms around each other's waists. She was still shaking, and her stomach felt like an acid swamp. She might not have been the best actress in Northwestern's theater department, but she still knew how to pull off a scene. In front of her, Ron held the gazebo door open for Sharon. His other hand strayed to her bottom. No mystery what they'd been up to last night. Now all she had to do was make certain none of them got an inkling of what she'd been up to.

As she let herself in through the screen door, everybody called out greetings, and she'd never seen a more sleep-deprived, sexually satisfied group. Molly had a rosy mark on her neck that looked like beard burn, and from the smug expression on Darnell's face, Charmaine didn't deserve her reputation as a prude. Phoebe and Dan sat on a wicker couch sharing a single muffin. And instead of nagging Webster as she usually did, Krystal was cooing and calling him "Baby." The only innocent faces belonged to Pippi, baby Danny, and Janine.

Annabelle turned her attention to the meal Molly had set out, even though she didn't feel like eating. A sunny yellow pottery vase filled with zinnias sat in the center of a nutmeg-colored tablecloth displaying frosty pitchers of juice, a French toast casserole, a basket of homemade muffins, and the B&B's specialty, baked oatmeal laced with brown sugar, cinnamon, and apples.

"Where's Heath?" Kevin asked. "Never mind. On the phone."

"He'll be along," she said. "He's getting a late start. I'm not sure what time he got to sleep last night, but he was still awake when I went to bed." As she headed for the buffet, she told herself the lie was an act of kindness, since the truth would have ruined more than a few breakfasts.

Janine, who was filling her plate, cast a disgruntled look at the gooey-eyed behavior going on behind her. "Tell me I'm not the only one feeling sexually deprived this morning."

Annabelle sidestepped. "Krystal should have been more sensitive toward the two of us."

"So we were wrong about you and Heath?"

Annabelle simply rolled her eyes. "You guys do love your drama."

She and Janine settled into a pair of wicker chairs not far from the Tucker family. Annabelle was nibbling at the corner of her baked oatmeal square when Heath made his appearance. He wore khaki shorts and a Nike T-shirt. At least part of what she'd told him was true. She did feel as though she'd laid the ghost of Rob to rest. Unfortunately, another ghost had taken its place.

Pippi, who'd been swiping bits of banana from her baby brother's high chair tray, flew across the gazebo and tackled Heath at the knees. *"Pwinz!"*

"Hey, kiddo." Heath awkwardly patted her head, and one of her Daphne the Bunny barrettes slid to the end of a blond curl.

Phoebe frowned. "What's she calling you?"

Annabelle slapped on her perkiest expression. "Prince. Isn't that adorable?"

Phoebe lifted an eyebrow. Dan kissed the corner of his wife's mouth, probably because he liked Heath and wanted to distract her. The three-year-old kept a firm grip on Heath's legs as she looked over at her mother. "Want Pwinz to get me juice." She gazed up at Heath. "I gotta stuffy nose." She wrinkled it to make her point.

Molly, who was wiping a glob of banana from the limestone floor, waved vaguely toward the table. "The juice is over there."

Pippi regarded him adoringly. "You gotta phone?"

Kevin's head shot up. "Don't let her near your cell. She's got a thing."

Heath started to reply, but Webster interrupted. "Where are we going on our hike?"

Kevin took the messy bib from Molly. "The trail runs around the lake. I figured we'd do the section between here and town—close to six miles. Nice views. Troy and Amy volunteered to drive us back when we're done."

"They're watching the kids," Molly said.

Troy and Amy were the young couple who ran the campground. Pippi patted Heath's bare leg. "Juice please."

"One juice coming up." Heath headed to the buffet table, filled a big glass all the way to the top, and gave it to her. She took half a sip, handed it back without spilling more than a few drops, and grinned. "I got moves."

This time Heath's mouth curled in genuine amusement. "Yeah?"

"Watch." She dropped to the sisal rug and did a somersault.

"Cool." Heath gave her a thumbs-up.

"Daddy says I'm cool, too."

Kevin smiled. "Come here, pumpkin. Leave Prince Man alone until he's had his breakfast."

"Good idea," Phoebe whispered. "That werewolf thing could happen at any minute."

Ignoring her, Heath took a sip from Pippi's juice glass. "So what time does the hike start?"

"As soon as we get our act together," Kevin replied.

Heath set down the glass and scooped up some of the French toast casserole. He said, a little too casually, "I was planning to take off for Detroit right after breakfast, but this sounds too good to pass up."

Annabelle took a dismal stab at her oatmeal square. She'd barely managed to get through her big scene this morning. How was she going to stay perky for a six-mile hike?

As it turned out, they were mostly separated. Annabelle tried to decide whether that was good or bad. Although she didn't have to keep pretending, she also couldn't be absolutely sure he'd bought her act this morning.

When they returned to the campground, Pippi threw herself at her parents as though she hadn't seen them in years. Kevin distracted her so Molly could nurse Danny, and Molly snuggled up with the baby in the gazebo's wicker rocker. Danny wanted to look around, and he batted away the faded receiving blanket she'd tossed over her shoulder for modesty.

"Could I have just a little privacy here, dude?" She cupped her hand around his small head.

Annabelle took a gulp from her iced tea glass. Molly deserved everything good that had happened to her, and Annabelle didn't begrudge her any of it, but she wanted those things, too: a great marriage, beautiful children, a fabulous career. Heath took a seat next to her on the glider. Since he was leaving soon, he'd opted for iced tea with the women instead of beer with the men.

"A bee!" Pippi exclaimed, pointing at the floor. "Look, Pwinz, a bee!"

"It's an ant, honey," her father said.

The men began talking about training camp, and Janine announced that she wanted to run an idea for a scene in her new book past the women. Danny finished his snack, and Molly set him on the floor to play. She'd just finished putting her clothes back together when a too familiar voice chirped from the path outside the gazebo. "There you all are."

Annabelle froze.

Everyone turned to watch through the screen as a tall, lovely, pregnant woman come toward them.

Annabelle couldn't believe it. Not now. Not while she was still trying to cope with last night's disaster.

"Gwen?" Krystal's face split in a smile. She jumped to her feet as the door opened, and the rest of them followed.

"Gwen! What are you doing here?"

"We thought you couldn't come."

"We're leaving today. Why did you wait till so late?"

"You're finally wearing maternity clothes."

And then, one by one, the women fell silent as the implications of Gwen's appearance hit them. Molly looked stricken. She turned to gaze at Annabelle, then at Heath. The other women were only a few beats behind. Dan's calculating expression indicated that Phoebe had told him about Annabelle's scam, but the rest of the men were oblivious.

Kevin snatched up his beer as Pippi made a grab for it. "Gwen called me yesterday to make sure we had room," he said with a grin. "She wanted to surprise you."

And did she ever.

"Where's your husband?" Webster asked.

"He'll be along in a second." With the women surrounding her, Gwen still hadn't spotted Heath, who'd come slowly to his feet. "Our closing got postponed," she said, accepting the glass of iced tea Sharon handed her. Annabelle was too queasy to take in much of her explanation—something about a problem with the bank, their furniture going into short term storage, and a week to kill before they could move in.

"Hey, guys." Ian stepped into the gazebo. He wore wrinkled plaid shorts and a Dell Computer T-shirt. The men called out greetings. Darnell slapped him on the back, sending him pitching into Kevin, who clasped him around the shoulders.

"You haven't met my agent yet." Kevin drew him past the women. "Ian, this is Heath Champion."

Ian's extended arm froze. Gwen drew in a quick breath, and her hand shot to her rounding stomach. She stared, first at Heath, then at Annabelle.

Annabelle managed a weak smile. "Busted."

Heath shook Ian's stalled hand without giving anything away, but Annabelle knew sudden death when she saw it.

"Nice to meet you, Ian," he said. "And, Gwen . . . Good to see you again." He nodded in the general direction of her stomach. "Fast work. Congratulations."

Gwen simply swallowed. Annabelle felt Heath's fingers coil around her upper arm. "Would you excuse us? Annabelle and I need to talk."

Just like that, the book club sprang into action. "No!"

"Don't move!"

"You're not taking her anywhere."

"Forget it."

Heath's expression was a cluster bomb about to detonate. "I'm afraid I'll have to insist."

Kevin looked puzzled. "What's going on?"

"Business." Heath marched Annabelle toward the screen door. If she'd tossed a sweater over her head, it would have been a bona fide perp walk.

Molly shot ahead of them. "I'm coming with you."

"No," Heath said flatly. "You're not."

Krystal shot Phoebe a frantic look. "You scare everybody in the NFL. Do something?"

"I'm thinking."

"I know . . ." Molly grabbed her daughter and thrust her toward Annabelle. "Take Pip with you."

"Molly!" Phoebe shot forward in outrage.

Molly regarded her sister helplessly. "How rough can he get if he has a three-year-old watching?"

Phoebe snatched her niece out of harm's way. "Never mind, sweetheart. Mommy's having one of her crazy spells."

Gwen made a faint, fluttery motion with her hand. "Annabelle, I'm sorry. I had no idea."

Annabelle managed a shrug. "Not your problem. I brought this on myself."

"Exactly," Heath said. And then he steered her out the door.

They walked without speaking for several minutes. Finally they reached a grove of trees, and that was where he turned on her. "You conned me."

More than once if she counted this morning, but she hoped he hadn't figured that out. "I needed a sure bet to get you to sign the contract, and Gwen was the best I had. I promise, I was going to tell you the truth sooner or later. I hadn't worked up the nerve."

"Now there's a surprise." Those cold green eyes could have cut glass. "Bait and switch."

"I—I'm afraid so."

"How did you get the husband to go along with it?"

"A—uh—year of free babysitting."

A blade of wind cut through the clearing, ruffling his hair. He stared at her for so long her skin started to itch. She thought of all she'd put herself through this morning . . . For nothing.

"You conned me," he said again, almost as if he were still trying to take it in.

Apprehension knotted her stomach. "I couldn't see another way."

A bird shrieked overhead. Another screeched in response. And then the edges of his mouth crinkled. "Way to go, Tinker Bell. This is exactly what I've been talking about."

• • •

Just because Heath approved of Annabelle's scam didn't mean
that she escaped a lecture about business ethics. She defended
herself by saying, truthfully, that it wouldn't have occurred to
her to do something so dishonorable to any other client.

He was only partially satisfied. "Once you start flirting with
the dark side, it's hard to turn back."

And didn't she just know it.

Kevin eventually popped through the trees. "Oh, good," he
said as he spotted Annabelle. "I told Molly you'd probably still
be alive."

She stayed at Kevin's side as they all walked back to the
gazebo. Shortly after that, Heath took off. As he left, she found
herself thinking that this deception crap was getting old. How
would Heath have reacted if she'd been honest? Right. Like
that wouldn't have been a recipe for destroying everything
from her self-esteem to her professional dreams. But she was
sick of deceit. She wanted to make love with someone she
didn't have secrets from, someone she could build a future
with. And didn't that just say it all. This was about chemistry. It
had nothing to do with an eternal meeting of kindred souls.

Chapter Sixteen

ortia hit the Enter key on her office computer to sort the data file. This time she'd searched by hair color, which was stupid because hair color could change from one week to the next, but surely someone lurked in her data bank whom she'd missed, someone who'd be perfect for Heath, and she kept envisioning a blonde. She winced as the aggressive whine of a power saw cut through the Sunday afternoon quiet. Non-union laborers were remodeling the office overhead, and the intrusion grated at her already frayed nerves.

Heath had taken off for the weekend with Annabelle Granger. Portia had gotten the news from his receptionist, a woman she'd befriended several months earlier with front-row seats at a Shania Twain concert. Portia still couldn't quite absorb it. *She* was the one who spent weekends with important clients: Vegas jaunts, Wisconsin winter excursions, lazy afternoons at one beach or another. She'd thrown wedding showers and baby showers, attended bar mitzvahs, anniversary parties, even funerals. Her Christmas card list had over five hundred names on it. Yet Annabelle Granger had spent the weekend with Heath Champion.

The power saw emitted another abrasive screech. Generally

she stayed away from the office on Sunday afternoons, but today she'd been more restless than usual. She'd begun the morning with mass in Winnetka. When she'd been a kid, she'd hated going to church, and in her twenties, she'd given it up altogether. But about five years ago, she'd started attending again. At first it had been a business tactic, another way to make the right contacts. She'd targeted four upscale Catholic churches and rotated among them: two on the North Shore, one in Lincoln Park, and one near the Gold Coast. But after a while, she'd begun to look forward to the services for reasons that had nothing to do with business and everything to do with the way the knots inside her unraveled as the familiar words of the liturgy washed over her. She still alternated churches—God helped those who helped themselves, didn't he?—but now her Sundays had become less about business and more about the possibility of peace. Not today, however. Today the serenity she needed so desperately had eluded her.

She'd met some acquaintances for coffee after mass, socially prominent friends from her brief marriage. How would they react if she introduced them to Bodie? Just the thought made her headache worse. Bodie inhabited a secret compartment in her life, a sordid, perverted chamber she could never let anyone peer into. He'd left two messages on her machine this week, but she hadn't returned either of them, not until today. An hour ago, she'd given in to temptation and dialed his number, then hung up before he could answer. If she could get one good night's sleep, she'd stop obsessing about him. Maybe she'd even be able to stop worrying so much about Heath and the feeling that her business was falling apart.

The power saw shrieked again, drilling through her temples. Before her marriage, she'd had her share of affairs. More than a few of them had brought her unhappiness, but none of them had degraded her. Which was what Bodie had done last week. He'd degraded her. And she'd let him do it.

Because it hadn't felt degrading.

That's what she couldn't understand. That's why her insomnia was growing unmanageable, why she hadn't been able to unwind during the mass, and why she'd forgotten last week's weigh-in. Because what he'd done had felt almost tender.

The columns on the computer monitor swam before her eyes, and hammering replaced the sound of the power saw. She had to get out of here. If she were still mentoring, she could have met with one of the women. Maybe she'd stop at the health club, or call Betsy Waits to see if she wanted to meet for dinner. But instead of doing either of those things, she returned her attention to the data on her screen. She had to prove to herself that she was still the best, and the only way she could do that was to find Heath's match.

The hammering turned to rapping, but not until it had become louder and more insistent did she realize it wasn't coming from overhead. She left her desk and made her way into the reception area. She was still dressed in the short, off-white Burberry jacket and Bottega Veneta slacks she'd worn to mass, but she'd kicked off her shoes while she worked, and she moved soundlessly across the carpet. Through the frosted glass, she made out a man's broad-shouldered form. "Who is it?"

A tough, flat voice replied. "The man of your dreams."

She squeezed her eyes shut and told herself not to open the door. This wasn't good for her. *He* wasn't good for her. But a dark, dissonant chorus overcame her willpower. She turned the lock. "I'm working."

"I'll watch."

"You'll be bored to tears." She stepped aside and let him in.

Muscle-bound men usually looked better in workout gear than street clothes, but not Bodie Gray. His chinos and tailored French blue shirt fit his body to perfection. He gazed at the reception area, taking in the cool green walls and Zen-like furnishings, but saying nothing. She refused to let him play another of his silent games. "How did you know I was here?"

"Caller ID."

She should never have called him. She cocked her head. "I hear your lord and master has gone off for the weekend with my rival."

"News travels. This place is nice."

The neediest part of her lapped up his feeble words of praise, but she remained outwardly impassive. "I know."

He gazed toward the reception desk. "Nobody handed you a thing, did they?"

"I'm not afraid of hard work. Women competing in business need to be tough or they won't survive."

"Somehow I can't see anybody giving you too much trouble."

"You have no idea. Successful women are always judged by a different standard than men."

"It's your breasts."

She'd never had a sense of humor about sexism, and she was shocked to feel herself smile, but his cocky, unrepentant machismo was difficult to resist.

"Show me the place," he said.

She did. He poked his head around the parchment screens, took in the quota charts she kept on a wall of the break room, asked questions. She heard the faint sound of Spanish as the workers decided they'd tortured her enough for today and left by the back staircase. She needed to know more about Heath's weekend away, but she waited until she led Bodie into her private office before she broached the subject.

"I'm surprised Heath didn't make you go with him this weekend. Apparently you're not as indispensable as you like to believe."

"I get a few days off now and then."

"I came in today because of him." She gestured toward her computer. "Little Miss Granger can wine and dine him for all she's worth, but I'm the one who'll find his wife."

"Probably."

She perched on the edge of her desk. "Tell me about the women he's dated in the past. He's not very forthcoming."

"I don't want to talk about Heath." He moved to the window, gazed out at the street, then pulled the drapery cord. The panels closed in a soft whoosh. He turned back toward her, and his eyes—so pale and remote they should have turned her to ice—felt like a warm balm to her shriveled soul.

"Take off your clothes," he whispered.

Chapter Seventeen

The week after the disastrous Wind Lake retreat, Annabelle immersed herself in work to keep from obsessing over what had happened. The Perfect for You Web site was up and running, and she received her first e-mail inquiry. She met separately with Ray Fiedler and Carole, who weren't going to be a love match but had learned something from each other. Melanie Richter, the Power Matches candidate Heath had rejected, agreed to have coffee with Shirley Miller's godson. Unfortunately, Jerry was intimidated by her Neiman's wardrobe and refused to ask her out again. A few more senior citizens arrived at her door, taking up too much of her time and doing nothing to improve her bottom line, but she understood loneliness, and she couldn't turn them away. At the same time, she knew she needed to think bigger if she intended to make a living wage. She examined her bank account balance and decided she could just afford to throw a wine and cheese party for her younger clients. All week, she waited for Heath to call. He didn't.

On Sunday afternoon she was listening to vintage Prince on the radio while she unpacked some groceries when her phone rang. "Hey, Spud. How's it going?"

Just the sound of her brother Doug's voice made her feel inept. She envisioned him as she'd last seen him: blond and good-looking, a male version of their mother. She stuffed a bag of baby carrots into the refrigerator and flicked off the radio. "Couldn't be better. How are things in LaLa Land?"

"The house next door just sold for one-point-two mil. On the market less than twenty-four hours. When are you coming out to visit again? Jamison misses you."

"I miss him, too." Not exactly true, since Annabelle barely knew him. Her sister-in-law had the poor kid so overscheduled with play dates and toddler enrichment classes that the last time Annabelle had visited, she'd mainly seen him asleep in his car seat. As Doug rattled on about their fabulous neighborhood, Annabelle imagined Jamison showing up on her doorstep as a twitchy, neurotic thirteen-year-old runaway. She'd nurse him back to mental health by teaching him her best slacker tricks, and when he grew up, he'd tell his children about his beloved, eccentric Auntie Annabelle who'd saved his sanity and taught him to appreciate life.

"So get this," Doug said. "I surprised Candace last week with a new Benz. I wish you could have seen the expression on her face."

Annabelle glanced out the kitchen window toward the alley where Sherman sat baking in the sun like a big green frog. "I'll bet she loved it."

"I'll say." Doug went on about the Benz—interior, exterior, GPS, like she cared. Once he put her on hold to take another call—shades of Heath. Finally he got to the point, and that was when she remembered the main reason Doug called. To lecture. "We need to talk about mom. Adam and I've been discussing the situation."

"Mom's a situation?" She opened a jar of Marshmallow Fluff and dug in.

"She's not getting any younger, Spud, but you don't seem to recognize that fact."

"She's only sixty-two," she said around the sweet gob. "Hardly ready for a nursing home."

"Remember that health scare she had last month?"

"It was a sinus infection!"

"You can minimize it all you want, but the years are catching up with her."

"She just registered for windsurfing lessons."

"She only tells you what she wants you to hear. She doesn't like being a nag."

"You could have fooled me." She tossed the dirty spoon in the sink with more force than necessary.

"Adam and I agree about this, and so does Candace. All the worrying Kate does about you and your . . . Why don't we just come right out and say it?"

Why don't we not? Annabelle screwed on the lid and shoved the jar in the cupboard.

"This anxiety about your fairly aimless lifestyle is putting a strain on her that she doesn't need."

Annabelle ordered herself to let his dig pass. This time she wouldn't let him get to her. "Mom thrives on worrying about me," she said semicalmly. "Retirement bores her, and trying to manage my life gives her something to do."

"That's not the way the rest of us see it. She's always stressed."

"Being stressed is her recreation. You know that."

"You're so clueless. When are you going to figure out that holding on to that house is a headache she doesn't need?"

The house. Another vulnerability. Even though Annabelle paid rent every month, she couldn't escape the fact that she was living under Mommy's roof.

"You need to move out of there so she can put the place on the market."

Her spirits sank. "She wants to sell it?" As she gazed around at the shabby kitchen, she could see her grandmother standing next to the sink as they did the dishes together. Nana didn't like messing up her manicures, so Annabelle always washed while she dried. They'd gossip about the boys Annabelle liked, about a new client Nana had just signed, talking about everything and nothing.

"I think it's pretty clear what she wants," Doug said. "She wants her daughter to step up to the plate and live responsibly. Instead, you're freeloading."

Was that what they called the rent money she barely managed to scrape up every month? Still, who was she kidding? Her mother would make a fortune if she sold this house to developers. Annabelle couldn't take any more. "If Mom wants to sell the house, she can talk to me about it, so butt out."

"You always do this. Can't you, just once, discuss a problem logically?"

"If you want logic, talk to Adam. Or Candace. Or Jamison, for God's sake, but leave me alone."

She hung up on him like the mature thirty-one-year-old she wasn't and promptly burst into tears. For a few moments she fought them, but then she grabbed a paper towel, sat down at the kitchen table, and gave in to her misery. She was tired of being the family outcast, tired of coming up short. And she was afraid . . . because no matter how much she fought it, she was falling in love with a man who was just like them.

By Monday morning, Heath still hadn't contacted her. She had a business to run, and as much as she might want to, she couldn't roll over and play dead any longer, so she left him a message. By Tuesday afternoon, he hadn't replied. She was fairly certain her Oscar-winning performance had convinced him at the time that he'd only been her sex therapist, but more than a week had passed since then, and he seemed to be having second thoughts. It wasn't in his nature to back away from confrontation, and sooner or later he'd contact her, but he'd want their showdown on his terms, which would put her at a disadvantage.

She still had Bodie's cell number from the day they'd spent with Arté Palmer, and she used it that evening.

• • •

An early morning jogger clipped past as she wedged Sherman into a miraculously vacant parking space a few doors down from the Lincoln Park address Bodie had given her the night before. She'd set her alarm for five-thirty, a fine time for Mr. Bronicki and his cronies to hop out of bed, but hell on earth for her. After a quick shower, she'd slipped into an acid yellow sundress with a corset-structured bodice that made her feel as though she had a bust, run a little styling gel through her second-day hair, dabbed on eye makeup and a slick of gloss, and set off.

The coffee she'd picked up at a Caribou on Halsted warmed her palm as she doubled-checked the address. Heath's house took her breath away. The free-form glass-and-brick structure, with its dramatic two-story wedge of windows angling toward the shady street, somehow managed to fit in with its neighbors, both the exquisitely renovated nineteenth-century town houses and the newer luxury homes built on the narrow, expensive lots. She walked down the sidewalk, then turned into a short brick path that curved to a carved mahogany front door and rang the bell. As she waited, she tried to refine her strategy, but the lock clicked and the door swung open before she'd gotten too far.

He wore a purple towel and a scowl, which didn't go away when he saw who'd come calling at 6:40 in the morning. He pulled the toothbrush from his mouth. "I'm not here."

"Now, now." She shoved the coffee into his free hand. "I'm starting a new company called Caffeine to Go Go. You're my first customer." She slipped past him into the foyer where an S-shaped staircase curved to a landing above. She took in the tumbled marble floors, the modern bronze chandelier, and the foyer's only real furnishing, an abandoned pair of sneakers. "Wow. I'm totally awestruck but pretending not to be."

"Glad you like it," he drawled. "Unfortunately, I'm not giving tours today."

She resisted the urge to run her fingertip over the dab of

shaving cream that clung to his earlobe. "That's all right. I'll look around while you finish getting dressed." She gestured toward the stairs. "Go on. Don't let me interrupt you."

"Annabelle, I don't have time to talk now."

"Squeeze me in," she said with her snarkiest smile.

The toothpaste had begun to bubble at the corner of his mouth. He wiped it away with the back of his hand. His gaze slid over her bare shoulders down to the fitted bodice of her sundress. "I haven't been avoiding you. I was going to call you back this afternoon."

"No, really, take as long as you need. I'm not in any hurry." She waved him away and headed toward the living room.

He grumbled something that sounded blasphemous, and, a moment later, she heard his bare feet padding upstairs. She peeked over her shoulder and caught a glimpse of a glorious pair of shoulders, a naked back, and a purple towel. Only when he disappeared did she return her attention to the living room.

Morning light splashed through the tall wedge of windows and dappled the pale hardwood floors. It was a beautiful space just begging to be lived in, but except for the gym equipment sitting on blue rubber mats, as empty as the foyer. No furniture, not even a sports poster on the wall. As she took it in, she began to see the room as it should be: a massive stone-topped coffee table sitting in front of a big, comfy sofa; chairs upholstered in spicy colors; splashy canvases on the walls; a streamlined CD cabinet; books and magazines strewn about. A kid's pull toy. A dog.

With a sigh, she reminded herself that she'd ambushed him this morning so they could get past their weekend at the lake. The old adage of being careful what you wished for sprang to mind. She'd wanted people to know that Heath had signed with Perfect for You, and the word had spread. Now, if she lost him as a client, everyone would assume she hadn't been good enough to keep him. Everything rested on how she handled herself this morning.

She passed through the empty dining room into the kitchen.

The counters were clear, the stainless-steel European appliances looked unused. Only the dirty glass in the sink signaled human habitation. She was struck by the notion that Heath had a place to live, but he didn't have a home.

She returned to the living room and gazed through the windows toward the street. A piece of the puzzle that made up the man she'd fallen in lust with settled into place. Because he was always on the move, she'd missed the fact that he was basically a loner. This unfurnished house brought his emotional isolation into focus.

He reappeared wearing gray slacks, a midnight blue shirt, and a patterned necktie, everything so perfectly pulled together he could have stepped out of a Barneys ad. He tossed his suit coat across the weight bench, set down the coffee she'd brought, and shot his cuffs. "I wasn't ditching you. I needed some time to reassess, and I'm not apologizing for it."

"Apology accepted." His frown didn't bode well, and she quickly shifted gears. "I'm sorry things didn't work out better with Phoebe at the lake. Despite what you might think, I was rooting for you."

"We had half a decent conversation." He picked up the coffee.

"What happened to the other half?"

"I let her push my buttons."

She'd have enjoyed hearing the details, but she needed to get rolling before he started looking at the watch peeking out from under his shirt cuff. "Okay, here's the real reason I'm here—and if you'd called me back, I wouldn't have had to bother you. I need to know if you said anything to anybody about you-know-who. If you did, I swear I'll never speak to you again. I told you in the strictest confidence. Truly, I'd die of embarrassment."

"Tell me you didn't barge in here to talk about Dream Boy."

She pretended to fidget with her ring, a turquoise Nana had bought in Santa Fe. "So do you think Dean might like me?"

"Gosh, I don't know. Why don't you wait till study hall and ask your girlfriends?"

She tried to appear offended. "I'm looking for the male perspective, that's all."

"Get it from Raoul."

"We're over. He was screwing around on me."

"Like everybody in town didn't already know that?"

Okay, they'd had their fun. She sank down on the edge of the weight bench. "I know you think Dean is too young for me . . ."

"Your age is only one item on a bullet list of calamities waiting to happen if you don't get past this. And I haven't seen Lover Boy, so your secret is safe. Are we done yet?"

"I don't know. Are we?" She rose from the bench. "The thing is . . . I'm afraid you still might be dealing with some emotional issues from the retreat, which, I'm sorry to say, is making you seem a little girly."

"Girly?" A dark eyebrow slashed upward.

"Only one woman's opinion."

"You think I'm being *girly*? You, the queen of Annabelle Junior High?"

"You haven't returned my calls."

"I wanted to think about it."

"Exactly." She advanced on him, working up a righteous head of steam. "Obviously you're still conflicted about my night of sexual liberation, but you're too macho to admit it. I should never have taken advantage of you. We both know that, but I thought you were okay with it. Apparently you're not."

"I'm sure this'll disappoint you," he said dryly, "but I wasn't traumatized by your rape and pillage."

"I respect you for holding on to your pride," she said primly.

He frowned. "Cut the crap. You were crystal clear about mixing business and pleasure, and you were right. We both know that. But Krystal threw her porn party, I don't like having people say no to me, and the rest is history. I'm the one who took advantage. The reason I haven't called is that I still haven't figured out how to make it up to you."

She hated the idea that he was seeing her as a victim. "Not by running, that's for sure. Smacks a little too much of the boss who sleeps with his secretary and then fires her for it."

She had the satisfaction of seeing him wince. "I'd never do that," he said.

"Great. Block off every evening starting tomorrow. We're kicking off with a brainy econ professor who looks a little like Kate Hudson, finds Adam Sandler at least mildly amusing, and knows a wineglass from a water goblet. If you don't like her, I have six more lined up. Now are you back in the game or are you wimping out?"

He didn't let her bait him. Instead, he wandered over to the windows, sipping his coffee and taking his time, no doubt thinking over how complicated this had gotten. "Are you sure about going on?" he finally said.

"Hey, I'm not the one who got all worked up. Of course I'm sure." *What a lie.* "I have a business to run, and frankly, you're making that difficult."

He shoved his hand through his hair. "All right. Set it up."

"Perfect." She gave him a smile so big her cheeks ached. "Now, down to business . . ."

They made their arrangements, setting up days and times, and she escaped as soon as they were done. On the drive back home, she made a promise to herself. From now on, she'd seal her emotions away where they belonged. In an internal Ziploc bag—extra heavy duty.

The next afternoon, Heath followed Kevin between the tables in the hotel ballroom as the quarterback shook hands, slapped backs, and worked the crowd of businesspeople who'd gathered to eat lunch and hear his motivational speech,

"Throwing the Long Ones in Life." Heath stayed just behind him, ready to intercede if anyone tried to get too up close and personal, but Kevin made it to the front table without incident.

Heath had heard his speech a dozen times, and as Kevin took his seat, he returned to the rear of the ballroom. The introductions began, and Heath's mind wandered back to Annabelle's ambush yesterday morning. She'd burst into his house, filling up the place with her sass, and despite what he'd said, he'd been glad to see her. All the same, he hadn't lied when he'd told her he'd needed time to think things over, including how he could torpedo that infantile crush she had on Dean Robillard. If she didn't come to her senses soon, Heath was going to lose all respect for her. Why did women leave their brains behind when it came to Dean?

Heath pushed away an uncomfortable memory of a former girlfriend saying exactly the same thing about him. He intended to have a pointed conversation with Dean to make sure Golden Boy understood Annabelle wasn't another bimbo he could stick in his trophy case. Except Heath was supposed to be courting Robillard, not antagonizing him. Once again, his matchmaker had put him in an impossible situation.

Kevin made a self-deprecating joke, and the crowd laughed. He had them right where he wanted, and Heath slipped into the hallway to check his messages. When he saw Bodie's number, he returned it first. "What's up?"

"A buddy of mine just phoned from Oak Street Beach," Bodie said. "Tony Coffield, remember him? His old man owns a couple of bars in Andersonville."

"Yeah?" Tony was one of a network of guys who fed Bodie information.

"So guess who else just showed up to catch some rays? None other than our good buddy Robillard. And it seems he's not alone. Tony says he's sharing a blanket with a red-haired chick. Cute, but not his usual type."

Heath backed against the wall and clenched his teeth.

Bodie chuckled. "Your little matchmaker sure knows how to keep herself busy."

A nnabelle lifted her head from the sandy blanket and gazed over at Dean. He lay on his back, muscles bronzed and oiled, blond hair gleaming, eyes shaded by space-age sunglasses with bright blue lenses. A pair of bikini-clad women made their fourth pass, and this time it looked as though they'd worked up the nerve to approach. Annabelle caught their eyes, pressed her index finger to her lips indicating that he was sleeping, and shook her head. Disappointed, the women walked on.

"Thanks," Dean said, without moving his mouth.

"Does this job pay?"

"I bought you a hot dog, didn't I?"

She propped her chin on her fists and dug her toes deeper into the sand. Dean had called her yesterday, a few hours after she'd left Heath's house. He'd asked if she could squeeze in a trip to the beach before T-camp started. She had a million things to do to get ready for the dating marathon she had planned, but she couldn't pass up the opportunity to feed the story of her infatuation in case Heath still had doubts.

"So explain it to me again," Dean said, eyes still shut. "About how you've been blatantly using me for your own nefarious purposes."

"Football players aren't supposed to know words like *nefarious*."

"I heard it on a beer commercial."

She smiled and adjusted her sunglasses. "All I'm saying is this. I got myself into a little jam—and, no, I'm not telling you who with. The easiest way to wiggle out was to pretend I'm smitten with you. Which, of course, I am."

"Bull. You treat me like a kid."

"Only to protect myself from your glory."

He snorted.

"Besides, being seen with you raises the profile of my business." She laid her cheek on her forearm. "It'll get people talking about Perfect for You, and free advertising is all I can afford right now. I'll pay you back. I promise." She reached over and patted one very hard, sun-warmed bicep. "Ten years from now, when we know for sure you've made it through puberty, I'm going to find you a great woman."

"Ten years?"

"You're right. We'll make it fifteen just to be safe."

Annabelle had a crappy night's sleep. She dreaded the start of Heath's dating marathon, but it was time to bite the bullet and hit him with everything she had. She arrived at Sienna's first. When he walked in, her heart gave a dopey little kick before it plunged to her toes. He'd been her lover, and now she had to introduce him to another woman.

He looked as grouchy as she felt. "I heard you played hooky yesterday," he said as he sat down.

She had hoped word of her outing with Dean would make its way back to him, and her spirits lifted. "Nope. I'm not saying a word." She made a zipping motion across her lips, turned the lock, and threw away the key.

His irritation deepened. "Do you know how juvenile that is?"

"You're the one who asked."

"All I said was that I heard you'd taken the day off. I was making conversation."

"I'm allowed to take a day off now and then. And Wind Lake doesn't count because I had to entertain a client. Specifically, you."

He got that sexy half-lidded look, the one that signaled he was about to say something raunchy. But then he seemed to think better of it. "So how is the course of true love progressing?"

"I think he's attracted to me. Maybe it's because I'm not

clingy. I could be clingy, but I'm forcing myself to give him plenty of room. Don't you agree that's the smart thing to do?"

"You are not sucking me into this discussion."

"I know he has gorgeous football groupies hanging all over him, but I think he might be growing out of that stage of his life. I get the sense that he's maturing."

"Don't hold your breath."

"You think I'm being stupid, don't you?"

"Tinker Bell, you've redefined stupid. For a woman who's supposed to have a head on her shoulders—"

"Shhh . . . Here comes Celeste."

Heath and Celeste had a boring discussion about the economy, a topic that always disheartened Annabelle. If the economy was good, she felt as though she wasn't taking proper advantage of it, and when the economy was bad, she couldn't see how she'd ever get ahead. She let the discussion drag on for the full twenty minutes before she put an end to it.

After Celeste left, Heath said, "I wouldn't mind hiring her, but I don't want to marry her."

Annabelle didn't think Celeste had liked Heath all that much either, and her mood brightened. Unfortunately, only temporarily, because her next candidate, a public relations executive, showed up right on schedule.

Heath was his normal charming self—respectful, interested in everything she had to say, but unwilling to take it any further. "Great taste in clothes, but I make her nervous."

For the rest of the week, Annabelle pulled out the stops, introducing him to a filmmaker, a floral shop owner, an insurance executive, and Janine's editor. He liked all of them but wasn't interested in dating any of them.

Portia got wind of the dating blitz and sent two more socialites. One drooled all over him, which he hated but Annabelle got a kick out of. The other disliked his lack of pedigree, which infuriated Annabelle. Next Portia insisted on setting up an introduction at the Drake for morning coffee. Heath finally agreed, so

Annabelle took advantage of the time slot to schedule a former classmate who taught adult night school.

Annabelle's candidate was a dud. Portia's wasn't. Portia had insisted on the morning meeting, Annabelle discovered, because she'd lined up WGN-TV's newest evening anchorwoman, Keri Winters. Keri was gorgeous, accomplished, and polished—too polished. She was Heath's female counterpart, and together they were slick enough to float an oil tanker.

Annabelle tried to put an end to the agony after twenty minutes, but Heath shot her the evil eye, and Keri didn't leave for another half hour. When the coast was finally clear, Annabelle rolled her eyes. "That was a waste of time."

"What do you mean? She's exactly what I'm looking for, and I'm asking her out."

"She's as plastic as you are. I'm telling you, it's a bad idea. If you ever have kids, they'll come out of the birth canal with Fisher-Price stamped on their butts."

He refused to listen, and the next day, he called Ms. News at Nine to set up a dinner date.

Chapter Eighteen

❧

Two weeks passed. Between getting ready for her wine and cheese party and brooding about Heath and Keri Winters, Annabelle lost enough weight to zip up the periwinkle blue mini she hadn't been able to wear all summer. "Go put some clothes on," Mr. Bronicki growled the night of the party when she came downstairs wearing the mini, along with a slinky ivory top.

"You're the hired help," she retorted. "You're not allowed to criticize."

"Showin' yourself off like a hussy . . . Irene, come out here and look at this."

Mrs. Valerio poked her head in from the kitchen. "You look very nice, Annabelle. Howard, come help me open this olive jar." After she'd started seeing Mr. Bronicki, Mrs. Valerio had dyed her hair Woody Woodpecker red, which matched the crimson sneakers she wore tonight with her Sunday best black dress.

Mr. Bronicki, spiffy in a long-sleeved white shirt, followed her into the kitchen. Annabelle moved to her office, where she'd converted her desk into a serving table with Nana's blue-and-yellow-plaid tablecloth and a gorgeous centerpiece of garden flowers Mrs. McClure had donated. Nana's charming pottery plates from the 1960s held the cheese and fruit. Mr. Bronicki had volunteered to answer the door and pour the wine while Mrs. Valerio kept the platters replenished. By shopping carefully and soliciting help from her seniors, Annabelle had managed to bring the evening together on budget. Even better, she'd picked up two more male clients through her new Web site.

Focusing on business didn't do much to erase the images of Heath in bed with Keri, but she did her best. The news that the WGN anchorwoman and the city's top sports agent were an item had recently hit talk radio, including the morning's top drive-time show, where disc jockeys Eric and Kathy had begun running a Name Their Weird Baby contest.

The doorbell rang. "I hear it," Mr. Bronicki grumbled from the kitchen. "I'm not deaf."

"Remember what I told you about smiling," Annabelle said as he shuffled past.

"Haven't been able to smile since I lost my teeth."

"You're funny as a box of Depends."

"Respect, young lady."

Annabelle had been worried people wouldn't mix, and she'd asked Janine to help. Her friend was the first to arrive, followed by Ernie Marks and Melanie Richter. Within an hour, Annabelle's tiny downstairs rooms were packed. Celeste, the University of Chicago economist, spent a lot of time talking to Shirley Miller's godson Jerry. Ernie Marks, the quiet elementary school principal, and Wendy, the vivacious Roscoe Village architect, seemed to hit it off. Annabelle's two newest clients, discovered through her Web site, clustered around the stylish Melanie. Unfortunately, Melanie seemed more interested in John Nager. In light of Melanie's having once married a man with a fetish for disinfecting doorknobs, Annabelle didn't think John the hypochondriac was her best match. The evening's most interesting development, however, came from an unexpected quarter. To Annabelle's surprise, Ray Fiedler latched onto Janine right away, and Janine didn't do one thing to shake him off. Annabelle had to admit that Ray's new haircut had done wonders for him.

By the time the last of the guests left, she was exhausted but satisfied, especially since everybody wanted to know the date of the next party, and a stack of her brochures had disappeared. All in all, Perfect for You had enjoyed a very successful night.

As Heath and Keri's courtship entered its third week, Annabelle stopped listening to talk radio. Instead, she followed up on the connections her clients had made at the party, tried to dissuade Melanie from seeing John, and signed another new client. She'd never been busier. She only wished she were happier.

A little before eleven o'clock on a Tuesday night, the doorbell rang. She set aside the book she'd been reading and went downstairs to find Heath standing on her porch, looking rumpled and travel weary. Although they'd spoken on the phone, this was the first time she'd seen him since the night he'd met Keri.

He took in her loose-fitting white cotton tank—no bra— and blue cotton drawstring pajama bottoms printed with pink martini glasses holding tiny green olives. "Were you asleep?"

"Reading. Is something wrong?"

"No." Behind him, a taxi pulled away from the curb. His eyes were red-rimmed, and a hint of stubble clung to his tough guy's jaw, which, sicko that she was, only made him more ruggedly attractive.

"Do you have anything to eat? Nothing but pretzels on the plane, even in first class." He was already inside. He set down his carry-on suitcase and a laptop. "I planned to call first, but I fell asleep in the cab."

Her emotions were too raw for this. "All I have is leftover spaghetti."

"Sounds great."

As she took in the lines of fatigue in his face, she didn't have the heart to turn him away, and she headed for the kitchen.

"You were right about Keri and me," he said from behind her.

She bumped into the doorjamb. "What?"

He gazed past her toward the refrigerator. "I wouldn't mind a Coke if you have one."

She wanted to grab him by his white shirt collar and shake him until he told her exactly what he meant, but she restrained herself. "Of course I was right about you and Keri. I'm a trained professional."

He loosened the knot on his necktie and unbuttoned his collar. "Refresh my memory. Exactly what kind of training have you had?"

"My nana was a superstar. It's in my blood." She was going to scream if he didn't tell her what had happened. She grabbed a Coke can from the refrigerator and passed it over.

"Keri and I were too much alike." He propped his shoulder against the wall and sipped his Coke. "It took half a dozen phone calls just to schedule lunch."

The gray cloud that had been following her for three weeks swept off to spoil somebody else's life. She withdrew an ancient powder blue Tupperware container from the refrigerator, along with what was left of the lunchtime Whopper she hadn't felt like finishing. "Was the breakup tough?"

"Not exactly. We played phone tag for so long we had to do it by e-mail."

"No broken hearts, then."

His jaw set in a stubborn line. "We should have been great together."

"You know my opinion about that."

"The Fisher-Price theory. How could I forget?"

As she cut up her leftover hamburger and mixed it with the spaghetti, she wondered why he hadn't phoned her with the news instead of showing up in person. She slid the plate into the microwave.

He wandered over to inspect the yellowed diet plan she'd stuck to the refrigerator when she'd moved in. "We didn't sleep together," he said, keeping his eyes firmly fixed on a low-carb fish dinner.

She reined in her joy. "Not my business."

"Damned right it's not, but you're nosy."

"Hey, I've been too busy building my empire to obsess over your sex life. Or lack thereof." She resisted the urge to do a little soft shoe as she grabbed a pot holder, pulled out the plate, and set it on the table. "You're not my only client, you know."

He found a fork in the silverware drawer then sat down and studied his plate. "Is that a french fry in my spaghetti?"

"Nouvelle cuisine." She reached into the freezer for the carton of Moose Tracks ice cream she hadn't felt like touching in three weeks.

"So how is business?" he asked.

As she pried off the lid, she told him about her party and her new clients. His smile held genuine pleasure. "Congratulations. Your hard work is paying off."

"It looks like it."

"So how are things with you and lover boy?"

It took her a moment to figure out who he was talking about. She dug into the Moose Tracks. "Better all the time."

"That's funny. I saw him at Waterworks a couple of nights ago in a lip-lock with a Britney Spears wannabe."

She excavated a ribbon of chocolate sauce. "All part of my plan. I don't want him to feel suffocated."

"Trust me. He doesn't."

"You see. It's working."

He cocked an eyebrow at her. "This is only one man's opinion, but I think you were better off with Raoul."

She grinned, stuck the lid back on the container, and returned the ice cream to the freezer. While he ate, she washed a saucepan she'd left soaking in the sink and answered more of his questions about the party. Considering how tired he was, she appreciated his interest.

When he finished eating, he brought his plate over. He'd devoured everything, even the french fry. "Thanks. That was the best meal I've had in days."

"Wow, you have been busy."

He retrieved what was left of the Moose Tracks from the freezer. "I'm too tired to go home. Do you have a spare bed where I can crash?"

She banged her shin against the dishwasher door. "Ouch! You want to stay *here* tonight?"

He looked up from the ice cream carton with a slightly puzzled expression, as if he didn't understand her question. "I haven't slept in two days. Is it a problem? I promise I'm too tired to jump you if that's what you're worried about."

"Of course I'm not worried." She occupied herself pulling the trash can out from under the sink. "I suppose it's okay. But Nana's old bedroom faces the alley, and tomorrow's garbage day."

"I'll survive."

Seeing how tired he was, she really couldn't understand why he hadn't waited until tomorrow and called with the news about Keri. Unless he didn't want to be alone tonight. Maybe his feelings for Keri went deeper than he was letting on. Some of the air leaked out of her happiness bubble.

"I'll carry that out." He stuck the ice cream back in the freezer and took the trash bag she'd just bundled up.

It was all too domestic. The late night, the cozy kitchen, shared chores. She in her pajamas with no bra. The mood-swing roller coaster she'd been riding for weeks took another dip.

When he returned from trash detail, he locked the door behind him and nodded toward the backyard. "That car . . . Let me guess. Nana's?"

"Sherman's more a personality than a car."

"You actually drive that thing where people can see you?"

"Some of us can't afford a BMW."

He shook his head. "I guess if this matchmaking gig doesn't work out, you could paint it yellow and stick a meter on the dashboard."

"I'm sure you amuse yourself."

He smiled and headed for the front of the house. "How about showing me my bedroom, Tinker Bell?"

This was too weird. She flipped off the light, determined to keep it laid-back. "If you happen to be one of those people who doesn't like mice, pull the sheet over your head. That generally keeps them away."

"I apologize for making fun of your car."

"Apology accepted."

He grabbed his suitcase and climbed the steps to the small, square upstairs hallway, which was cut up with a series of doors.

"You can take Nana's old bedroom," she said. "Bathroom next to it. That's the living room. It was my mother's bedroom when she was a kid. I sleep on the third floor."

He set down his suitcase and went over to stand in the living room doorway. The outdated gray-and-mauve decorating scheme looked hopelessly shabby. A section of yesterday's newspaper had fallen to the sculpted tweed carpet, and the book she'd been reading lay open on the gray sofa. A pickled oak armoire holding a television occupied the space between two rattly double-hung windows, which were topped with poofy valances in faded gray and mauve stripes. In front of the windows, a matching pair of white metal stands with curly legs held more of Nana's African violet collection.

"This is nice," he said. "I like your house."

At first she thought he was kidding, but then she realized he was sincere. "I'll trade you," she said.

He gazed toward the open door in the hallway. "You sleep in the attic?"

"It's where I stayed when I was a kid, and I kind of got used to it."

"Tinker Bell's lair. This I have to see." He headed for the narrow attic stairs.

"I thought you were so tired," she called out.

"Making this the perfect time for me to see your bedroom. I'm harmless."

She didn't believe that for a moment.

The attic with its twin dormers and sloping ceilings had become the repository for all of Nana's discarded antiques: a cherry four-poster bed, an oak bureau, a dressing table with a gilded mirror, even an old dressmaker's mannequin from the days when Nana had kept herself busy by sewing instead of matchmaking. One dormer held a cozy armchair and ottoman, the other a small walnut desk and an ugly, but efficient, window air conditioner. Annabelle had recently added blue-and-white toile curtains to the dormer windows, a matching toile bed-spread, and some French prints to complement the miscella-neous landscapes that had drifted up here.

She was glad she'd tidied up earlier, although she wished she hadn't overlooked the pink bra lying on the bed. His eyes wandered to it, then drifted to the mannequin, currently outfit-ted in an old lace tablecloth and a Cubs hat. "Nana?"

"She was a fan."

"So I see." He gazed up at the sloping ceiling. "All this needs is a couple of skylights, and it'd be perfect."

"Maybe you should concentrate on decorating your own place."

"I guess."

"Honestly, Heath, if I had that gorgeous house and your money, I'd turn it into a showplace."

"What do you mean?"

"Big furniture, stone tables, great lighting, contemporary art on the wall—huge canvases. How can you stand living in such an amazing house and not doing anything with it?"

He looked at her so strangely that she grew uncomfortable and turned away. "Nana's bedroom has a temperamental window shade. I'll go fix it and get you some towels."

She hurried downstairs. The faint scent of Avon's To a Wild Rose still clung to Nana's room. She turned on the small china dresser lamp, put away the extra blanket she'd left at the foot of the bed, and fixed the shade. In the bathroom, she stowed the Tampax box from last week and draped a clean set of towels over the old chrome rod.

He still hadn't come downstairs. She wondered if he'd spotted her old Tippy Tumbles doll propped on the bureau. Even worse, what about the sex toy catalog that she hadn't gotten around to throwing away? She rushed up the stairs.

He lay on her bed, fully dressed except for his shoes, and sound asleep.

His lips were slightly parted, and his ankles, clad in plain black socks, crossed. One hand rested on his chest. The other lay at his side, next to the scrap of pink bra peeking from under his hip. It nested by his fingertips, not quite touching them, but close enough to make her queasy. Call her crazy, but she couldn't stand seeing abandoned lingerie anywhere near him.

A floorboard squeaked as she tiptoed to the bed. Slowly, carefully, she snagged the bra strap and tugged.

It didn't budge.

He expelled a little puff of air. This was nuts. She felt vulnerable enough as it was. She should go away and let him sleep. But she tugged again.

He rolled toward her, onto his side, trapping all but a loop of lacy strap under his hip.

She started to perspire. She knew this was insane, but she couldn't make herself walk away. Another floorboard creaked as she knelt at the side of the bed, the same floorboard that creaked every time she stepped on it, so she should have been more careful. Her heart was pounding. She pressed down on the mattress with one hand and slipped her finger through the

loop of strap sticking out from under his hip with the other.
She pulled hard.

One heavy eyelid drifted open, and his sleep-rusty voice
made her jump. "Either get in here with me or go away."

"This is"—she pulled a little harder—"my bed."

"I know. I'm resting."

He didn't look like he was resting. He looked like he'd settled in for the night. With her underwear. Which refused to
budge. "Could I . . ."

"I'm dead on my feet." His eyes drifted shut. "You can
have your bed back in the morning. Promise." His voice faded
on a slur.

"Okay, but . . ."

"Go 'way," he muttered.

"I will. First, though, would you mind—"

He rolled to his back again, which should have freed the bra
but didn't. Instead, it wedged between his hip and hand.

"I, uh, need one little thing. Then I won't bother you
any—"

His fingers clamped her wrist, and this time when his lids
opened, his eyes were completely focused. "What do you *want*?"

"My bra back."

He lifted his head and glanced to his side, still holding her
wrist. "Why?"

"I'm a neat freak. Messy rooms drive me crazy." She yanked
hard and jerked it free.

Heath gazed at the bra dangling from her fingers. "Are you
going somewhere tonight?"

"No, I—" She'd awakened the sleeping lion for sure, and
she wadded the bra in her hands, trying to make it invisible.
"Go back to sleep. I'll take Nana's bed."

"I'm awake now." He propped himself on his elbows.
"Usually I can see through your latest craziness, but I have to
say, this time you've got me stumped."

"Just forget it."

"One thing I do know . . ." He nodded toward her hand. "This isn't about a bra."

"That's what you think." She scowled at him. "Until you've walked a mile in my shoes, don't judge."

"Judge what?"

"You wouldn't understand."

"I spend most of my life around football players. You'd be surprised how many weird things I understand."

"Not this weird."

"Try me."

The stubborn set of his mouth told her he wasn't going to let this go, and she had no explanation but the truth. "I can't stand seeing . . ." She swallowed and licked her lips. "It's hard for me to see . . . uh . . . female lingerie too near a man's hand. That is . . . when the lingerie isn't actually on a female body."

He groaned and sank back into her pillows. "Oh, my God. Don't tell me."

"It upsets me." Which was putting it mildly.

She knew he'd laugh, and he did, a big sound that bounced around the attic's odd angles.

She stared him down.

He threw his feet over the side of the bed. "You're afraid *I'm* going to start cross-dressing?"

Hearing it spoken aloud made her wince. How had she lived to be thirty-one years old without someone locking her up? "Not afraid exactly. But . . . The thing is . . . Why expose yourself to temptation?"

He loved that.

She understood his amusement—she'd be amused herself if she were him—but she couldn't find a smile anywhere. Dispirited, she turned back toward the stairs. His laughter faded, and another floorboard creaked as he came up behind her. He set his hands on her shoulders. "Hey, you really are upset, aren't you?"

She nodded.

"I'm sorry. I spend too much time in locker rooms. I won't tease you anymore. I promise."

His sympathy was worse than his teasing, but she turned into his chest all the same. He stroked her hair, and she told herself to back away, but she felt as though she belonged exactly where she was. And then she grew aware of the powerful erection pressing against her body.

So did he. He quickly stepped back, abruptly releasing her. "I'd better go downstairs so you can have your bedroom back," he said.

She managed a shaky nod. "Okay."

He picked up his shoes, but he didn't leave right away. Instead, he made his way to her desk and gestured toward the magazines stacked on top. "I like to read before I fall asleep. I don't suppose you've got a spare copy of *Sports Illustrated* lying around?"

" 'Fraid not."

"Of course you don't. Why would you?" His hand shot out. "I'll take this instead?"

And there went her sex toy catalog.

Heath smiled to himself as he set off down the stairs, but his smile had faded by the time he reached Nana's bedroom. What the hell was he doing here? He pulled off his shirt and tossed it on a chair. He hadn't planned on showing up at Annabelle's door, but the past week had been brutal. With the preseason about to begin, he'd flown all over the country, touching base with each of his clients. He'd played big brother, cheerleader, lawyer, and shrink. He'd endured flight delays, car rental mix-ups, bad food, loud music, too much booze, and not enough sleep. Tonight, when he'd gotten into the cab, the image of his empty house looming in front of him had been more than he could handle, and he'd heard himself giving the driver Annabelle's address.

This sense that he was thrashing around threatened his mental toughness. He'd signed with Portia in May, Annabelle early in June. Now it was mid-August, but he was no closer to reaching his goal than when he'd started. As he unzipped his pants, he knew that his frustrating breakup with Keri proved one thing. He couldn't keep going on like this, not with the football season starting, not if he wanted to stay mentally sharp. The time had come to make some changes . . .

Portia watched the woman's breasts leak into the platter of raw oysters, a steady drip, drip, drip. An ice sculpture of a classical female figure might have made sense in the abstract, but tonight's silent auction and cocktail party benefited a shelter for abused women, and watching a woman melt into the hors d'oeuvres sent the wrong message. The restaurant's air-conditioning couldn't handle either the ice sculpture or the crowd, and Portia was hot even in her strapless dress. She'd bought the short red cocktail number just that afternoon, hoping something new and extravagant would lift her spirits, as if a new dress could fix what was wrong with her. She'd been so optimistic about Heath and Keri, basking in the publicity they'd stirred up. She should have realized they were too much alike, but she'd lost her instincts right along with her passion for manufacturing other people's happy endings.

She felt scattered and depressed, sick of Power Matches, sick of herself and of everything that had once given her so much pride. She moved away from the buffet table and the disappearing woman. She had to pull herself together before the meeting Heath had set up for tomorrow morning. Why had he called it? Probably not to sing her praises. Well, she refused to lose this thing. Bodie said she was obsessed. *Just tell Heath to go to hell*. She'd tried to explain that failure bred failure, but Bodie had grown up in a trailer park, so some things didn't compute with him.

She'd been trying with little success not to think about Bodie. They'd become creatures of the dark. For the past month, they'd seen each other several times a week, always at her place, always at night, a couple of sex-crazed vampires. Whenever Bodie suggested they go out to dinner or to a movie, she made an excuse. She could no more explain Bodie and his tattoos to her friends than she could explain the bizarre need she sometimes felt to parade him in front of everyone. It had to end. Any day now, she'd break it off.

Toni Duchette appeared at her elbow, fresh blond chunks in her short brown hair, fireplug figure stuffed into a black sequined number. "Did you bid on anything?"

"The watercolor." Portia gestured toward a rip-off Berthe Morisot on the nearest table. "It's perfect to hang over my dresser."

She remembered the startled expression on Bodie's face the first time he'd seen her extravagantly feminine bedroom. His outrageous masculinity should have looked ridiculous in her billowy white fairy princess bed, but seeing those sinewy muscles outlined against her silky ecru sheets, his shaved head denting her satin pillows, a frill of lace veiling the tattoos that banded his arm, had merely fueled her desire.

As Toni went on about the donations they'd received, Portia automatically scanned the room for interesting prospects, but this was an older crowd, and supporting the women's shelter had never been about business for her. She couldn't imagine anything worse than being under the power of an abusive man, and she'd given the shelter thousands of dollars over the years.

"The committee's done a wonderful job," Toni said, surveying the crowd. "Even Colleen Corbett showed up, and she hardly ever comes to these things anymore." Colleen Corbett was a bastion of old Chicago society, seventy years old, and a former intimate of both Eppie Lederer, otherwise known as Ann Landers, and the late Sis Daley, wife of Boss Daley and mother of the current mayor. Portia had been trying to ingratiate herself with her for years without success.

When Toni finally moved away, Portia decided she'd try again to break through Colleen Corbett's reserve. Tonight, Colleen wore one of her signature Chanel suits, this one peach with beige trim. Her permed and shellacked hairstyle hadn't changed since her photos from the 1960s, except for its color, now a polished steel gray.

"Colleen, it's lovely to see you again." Portia offered her most ingratiating smile. "Portia Powers. We chatted at the Sydneys' party last spring."

"Yes. Nice to see you." Her voice was faintly nasal, her manner cordial, but Portia could tell she didn't remember. Several beats of silence ticked by, which Colleen didn't try to fill.

"Some interesting auction pieces." Portia resisted the urge to grab a gin and tonic from a passing waiter.

"Yes, very interesting," Colleen replied.

"A little warm in here tonight. The ice sculpture seems to be fighting a losing battle."

"Oh? I hadn't noticed."

This was hopeless. Portia hated looking like a sycophant, and she'd just decided to cut her losses when she noticed a subtle shift in the room's atmosphere. The noise level dropped; a head pivoted here and there. She turned to see what had caused the rustle of interest.

And felt the floor drop out from under her.

Bodie stood just inside the doorway, his massive frame clad in a perfectly cut, pale beige summer suit with a chocolate-colored shirt and subtly patterned necktie. He looked like a very expensive, very deadly, Mafia hit man. She wanted to run into his arms. At the same time, she felt a wild urge to dive under the buffet table. The biggest gossips in the city were here tonight. Just by herself Toni Duchette broadcast to more people than WGN Radio.

Her knees felt weak, the tips of her fingers numb. What was he doing here? Her mind raced then fastened on an image of him standing naked in front of the small console in her living room where she kept her personal mail. He'd moved away as she approached, but he must have seen the stack of invitations she never mentioned to him: the Morrisons' pool party, the new River North gallery opening, tonight's benefit. He would have known exactly why she hadn't invited him to go with her. Now, he intended to make her pay.

The cloying scent of Colleen's Shalimar made her stomach pitch. Bodie's gangster's smile offered no reassurance as he headed straight toward her. A trickle of perspiration slid between her breasts. This wasn't a man who took slights well.

Colleen had her back to him. Portia didn't know how to brace herself for a disaster of this magnitude. He stopped just behind Colleen. If the older woman looked around, she'd have a heart attack. Mockery turned his blue eyes to slate. He raised his arm. And set his hand on Colleen's shoulder.

"Hello, sweetheart."

Portia sucked in her breath. Bodie had just called Colleen Corbett "sweetheart"?

The older woman tilted her head. "Bodie? What on earth are you doing here?"

Portia's world spun.

"I heard they were handing out free drinks," he said. And then he pressed a kiss to Colleen's papery cheek.

Colleen slipped her hand into his big paw and said peevishly, "I got that dreadful birthday card you sent me, and it wasn't one bit funny."

"I laughed."

"You should have sent flowers like everyone else."

"You liked that card a hell of a lot more than a bunch of roses. Admit it."

Colleen pursed her lips. "I admit nothing. Unlike your mother, I refuse to encourage your behavior."

Bodie's gaze drifted to Portia, recalling Colleen to the amenities. "Oh, Paula . . . This is Bodie Gray."

"Her name is Portia," he said. "And we've met."

"Portia?" Her forehead wrinkled. "Are you sure?"

"I'm sure, Auntie Cee."

Auntie Cee?

"Portia? How Shakespearian." Colleen patted Bodie's arm and smiled at her. "My nephew is relatively harmless, despite his terrifying appearance."

Portia wobbled ever so slightly on her needle-sharp heels. "Your nephew?"

Bodie reached out to steady her. As he touched her arm, his soft, menacing voice slid over her like inky silk. "Maybe you should put your head between your knees."

What about the trailer park, and the drunken father? What about the cockroaches and the trashy women? He'd made it all up. This whole time he'd been playing her.

She couldn't bear it. She turned and pushed her way through the crowd. Faces flashed by as she dashed into the hallway, out of the restaurant. The night air hung thick and heavy with heat and exhaust. She set off down the street, past the shuttered shops, past a graffiti-splattered wall. The Bucktown restaurant edged the border of less fashionable Humbolt Park, but she kept walking, not caring where she was going, only knowing that she had to keep moving. A CTA bus roared by, and a punk with a pit bull gave her a sly, assessing eye. The city closed around her, hot, suffocating, filled with menace. She stepped off the curb.

"Your car's the other way," Bodie said from behind her.

"I don't have anything to say to you."

He caught her arm and dragged her back up on the curb. "How about apologizing for treating me like nothing more than a piece of meat?"

"Oh, no, you don't. You're not turning this back on me. You're the one who lied. All those stories . . . The cockroaches, the drunken father. Right from the beginning you lied to me. You aren't Heath's bodyguard."

"He can pretty much take care of himself."

"This whole time you've been laughing at me."

"Yeah, sort of. When I wasn't laughing at myself." He pushed her into the recessed doorway of a shabby flower shop with a dirty window. "I told you what you needed to hear if the two of us were ever going to have a chance."

"Lies are your idea of how to start a relationship?"

"They're my idea of how this one needed to start."

"So this was all premeditated?"

"Now, there you've got me." He rubbed his thumbs over her arms where he'd been holding her, then let her go. "At first I was jerking your chain because you pissed me off. You wanted a stud, and I was more than happy to comply, but it didn't take me long to start resenting being your dirty little secret."

She squeezed her eyes shut. "You wouldn't have been a secret if you'd told me the truth."

"Right. You'd have loved that. I can just imagine how you'd have paraded me in front of your friends, letting everybody know that my mother and Colleen Corbett are sisters. Sooner or later you'd have found out that my father's family is even more respectable. Old Greenwich. That would have made you real happy, wouldn't it?"

"You act like I'm some terrible snob."

"Don't even try to deny it. I've never known anyone as frightened of other people's opinions as you."

"That's not true. I'm my own person. And I won't tolerate being manipulated."

"Yeah. Not being in control scares the hell out of you." He ran his thumb down her cheek. "Sometimes I think you're the most frightened person I've ever known. You're so afraid you'll come up short that you're making yourself sick."

She shoved his hand away, so furious she could barely speak. "I'm the strongest woman you've ever known."

"You spend so much time trying to prove how superior you are that you've forgotten how to live. You obsess over all the wrong things, refuse to let anybody see inside you, and then you can't figure out why you're not happy."

"If I wanted a shrink, I'd hire one."

"You should have done that a long time ago. I've lived in the shadows, too, babe, and I don't recommend staying there." He hesitated, and she thought he'd finished, but he went on. "After I had to quit football, I had a big problem with drugs. You name it; I tried it. My family convinced me to go into re-hab, but I told everybody the counselors were assholes and left after two days. Six months later Heath found me passed out in a bar. He banged my head into the wall a couple of times, told me he used to admire me but that I'd turned into the sorriest son of a bitch he'd ever seen. Then he offered me a job. He didn't give me any lectures about staying clean, but I knew that was part of the deal, so I asked him to give me six weeks. I put myself in rehab, and this time I paid attention. Those counselors saved my life."

"I'm hardly a drug addict."

"Fear can be an addiction."

Even as his poisoned dart hit home, she refused to blink. "If you have so little respect for me, why are you still around?"

He slipped a gentle hand into her hair and pushed a curl behind her ear. "Because I'm a sucker for beautiful, wounded creatures."

Something broke apart inside her.

"And because," he want on, "when you let down your guard, I see someone who's brilliant and passionate." He brushed her cheekbone with his thumb. "But you're so afraid to lead with your heart that you're dying inside."

She felt herself coming apart, and she punished him in the only way she knew how. "What a bunch of crap. You're still around because you like to fuck me."

"That, too." He kissed her forehead. "There's a hell of a

woman hidden away behind all that fear. Why don't you let her come out and play?"

Because she didn't know how.

The tightness in her chest made it hard to breathe. "Go to hell." Pushing past him, she took off down the street, half walking, half running. But he'd already seen her tears, and for that, she would never forgive him.

B odie heard the sound of a baseball game coming from his television as he let himself into his Wrigleyville condo. "Make yourself right at home," he muttered, tossing his keys on the mission-style table that sat in the foyer.

"Thanks," Heath said from the big sectional sofa in Bodie's living room. "Sox just gave up a run in the seventh."

Bodie sank into the armchair across from him. Unlike Heath's house, Bodie's was furnished. Bodie liked the clean design of the Arts and Crafts period, and over the years he'd bought some good Stickley pieces and added Craftsman-style built-ins. He kicked off his shoes. "You should either sell your fucking house or live in it."

"I know." Heath set down his beer. "You look like shit."

"A thousand beautiful women in this town, and I've got to fall for Portia Powers."

"You set yourself up for grief that first night when you blackmailed her with that bodyguard bullshit."

Bodie rubbed his hand over his head. "Tell me something I don't know."

"If that woman ever realizes how scared you are of her, you'll really be screwed."

"She's such a pain in the ass. I keep telling myself to walk away, but . . . Hell, I don't know . . . It's like I've got X-ray vision, and I can see who she really is underneath all the bullshit." He shifted in his chair, uncomfortable with saying so much, even to his best friend.

Heath understood. "Tell me we're not sharing our feelings, Mary Lou."

"Fuck you."

"Shut up and watch the game."

Bodie relaxed into the chair. Initially he'd been attracted by Portia's beauty, then by her sheer gall. She had as much grit and determination as any teammate he'd ever played with, and those were qualities he respected. But when they made love, he saw another woman, one who was insecure, generous, and full of heart, and he couldn't get past thinking that this softer, unguarded woman was the real Portia Powers. Still, what kind of idiot fell for someone who needed so badly to be fixed?

As a kid, he used to bring home injured animals and try to nurse them back to health. Apparently he was still doing it.

Chapter Nineteen

nnabelle had trouble finding a parking spot for Sherman, but she was only two minutes late for the meeting Heath had scheduled, which hardly justified the censorious look from his Evil Receptionist. ESPN played on the television screen in the lobby, phones rang in the background, and one of Heath's interns struggled to change a printer cartridge in the equipment closet. The office door on her left had been closed the first time she was here, but now it stood open, and she saw Bodie with his feet propped on a desk and a telephone pressed to his ear. He waved as she passed. She opened the door to Heath's office and heard a throaty female voice.

". . . and I'm very optimistic about her. She's incredibly beautiful." Portia Powers sat in one of two chairs positioned in front of Heath's desk. His voice mail message hadn't mentioned this would be a threesome.

Just looking at the Dragon Lady made Annabelle feel dowdy. Summer fashion was supposed to be all about color, but maybe Annabelle had gotten a little carried away with her melon-colored blouse, lemon yellow skirt, and the drop earrings set with tiny lime green stones she'd found at TJ Maxx. At least her hair looked decent. Now that it was longer, she'd been able to use a big barrel curling iron, then finger-comb the results into a casual tousle.

Portia was all cool elegance in pewter silk. Against her dusky hair, the effect was dazzling. Small, petal pink earrings provided a subtle touch of color against her porcelain skin, and a Kate Spade handbag in the same pink shade sat on the floor at her side. She hadn't made the mistake of going into pink overkill with her shoes, which were stylish black mules.

Or one of them was.

Annabelle stared at her competitor's feet. At first glance, the shoes looked the same. They both had open toes and low heels, but one was a black mule and the other a navy sling-back. What was that about?

Annabelle drew her eyes away and slipped her sunglasses in her purse. "Sorry I'm late. Sherman didn't like any of the parking spots I showed him."

"Sherman is Annabelle's car," Heath explained as he rose from behind the desk and gestured to the chair next to Portia's. "Have a seat. I don't believe you and Portia have met in person."

"As a matter of fact we have," Portia replied smoothly.

Through the long wall of windows behind his desk, Annabelle spotted a sailboat skimming over Lake Michigan in the distance. She wished she were on it.

"We've been at this since spring," Heath said, "and now football season is starting. I think both of you know that I'd hoped to be further along."

"I understand." Portia's smooth confidence belied her mismatched shoes. "We all hoped this would be easier. But you're an extremely discriminating man, and you deserve an extraordinary woman."

Suck up, Annabelle thought. Still, when it came to Heath, Annabelle didn't exactly deserve high marks for professionalism, and she could do a lot worse than follow Portia's example.

Portia shifted slightly in her chair, which cast her face into a harsher light. She wasn't as young as Annabelle had thought when they'd met, and her expertly applied makeup couldn't camouflage the dark circles under her eyes. Too much nightlife or something more serious?

Heath set his hip on the corner of the desk. "Portia, you found Keri Winters for me, and even though that didn't work out, you were on the right path. But you've sent too many candidates who aren't in the ballpark."

Portia didn't make the mistake of getting defensive. "You're right. I should have eliminated more of them, but every woman I've chosen has been so special, and I hate second-guessing my most discriminating clients. I'll be more careful from now on."

The Dragon Lady was good. Annabelle had to give her that.

Heath turned his attention to Annabelle. No one could have imagined that he'd fallen asleep in her attic bedroom two nights ago, or that once, in a pretty cottage by the side of a Michigan lake, they'd made love. "Annabelle, you've done a better job screening, and you've introduced me to a lot of also-rans, but you haven't produced a single winner."

She opened her mouth to respond, but before she could say a word, he cut her off. "Gwen doesn't count."

Unlike Portia, Annabelle thrived on being defensive. "Gwen was almost perfect."

"As long as we overlook her husband and that inconvenient pregnancy."

Portia sat straighter in her chair. Annabelle crossed her hands primly in her lap. "You have to admit she was exactly what you're looking for."

"Yeah, bigamy's my life's dream, all right."

"You cornered me," she replied. "And, let's be honest. Once she got to know you, she'd have dumped you. You're way too high maintenance."

Portia's eyes had widened like butterfly wings. She studied Annabelle more closely. Then she got a little twitchy. She uncrossed the legs she'd crossed, crossed them again. Her top foot—the one in the navy sling-back—began tapping away.

"I'm sure Annabelle has learned by now to be more careful with her background checks."

Annabelle pretended surprise. "I was supposed to check Heath's background?"

"Not Heath's background," Portia retorted. "The women!"

Heath fought a smile. "Annabelle is baiting you. I've learned it's best to ignore her."

Now Portia looked genuinely rattled. Annabelle almost felt sorry for her as she watched the navy sling-back move faster and faster.

Heath, in the meantime, made a sprint for the goal line. "Here's the way it's going to be, ladies. I made a mistake by not signing contracts with a shorter term, but it's a mistake I'm correcting right now. You each have one shot left. That's it."

The sling-back froze. "When you say one shot . . ."

"One introduction each," Heath said firmly.

Portia twisted in her chair, knocking the Kate Spade handbag over with her heel. "That's not realistic."

"Work with it."

"Are you sure you really want to get married?" Annabelle said. "Because, if you do, maybe you should think about the possibility—more than a possibility, in my judgment, but I'm trying to be diplomatic . . . Have you thought about the possibility that you're the one who's sabotaging this process, not us?"

Portia shot her a warning look. "*Sabotage* is a strong word. I'm sure what Annabelle means to say is that—"

"What Annabelle means to say"—she rose from her chair—"is that we introduced you to some terrific women, but you only gave one of them a chance. The *wrong* one—again, only my opinion. We're not magicians, Heath. We have to work with flesh-and-blood human beings, not some fantasy woman you've conjured in your mind."

Portia plastered a phony smile on her face and rushed to save the sinking ship. "I hear what you're saying, Heath. You're not satisfied with the service you've been getting from Power

Matches. You want us to vet the candidates more carefully, and that's certainly a reasonable request. I can't speak for Miss Granger, but I promise that I'll proceed more conservatively from now on."

"Very conservatively," he said. "You have one introduction. The same goes for you, Annabelle. After that, I'm calling it quits."

Portia's plastic smile melted at the edges. "But your contract runs into October. It's only mid-August."

"Save your breath," Annabelle said. "Heath wants an excuse to fire us. He doesn't believe in failure, and if he fires us, he can transfer the blame."

"Fire us?" Portia looked sick.

"It'll be a new experience for you," Annabelle said glumly. "Fortunately for me, I've had practice."

Portia pulled herself back together. "I know this has been frustrating, but it's frustrating for everyone who goes through the process. You deserve results, and you'll get them, but only with a little patience."

"I've been patient for months," he said. "That's long enough."

Annabelle looked into his proud stubborn face and couldn't keep silent. "Are you going to take ownership for any part of the problem?"

He met her gaze dead-on. "Absolutely. That's what I'm doing right now. I told you I was looking for someone extraordinary, and if I'd thought it would be easy to find her, I'd have done it myself." He rose from the corner of the desk. "Take as long as you need to come up with your last introduction. And believe me, nobody hopes that one of you gets it right more than I do."

He made his way to the door, then stood back to let them out, his head outlined against the sign for the Beau Vista Trailer Park hanging on the wall behind him.

Annabelle retrieved her purse and gave him her most dignified nod, but she was fuming as she left his office, definitely in no mood to share an elevator with Portia, so she moved quickly through the lobby to the elevator bank.

As it turned out, she had no need to rush.

Portia slowed her steps as she watched Annabelle disappear. Bodie's office lay just ahead on her right. When she'd walked past it earlier, she'd forced herself not to look in, but she'd known he was there. She could feel him through her skin. Even during that horrible meeting with Heath when she'd most needed to keep her wits, she'd felt him.

All last night she'd lain awake reliving the horrible things he'd said to her. Maybe she could have forgiven the lies he'd told her about his upbringing, but she could never forgive the rest. Who did he think he was to psychoanalyze her? The only thing wrong with her was him. Maybe she'd been a little depressed before she met him, but it hadn't been significant. Last night he'd made her feel like a failure, and she wouldn't let anyone do that to her.

Her hands were trembling as she stopped inside his office door. He was on the phone, his massive frame tilted back in his chair. As he spotted her, his face broke into a smile, and he dropped his feet to the floor.

"Let me call you back, Jimmie . . . Yeah, sounds good. We'll get together." He set the phone aside and rose. "Hey, babe . . . Are you still talking to me?"

His silly, hopeful grin made her falter. Instead of looking dangerous, he looked like a kid who'd spotted a new bike sitting on his front porch. She turned away to compose herself and came face-to-face with a wall of memorabilia. She took in a pair of framed magazine covers, some team pictures from his playing days, newspaper clippings. But it was a black-and-white photo that caught her attention. The photographer had captured Bodie with his helmet tilted back on his head, chin strap dangling, a scrap of turf caught in the corner of his face mask. His eyes shone with triumph, and his radiant grin owned the world. She bit her lip and made herself turn back to confront him. "I'm breaking it off, Bodie."

He came around the side of the desk, his smile fading. "Don't do this, sweetheart."

"You couldn't have been more wrong about me." She forced herself to say the words that would keep her safe. "I love my life. I have money and a beautiful home, a successful business. I have friends—good, dear friends." Her voice caught. "I love my life. Every part of it. Except the part that involves you."

"Don't, babe." He reached toward her with one of his gentle, meat hook hands, not touching her, a gesture of entreaty. "You're a fighter," he said softly. "Have the guts to fight for us."

She steeled herself against the pain. "It was a fling, Bodie. An amusement. Now it's over."

Her lips had begun to tremble, just like a child's, and she didn't wait for him to respond. She turned away . . . left his office . . . rode numbly down to the street in the elevator. Two pretty young things passed her as she stepped outside. One of them pointed toward her feet, and the other laughed.

Portia brushed past them, blinking back tears, suffocating. A red double-decker tour bus crawled by, the guide quoting Carl Sandburg in a booming, overly dramatic voice that felt like fingernails scraping the chalkboard of her skin.

"Stormy, husky brawling . . . City of the big shoulders: They tell me you are wicked, and I believe them . . ."

Portia swiped at her eyes and picked up her step. She had work to do. Work would fix everything.

Sherman's air-conditioning was on the fritz, and Annabelle's appearance had degenerated into a mass of curls and wrinkles by the time she got home from the meeting with Heath, but she didn't go inside right away. Instead, she stayed in the car with the windows rolled down and braced herself for the next step. He was only giving her one more introduction. That meant she couldn't put it off any longer. Even so, it took all her willpower to pull her cell from her purse and make the call.

"Delaney, hi. It's Annabelle. Yes, I know. It's been ages . . ."

W e're poor as church mice," Delaney Lightfield told Heath the night of their first official date, a mere three days after they'd been introduced. "But we still maintain appearances. And thanks to Uncle Eldred's influence, I have a great sales job at the Lyric Opera."

She relayed this information with a charming, self-deprecating laugh that made Heath smile. At twenty-nine, Delaney reminded him of a blond, more athletic Audrey Hepburn. She wore a sleeveless navy cotton sweater dress with a strand of pearls that had belonged to her great-grandmother. She'd grown up in Lake Forest and graduated from Smith. She was an expert skier and a competent tennis player. She golfed, rode horseback, and spoke four languages. Although several decades of outdated business practices had depleted the Lightfield railroad fortune and forced the sale of the family's summer house in Bar Harbor, Maine, she liked the challenge of making it on her own. She loved to cook and confessed that she sometimes wished she'd gone to culinary school. The woman of his dreams had finally appeared.

As the evening progressed, he switched from beer to wine, reminded himself to watch his language, and made it a point to mention the new Fauvist exhibit at the Art Institute. After dinner, he drove her back to the apartment she shared with two roommates and gave her a gentleman's kiss on the cheek. As he drove away, the faint scent of French lavender lingered in the car. He grabbed his cell to phone Annabelle, but he was too revved to go home. He wanted to talk to her in person. Singing along with the radio in his off-key baritone, he headed for Wicker Park.

Annabelle opened the door. She wore a V-necked striped top and a blue mini that did great things for her legs. "I should have issued my ultimatum sooner," he said. "You definitely know how to deliver under pressure."

"I thought you'd like her."

"Did she call you yet?"

Annabelle nodded but didn't say more, and he tensed. Maybe the date hadn't gone as well as he thought. Delaney was a blue blood. What if she'd caught too strong a whiff of the trailer park?

"I talked with her a few minutes ago," Annabelle finally said. "She's smitten. Congratulations."

"Really?" His instincts had been on target. "That's great. Let's celebrate. How about a beer?"

Annabelle didn't move. "It's . . . not a good time."

She glanced over her shoulder, and that's when it hit him. She wasn't alone. He took in her fresh lip gloss and the blue mini. His good mood fizzled. Who did she have with her?

He gazed over the top of her head, but the front room was empty. Which didn't mean the same thing was true of her bedroom . . . He fought the urge to charge past her and see for himself. "No problem," he said stiffly. "I'll talk to you next week."

But instead of walking away, he stood there. Finally she nodded and shut the door.

Five minutes ago he'd been on top of the world. Now he wanted to kick something. He headed down the sidewalk and climbed into his car, but it wasn't until he edged out of his parking space that his headlights caught the vehicle across the street. Earlier, he'd been too preoccupied to notice, but he wasn't preoccupied now.

The last time he'd seen that bright red Porsche, it had been parked at Stars headquarters.

• • •

A nnabelle trudged into the kitchen. Dean was sitting at the table, a Coke in one hand, a deck of cards in the other. "It's your deal," he said.

"I don't feel like playing anymore."

"You're no fun tonight." He tossed down the cards.

"Like you're a barrel of laughs?" Kevin had sprained an ankle in Sunday's game, so Dean had taken over in the second quarter and thrown four interceptions before the final whistle. The press was all over him, which was why he'd decided to hide out at her place for a while.

Water dripped from the sink faucet, its irritating *plunk plunk* getting on her nerves. She'd known Delaney and Heath would be a match. The enticing combination of Delaney's appearance, her tomboyish athleticism, and her impeccable pedigree had predictably knocked Heath off his feet. And Delaney'd always had a weakness for macho men.

Annabelle had met Delaney twenty-one years ago at summer camp, and they'd become best friends, even though Delaney was two years younger. After their camp days had ended, they'd seen less of each other, mainly meeting in Chicago when Annabelle had visited Nana. During college, they'd drifted apart, only to reconnect a few years ago. Now they met every few months for lunch, no longer best friends, but friendly acquaintances with a shared history. For weeks now, Annabelle had been thinking about how perfect Delaney and Heath were for each other, so why had she waited so long to introduce them?

Because she'd known how perfect they'd be for each other.

She gazed over at Dean, who was tossing popcorn kernels in the air and catching them in his mouth. If only his passing game had been as accurate. She turned off the dripping faucet then slumped down at the table, a kindred soul in depression.

The refrigerator's compressor clicked off, and the kitchen

fell quiet except for the ticktock of the daisy wall clock and the soft plop of popcorn finding its target.

"Do you want to make out?" she said glumly.

He coughed up a kernel. "No!"

"You don't have to look so outraged."

His chair banged back down on all four legs. "It'd be like making out with my sister."

"You haven't got a sister."

"No, but I've got an imagination."

"Fine. I didn't want to anyway. I was just making conversation."

"You were just trying to distract yourself because you've fallen in love with the wrong guy."

"You're so full of it."

"I heard Heath's voice at the door."

"Business."

"Whatever gets you through the day." He pushed the popcorn bowl back from the edge of the table. "I'm glad you didn't let him in. It's bad enough having Bodie tail me. He won't give up."

"It's been over two months. I can't believe you still haven't found an agent. Or have you? No, never mind, I'd just tell Heath, and I don't want to be in the middle."

"You're not in the middle. You're on his side." He tilted back in the chair again. "So why didn't you take advantage of this golden opportunity to make him jealous and ask him in?"

Exactly what she'd been wondering herself except, really, what was the point? She was sick of deception, sick of keeping her guard up. She'd only invented her crush to keep from losing Heath as a client, and she no longer had to worry about that.

"I didn't feel like it."

For all his dumb-jock ways, Dean was smart as a whip, and she didn't like the way he was looking at her, so she frowned at him. "Are you wearing makeup?"

"Tinted sunblock on my chin. I've got a zit."

"It sucks being a teenager."

"If you'd invited him in, I'd have nibbled on your neck and everything."

With a sigh, she picked up the deck of cards and began to shuffle. "My deal."

Delaney stayed by Heath's side as he spent halftime traveling between the skyboxes at the Midwest Sports Dome to press the flesh of the city's movers and shakers. While he attended the Stars game, text messages were arriving from all over the country updating him on his other clients' games. He'd been working the phones on and off since early morning, talking to wives, parents, and girlfriends—even Caleb Crenshaw's grandmother—letting everybody know he was on the job. He glanced at his Black-Berry and saw a message from Bodie, who was at Lambeau Field with Sean. So far, their rookie fullback was having a great year.

Heath had been seeing Delaney for a month, although he'd been traveling so much they'd only gone out five times. Still, they talked nearly every day, and he already knew he'd found the woman he'd been searching for. This afternoon Delaney wore a black V-neck sweater, her great-grandmother's pearls, and a trendy pair of jeans perfectly cut to fit her tall, thin figure. To his surprise, she broke away from his side and headed for Jerry Pierce, a ruddy-faced man in his early sixties and the head of one of Chicago's largest brokerage firms.

She greeted Jerry with a hug that spoke of long familiarity. "How's Mandy doing?"

"In her fifth month. We have our fingers crossed."

"She'll make it full term this time, I just know it. You and Carol are going to be the best grandparents."

Heath and Jerry played in the same charity Pro Am every year, but Heath hadn't known Jerry had a daughter, let alone that she suffered problem pregnancies. This was the kind of thing

Delaney kept on top of, right along with knowing where to find the last remaining bottle of a 2002 Shotfire Ridge *cuvée* and why it was worth the effort to locate it. Even though he was a beer man, he admired her expertise, and he'd been making an effort to appreciate the vino. Football seemed to be one of the few areas where she wasn't knowledgeable, preferring more genteel sports, but she'd been making an effort to learn more.

Jerry shook Heath's hand. "Robillard's finally looking like himself this week," the older man said. "How come you haven't signed that boy yet?"

"Dean believes in taking his time."

"If he signs with anybody else, he's a fool," Delaney said loyally. "Heath is the best."

Jerry turned out to be an opera buff, another thing Heath hadn't known, and the conversation drifted to the Lyric. "Heath's a country music fan." Delaney's voice held a sweetly tolerant note. "I'm determined to convert him."

Heath glanced around the skybox, looking for Annabelle. She usually came to Stars games with Molly or one of the others, and he'd been sure he'd run into her, but no luck so far. As Delaney went on about *Don Giovanni,* Heath remembered one evening in between introductions when Annabelle had sung every word to Alan Jackson's "It's Five O'Clock Somewhere." But then Annabelle knew all kinds of useless information. Like the fact that only people with a special enzyme in their body got smelly pee when they ate asparagus, which, he had to admit, was interesting.

The door of the skybox opened, and Phoebe came in wearing the team colors, a figure-molding pale aqua knit dress with a gold scarf tossed around her neck. Heath excused himself from Jerry and guided Delaney over to introduce her.

"It's a pleasure," Delaney said with obvious sincerity.

"Annabelle's told me so much about you," Phoebe replied with a smile.

He let the women chat without worrying about Delaney

saying the wrong thing. She never did, and everybody but Bodie liked her. Not that Bodie disliked her. He just didn't think Heath should marry her. *"I'll admit the two of you look good on paper,"* he'd said last week, *"but you don't ever relax around her. You're not yourself."*

Maybe because Heath was becoming someone better. Considering the train wreck that passed for Bodie's current love life, Heath felt safe in ignoring him.

Later, Heath met up with Phoebe in the hallway outside the owner's skybox. Delaney had just headed off for the ladies' room, and Heath was chatting with Ron and Sharon McDermitt when the Stars' owner came around the corner. "Heath, can I steal you away for a minute?"

"I swear to God, whatever it is, I didn't do it. Tell her, Ron."

Ron grinned. "You're on your own, buddy." He and Sharon disappeared into the skybox.

Heath regarded Phoebe warily. "I knew I should have gotten a booster on my tetanus shot."

"I might owe you an apology."

"That's it. No more beer for me. You'll never guess what I thought you just said."

"Pay attention." She shifted her purse higher on her shoulder. "All I'm trying to say is that I might have jumped to the wrong conclusion when we were at the lake."

"Which of about a hundred wrong conclusions would that be?" He knew the answer, but she'd lose respect for him if he gave in too easily.

"That you were taking advantage of Annabelle. I hope I'm a big enough person to admit when I'm wrong, but you have to remember that you've programmed me to expect the worst. Anyway, every time I see Annabelle she talks about how thrilled she is to be making this match between you and Delaney. Her business is blossoming. And Delaney's lovely." She reached up and patted his cheek. "Maybe our little boy is finally growing up."

He couldn't believe it. After all these years had he cracked the ice with Phoebe? If so, he owed it all to Delaney.

As Phoebe disappeared into the owner's skybox, he pulled out his cell so he could share the news with Annabelle, but before he punched in her number, Delaney reappeared. He probably couldn't have reached Annabelle anyway. Unlike him, she didn't believe in leaving her phone on.

A nnabelle had never been a big opera fan, but Delaney had box seats for *Tosca*, and the Lyric's lavish production was exactly the distraction she needed to take her mind off her mother's phone call that afternoon. Her family, it seemed, had decided to descend on Chicago next month to help Annabelle celebrate her thirty-second birthday.

"Adam has a conference," Kate had said, *"and Doug and Candace want to visit some old friends. Dad and I were planning a trip to St. Louis anyway, so we'll drive up from there."*

One big, happy family.

Intermission came. "I can't believe how much I'm enjoying this," Annabelle said as she bought Delaney a glass of wine.

Unfortunately, her old friend was more interested in talking about Heath than in discussing the trials and tribulations of Tosca's doomed lovers. "Did I remember to tell you that Heath introduced me to Phoebe Calebow on Saturday? She's lovely. The whole weekend was fabulous."

Annabelle didn't want to hear about it, but Delaney was on a roll.

"I told you that Heath left for the coast yesterday, but I didn't tell you that he sent flowers again. Unfortunately, more roses, but he's basically a jock, so how much imagination can you expect?"

Annabelle loved roses, and she didn't think they were all that unimaginative.

Delaney tugged on her pearls. "Of course, my parents adore

him—you know how they are—and my brother thinks he's the best guy I've ever dated."

Annabelle's brothers would have liked Heath, too. For all the wrong reasons, but still . . .

"We'll have been together five weeks this coming Friday. Annabelle, I think this might be it. He's as close to perfect as I'll ever get." Her smile faded. "Well . . . Except for that small problem I've been telling you about."

Annabelle slowly released the air she'd been holding in her lungs. "No change?"

Delaney lowered her voice. "I was all over him in the car on Saturday. It was obvious I was getting to him, but he didn't follow up on it. I know I'm being paranoid—and I'd never say this to anybody else—but are you absolutely sure he's not gay? There was this guy in college, totally macho, but he turned out to have a boyfriend."

"I don't *think* he's gay," Annabelle heard herself say.

"No," Delaney shook her head firmly. "I'm sure he's not."

"You're probably right."

The bell rang to announce the end of intermission, and Annabelle slithered back to her seat like the miserable snake she was.

R ain pummeled the window behind Portia's desk, and a bolt of lightning split the late afternoon sky.

". . . and so we're giving our two weeks' notice," Briana said.

Portia felt the storm's fury pricking her skin.

The slit of Briana's black skirt fell open as she crossed her long legs. "We only finalized the details yesterday," she said, "which is why we couldn't tell you earlier."

"We'll stretch it to three weeks if you really need us." Kiki leaned forward in her chair, her brow furrowed with concern "We know you haven't replaced Diana yet, and we don't want to leave you in a bind."

Portia repressed a hysterical bubble of laughter. How much worse could things get than to lose her two remaining assistants?

"We've been talking about this for six months." Briana's bright smile invited Portia to be happy right along with her. "We both love to ski, and Denver's a great city."

"A fabulous city," Kiki said. "There are tons of singles, and with everything we've learned from you, we know we're ready to start our own business."

Briana tilted her head, her straight blond hair falling over her shoulder. "We can't thank you enough for showing us the ropes, Portia. I'll admit, there were times when we resented how tough you were, but now we're grateful."

Portia pressed her sweaty palms together. "I'm glad to hear it."

The two women exchanged glances. Briana gave Kiki an almost imperceptible nod. Kiki fiddled with the top button on her blouse. "Briana and I were wondering—hoping, really—that maybe . . . Would you mind if we called you every once in a while? I know we're going to have a million questions starting out."

They wanted her to mentor them. They were walking out, leaving her with no trained assistants, and they wanted her to help them. "Of course," Portia said stiffly. "Call me whenever you need to."

"Thanks so much," Briana said. "Really. We mean it."

Portia managed what she hoped was a gracious nod, but her stomach roiled. She didn't plan what she said next. The words just came out. "I can tell that you're anxious to get started, and I wouldn't dream of holding you back. Things have been quiet lately, so there's really no need for either of you to hang around another two weeks. I'll manage fine." She waved her fingers toward the door, shooing them away, as if they were a pair of mischievous schoolgirls. "Go on. Finish up what you need to and take off."

"Really?" Briana's eyes turned to saucers. "You don't mind?"

"Of course not," Portia said. "Why would I mind?"

They weren't about to look a gift horse in the mouth, and they rushed toward the door. "Thanks, Portia. You're the best."

"The best," Portia whispered to herself when she was finally alone. Another thunderclap rattled the window. She folded her arms on her desk and put her head down. She couldn't do this anymore.

That night she sat in her darkened living room and stared at nothing. It had been almost six weeks since she'd last seen Bodie, and she ached for him. She felt rootless, adrift, lonely to the very bottom of her soul. Her personal life lay in pieces around her, and Power Matches was falling apart. Not only because of her assistants' desertion, but also because she'd lost her focus.

She thought of what had happened with Heath. Unlike Portia, Annabelle had seized her opportunity and used it brilliantly. *One introduction each,* he'd said. While Portia had followed her seriously flawed instincts and waited, Annabelle had pounced and introduced him to Delaney Lightfield. It couldn't have been more ironic. Portia had known the Lightfields for years. She'd watched Delaney grow up. But she'd been so busy falling apart that she'd never once thought of introducing her to Heath.

She glanced at the clock. Not even nine. She couldn't face another sleepless night. For weeks she'd been resisting taking a sleeping pill, hating the idea of being dependent. But if she didn't get a decent night's rest soon, she'd go crazy. Her heart started its panicky flutter. She pressed her hand to her chest. What if she died right here? Who would care? Only Bodie.

She couldn't bear it any longer, so she tossed on her hot pink trench coat, grabbed her purse, and took the elevator down to the lobby. Even though it was dark, she slipped on her Chanel sunglasses in case she ran into one of her neighbors. She couldn't bear the thought of anyone seeing her like this—without her makeup, a pair of ratty sweatpants peeking out from under a Marc Jacobs trench coat.

She hurried around the corner to the all-night drugstore. As she reached the aisle with the sleeping remedies, she saw them. Piled in a wire bin marked 75% OFF. Dusty purple boxes of aging yellow marshmallow Easter chicks. The bin sat at the end of the aisle across from the sleep aids. Her mother had bought those chicks every Easter and set them out in her Franklin Mint teddy bear bowl. Portia still remembered the grit of the sugar crystals between her teeth.

"You need some help?"

The clerk was a chubby Hispanic girl who wore too much makeup and wouldn't be able to comprehend that some things were beyond help. Portia shook her head, and the girl disappeared. She turned her attention to the sleeping pills, but the boxes swam before her eyes. Her gaze drifted back to the bin of chicks. Easter had been five months ago. They'd be rubbery by now.

A patrol car blew past outside, its siren blaring, and Portia wanted to shove her fingers in her ears. Some of the purple Easter chick cartons were dented, and a couple of the cellophane windows had split open. Disgusting. Why didn't they throw them out?

Overhead, the fluorescent light fixture hummed. The overly made-up clerk was staring at her. With a good night's sleep, Portia'd feel like her old self again. She had to choose something quickly. But what?

The noise from the fluorescent lights bored through her temples. Her pulse raced. She couldn't keep standing here. Her feet began to move, and her purse fell low on her arm. Instead of reaching for a sleeping aid, she reached into the bin for the marshmallow chicks. A trickle of perspiration slid between her breasts. She scooped up one box, then another, and another. Outside, a taxi horn blared. Her shoulder bumped a display of cleaning supplies, and a stack of sponges fell to the floor. She stumbled to the register.

Another kid stood behind the counter, this one pimply-faced and chinless. He picked up a box of chicks. "I love these things."

She fixed her eyes on the rack of tabloids. He ran the box over the scanner. Everyone in her building shopped at this drugstore, and a lot of them walked their dogs at night. What if someone wandered in here and saw her?

The boy held up a box with a torn cellophane window. "This is ripped."

She flinched. "They're . . . for my niece's kindergarten class."

"Do you want me to get another one?"

"No, it's fine."

"But it's ripped."

"I said it's fine!" She'd shouted, and the kid looked startled. She contorted her mouth into a travesty of a smile. "They're . . . making necklaces."

He looked at her as if she were crazy. Her heart raced faster. He started scanning again. The door opened, and an elderly couple entered the store. No one she knew, but she'd seen them before. He scanned the last box. She thrust a twenty at him, and he scrutinized it like a treasury agent. The chicks lay scattered across the counter for anyone to see, eight purple boxes, six chicks to a box. He handed over her change. She shoved it in her purse, not bothering with her wallet, just throwing it inside.

The phone by the register rang, and he answered it. "Hey, Mark, what's up? No, I don't get off till midnight. Sucks."

She snatched the sack from him and shoved the rest of the boxes inside. One fell to the floor. She left it there.

"Hey, lady, you want your receipt?"

She hurried into the street. It had started to rain again. She clutched the sack to her chest and dodged a fresh-faced young woman who still believed in happily-ever-after. Rain soaked her hair, and by the time she got back home, she was shivering. She dumped the sack on her dining room table. Some of the boxes spilled out.

She shrugged off her trench coat and tried to catch her breath. She should make herself a cup of tea, turn on some music, maybe the television. But she did none of those things. Instead, she sank into the chair at the foot of the table and slowly began lining up the boxes in front of her.

Seven boxes. Six chicks to a box.

Hands trembling, she started peeling off the cellophane and tearing open the flaps. Bits of purple cardboard dropped to the floor. Chicks tumbled out along with a gritty snow of yellow sugar.

Finally all the boxes were opened. She pushed the last remnants of cardboard and cellophane to the carpet. Only the chicks were left. As she gazed at them, she knew Bodie had been right about her. All her life, she'd been driven by fear, so frightened of falling short that she'd forgotten how to live.

She began to eat the chicks, one by one.

Chapter Twenty

♥

Construction had clogged Denver's midday traffic, dampening Heath's already foul mood. For six weeks, he'd shown Delaney nothing but respect. This was his future wife, after all, and he didn't want her to think he was only after her for sex. An image of Annabelle naked sprang into his mind. He gritted his teeth and laid on the horn of the rental car. The only reason he kept thinking about Annabelle was because he was worried. No matter how much he nosed around, he couldn't find out for sure if she and Dean were sleeping together.

The distinct possibility that Dean was taking advantage of Annabelle made him crazy, but he forced his thoughts back to Delaney where they belonged. During their last couple of dates, she'd started sending strong signals that she was ready for sex, which meant he had to make plans, but that wasn't as simple as it seemed. For one thing, she had roommates, so he'd have to take her to his house, and how could he do that until he'd moved his workout equipment to the basement? He wanted her to like his house, but he'd already discovered that she didn't care much for contemporary architecture, so he'd probably have to sell it. A couple of months ago, that would have been fine, but something about seeing it through Annabelle's eyes had made him start to look at the place differently. He hoped he could talk Delaney into changing her mind.

He flipped the bird at the jerk who'd just cut him off and pondered a bigger problem. He couldn't shake the old-fashioned notion that he should propose to Delaney before they slept together. She was Delaney Lightfield, not some football groupie. True, they'd only dated for six weeks, but it was obvious to everybody except Bodie that they were perfect for each other, so why wait?

Except how could he propose without a ring?

For a brief moment, he considered asking Annabelle to pick one out, but even he knew he could only delegate so much. Traffic ground to a stop. He'd be late for his eleven o'clock meeting. He drummed his fingers on the steering wheel. The difficulty of trying to propose to Delaney without mentioning the *love* word flashed through his mind, but he'd work that out later. For now, he had to figure out what to do about the ring. She'd have lots of opinions about diamonds, and he suspected his philosophy of "the bigger the better" might not be in line with her upper-crust way of thinking. She'd want something discreet with a perfect cut. Then there was that color crap people talked about. Frankly, one diamond looked pretty much like another to him.

The traffic still wasn't moving. Heath thought it over. What the hell. He reached for his cell and made the call.

For once, Annabelle answered instead of her voice mail.

He kept it brief, but she was in one of her uncooperative moods, and even with horns blaring around him, she shouted so loud he had to hold the phone away from his ear.

"You want me to do *what*?"

Annabelle stormed around the house, slamming cupboard doors and kicking over her office wastebasket. She couldn't believe she'd let herself fall for such a complete and utter idiot.

Heath wanted her to check out engagement rings for De-laney! What a shitty day. And with her family birthday party coming up in a couple of weeks, the future didn't look any cheerier.

She grabbed her jacket and headed out for a walk. Maybe the sunny October afternoon would brighten her spirits. The truth was, she should be on top of the world. Mr. Bronicki and Mrs. Valerio were moving in together. *"We'd like to get married,"* they'd explained to Annabelle, *"but we can't afford it, so we're doing the next best thing."* Even more exciting, Annabelle might have made her first permanent match. Janine and Ray Fiedler seemed to be falling in love.

She couldn't have been happier for her friend, and she finally smiled. Once Ray had gotten rid of his comb-over, his attitude had also improved, and he'd turned out to be a decent guy. Janine had been afraid he'd be repulsed by her mastectomy, but he thought she was the most beautiful woman in the world.

Annabelle had other reasons to be happy. Things were looking serious between Ernie Marks, her shy elementary school principal, and Wendy, the bubbly architect. She'd talked Melanie out of her infatuation with John Nager. And thanks to the publicity from Heath's match with Delaney, her business had been growing like crazy. Finally, she had enough money in the bank to start thinking about buying a new car.

Instead, she thought about Heath and Delaney. How could he be so blind? Despite everything Annabelle had once believed, Delaney wasn't the right woman for him. She was too contained, too polished. Too perfect.

Heath had the ring in his pocket, but his tongue kept sticking to the roof of his mouth. This was stupid. He never let pressure get to him, yet here he was with a bad case of flop sweat.

This afternoon he'd sent his secretary to pick up the ring he'd chosen as soon as he'd gotten back from Denver two weeks ago. He and Delaney had just finished a five-hundred-dollar dinner at Charlie Trotter's. The lighting was muted, the music soft, the atmosphere perfect. All he had to do was take her hand and say the magic words. *Would you do me the honor of being my wife?*

He'd decided to dodge the whole "I love you" thing by keeping it specific. He'd tell her he loved her intelligence; he loved the way she looked. He definitely loved playing golf with her. Most of all, he loved her polish, the sense that she'd finish him. If she pressed him on the love thing, he could always tell her he was fairly sure he *would* love her at some time in the future, after they'd been married for a while and he was certain she'd stick, but somehow he didn't think she'd see his reassurance in the same positive light he did, so best to deflect.

He wondered if she'd get teary-eyed when he gave her the ring. Probably not. She wasn't too emotional, which was another positive. Afterward, they'd go back to his place and celebrate their engagement in bed. He'd make sure he took it slow. He sure as hell wouldn't rush her like he'd rushed Annabelle.

Damn, that had been fun.

Fun, but not serious. Making love with Annabelle had been exciting, crazy, definitely hot, but it hadn't been important. The only reason he thought about it so often was because he couldn't repeat the experience, so it had taken on the lure of the forbidden.

He fingered the robin's egg blue jewelry box in his pocket. He didn't much care for the ring he'd chosen. It was only a little over a carat because Delaney didn't like anything ostentatious. But he liked a little ostentation, especially when it came to the ring he'd be putting on his future wife's finger. Still, he wasn't the one who'd have to wear the puny son of a bitch, so he'd keep his opinions to himself.

Okay . . . Time to get to work here. Steer a careful path around the love discussion, give her the fucking ring, and propose. Then take her back to his place and seal the deal.

His cell vibrated in his pocket, right next to the ring box. Annabelle had given him strict orders not to take calls when he was with Delaney, but wouldn't she have to get used to this if they were going to get married? "Champion." He shot his future wife an apologetic look.

Annabelle's voice hissed through the receiver like a leaky radiator. "Get over here right now."

"I'm kind of in the middle."

"I don't care if you're in Antarctica. Get your sorry ass over here."

He heard a male voice in the background. Make that male voices. He sat straighter in his chair. "Are you okay?"

"Does it sound like I'm okay?"

"It sounds like you're pissed."

But she'd already hung up.

Half an hour later, he and Delaney were rushing up the sidewalk toward Annabelle's front porch. "It's not like her to get hysterical," Delaney said for the second time. "Something must really be wrong."

He'd already explained that Annabelle had been more enraged than hysterical, but the concept of rage seemed foreign to Delaney, which didn't bode well for the times when he had to watch the Sox lose another close one.

"It sounds like some kind of party." She pressed the bell, but nobody was going to hear anything over the hip-hop music blaring from inside, and he reached in front of her to push the door open.

As they stepped inside, he saw Sean Palmer and half a dozen of his Bears teammates draped around Annabelle's reception room, which wasn't alarming in itself, but through the door leading to the kitchen, he spotted another batch of players, all of them Chicago Stars. Annabelle's office seemed to be neutral territory with five or six players not exactly mingling, but scoping one another out from opposite corners while Annabelle stood in the middle of the archway. Heath could see why she might be nervous. Neither team had forgotten last year's controversial call that had given the Stars a narrow and highly disputed victory over their rivals. He couldn't help wondering what part of her brain had been on vacation when she'd let all of these guys in at the same time.

"Hey, everybody, Jerry Maguire's here."

Heath responded to Sean Palmer's greeting with a wave. Delaney moved a little closer to his side.

"How come you ain't got no cable, Annabelle?" Eddie Skinner protested over the top of the music. "You got cable upstairs?"

"No," Annabelle retorted, pushing her way into the reception room. "And get your big-ass shoes off my sofa cushions this minute." She did a one-eighty, her finger pointed like a gun at Tremaine Russell, the best running back the Bears had seen in a decade. "Use a freakin' coaster under your glass, Tremaine!"

Heath stood back and grinned. She looked like a harried Cub Scout den mother, hands on hips, red hair flying, eyes shooting firecrackers.

Tremaine snatched up his glass and wiped the end table with the sleeve of his designer sweater. "Sorry, Annabelle."

Annabelle caught Heath's grin and marched forward, pinning her wrath on him. "This is all your fault. You have at least four clients here, none of whom I knew personally a year ago. If it weren't for you, I'd be just another fan watching them destroy each other from a safe distance."

Her hissy fit was getting everybody's attention, and someone turned the music down so they could all listen in. She jerked her head toward the kitchen. "They've drunk everything in the house, including a pitcher of African violet plant food I'd just mixed up and was stupid enough to leave on the counter."

Tremaine punched Eddie in the shoulder. "I told you it tasted weird."

Eddie shrugged. "Tasted okay to me."

"They've also ordered hundreds of dollars' worth of Chinese food, which I do not intend to see all over this rug, so everybody is going to . . . *eat in the kitchen*."

"And pizza." Jason Kent, a Stars second stringer, called out from someplace near the refrigerator. "Don't forget we ordered pizzas, too."

"When did my house turn into a hangout for every grossly overpaid, terminally pampered professional football player in northern Illinois?"

"We like it here," Jason said. "It reminds us of home."

"Plus, no women around." Leandro Collins, the Bears' first-string tight end emerged from the office munching on a bag of chips. "There's times when you need a rest from the ladies."

Annabelle shot out her arm and smacked him in the side of the head. "Don't forget who you're talking to."

Leandro had a short fuse, and he'd been known to take out a ref here and there when he didn't like a call, but the tight end merely rubbed the side of his head and grimaced. "Just like my mama."

"Mine, too," Tremaine said with happy nod.

Annabelle spun on Heath. "Their *mother*! I'm thirty-one years old, and I remind them of their mothers."

"You act like my mother," Sean pointed out, unwisely as it transpired, because he got a swat in the head next.

Heath exchanged sympathetic looks with the boys, then gave Annabelle his full attention, speaking softly and patiently. "Tell me how this happened, sweetheart."

Annabelle threw up her hands. "I have no idea. In the summer it was just Dean dropping in. Then he brought Jason and Dewitt with him. Then Arté asked me to keep my eye on Sean, so I invited him over—just once, mind you—and he showed up with Leandro and Matt. A Star here, a Bear there . . . One thing led to another. And now I have a potentially deadly riot on my hands, right in the middle of my living room."

"I told you not to worry about that," Jason said. "This is neutral territory."

"Yeah, right." Her nostrils flared. "Neutral territory until somebody gets mad, and then you guys'll be all, 'We're sorry, Annabelle, but you seem to be missing your front windows and *half the second floor.*'"

"Only person's been mad since we got here is you," Sean muttered.

Annabelle's expression turned so hilariously murderous that Eddie snorted beer—or maybe African violet fertilizer—right out through his nose, which cracked everybody up.

Annabelle lunged for Heath, grabbing his shirtfront in her fists, pulling herself up on her toes, and hissing at him through clenched teeth. "They're going to get drunk, and then one of these idiots is going to plow his Mercedes into a car full of nuns. And I'll be liable. This is Illinois. We have host laws in this state."

For the first time Heath was disappointed in her. "Didn't you get their keys?"

"Of course I got their keys. Do you think I'm nuts? But—"

The front door blew open, and Mr. Hot Shit Robillard waltzed in all decked out in Oakleys, diamonds, and cowboy boots. He gave a two-finger wave like the fucking king of England.

"Oh, shit. Kill me now." Annabelle's grip on his shirt tightened. "Somebody's going to take him out tonight. I can feel it. He'll end up with a broken arm or crippled, and then I'll have to deal with Phoebe."

Heath gently pried her fingers loose. "Relax. Lover Boy can take care of himself."

"All I wanted was to be a matchmaker. Is that so hard to understand? A simple matchmaker." She slumped back on her heels. "My life is crap."

Leandro frowned. "Annabelle, you're starting to get on my nerves."

Three long strides brought Robillard to her side. He gave Heath a long look, then looped his arm around Annabelle and kissed her hard on the lips. Fury exploded behind Heath's eyelids. His right hand curled into a fist, but this was Annabelle's house, and she'd never forgive him if he did what he wanted to.

"Annabelle's my woman," Dean announced as he broke the kiss and gazed into her eyes. "Anybody gives her trouble has to deal with me . . . and my offensive line."

Annabelle looked annoyed, which made Heath feel a hell of a lot better. "I can take care of myself. What I can't deal with is a house full of drunken morons."

"That is so harsh," Eddie said, looking injured.

Dean stroked her shoulder. "You guys know how irrational pregnant women can get."

Way too many heads started nodding.

"Did you take that test like I told you, baby doll?" Dean slipped his arm around her again. "Do you know yet if you're carryin' my love child?"

Apparently that was too much for Annabelle, because she started to laugh. "I need a beer." She grabbed Tremaine's bottle and drained what was left.

"You shouldn't drink if you're pregnant," Eddie Skinner said with a frown.

Leandro swatted him in the head.

Heath realized he was having the best time he'd had in weeks.

Which reminded him of Delaney.

Annabelle had been too preoccupied to spot her through the crowd, and Delaney hadn't moved from her place inside the front door. She stood with her back to the wall and that ever-pleasant smile frozen on her face, but her eyes were glazed and just a little wild. Delaney Lightfield, horsewoman, champion trapshooter, golfer, and expert skier, had just glimpsed her future, and she didn't like what she saw.

"Don't anybody let me eat more than one egg roll."

Annabelle set her empty bottle on a stack of magazines. "I can hardly zip my jeans now." She rolled her eyes at Eddie, who was frowning at her. "And I'm *not* pregnant."

Robillard still wanted to make trouble. "Only because I haven't been trying hard enough. We'll take care of that tonight, baby doll."

Annabelle rolled her eyes and looked around for a place to sit, but every chair was occupied, so she ended up in Sean's lap. She sat there primly, but comfortably. "And I can only have one slice of pizza."

Heath needed to do something about Delaney, and he made his way over to her. "Sorry about this."

"I should mix," Delaney said determinedly.

"Not if you don't want to."

"It's just . . . It's a little overwhelming. The house is so small. And there are so many of them."

"Let's go outside."

"Yes, that's probably the best idea."

Heath drew her onto the front porch. For a few moments, they didn't speak. Delaney gazed at the house across the street, wrapping her arms around herself. He rested his shoulder against a post, the ring box heavy against his hip. "I can't leave her," he said.

"Oh, no, no. I wouldn't expect you to."

He stuffed his hands in his pockets. "I guess you needed to see my life for what it is. This is a pretty good sample."

"Yes. It was silly of me. I didn't . . ." She gave a tight, self-deprecating laugh. "I like the skybox better."

He understood, and he smiled. "The skybox does keep reality at a distance."

"I'm sorry," she said. "I imagined it differently."

"I know you did."

Somebody turned the music up again. She slipped her thumbs under the collar of her jacket and gazed around. "It's only a matter of time before the neighbors call the police."

The cops tended to look the other way when the city's top athletes misbehaved, but he doubted that would reassure her.

Her fingers crept to her pearls. "I don't understand how Annabelle can be so comfortable with all that chaos."

He settled on the simplest explanation. "She has brothers."

"So do I."

"Annabelle is one of those people who gets bored easily. I guess you could say she creates her own excitement." Just like him.

She shook her head. "But it's so . . . disruptive."

Which was exactly why Annabelle got herself into this sort of thing.

"My life's pretty disruptive," he said.

"Yes. Yes, I see that now."

A few moments of silence ticked by. "Would you like me to call you a cab?" he asked quietly.

She hesitated, then nodded. "That might be for the best."

While they waited, they apologized to each other, both of them saying pretty much the same thing, that they'd thought it would work out, but it was better they'd found out now that it wouldn't. The ten minutes it took for the cab to arrive lasted forever. Heath gave the driver a fifty and helped Delaney in. She smiled up at him, more thoughtful than sad. She was a terrific person, and he experienced a fleeting moment of regret that he wasn't the kind of man who could be satisfied with beauty, brains, intelligence, and athletic ability. No, it took the Tinker Bell factor to suck him in. As the cab drove away, he felt himself relax for the first time since the night they'd met.

The food had arrived while they'd waited outside, but when he reentered the house, nobody was eating. Instead, they were all jammed into the living room, the music turned down, their attention focused on an upturned NASCAR cap sitting in the general vicinity of Annabelle's feet. As he moved closer, he saw an assortment of diamond studs shining in the bottom.

Annabelle spotted him and grinned. "I'm supposed to close

my eyes, pick a stud, and sleep with whoever it belongs to. A stud for a stud. How fun is that?"

Dean raised his head from across the room. "Just so you know, Heathcliff, both of mine are still in my ears."

"That's because you cheap, bitch." Dewitt Gilbert, Dean's favorite wide receiver, slapped him on the back.

Annabelle smiled at Heath. "They're just goofing around. They know I won't do it."

"You might," Gary Sweeney said. "There's a good fifteen carats in that hat."

"Damn. I've always wanted to sleep with a natural red-head." Reggie O'Shea whipped the jewel-encrusted crucifix from around his neck and dropped it in the hat.

The men gazed down at it.

"That's just wrong," Leandro said.

There were enough mutters of agreement that Reggie retrieved his necklace.

Annabelle sighed, and Heath heard honest-to-God regret in her voice. "This has been fun, but the food's getting cold. Sean, that is a gorgeous set of studs, but your mother would kill me."

Not to mention what Heath would do.

Sometime around two in the morning, the beer supply a couple of the guys had been secretly replenishing finally ran out, and the crowd began to thin. Annabelle put Heath in charge of conducting field sobriety tests. He called cabs and shoved drunks into the few cars with sober drives. Just one fight had erupted all evening, and it wasn't over car keys. Dean took exception to his teammate Dewitt's statement that the only reason a guy would buy a Porsche instead of a kick-ass car like an Escalade was to match the color of his lace panties. Two Bears players had to pull them apart.

"So tell me the truth," Annabelle had said to Heath at the time. "Did they really go to college?"

"Yeah, but not necessarily to their classes."

By two-thirty, Annabelle had fallen asleep at one end of the couch with Leandro on the other, while Heath and Dean cleaned up the worst of the mess in the kitchen. Heath tossed Dean a plastic trash bag. "Hide those empty whiskey bottles."

"Since nobody got killed, she probably won't care."

"No sense in taking chances. She was pretty riled up tonight."

They shoved the worst of the food mess into trash bags and carried them out to the alley. Dean gazed at Sherman in disgust. "She actually tried to talk me into trading cars with her. She said driving that heap for a couple of days would help me stay in touch with the real world."

"Not to mention giving her a shot at your Porsche."

"I do believe I pointed that out." They headed toward the house. "So how's come you haven't tried to shove a contract under my nose tonight?"

"Losing interest." Heath held the back door open for him. "I'm used to guys who are more decisive."

"I'm decisive as hell. I'll have you know the only reason I haven't signed with anybody yet is because I'm having too much fun being courted. You wouldn't believe the shit agents'll send you, and I'm not just talking about front-row concert tickets. The Zagorskis bought me a Segway."

"Yeah, well, while you're enjoying yourself, remember that Nike's forgetting all the reasons they need your candy-ass face smiling down on the homeless from their billboards."

"Speaking of presents . . ." Dean leaned against the counter, his expression cagey. "I've been admiring that new Rolex Submariner watch I've seen in the stores. Those folks sure do know how to make a great timepiece."

"How about I send you a flower arrangement that matches your pretty blue eyes instead?"

"That's cold, man." He dredged his keys from Annabelle's

Hello Kitty cookie jar along with an Oreo. "It's hard to see how you got to be such a hotshot agent with that kind of attitude."

Heath smiled. "It looks like you'll never find out. Your loss."

Robillard snapped the Oreo in two with his teeth, gave him a cocky grin, and sauntered from the kitchen. "Later, Heathcliff."

Heath sent Leandro off in a cab. He couldn't stop grinning. There wasn't one thing between Dean and Annabelle except mischief. Annabelle didn't love him. She treated him exactly the same way she treated the other players, like they were overgrown kids. All that crap she'd fed Heath was totally bogus. And if Dean had been in love with her, he sure as hell wouldn't have left her alone with another man tonight.

She lay on her side, little puffs of air stirring the lock of hair that had fallen over her mouth. He fetched a blanket, and she didn't stir as he covered her with it. He found himself wondering how bad it would be to reach under that blanket and slip off her jeans so she could sleep more comfortably?

Bad.

Try as he might, he could only come up with one reason Annabelle had set up her charade with Dean. Because she was in love with Heath, and she wanted to save her pride. Funny, feisty, glorious Annabelle Granger loved him. His grin grew broader, and he felt lighthearted for the first time in months. Amazing what clarity could do for a man's peace of mind.

The phone awakened him. He reached across the nightstand for it and muttered into the mouthpiece. "Champion."

There was a long silence. He turned his face deeper into the pillow and drifted.

"Heath?"

He rubbed his hand over his mouth. "Yeah?"

"Heath?"

"Phoebe?"

He heard an angry, in-drawn breath and then the crack of a broken connection. His eyes shot open. Another few seconds passed before he confirmed what he feared. This wasn't his bedroom, the phone he'd answered didn't belong to him, and it was—he gazed at the clock—not quite eight in the morning.

Great. Now Phoebe knew he'd spent the night at Annabelle's. He was screwed. Double screwed, once Phoebe heard that he'd broken up with Delaney.

Wide awake, he climbed out of Annabelle's bed, which unfortunately didn't contain Annabelle. Despite the career implications of what had just happened, his good mood from last night wouldn't go away. He headed downstairs from the attic to shower, then shaved with Annabelle's Gillette Daisy. He didn't have a change of clothes, which meant he could either pull on yesterday's boxers or go commando. He opted for the latter, then slipped into last night's dress shirt, badly wrinkled from Annabelle's fists.

When he got downstairs, he found her still curled into a ball on the couch, the blanket pulled up to her chin, one bare foot sticking out. He'd never had a foot fetish, but there was something about that sweet little arch that made him want to do all kinds of semiobscene things with it. But then most parts of Annabelle's body seemed to have that effect on him, which should have been a big clue. He pulled his eyes away from her toes and headed for the kitchen.

He and Dean hadn't done the best job of cleaning, and the morning light revealed remnants of Chinese food stuck to the counters. While the coffee brewed, he grabbed some paper towels and got up the worst of it. By the time he looked into the other room again, Annabelle had made it into a sitting position. Her hair draped most of her face except for the tip of her nose and one cheekbone.

"Where are my jeans?" she muttered. "Never mind. We'll

talk about it later." She pulled the blanket around her and staggered toward the stairs.

He went back into the kitchen and poured himself coffee. As he was about to take the first sip, he noticed that a big pot of African violets had been shoved under the table. He didn't know much about plants, but the foliage on this one looked a lot the worse for wear. He couldn't actually prove anybody had peed in it, but why take the chance? He took it outside and hid it under the back steps.

He'd just finished reading the motivational messages on Annabelle's refrigerator when he heard a rustling noise. He turned to enjoy the sight of Annabelle shuffling into the kitchen. She hadn't made it as far as the shower, but she'd twisted her hair up and washed her face, leaving her eyelashes spiky and her cheeks flushed. A pair of plaid cotton sleeping boxers stuck out from beneath an oversize purple sweatshirt. He followed the line of her bare legs down to her feet, which were tucked into ratty chartreuse running shoes. All in all, she looked sleepy, rumpled, and sexy.

He handed her a mug of coffee. She waited until she'd had her first sip before she acknowledged him, a little gravel still in her voice. "Do I want to know who took off my jeans?"

He thought it over. "Robillard. Guy's a sleaze."

She glowered at him. "I wasn't that out of it. You copped a feel when you unzipped them."

He couldn't have looked repentant if he tried. "Hand slipped."

She sank down at the kitchen table. "Did I imagine it, or was Delaney here last night?"

"She was here."

"Why didn't she stay and help out?"

Now came the tricky part. He made a play of rooting around in the cupboard for something to eat, even though he knew she'd been cleaned out. After he'd shuffled around a couple of cans of

stewed tomatoes, he closed the door. "The whole thing was a little too much for her."

She sat up straighter. "What do you mean?"

Too late, he realized he should have been figuring out how
he wanted to spin this instead of hiding African violets and
standing in front of the refrigerator reading inspiring quotes
from Oprah. Maybe a shrug would help stave off this particular
discussion until she was wide awake. He gave it a try.

It didn't work.

"I don't understand." Annabelle untucked the leg she'd
crooked under her hip and started looking worried. "She told
me she was starting to like football."

"As it turns out, not when it's quite so up close and personal."

The lines on her forehead deepened. "I'll coach her
through it. They're only intimidating if you let them get the
upper hand."

He shouldn't smile, but wasn't this exactly why his new
plan would work so much better than the old one? From the
very beginning, Annabelle had made him happy, but he'd been
so focused in the wrong direction that he hadn't understood
what that meant. Annabelle wasn't the woman of his dreams.
Far from it. His dreams had been the product of insecurity, im-
maturity, and misdirected ambition. No, Annabelle was the
woman of his future . . . the woman of his happiness.

His clearer vision told him she wouldn't take his news
about Delaney well, especially when he couldn't quite rein in
his smile. "The thing is . . . Delaney and I are over."

Annabelle's coffee mug dropped to the table with a thud,
and she rose from the chair. "No. You're not over. This is just a
bump in the road."

"I'm afraid not. Last night she got a good look at my life,
and what she saw didn't make her happy."

"I'll fix it. Once she understands—"

"No, Annabelle," he said firmly. "This one can't be fixed. I
don't want to marry her."

She exploded. "You don't want to marry *anyone*!"

"That's not . . . exactly true."

"It *is* true. And I'm sick of it. I'm sick of you." Her arms started to flail. "You're making me crazy, and I can't take it anymore. You're fired, Mr. Champion. This time *I'm* firing *you*."

It was an impressive display of temper, so he proceeded cautiously. "I'm a client," he pointed out. "You can't fire me."

She bored into him with those honey eyes. "I just did."

"In my defense, I had good intentions." He reached into his pocket and pulled out the jeweler's box. "I was planning to propose last night. We were at Charlie Trotter's. The food was great, the mood perfect, and I had the ring. But just as I got ready to give it to her . . . you called."

He paused and let her draw her own conclusions, which she, being female, was quick to do.

"Oh, my God. It was me. I'm responsible."

A good agent always shifted the blame, but as her consternation grew, he knew he had to come clean. "Your phone call wasn't the real problem. I'd been trying to give her the ring all evening, but I couldn't seem to get it out of my pocket. That's got to tell you something right there."

By putting the blame where it belonged, he set her off again. "Nobody's right for you! I swear, you'd find something wrong with the Virgin Mary." She snatched the ring box from him, flipped it open, and curled her lip. "This was the best you could do? You're a multimillionaire!"

"Exactly!" If he'd needed any more proof that Annabelle Granger was a woman in a million, this was it. "Don't you see? She likes everything subtle. If I'd chosen anything bigger, she'd have been embarrassed. I hate that ring. Imagine how the guys would react if they saw a puny rock like that on my wife's finger."

She snapped the lid shut and shoved the box back into his hand. "You're still fired."

"I understand." He slipped it into his pocket, took a last swig of coffee, and headed for the door.

"I think it'll be better for both of us if we cut if off right here."

He hoped that tremor he heard in her voice wasn't all in his imagination. "Do you now?" The urge to kiss away her outrage nearly overwhelmed him. But while short-term gratification was tempting, he needed to focus on the long term, so he merely smiled and left her alone.

Outside, the morning air held the crisp smoky scent of autumn. He breathed it in and, with a light step, headed down the street to his car. Watching her with the men last night had opened his eyes to something he should have realized weeks ago. Annabelle Granger was his perfect match.

Chapter Twenty-one

Ever since the day Annabelle had walked into Heath's office, her life had been a Ferris wheel spinning at triple speed. She'd soar to the top, hang there for a few blissful seconds, then take a stomach-turning plummet to the bottom. As she got ready for her birthday party, she told herself she was glad she'd fired him. He was crazy. Even worse, he'd made her crazy. At least tonight she wouldn't have time to think about him. Instead, she'd be making sure her family saw her as she was, no longer a failure but an almost-successful, just-turned-thirty-two-year-old businesswoman who didn't need anybody's advice or pity. Perfect for You might not be a candidate for the Fortune 500, but at least it was finally turning a profit.

She screwed the top back on a tube of lip gloss and headed across the hall from the bathroom to the full-length mirror in Nana's bedroom. She liked what she saw. Her cocktail dress, a long-sleeved A-line, had been a splurge, but she didn't regret a penny. The flattering off-the-shoulder neckline made her neck look long and graceful, as well as dramatizing her face and hair. She could have chosen the dress in safe, conservative black, but she'd opted for peach instead. She loved the dramatic juxtaposition of the soft pastel with her red hair, which was behaving perfectly for a change, floating around her face in a pretty tousle and providing peekaboo glimpses of a delicate pair of lacy gold chandeliers. Her butter-cream stilettos gave her a few extra inches of height, but not nearly as much stature as the man on her arm would provide.

"You're bringing a date?" Kate's astonishment over break-fast at her parents' hotel that morning still grated, but Annabelle had held her tongue. While Dean's relative youth might work against her, the Grangers were huge football fans. With the ex-ception of Candace, the family had followed the Stars for years, and she could only hope that Dean's status would compensate for his youth and diamond studs.

She took one last look at her reflection. Candace would be wearing Max Mara, but so what? Her sister-in-law was an inse-cure, social-climbing dork. Annabelle wished Doug had brought Jamison instead, but her nephew was home in California with a nanny. Annabelle glanced at her watch. Her trophy date wouldn't be picking her up for another twenty minutes. Before Dean had agreed to do this, she'd had to promise to be at his beck and call for the rest of her natural life, but it would be worth it.

As she headed downstairs, she grew uncomfortably aware that there was something pathetic about a now thirty-two-year-old woman still trying to earn her family's approval. Maybe when she was forty she'd have gotten past this. Or maybe not. Face it, she had reason to be apprehensive. The last time she'd been with her family, they'd staged an intervention.

"You have so much potential, darling," Kate had said over Christmas Eve eggnog on the lanai of their Naples home. *"We love you too much to stand by and watch you waste it."*

"It's fine to be a screwup when you're twenty-one," Doug had said. *"But if you haven't gotten serious about a career by the time you're thirty, you start looking like a loser."*

"Doug's right," Dr. Adam had said. *"We can't always be watching out for you. You need to dig in."*

"At least think about how your lifestyle reflects on the rest of the family." That had come from Candace, after she'd tossed back her fourth eggnog.

Even her father had piled on. *"Take some golf lessons. There's no better place to make the right kind of connections."*

Tonight's "party" would be at the stodgy Mayfair Club, where Kate had booked a private room. Annabelle had wanted to invite the book club for protection but Kate had insisted it be "just family." Adam's newest girlfriend and Annabelle's mystery date were the only exceptions.

Annabelle tested the temperature outside. It was chilly, almost Halloween, but not cold enough to ruin her outfit with one of her ratty jackets. She stepped back inside and began to pace. Another fifteen minutes until Dean was due to pick her up. Surely tonight her family would finally see that she wasn't a failure. She looked good, she had a very hot, make-believe boyfriend, and Perfect for You had begun to turn the corner. If only Heath . . .

She'd been trying so hard not to gnaw over her unhappiness. She hadn't talked to him since the party last weekend, and, so far, he'd honored her demand to leave her alone. She'd even managed to resist calling him to acknowledge the boxes of gourmet groceries and pricey liquors he'd had delivered to replenish her pantry. Why he'd included the lone African violet remained a mystery.

As painful as it was, she knew he was an emotional investment she could no longer afford. For months, she'd tried to convince herself that her feelings for him centered more on lust than love, but it wasn't true. She loved him in so many ways she'd lost count: his basic decency, his humor, the way he understood her. But his emotional hang-ups had roots a mile deep, and they'd caused him irreparable damage. He was capable of absolute loyalty, of total dedication, of offering strength and comfort, but she no longer believed he was capable of love. She had to cut him out of her life.

The phone rang. If Dean was canceling, she'd never forgive him. She rushed into her office and snatched up the receiver before the voice mail could kick in. "Hello?"

"This is personal, not business," Heath said, "so don't hang up. We have to talk."

Just the sound of his voice made her heart leap. "Oh, no, we don't."

"You fired me," he said calmly. "I respect that. You're not my matchmaker any longer. But we're still friends, and in the interest of our friendship, we need to discuss page thirteen."

"Page thirteen?"

"You've accused me of being arrogant. I've always thought of myself as confident, but I'm here to tell you, no more. After studying these pictures . . . Honey, if this is what you're looking for in a man, I don't think any of us are going to measure up."

She had a sinking feeling that she understood exactly what he was talking about, and she sank down on the corner of her desk. "I have no idea what you're talking about."

"Who knew flexible silicone came in so many colors?"

Her sex toy catalog. He'd taken it months ago. She'd hoped he'd forgotten it by now.

"Most of these products seem to be hypoallergenic," Heath went on. "That's good, I guess. Some with batteries, some without. I suppose that's a matter of preference. There's a harness on this one. That's pretty kinky. And . . . Son of a bitch! It says this one is dishwasher safe. As much as I like— I'm sorry, but there's just something unappetizing about that."

She should hang up, but she'd missed him so much. "Sean Palmer, is that you? If you don't stop talking dirty, I'm telling your mother."

He didn't bite. "The top of page fourteen . . . That model comes with some kind of pump. You've got the corner turned down, so you must be interested."

She was fairly sure she hadn't turned any pages down, but who knew?

"And how about this one with the suction cup? The question is, exactly what would you stick it to? A word of caution, sweetheart. You suction something like that to your bedroom window or, hell, the dashboard of your car—it's going to attract the wrong kind of attention."

She smiled.

"Just tell me one thing, Annabelle, and then I have to go." His voice dropped to a low, intimate note that made her shiver. "Why would a woman be so interested in an artificial one when the real thing works a hell of a lot better?"

As she searched for just the right comeback, he hung up. She took a few deep breaths, but they didn't begin to steady her. No matter how much she tried to inoculate herself, he got to her every time, which was the biggest reason of all why she couldn't afford these conversations.

The doorbell rang. Thank God, Dean was early. She jumped up from the desk and pressed her hands to her cheeks to cool herself off. Plastering a smile on her face, she opened the front door.

Heath stood on the other side.

"Happy birthday." He slipped his cell into his pocket, tossed her catalog down, and brushed her lips with a soft, quick kiss, which she could barely keep from returning.

"What are you doing here?"

"You look beautiful. More than beautiful. Unfortunately, your present won't get here until tomorrow, but I don't want you to think I forgot."

"What present? Never mind." She made herself block the doorway instead of opening her arms. "Dean's picking me up in ten minutes. I can't talk to you now."

He moved her out of the way so he could get inside. "I'm afraid Dean's indisposed. I'm taking his place. I like your dress."

"What are you talking about? I spoke to him three hours ago, and he was fine."

"Those stomach viruses come on fast."

"Bull. What have you done with him?"

"It wasn't me. It was Kevin. I don't know why he had to insist on watching game film with him tonight. Don't quote me, but your pal Kevin can be a real prick when he wants to." He nuzzled her neck, right behind her chandelier earring. "Damn, you smell good."

It took her a few beats too long to push herself away. "Does Molly know about this?"

"Not exactly. Unfortunately, Molly's gone over to the dark side along with her sister. Those two women are way too protective of you. It's me they should be worrying about. I don't know why they haven't figured out you can take care of yourself."

She liked knowing he understood that about her, but she still wouldn't give in to his smarmy agent's charm. "I don't want to go to my birthday party with you. As far as my family knows, you're still my client, so it would look a little odd. Besides, I want to go with Dean. Someone who'll *impress* them."

"And you think I won't?"

She took in his dark gray suit, probably Armani, his designer necktie, and tonight's watch, an incredible white gold Patek Philippe. Her family would roll on their backs and beg him to scratch their stomachs.

He knew he'd boxed her in. She saw it in his crafty smile. "Oh, all right," she said grouchily. "But I'm warning you now, my brothers are the most clueless, obnoxious, opinionated men you'll ever meet." She threw up her hands. "Why am I wasting my breath? You're going to love them."

And they loved him right back. Their shocked expressions when she walked into the Mayfair Club's walnut-paneled private dining room with Heath at her side fulfilled all her fantasies. First they checked to make sure he wasn't wearing high heels, then they mentally priced out his wardrobe. Even before introductions were exchanged, he was one of them, a certified member of the high-achievers' club.

"Mom and Dad, this is Heath Champion, and I know what you're thinking. It sounded phony to me, too. But he was born Campione, and you've got to admit the name Champion is good for marketing."

"Very good for marketing," Kate said approvingly. Her favorite bracelet, an engraved gold cuff, clinked against Nana's old charm bracelet. At the same time, she shot Annabelle an inquisitive glance, which Annabelle pretended not to see, since she still hadn't figured out how to explain why the man they knew as her most important client had shown up as her date.

Tonight Kate was clad in one of her St. John knit suits, the champagne color perfectly matching her ash blond hair, which she'd worn in a jaw-length Gena Rowlands pageboy for as long as Annabelle could remember. Her dad sported his favorite navy blazer, a white shirt, and a gray necktie the same color as what remained of his curly hair. Once it had been auburn like hers. An American flag pin graced his lapel, and as she hugged him, she drew in his familiar daddy scent: Brut shaving cream, dry-cleaning fluid, and well-scrubbed surgeon's skin.

Heath started pumping hands. "Kate, Chet, it's a pleasure."

Although Annabelle had met her parents earlier for breakfast, her brothers had only flown in a few hours ago, and she exchanged hugs with them. Doug and Adam had inherited their blond, blue-eyed good looks from Kate, although not her tendency to carry a few extra pounds at the waist. They were looking especially handsome tonight, hard-bodied and successful.

"Doug, you're the accountant, right?" Respect shone in Heath's eyes. "I heard you made VP at Reynolds and Peate. Very impressive. And, Adam . . . The top heart surgeon in St. Louis. It's an honor."

Her brothers were honored right back, and the men did a

friendly little shoulder slapping. "Read about you in the paper . . ."

"You've built quite a reputation . . ."

". . . amazing client roster you have."

Her sister-in-law used perfume like bug repellant, so Annabelle hugged her last. Overly tanned, aggressively made-up, and undernourished, Candace wore a short black strapless dress to showcase her toned arms and trim calves. Her diamond studs were nearly as big as Sean Palmer's, but Annabelle still thought she looked like a horse.

Heath gave Candace his double whammy—sexy smile and patented dead-eyed sincerity. "Wow, Doug, how'd an ugly guy like you manage to land such a beauty?"

Doug, who knew exactly how good-looking he was, laughed. Candace gave a coquettish toss of her mahogany brown hair extensions. "The question is . . . How did a girl like Annabelle manage to talk a man like you into joining our silly little family party?"

Annabelle smiled sweetly. "I promised he could tie me up afterward and spank me."

Heath enjoyed that, but her mother huffed. "Annabelle, not everyone here is familiar with your sense of humor."

Annabelle turned her attention to the stranger in the room, Adam's latest conquest. Like the others, including his ex-wife, this one was well tailored and attractive with square features, a blunt-cut dark brown bob, and a total lack of charm. Just the sight of those thin, unsmiling lips announced that her brother had chosen still another emotionally robotic female.

"This is Dr. Lucille Menger." He slipped a protective arm around her shoulders. "Our very talented new pathologist."

Good job choice, Lucy. Not much need to worry about bedside manner.

Heath gave her a megawatt smile. "You and I seem to be the only outsiders tonight, so we'd better stick together. For all we know, these people could be serial killers."

Her parents and brothers chuckled, but Lucille looked mystified. Finally her mental fog cleared. "Oh, that's a joke."

Annabelle shot a quick look at Kate, but beyond the flicker of an eyebrow, her mother wasn't giving anything away. Annabelle's irritation grew. Her brother had a track record for choosing these humorless brainiacs, but did anybody stage an intervention for Dr. Adam? No, they did not. Only for Annabelle.

Heath looked boyishly repentant. "A bad joke, I'm afraid."

Lucille seemed relieved to know it wasn't her.

Kate always booked the Mayfair Club's second-floor private dining room for the Granger family's Chicago gatherings. Decorated like an English manor house with polished brass and chintz, the room offered a cozy seating area near a mullioned bay window that looked down on Delaware Place, and they settled there for cocktails and birthday presents. Doug and Candace presented her with a gift certificate for a makeover at a local salon. No mystery who'd come up with that idea. Adam gave her a new DVD player along with a collection of workout videos, thank you very much. When she unwrapped her parents' gift, she found an expensive navy suit she wouldn't have been caught dead wearing, but couldn't return because Kate had ordered it from her favorite working woman's boutique in St. Louis, and the manager would squeal.

"Every woman needs a power suit as she gets older," her mother said.

The corner of Heath's mouth twitched. "I have a gift for Annabelle, too. Unfortunately, it won't be ready until Monday."

Candace pressed him for details, but he refused to say more. Kate could no longer hold back her curiosity about why he was here. "We never mind when Annabelle shows up without a date, even though she says it makes her feel like a fifth wheel. As her client, you certainly had no obligation to be her escort, but . . . Well, I must say we're all glad you agreed to join us . . . ?"

She ended her sentence with an implied question mark. Annabelle hoped Heath would somehow put an end to her mother's assumption that this was a mercy date for him, but he was more intent on playing the charm card. "It's my pleasure. I've been looking forward to meeting all of you. Annabelle's told me the most amazing stories about your banking career, Kate. You were a real trailblazer for women."

Kate melted all over him. "I don't know about that, but I will say things were a lot more difficult for women back then than they are now. I keep telling Annabelle that she doesn't know how lucky she is. These days, the only obstacles standing in the way of a woman's success are ones of her own making."

Zing.

"You've obviously taught her well," Heath said smoothly. "It's amazing what she's been able to create in such a short time. You must be enormously proud of her."

Kate looked hard at Heath to see if he was kidding. Candace snickered. Annabelle didn't exactly hate her sister-in-law, but she wouldn't be the first person standing in line if Candace turned up needing a kidney.

Kate reached across the arm of her chair to pat Annabelle's knee. "Tactfully put, Heath. My daughter has always been a free spirit. And you look lovely tonight, sweetheart, although it's too bad they didn't have that dress in black."

Annabelle sighed. Heath smiled, then turned his attention to Candace, who'd maneuvered a position on the leather sofa between him and Doug. "I understand that you and Doug have a gifted little boy."

Gifted? The most Annabelle had said about Jamison was that he'd learned to get everybody's attention by peeing on the living room rug. But the Granger clan ate it up.

Kate beamed. "He reminds me so much of Doug and Adam at that age."

Tiny penises?

"We're having him tested," Doug said. "We don't want him to be bored in school."

"He loves his nature enrichment class." A strand from Candace's hair extensions was sticking to her lip gloss, but she didn't seem to notice. "We're teaching him to recycle."

"It's amazing how well coordinated he is for a three-year-old," Adam said. "He's going to be quite an athlete."

Kate puffed up with maternal pride. "Doug and Adam were swimmers."

Annabelle had been a swimmer, too.

"Annabelle swam, too." Kate hooked a sickle of blond hair behind her ear. "Unfortunately, she didn't take to it like her brothers."

Translation: Annabelle had never won any medals. "I just had fun," she muttered, but no one was paying attention because her father had decided to enter the conversation.

"I'm cutting down my old seven iron for Jamison. It's never too early to get them interested in the game."

Candace launched into a description of Jamison's academic prowess, and Mr. Charm made all the right responses. Kate regarded her sons fondly. "Both Doug and Adam were reading by the time they were four. Not just words, but entire paragraphs. I'm afraid it took Annabelle a little longer. Not that she was slow—not at all—but she had a hard time sitting still."

She still did.

"A little attention deficit disorder isn't necessarily a bad thing," Annabelle said, feeling the need to interject. "At least it gives you a broad range of interests."

Everybody stared at her, even Heath. It figured. In less than half an hour, he'd deserted the loser's lunch table and taken up permanent residence with the cool kids.

The agony continued as the appetizers arrived and they resettled around the table, which was set with white linen, pink roses, and silver candlesticks. "So, Spud, when are you coming to St. Louis to see the new cardiac wing?" Adam took the seat next to her, his date on his opposite side. "Funniest damn thing,

Lucille. The last time Annabelle visited, somebody left a cleaning bucket in the hall. Annabelle was talking as usual, so she didn't see it. Splat!"

They all laughed as though they hadn't heard the story at least a dozen times.

"Remember that party we had before our senior year in college?" Doug snorted. "We mixed everybody's leftover drinks together and dared Spud to down the whole damn thing. God, I never thought she'd stop puking."

"Yeah, those are some great memories, all right." Annabelle drained her wineglass.

Fortunately, they were more interested in grilling Heath than in torturing her. Doug wanted to know if he'd considered opening an office in L.A. Adam asked if he'd taken on any partners. Her father inquired into his golf game. All of them agreed that hard work, clear-cut goals, and a smooth backswing were the secrets to success. By the time they dug into their entrées, she could see that Heath had fallen as much in love with her family as her family had with him.

Kate, however, still hadn't satisfied her curiosity about why he'd shown up as her escort. "Tell us how your hunt for a wife is coming along. I understand you're working with two matchmakers."

Annabelle decided to get it over with. "One matchmaker. I fired him."

Her brothers laughed, but Kate regarded her severely over her dinner roll. "Annabelle, you have the most bizarre sense of humor."

"I'm not joking," she said. "Heath was impossible to work with."

An embarrassed silence fell over the table. Heath shrugged and set down his fork. "I couldn't seem to stay on task, and Annabelle doesn't put up with a lot of nonsense when it comes to business."

Her family gaped, all except Candace, who'd finished her

third chardonnay and decided it was time to launch her very favorite topic of conversation. "You'll never hear it from any of them, Heath, but the Granger family is old, *old* St. Louis, if you know what I mean."

Heath's fingers curled around the stem of his wineglass. "I'm not sure I do."

As much as Annabelle appreciated the change of topic, she wished Candace could have chosen something else. Kate wasn't happy, either, but since Candace had decided to misbehave instead of Annabelle, she merely asked Lucille to pass the salt.

"Salt leads to high blood pressure," Lucille felt duty bound to point out.

"Fascinating." Kate reached past her for the shaker.

"The Grangers are one of St. Louis's original brewery families," Candace said. "They practically settled the town."

Annabelle stifled a yawn.

Heath, however, abandoned his prime rib to give Candace his full attention. "You don't say?"

Candace, a natural-born snob, was more than happy to elaborate. "My father-in-law waited until he graduated from college to announce that he intended to go into medicine instead of beer. His family was forced to sell out to Anheuser-Busch. Apparently, it was quite the news story."

"I can imagine." Heath gazed across the table at Annabelle. "You never mentioned any of this."

"None of them do," Candace said in a conspiratorial whisper. "They're ashamed of being born with money."

"Not ashamed," her father said firmly. "But Kate and I have always believed in the value of hard work. We had no intention of raising children with nothing better to do than count the money in their trust funds."

Since none of them could touch the money in their trust funds until they were about 130, Annabelle had never understood why it was such a big hairy deal.

"We've watched too many young people get ruined that way," Kate said.

Candace had another tidbit to disclose. "Apparently quite a dustup occurred when Chet brought Kate home. The Grangers saw it as marrying down."

Far from taking offense, Kate looked smug. "Chet's mother was a horrible snob. She couldn't help it, poor thing. She was a product of that insular St. Louis socialite culture, which was exactly why I tried so hard—and so *futilely*, I might add—to talk Annabelle out of being a debutante. My family might have been working class—God knows my mother was—but—"

"Don't you *dare* say one bad word about Nana." Annabelle stabbed a green bean.

"—but I knew how to read an etiquette book as well as anyone," Kate went on smoothly, "and it didn't take me long to fit right in with the high and mighty Grangers."

Chet regarded Kate with pride. "By the time my own mother died, she cared more about Kate than she did about me."

Heath hadn't taken his eyes off Annabelle. "You were a debutante?"

Her spine stiffened, and her chin came up. "I loved the gowns, and it seemed like a good idea at the time. You got a problem with that?"

Heath started to laugh, and he kept at it so long that Kate had to dig a tissue from her purse and hand it over so he could wipe his eyes. Frankly, Annabelle didn't see what was so gosh darned funny.

Candace unwisely permitted the waiter to refill her wineglass. "Then there was River Bend, the house where they all grew up . . ."

Heath gave a snort of amusement. "Your house had a name?"

"Don't look at me," Annabelle retorted. "It happened before I was born."

"River Bend was an estate, not just a house," Candace explained. "We still can't quite believe that Chet talked Kate into selling the property, although their home in Naples has to be seen to be believed."

Heath started laughing all over again.

"You're annoying," Annabelle said.

Candace went on to describe the beauty of River Bend, which made Annabelle nostalgic, even though Candace neglected to mention the drafty windows, smoking fireplaces, and frequent infestations of mice. Finally, even Doug had heard enough, and he switched the subject.

Heath loved the Grangers, every one of them, with the exception of Candace, who was a self-important pain in the ass, but she had to live in Annabelle's shadow, so he was prepared to be tolerant. As he gazed around the table, he saw the rock solid family he'd dreamed of as a boy. Chet and Kate were loving parents who'd dedicated themselves to turning their kids into successful adults. Her brothers' teasing drove Annabelle crazy—they did everything but give her noogies—but as the youngest child and only girl, she was clearly their pet, and watching Adam's and Doug's not-so-subtle competition for her attention was one of the highlights of his evening. The complexities of the mother-daughter relationship were beyond him. Kate was a nag, but she made excuses to touch Annabelle whenever she could and smiled at her when she wasn't looking. As for Chet . . . His fond expression left no doubt who was Daddy's Little Girl.

As he gazed across the table at her, his throat tightened with pride. He'd never seen her look so beautiful or so sexy, but then his thoughts always seemed to take that direction. Her bare shoulders gleamed in the candlelight, and he wanted to lick the sprinkle of freckles on that graceful little nose. Her shiny swirl of hair reminded him of autumn leaves, and his fingers ached to rumple it. If he hadn't been so wrapped up in his outdated, misdirected notions of what made up a trophy wife, he would have realized months ago the place she occupied in his life. But it had taken last weekend's party to open his eyes. Annabelle made everybody happy, including him. With Annabelle, he remembered that life was about living, not just about work, and that laughter was as precious a commodity as cash.

He'd canceled a morning's worth of appointments to pick out her engagement ring, only two and a half carats because her hands were small, and lugging three carats around all day might leave her too tired to take off her clothes at night. He'd planned exactly how he intended to propose to her, and this morning he'd put the first part of that plan in motion.

He'd hired the Northwestern University Marching Band.

He envisioned exactly how it would unfold. Right now, she was angry, so he had to make her forget that, up until a few weeks ago, he'd intended to marry Delaney Lightfield. He had a pretty good idea Annabelle loved him. The Dean Robillard scam proved that, didn't it? And if he was wrong, he'd make her love him . . . starting tonight.

He'd kiss her breathless, carry her upstairs to that attic bedroom, turn Nana to the wall, and make love with her until they were both senseless. Afterward, he'd follow up with a boatload of flowers, some ultraromantic dates, and a slew of salacious phone calls. When he was absolutely certain he'd crumbled the last of her defenses, he'd invite her to a special dinner at Evanston's top restaurant. After she'd been lulled by good food, champagne, and candlelight, he'd tell her he wanted to see her old college hangouts and suggest a walk around the Northwestern campus. Along the way, he'd pull her into one of those big arched doorways, kiss her, probably feel her up a little because, who was he kidding, there was no way he could kiss Annabelle without touching her. Finally, they'd reach the campus lakefront, and that's where the Northwestern marching band would be waiting, playing something old-fashioned and romantic. He'd drop down on one knee, pull out the ring, and ask her to marry him.

He held on to the image, savored it, and then, with a pang of regret, let it go. There'd be no marching band, no proposal by the lakefront, not even a ring to seal the exact moment he asked her to marry him, since the one he'd chosen wouldn't be ready until next week. He was abandoning his perfect plan because, after meeting the Granger family and seeing how much they meant to one another—how much Annabelle meant to them—he knew they had to be part of this.

The waiter disappeared, leaving them with fresh coffee and dessert. Across the table Annabelle was hissing at St. Louis's preeminent heart surgeon, who'd twisted a lock of her hair around his finger and announced he wouldn't let go until she told everyone about the time she wet her pants at Laurie somebody's birthday party.

Heath rose to his feet. Adam dropped Annabelle's hair, and she kicked him under the table. "Ouch!" Adam rubbed his leg. "That hurt!"

"Good."

"Children . . ."

Heath smiled. He loved this. "I hope nobody minds, but I have a couple of things to say. First, you're terrific people. Thanks for letting me be a part of this evening."

A chorus of "Here, here" followed, accompanied by the clink of wineglasses. Only Annabelle remained silent and suspicious, but what he was about to say should wipe that frown right off her face.

"I wasn't fortunate enough to grow up with a family like yours. I think all of you know how lucky you are to have one another." He gazed at Annabelle, but she was trying to find her napkin, which Adam had passed under the table to Doug. He waited until her head came back up.

"It's been almost five months since you barged into my office wearing that awful yellow suit, Annabelle. In that time, you've turned my life upside down."

Kate's hand shot out, bracelets jangling. "If you'll just be patient, I'm sure she'll do her very best to make things right. Annabelle is an extremely hard worker. Granted, her professional methods might not be what you're accustomed to, but her heart's in the right place."

Doug snapped a pen from his pocket. "I'm planning to go over all her records before I leave. With a little reorganization, a firmer hand on the reins, her operation should be stabilized in no time."

Annabelle set her chin in her hand and sighed.

"This isn't about Perfect for You," Heath said.

They regarded him blankly.

"She renamed her company," he said patiently. "It's no longer Marriages by Myrna. She calls it Perfect for You."

Adam gazed at her in puzzlement. "Is that true?"

Candace adjusted an earring. "Couldn't you have found something catchier?"

"I don't remember hearing about this," Doug said.

"Neither do I." Chet set down his coffee cup. "Nobody tells me anything."

"*I* told you," Kate replied tartly. "Unfortunately, I didn't have it announced on the Golf Channel."

"What kind of company?" Lucille said.

While Adam explained that his sister was a matchmaker, Doug pulled out his BlackBerry. "I'm sure it didn't occur to you to investigate trademark protection."

Heath realized he was losing them, and he turned up the volume. "The point is . . . Until I met Annabelle, I thought I had my life figured out, but it didn't take her long to point out that I'd made some serious errors in my calculations."

Kate winced. "Oh, dear. I know she's not always tactful, but she means well."

Annabelle picked up Adam's wrist and looked at his watch. Heath wished she had a little more trust. "I know everyone here recognizes how special Annabelle is," he said, "but I haven't known her as long, and it took me a while to figure it out."

Annabelle went after a gravy spot on the tablecloth.

"Just because I was slow to catch on," he said, "doesn't mean I'm stupid. I recognize quality when I see it, and Annabelle is an amazing woman." Now he had her full attention, and he got that familiar adrenaline rush that signaled the final moments before he closed on a deal. "I know today is your birthday, sweetheart, and that means you should be the one getting the present instead of me, but I'm feeling greedy." He turned, first to one end of the table, and then to the other. "Chet, Kate, I'd like to ask permission to marry your daughter."

Shocked silence fell over the room. A candle sputtered. A spoon clattered against a dish. Annabelle sat frozen while the rest of her family gradually came back to life.

"Why would you want to marry Annabelle?" Candace wailed.

"But I thought you were—"

"Oh, sweetheart . . ."

"Marry her?"

"Our Annabelle?"

"She never said anything about—"

Kate dove for her tissues. "This is the happiest moment of my life."

"Permission granted, Champion."

Grinning, Doug reached across the table to poke his mother. "Make it a Christmas wedding before he realizes what he's gotten into and changes his mind."

Heath stayed focused on Annabelle, giving her time to adjust. Her lips formed a lopsided oval; her eyes turned into puddles of spilled honey . . . And then her eyebrows slammed together. "What are you talking about?"

At the very least, he'd expected a joyous gasp. "I want to marry you," he said again.

Her frown grew more ominous, and he found himself remembering Annabelle seldom did what he expected, something he should possibly have recalled before he'd stood up.

"And when did you have this magical revelation?" she asked. "No, let me guess. Tonight after you met my family."

"Wrong." Here, at least, he was on solid ground.

"Then when?"

"Last weekend, at the party."

Disbelief shone in her eyes. "Why didn't you say something then?"

Too late, he realized he should have stuck with his original plan, but he refused to let himself panic. Always meet strength with strength. "I'd only broken up with Delaney a few hours earlier. It seemed a little *premature.*"

"This whole thing seems a little *premature.*"

Kate braced her hand on the tablecloth. "Annabelle, you're being peevish."

"That doesn't begin to describe how I feel." He winced as Annabelle shot up from her chair. "Did anybody hear him mention the *L*-word? Because I sure didn't."

Just like that, she'd cornered him. Had he really thought she wouldn't notice? Was that why he'd decided to do this in front of her family? He began to sweat. If he didn't handle this exactly right, the whole deal would collapse around him. He knew what he had to do, but at the precise moment when he most needed to keep his head, he lost it. "I hired the *Northwestern marching band!*"

Stunned silence greeted this revelation.

He'd made himself look like an ass. Annabelle shook her head with a quiet dignity that unnerved him. "You have lost your mind. I only wish you could have done it privately."

"Annabelle!" Kate's neck was turning red. "Just because Heath doesn't want to air his most intimate feelings in front of virtual strangers doesn't mean he's not in love with you. How could anybody not love you?"

Annabelle kept her eyes locked with his. "Here's what I've learned about pythons, Mother. Sometimes it's more important to pay attention to what they don't say than to what they do."

Kate came to her feet. "You're too upset to discuss this now. Heath is a wonderful man. Just look at the way he fits in. Wait until tomorrow when you've had a chance to cool down, and then the two of you can talk this through."

"Save your breath," Doug muttered. "All you have to do is look at her, and you know she's going to blow it."

"Come on, Spud," Adam pleaded. "Tell the guy you'll marry him. For once in your life, do the smart thing."

Help from her brothers was the last thing Heath needed. These were guys you wanted by your side in a foxhole, not around a pissed off female. Proposing in front of her family was the worst idea he'd ever had, but deals had turned sour on him before, and he'd still managed to pull them off. All he needed to do was get her alone . . . and avoid the one topic she'd most want to discuss.

Chapter Twenty-two

Annabelle rushed into the deserted hallway. Soft music played through the speakers, and dim, romantic lighting cast a soothing glow over the garnet walls, but she couldn't stop shaking. She'd thought Rob had broken her heart, but that pain was nothing compared to what she felt now. Just past the dining room, she stumbled into a nook furnished with a love seat and a pair of Sheraton chairs. Heath followed her, but she kept her back to him, and he was smart enough not to touch her.

"Before you say anything you're going to regret, Annabelle, let me suggest you turn on your fax machine when you get home. I'm sending you a jeweler's receipt for a very large diamond ring. Notice when I ordered it. On Tuesday, four days ago."

So he'd been telling the truth when he'd said he'd decided to marry her the night of the party. She didn't feel comforted. Even though she'd known he had this emotional hole inside him, she'd thought she could keep herself from ever tumbling into it.

"Are you listening to me?" he said. "I'd already made up

my mind to marry you before I met a single member of your family. I'm sorry it took me so long to get my head straight, but, as you've been quick to point out, I'm an idiot, and all I did tonight was prove you're right. I should have talked to you privately, but I started thinking how much it would mean to them to be part of this. Obviously, I got carried away."

"It didn't occur to you that I'd refuse, did it?" She stared blindly at her watery reflection in the window. "You were so sure I was head over heels in love with you that you didn't even hesitate."

He moved behind her, standing so close that she felt the heat of his body. "Aren't you?"

She'd thought she was being so clever dangling Dean in front of him, but he'd seen through her charade, and now he'd stolen what was left of her pride, in addition to everything else. "Yeah, but so what? I fall in love easily. Thankfully, I get over it just as easily." What a lie.

"Don't say that."

She finally turned to face him. "I know you so much better than you think I do. You saw how well I got along with the guys at the party, and that was when you realized I'd be enough of a business asset to compensate for not being gorgeous."

"Stop putting yourself down. You're the most beautiful woman I've ever known."

She might have been able to laugh at his sheer gall if it didn't hurt so much. "Quit lying. I'm a compromise, and we both know it."

"I never compromise," he retorted. "And I sure as hell didn't compromise with you. Sometimes two people fit together, and that's what happened to us."

He was slick as an eel, and she couldn't let him get to her. "It's starting to make sense. You don't believe in blowing deadlines. Your thirty-fifth birthday is coming up. Time to get a move on, right? At the party, you saw that I could be a business asset. You like being with me. Then tonight you found out I was born with that silver spoon you've been looking for. I guess that hit it out of the ballpark for you. But you forgot something, didn't you?" She made herself meet his eyes. "What about love? What about that?"

He didn't miss a beat. "What about it? Pay attention, because I'm going to start at the top. You're beautiful, every part of you. I love your hair, the way it looks, the way it feels. I love touching it, smelling it. I love the way you wrinkle your nose when you laugh. It makes me laugh, too, every time. And I love watching you eat. Sometimes you can't shovel it in fast enough, but when you get interested in a conversation, you forget there's anything in front of you. God knows, I love making love with you. I can't even talk about that without wanting you. I love your pathetic attachment to those seniors. I love how hard you work . . ." On and on he went, pacing the small square of carpet, cataloging her virtues.

He began describing their future, painting a rosy picture of their life together living in his house, the parties they'd have, the vacations they'd take. He even had the temerity to mention children, which brought her to her feet.

"Stop it! Just stop it." She balled her hands into fists. "You've said everything except what I need to hear. I want you to love *me,* Heath, not my awful hair, or the way I get along with your clients, or the fact that I have the family you've always dreamed of. I want you to love *me,* and you don't know how to do that, do you?"

He didn't even blink. "Have you been listening to anything I've said?"

"Every word."

He drilled her with his eyes, tried to swamp her with his lethal confidence. "Then how could I not love you?"

If she hadn't been so painfully wise to his tricks, she might have been taken in, but his words fell flat. "I don't know," she said quietly. "You tell me."

He threw up his hand, but she could feel him scrambling. "Your family's right. You're a personal disaster. What do you want? Just tell me what you want."

"I want your best offer."

He stared at her, his gaze intense, intimidating, overpowering. And then he did the unthinkable. He looked away. With a sinking heart, she watched his hands slide into his pockets, his shoulders drop almost imperceptibly. "You already have it."

She bit her lip, nodded. "That's what I thought." And then she walked away.

She had no money with her, but she climbed into a cab anyway, then made the driver wait at her house while she went inside to get the cash to pay him. Her family would be descending at any minute. She grabbed a suitcase before that could happen and began stuffing it with whatever her fingers closed around, not letting herself feel or think. Fifteen minutes later, she was in her car.

Just before midnight on Saturday, Portia got the news about Heath's marriage proposal in a phone call from Baxter Benton, who'd waited tables at the Mayfair Club for a thousand years and had eavesdropped on the Granger family party. Portia had been curled up on the couch in an old beach towel and sweatpants—her jeans no longer fit—with a sea of candy wrappers and crumpled tissues surrounding her like a barbed-wire fence. By the time she hung up, she was on her feet, excited for the first time in weeks. She hadn't lost her instincts after all. This was why she hadn't been able to find the perfect woman for that final introduction. The chemistry she'd detected between Heath and Annabelle that day in his office hadn't been imaginary.

She stepped over the beach towel she'd dropped and snatched up an unread copy of the *Tribune* to check the date. Her contract with Heath ran out on Tuesday, three days from now. She set the newspaper aside and began to pace. If she could pull this off, maybe, just maybe, she could leave Power Matches behind without feeling like a failure.

It was midnight, and she couldn't do anything until morning. She gazed at the mess that had accumulated around her. Her cleaning lady had quit a couple of weeks ago, and Portia hadn't replaced her. A film of dust covered everything, the trash cans overflowed, and the rugs needed vacuuming. She hadn't even gone to work yesterday. What was the point? She had no assistants, just Inez and the IT guy who ran the Power Matches Web site, the one part of the business that interested her the least.

She touched her face. This morning, she'd gone to her dermatologist. Catastrophic timing, but then so was her life. Still, for the first time in weeks, she felt a sliver of hope.

Heath got drunk Saturday night, just like his old man used to. All he needed was a woman to smack around, and he'd be a chip right off the old block. Come to think of it, the old man would be proud of him, because a couple of hours ago, Heath had smacked one around real good, not physically maybe, but he'd beat the hell out of her emotionally. And she'd smacked him right back. Got him right where it hurt. As he fell into bed sometime near dawn, he wished he'd told her he loved her, said the words she needed to hear. But he couldn't give Annabelle anything but the truth. She meant too much to him.

When he finally woke up, it was Sunday afternoon. He staggered into the shower and shoved his throbbing head under the water. He should be at Soldier Field right now with Sean's family, but as he climbed out of the shower, he pulled on a robe instead, then made his way to the kitchen and reached for the coffeepot. He hadn't called a single client to wish him well, and he didn't even care.

He pulled a mug from the cupboard and tried to work up some more indignation against Annabelle. She'd derailed him, and he didn't like it. He had a plan, a damn good one for both of them. Why couldn't she have trusted him? Why did she need to hear a bunch of meaningless bull? Actions spoke louder than words, and once they were married, he'd have shown her how much he cared in every way he knew how.

He grabbed some aspirin and drifted downstairs to his pricey, barely furnished media room so he could catch a few games. He wasn't dressed, hadn't shaved or eaten, and he didn't give a damn. As he began surfing the sports channels, he thought of the way her family had attacked him after she'd walked out. Like a school of piranhas.

"What's your game, Champion?"

"Do you love her or not?"

"Nobody hurts Annabelle and gets away with it."

Even Candace had jumped in. *"I'm sure you made her cry, and she hates it when she gets all blouhy."*

Finally, Chet had said it all. *"You'd better leave now."*

For the rest of Sunday afternoon into the night, Heath flicked from one game to the next, not taking in a single play. He'd been ignoring the phone all day, but he didn't want anybody calling out the cops, so he'd managed to fake his way through a conversation with Bodie where he'd pleaded the flu. Afterward, he went upstairs and grabbed a bag of potato chips. They tasted like dryer lint. Still dressed in his white cotton bathrobe, he settled into the living room's lone chair with a fresh bottle of scotch.

His perfect plan lay in shambles around him. In one disastrous night, he'd lost a wife, lover, friend, and they'd all been the same person. The long, lonely shadow of the Beau Vista Trailer Park crept over him.

Portia spent Sunday holed up in her apartment, a telephone propped to her shoulder, trying to locate Heath. She finally reached his receptionist and promised to treat her to a spa weekend if she could find out where he was. The woman didn't get back to her until eleven that night. "Sick at home," she said. "On a game day. Nobody can believe it."

Portia needed to say his name. "Has Bodie talked to him?"

"That's how we found out he was sick."

"So . . . did Bodie check on him?"

"No. He's still on his way back from Texas."

As Portia hung up, her heart ached, but she couldn't give in to it, not now. She didn't believe for a minute that Heath was sick, and she dialed his number. When his voice mail picked up, she tried again, but he wasn't answering. Once again, she touched her face. How could she do this?

How could she not?

She dashed into her bedroom and rooted through her drawers until she found her largest Hermès scarf. Still, she hesitated. She walked over to the window and gazed out into the darkness.

To hell with it.

With Willie Nelson on the stereo, Heath dozed. Sometime around midnight, his doorbell rang. He ignored it. It rang again and again. When he couldn't stand it any longer, he stalked into the hallway, snatched up his running shoes, and hurled them against the door. "Go away!" He stomped back to the empty living room and picked up the tumbler of scotch he'd abandoned earlier. A sharp rapping at the window made him whirl around . . . and stare into a vision straight from hell.

"Fuck!"

His tumbler shattered to the floor, scotch sloshing over his bare calves. "What the—"

The nightmare face ducked into the shrubbery. "Open the damn door!"

"Portia?" He stepped over the broken glass but saw only

rustling branches outside the window. He couldn't have conjured up that dark, shrouded face, which was stripped of all human features except for a pair of gaping eyes. He returned to the foyer and threw open the door. The porch was empty.

He heard a hiss from behind the bushes. "Come over here."

"No way. I've read Stephen King. You come to me."

"I can't."

"I'm not moving."

A few seconds ticked by. "All right," she said, "but turn around."

"Okay." He didn't move.

Gradually Portia emerged from the shadows onto the walk. She wore a long black coat with a very expensive scarf pulled forward around her head. She held her hand over her forehead like a visor. "Are you looking?"

"Of course I'm looking. Do you think I'm nuts?"

Seconds ticked by, and then she dropped her hand.

She was blue. Her entire face and what he could see of her neck. Not a faint bluish tint, but bright, bold, Blue Man Group blue. Only the whites of her eyes and her lips had escaped.

"I know," she said. "I look like a Smurf."

He blinked his eyes. "I was thinking of something else, but you're right. Does it wash off?"

"Do you think I'd come out like this if it washed off?"

"I guess not."

"It's a special cosmetic acid peel. I had it done yesterday morning." She sounded angry, as if it were his fault. "Obviously I didn't intend to show my face until it faded."

"But here you are. How long does the Smurf thing last?"

"Another few days, and then it peels off. It was worse yesterday."

"Hard to imagine. And you've done this to yourself because . . . ?"

"It removes dead cells and stimulates new— Never mind."

She took in his unshaven jaw, white bathrobe, bare legs, and
Gucci loafers. "I'm not the only one who looks like hell."

"Can't a man take a day off now and then?"

"A Sunday in the middle of the football season? I don't
think so." She charged past him into the house where she
promptly turned off the overhead foyer light. "We need to
have a serious conversation."

"I don't know why."

"Business, Heath. We have business to discuss."

Normally, he'd have thrown her out, but he'd lost his
appetite for scotch, and he needed to talk to somebody who
wasn't predisposed to take Annabelle's side. He moved ahead of
her into the living room and—because he wasn't his damned
father and knew something about simple courtesy—turned down
the dimmer on the room's only lamp. "There's broken glass by
the fireplace."

"I see." She took in the room's lack of furnishings but
made no comment. "I heard that you proposed to Annabelle
Granger last night. But what I don't know is why the little twit
turned you down. Given that she rushed out of the Mayfair
Club without you, I'm assuming that's what happened."

His sense of being ill-used erupted. "She's a nutcase, that's
why. Way more trouble than I need in my life. And don't call
her a twit."

"Apologies," she drawled.

"It's not like she had a whole truckload of guys lining up to
marry her."

"I heard her last fiancé had a gender identity problem, so I
think it's safe to say you were a step up."

"Apparently not."

Portia didn't seem to notice her scarf slipping off her head.
Beneath it, her hair was a mess, matted on one side, sticking up
on the other. Hard to reconcile her lunatic appearance with
the fashion plate he remembered. "I tried to tell you she was a

loose cannon," she said. "You should never have done business with her in the first place." She moved closer, her eyes piercing in their eerie blue craters. "You certainly shouldn't have fallen in love with her."

A knife shot through his belly. "I'm not in love with her! Don't try to stick a label on this."

She eyed the empty scotch bottle. "You could have fooled me."

No way was he going to let her do this to him. "What is it with you women? Can't you leave things alone? The fact is, Annabelle and I get along great. We understand each other, and we have fun together. But that's not good enough for her. She's so frickin' insecure." He began pacing the room, nursing his sense of being ill-used and searching for an example that would prove his point. "She's got this thing about her hair."

Portia finally remembered her own and touched the flattened mess. "With hair like hers, I suppose she can be forgiven a little vanity."

"She hates it," he said triumphantly. "I told you she was a nutcase."

"Yet this is the woman you chose to marry."

His anger faded. He felt wrung out, and he wanted another drink. "The whole thing sort of sneaked up on me. She's sweet, smart—really sharp, not just book smart. She's funny. God, but she makes me laugh. Her friends love her, and that tells you something right there, because they're incredible women. I don't know . . . When I'm with her, I forget about work, and . . ." He stopped. He'd already said too much.

Portia wandered to the fireplace, her coat gaping to reveal red sweatpants and what looked like a pajama top. Normally, he couldn't have taken a woman with a Smurf-blue face and an advanced case of bed head too seriously, but this was Portia Powers, and he kept his guard up, which was fortunate, because she hit him again. "But despite all that, you seem to love her."

He could barely control his turmoil. "Come on, Portia. You and I are two of a kind. We're both realists."

"Just because I'm a realist doesn't mean I don't believe love exists. Maybe not for everyone, but . . ." She made a small, awkward gesture that seemed out of character. "Your proposal must have thrown her for a loop. She loves you, of course. I had an inkling of that during our ill-fated meeting. I'm surprised she wasn't willing to overlook your emotional constipation and take you up on your offer."

"The fact that I wouldn't lie to her doesn't mean it wasn't a damn good offer. I'd have given her everything she needed."

"Except love. That's what she was waiting to hear, right?"

"It's a word! Action is what counts."

She nudged the scotch bottle he'd left on the floor with the toe of her shoe. "Has it occurred to you—and I'm merely asking because it's my job—it is possible Annabelle's the sane one, and you're the nutcase?"

"I think you'd better go home."

"And I think you're protesting too much. You've been introduced to a dazzling array of women, but Annabelle is the only one you've wanted to marry. That in itself has to give you pause."

"I looked at the situation logically, that's all."

"Oh, yes, you're the master of logic, all right." She stepped around the broken glass. "Come on, Heath. Cut the crap. I can't help you if you won't tell me the truth about that wall you've built around yourself."

"What is this? Shrink time?"

"Why not? God knows, your secrets are safe with me. It's not like I have an army of intimate friends waiting to tear them out of me."

"Believe me, you don't want to hear about my childhood traumas. Let's just say that, right around the time I turned fifteen, I figured out my survival depended on making sure I didn't keep throwing my heart at people. I backslid once, and I paid the price. Do you know what? It's turned out to be a saner way to live. I recommend it." He advanced on her. "I also resent like hell your implication that I'm some kind of cold-blooded monster, because I'm not."

"Is that what you're hearing? You do have all the classic symptoms."

"Of what?"

"A man in love, of course."

He flinched.

"Look at yourself." Her voice softened, and he thought he heard a note of genuine sympathy. "This isn't about a deal gone bad. This is about your heart breaking."

He heard a roaring inside his head.

She walked to the window. Her words drifted back to him muffled, as if she were having a hard time getting them out. "I think . . . I think this is the way love feels to people like you and me. Threatening and dangerous. We have to be in control, and love takes that away. People like us . . . We can't tolerate vulnerability. But despite our best efforts, sooner or later love seems to catch up with us. And then . . ." She drew a jagged breath. "And then we fall apart."

He felt like he'd been sucker punched.

Slowly she turned back to him, her head high, silvery tracks running down her bright blue cheeks. "I'm claiming my introduction."

He heard what she was saying, but the words made no sense.

"You promised Annabelle and me one last introduction. Annabelle used hers up with Delaney Lightfield. Now it's my turn."

"You want to introduce me to someone? Now? After you've just told me I'm in love with Annabelle?"

"We have a deal." She swiped at her nose with the sleeve of her trench coat. "You're the one who outlined the terms, and I have a lovely young woman who's just what you need. She's high-spirited and intelligent. She's also impulsive and a little temperamental, which will keep you interested. Attractive, of course, like all Power Matches candidates. She has this amazing red hair . . ."

He wasn't usually so slow on the uptake, and he finally understood. "You want to introduce me to Annabelle?"

"Not *want*. I *will*," she said fiercely. "We have a deal. Your contract doesn't run out until midnight Tuesday."

"But—"

"You can't go any further by yourself. It's time for a professional to take over." Just like that, she ran out of steam, and a fresh tear rolled down her cheek. "Annabelle has . . . She has the breadth of character you lack. She's the woman who'll . . . keep you human. She won't put up with anything less." Her chest rose as she drew a long, unsteady breath. "Unfortunately, you'll have to find her first. I made inquiries. She's not home."

The news jolted him. He wanted her tucked safely away in her grandmother's house. Waiting for him.

The pink seam of Portia's lips tightened below her damp blue cheeks. "Listen to me, Heath. As soon as you find her, call me. Don't try to handle this yourself. You need help. Do you understand me? This is *my* introduction."

Right now, the only thing he understood was the depth of his own foolishness. He loved Annabelle. Of course he loved her. This explained all these feelings he'd been too frightened to label.

He needed to be alone to think this through. Portia seemed to understand, because she tugged her trench coat closed and left the room. He felt like he'd been hit in the head with a fly ball. He sagged down in the chair and buried his head in his hands.

Portia's heels clicked on the marble floor in the foyer. He heard her open the front door, and then, unexpectedly, Bodie's voice.

"Fuck!"

Chapter Twenty-three

P ortia fell into Bodie's arms. Just fell. He wasn't expecting it, and he stumbled backward. She went with him,
wrapped her arms around him, and wouldn't let him
go. Not ever again. This man was solid as a rock.

"Portia?" He gripped her shoulders and pushed her a few
inches away so he could study her face.

She gazed up into his horrified eyes. "Everything you said
about me was right."

"I know that, but . . ." He ran his thumb over her papery
blue cheek. "Did you lose a bet or something?"

She rested her head against his chest. "It's been a really bad
couple of months. Could you just hold me?"

"I could do that." He pulled her close, and they stood like
that for a while, surrounded by a pool of light from the copper
porch fixtures. "A paintball game gone bad?" he finally asked.

She gripped him tighter. "An acid treatment. It burned so
bad. I thought maybe I could . . . peel away the old me."

He rubbed the back of her neck. "Let's sit over there so
you can tell me all about it."

She snuggled closer. "Okay. But don't let me go."

"I won't." True to his word, he kept his arm around her as he drew her across the street to the tiny neighborhood park with its single green iron bench. Even before they reached it, she began to talk, and as the dry leaves blew over their shoes, she told him everything: about the marshmallow chicks, about her acid peel, about Heath and Annabelle. She told him about getting fired as a mentor and about her fear.

"I'm scared all the time, Bodie. All the time."

He stroked her matted hair. "I know, babe. I know."

"I love you. Do you know that, too?"

"That I didn't know." He kissed the top of her head. "But I'm glad to hear it."

The tail of her scarf blew across her cheek. "Do you love me?"

"I'm afraid so."

She smiled. "Will you marry me?"

"Let me see if I can make it through the next few months without killing you first."

"Okay." She cuddled closer. "You might have noticed I'm not the most nurturing person."

"In your own odd way, you are." He pushed her scarf aside. "I still can't believe you had the guts to come out looking like this."

"I had a job to do."

"I love a woman who's willing to take one for the team."

She heard only awe in his voice, and it made her love him even more. "I have to make this match, Bodie."

"Haven't you learned enough yet about the perils of ruth-less ambition?"

"It's not exactly what you're thinking. The best part of me wants to do this for Heath. But I want to go out on a high note, too. One last match—this match—and then I'm selling my business."

"Really?"

"I need a new challenge."

"Lord, help us."

"I mean it, Bodie. I want to run free. Be wild. I want to go where my passion leads me. I want to work hard at something that only the strongest woman in the world can do."

"Okay, now I'm scared."

"I want to eat. Really eat. And to be kinder and more generous. Real generosity, without expecting anything in return. I want to have great skin when I'm eighty. And I don't ever again want to care what anybody thinks. Except you."

"Oh, God, I'm so turned on right now I'm going to explode." Abruptly, he pulled her from the bench. "Let's go back to my place. Now."

"Only if you promise not to tell me any of those bag-over-the-head sex jokes."

"I'll cut an airhole in it."

She smiled. "You know I have no sense of humor."

"We'll work on it." And then he kissed her, blue lips and all.

Even before he hit the shower on Monday morning, Heath started working the phones. He was hung over, nauseated, scared, and exuberant. Portia's shock therapy had made him face what his subconscious had known for a long time but his fear had kept him from acknowledging, that he loved Annabelle with all his heart. Everything Portia said had struck home. Fear had been his enemy, not love. If he hadn't been so busy measuring his character with a crooked ruler, he might have understood what was missing from inside him. He'd taken pride in his work ethic and his intellectual dexterity, in his incisiveness and his high tolerance for risk, but he'd failed to acknowledge that his crapped-up childhood had left him an emotional coward. As a result, he'd been living half a life. Maybe having Annabelle at his side would finally let him relax into becoming the man he'd never quite had the courage to be. But before that could happen, he had to find her.

She wasn't answering either her home phone or her cell, and he soon discovered her friends wouldn't talk to him either. After a quick shower, he got hold of Kate. First she reamed his ass, then she acknowledged that Annabelle had called on Sunday morning to say she was okay, but she hadn't been willing to tell her mother where she was.

"I'm personally blaming you for this," Kate said. "Annabelle is extremely sensitive. You should have realized that."

"Yes, ma'am. And as soon as I find her, I promise I'll set this right."

That softened her up enough to divulge that the Granger brothers were gunning for him, so he'd better watch himself. He loved those guys.

He set off for Wicker Park. Messages were coming in fast and furiously from his office, but he ignored them. For the first time in his career, he hadn't contacted a single client to talk about yesterday's game. He didn't intend to either, not until he'd found Annabelle.

Wind whistled off the lake, and the cloudy October morning held a chill. He pulled into the alley behind Annabelle's house and found the sporty new silver Audi TT Roadster he'd ordered for her birthday, but not her Crown Vic. Mr. Bronicki spotted him right away and came over to see what Heath was up to, but other than passing on the information that Annabelle had driven off like a crazy person Saturday night, he had nothing more to add. He did, however, want to know about the Audi, and when he learned it was a birthday gift, he told Heath he'd better not be expecting any "relations" with her in exchange for the fancy wheels.

"Just because her grammie's not around don't mean people aren't watching out for her."

"Tell me about it," Heath muttered.

"What's that you say?"

"I said, I'm in love with her." He liked the way the words sounded, and he said them again. "I love Annabelle, and I plan to marry her." If he could find her. And if she'd still have him.

Mr. Bronicki scowled. "Just make sure she don't raise her rates. A lot of people are on a fixed income, you know."

"I'll do my best."

After Mr. Bronicki had parked the Audi in his garage for safekeeping, Heath circled the house and pounded on the front door, but it was closed up tighter than a drum. He pulled out his phone and decided to try Gwen again, but got her husband instead. "No, Annabelle didn't spend the night here," Ian said. "Dude, you'd better watch your back. She talked to somebody in the book club yesterday, and the women are pissed. Here's a word of advice, chump. Most women aren't too anxious to marry a guy who's not in love with them, no matter how much hair he's got."

"I *am* in love with her!"

"Tell her, not me."

"I'm trying to, damn it. And I can't tell you how comforting it is to know that everybody in the city is in on my private business."

"You brought it on yourself. The price of stupidity."

Heath hung up and tried to think, but until he could get somebody to talk to him, he was screwed. As he stood on Annabelle's porch, he flicked through his messages. None of them were from her. Why the hell couldn't everybody leave him alone? He rubbed his jaw and realized he'd forgotten to shave for the second day in a row, and with the way he was dressed, he'd be lucky if he didn't get arrested for vagrancy, but he'd pulled on the first things he grabbed: designer navy slacks, a ripped black-and-orange Bengals T-shirt, and a paint-smeared red Cardinals windbreaker Bodie had picked up somewhere and left in his closet.

Finally, he got hold of Kevin. "It's Heath. Have you—"

"All I'm saying is this . . . For a supposedly bright guy, you're—"

"I know, I know. Did Annabelle spend the night at your house?"

"No, and I don't think she was with any of the other women either."

Heath sank down on Annabelle's front step. "You've got to find out where she went."

"You think they'd tell me? The girls have a big NO BOYS ALLOWED sign plastered all over their little pink clubhouse."

"You're my best shot. Come on, Kev."

"All I know is that the book club is meeting at one o'clock today. Phoebe takes Mondays off during the season, and it's at her house. Molly's been making leis, so they've got some kind of Hawaiian theme going."

Annabelle loved the book club. Of course, she'd be there. She'd run to those women for comfort and support as fast as those small feet would carry her. They'd give her what she wasn't getting from him.

"One more thing," Kevin said. "Robillard's been calling everybody trying to get hold of you."

"He can wait."

"Did I hear you right?" Kevin said. "This is Dean Robillard we're talking about. Apparently, after months of screwing around, he's developed an urgent need for an agent."

"I'll get to him later." Heath headed for the street and his car.

"Would that be about the same time you get around to congratulating me on yesterday's game, arguably the best of my career?"

"Yeah, congratulations. You're the best. I've got to go."

"Okay, slimeball, I don't know who you are or what you're up to, but put my agent back on the phone right now."

Heath hung up. And then it hit him. He'd seen Dean's

number on his phone log, but he'd been ignoring the calls. What if Annabelle hadn't spent the last two nights with one of her girl-friends? What if she'd gone running to her pet quarterback?

Dean picked up his phone on the second ring. "Daffy Dan's Porno Palace."

"Is Annabelle with you?"

"Heathcliff? Damn, man, you really screwed her over."

"I know that, but how do you know it?"

"Phoebe's secretary."

"Are you sure it wasn't Annabelle who told you? Has she been with you?"

"I haven't seen her or talked to her, but if I do, I'm going to strongly suggest she tell you to—"

"I love her!" Heath hadn't meant to shout, but he couldn't stop himself, and the woman who'd just emerged from the house across the street scurried back inside. "I love her," he re-peated in a voice that was only marginally quieter, "and I need to tell her that. But I have to find her first."

"I doubt she'll call me. Not unless that pregnancy test—"

"I'm warning you, Robillard, if I find out you know where she went, and you aren't telling me, I'll break every goddamn bone in that million-dollar shoulder of yours."

"The boy's talkin' smack, and it's not even lunchtime. You are so whipped. Now here's the thing, Heathcliff, the reason I've been calling you. A couple of high rollers at Pepsico con-tacted me, and—"

Heath hung up on God's gift to the NFL, hit the button to unlock his car, and set off for the Loop and Birdcage Press. The book club meeting wasn't scheduled until one, which gave him time to cover an extra base.

"I spoke with Molly this morning." Annabelle's former fiancé surveyed Heath's unshaven jaw and mismatched outfit from behind her desk in the marketing department of Molly's publishing company. "I hurt Annabelle more than enough. Did you have to dump on her, too?"

Rosemary wasn't the most attractive woman Heath had ever seen, but she was well dressed and dignified. Way too dignified. Completely the wrong person for Annabelle. What the hell had she been thinking? "I didn't set out to dump on her."

"I'm sure you thought you were doing her a huge favor when you proposed," Rosemary drawled. Then she proceeded to blister Heath with a way too insightful lecture on male insensitivity, exactly what he didn't need to hear right now. He escaped as quickly as he could.

As he made his way back to his car, he saw that half a dozen more calls had come in, none of them from the person he wanted to talk to. He tore the parking ticket off his windshield and headed for the Ike. By the time he reached the expressway, his stomach was a mass of knots. He told himself she'd come home sooner or later, that this wasn't an emergency. But nothing could still his sense of urgency. She was in pain because of him—suffering from his stupidity—and that was intolerable.

He hit a traffic backup on the East West Tollway and didn't reach the Calebow house until one-fifteen. He scanned the cars lining the driveway for an ugly green Crown Victoria, but Annabelle's car was MIA. Maybe she'd ridden with somebody else. But as he rang the bell, he couldn't shake off a sense of foreboding.

The door swung open, and he gazed down at Pippi Tucker. Stumpy blond pigtails stuck out on each side of her head, and she held a menagerie of stuffed animals against her flat chest. "Pwince! I didn't go to preschool today 'cause my school got busted water pies."

"Is that right? Is, uh, Annabelle here?"

"I been playing with Hannah's stuffed animals. Hannah's at school. She don't have busted water pies. Can I see your phone?"

"Pip?" Phoebe appeared in the hallway. She wore black slacks and a purple turtleneck draped with a blue and yellow paper lei. She took in Heath's unkempt appearance through a pair of rimless half glasses. "I hope the police caught whoever mugged you."

Pippi hopped up and down. "Pwince is here!"

"I see." Phoebe set her hand on the child's shoulder without taking her eyes off Heath. "Did you come all the way out here to gloat? I wish I were a big enough person to congratulate you on your new client, but I'm not."

He wedged past her into the foyer. "Is Annabelle here?"

She pulled off her glasses. "Go ahead. Tell me all the ways you plan to bankrupt me."

"I don't see her car."

Her cat's eyes narrowed. "You've talked to Dean, right?"

"Yeah, but he didn't know where Annabelle was." Grilling Phoebe was a waste of time, and he headed for the living room, which was spacious and rustic, with exposed beams and a loft. The book club had gathered in a nook beneath it, all of them except Annabelle. Even casually dressed and draped in paper leis, they were an intimidating bunch of women, and as he crossed the room, he felt their eyes on him like hypodermics. "Where is she? And don't tell me you don't know."

Molly uncrossed her legs and rose. "We do know, and we've been ordered to keep our mouths shut. Annabelle wants time to herself."

"She just thinks she does. I have to talk to her."

Gwen regarded him over her enormous stomach like a hostile Buddha. "Are you planning to give her more reasons she should marry a man who doesn't love her?"

"It's not like that." He gritted his teeth. "I do love her. I love her with all my frickin' heart, but I can't convince her of that if somebody won't tell me where the hell she's gone."

He hadn't meant to sound so angry, and Charmaine took offense. "When did you have this miraculous realization?"

"Last night. A blue woman and a bottle of scotch opened my eyes. Now where is she?"

"We're not going to tell you," said Krystal.

Janine glared at him. "If she calls, we'll relay your message. And we'll also tell her we don't like your attitude."

"I'll relay my own damned message," he retorted.

"Not even the great Heath Champion can bulldoze his way through this." Molly's quiet stubbornness sent a chill up his spine. "Annabelle will contact you in her own way and in her own time. Or maybe not. That's up to her. I know it goes against your nature, but you'll have to be patient. She's calling the shots now."

"It's not as though you won't be busy," Lady Evil drawled from behind him. "Now that Dean has turned his back on the goodwill of the woman who holds his contract—"

He spun on her. "I don't give a damn about Dean right now, Phoebe, and here's a news flash. Some things in life are more important than football."

Her eyebrows rose ever so slightly. He turned back to the women, ready to strangle the information out of them if he needed to, only to discover he had no anger left. He lifted his hands, shocked to see they were unsteady, but not as unsteady as his voice. "She's . . . I—I have to make this right. I can't stand knowing she's . . . That I've made her suffer. Please . . ."

But they had no hearts, and one by one, they looked away.

He walked blindly out of the house. The wind had picked up, and a blast of chilly air cut through his jacket. Mechanically, he reached for his phone, hoping against hope that she'd called, knowing she hadn't.

The Chiefs were trying to reach him. So were Bodie and Phil Tyree. He set the heels of his hands on the hood of his car and bowed his head. He deserved to suffer. She didn't.

"Are you sad, Pwince?"

He looked back toward the house to see Pippi standing on the top step of the porch, a monkey under one arm, a bear under the other. He fought a wild urge to pick her up and carry her around for a while, to tuck her under his chin and hold her close, just like one of those stuffed animals. He drew in a little air. "Yeah, Pip. I'm kind of sad."

"You gonna cry?"

He pushed his response around the lump in his throat. "Naw, guys don't cry."

The door behind her opened, and Phoebe emerged, blond, powerful, and merciless. She paid no attention to him. Instead, she crouched at Pippi's side and adjusted one of her pigtail stubs, speaking softly to her. He reached in his pocket for his keys.

Phoebe headed back into the house. Pippi dropped her stuffed animals and scampered down the steps. "Pwince! I gotta tell you something." She ran toward him, pink sneakers flying. When she reached his side, she tilted her head back to gaze up at him. "I gotta secret."

He crouched next to her. She smelled innocent. Like crayons and fruit juice. "Yeah?"

"Aunt Phoebe said don't tell nobody but you, not even Mommy."

He glanced toward the porch, but Phoebe had disappeared. "Tell me what?"

"Belle!" Pippi grinned. "She went to our campground!"

A surge of adrenaline shot through his veins. His head reeled. He pulled Pippi off her feet, drew her against him, and kissed the hell out of her cheeks. "Thanks, sweetheart. Thanks for telling me."

She cupped his jaw and pushed him away with a frown. "Scratchy."

He laughed, gave her another kiss for good measure, and set her back on her feet. He'd forgotten to turn his phone off, and it rang. Her eyes widened. He automatically reached for it. "Champion."

"Heathcliff, I need an agent, man," Dean barked, "and I swear to God, if you hang up on me again—"

He thrust his phone to Pippi. "Talk to the nice man, sweetheart. Tell him all about how your daddy's the greatest quarterback who'll ever play the game."

As he pulled out of the driveway, he watched Pippi heading back to the porch, his phone pressed to her ear, her pigtails twitching while she chatted away for all she was worth.

Inside the house, the front draperies moved, and through the window, he glimpsed the most powerful woman in the NFL. Maybe it was his imagination, but it looked like she was smiling.

Chapter Twenty-four

❦

Heath reached the Wind Lake Campground a little before midnight. Only the watery glow of the Victorian streetlamps on the commons and the single porch light at the bed-and-breakfast shone through the rain-swept darkness. His wiper blades beat at the Audi's windshield. The unheated cottages sat empty and shuttered for the season. Even the caged yellow dock lights in the distance had been turned off. He'd originally planned to fly, but foul weather had closed the small airport, and he hadn't been patient enough to wait out the delay. He should have, because the storm had stretched the eight-hour trip to ten.

He'd gotten a late start leaving Chicago. Not having Annabelle's engagement ring in his pocket bothered him—he wanted to give her something tangible—so he'd driven back to Wicker Park to pick up her new car. Maybe she couldn't wear it on her finger, but at least she'd see how serious he was. Unfortunately, the Audi Roadster hadn't been built for a six-footer, and after ten hours, he had stiff legs, a cramped neck, and a killer headache he'd been feeding with black coffee. Ten Disney

balloons bobbed in the backseat. He'd seen them tied together
when he'd stopped for gas and impulsively bought them. For
the last sixty miles, Dumbo and Cruella De Vil had been slapping the back of his head.

Through the rain-drenched windshield, he made out a row
of empty rocking chairs swaying on the front porch. Even
though the cottages were closed up, Kevin had told him the
B&B did a decent business this time of year with tourists searching for fall foliage, and the Roadster's headlights picked out
half a dozen cars parked off to the side. But Annabelle's Crown
Vic wasn't one of them.

The Audi lurched in a rain-filled pothole as Heath turned
into the lane that ran parallel to the dark lake. Not for the first
time did it occur to him that setting off for the north woods
based on information fed to a three-year-old from a woman
who held a giant grudge against him might not have been his
smartest move, but he'd done it anyway.

He hit the brakes as his headlights picked out what he'd
spent the last ten hours praying to see: Annabelle's car, parked in
front of Lilies of the Field. Relief made him light-headed. As
he pulled up behind the Crown Vic, he gazed through the rain
at the darkened cottage and fought the urge to wake her and set
things straight. He was in no condition to negotiate his future
happiness until he'd had a few hours' sleep. The B&B was
closed up for the night, and he couldn't stay in town, not when
Annabelle might decide to take off before he got back. Only
one thing to do . . .

He backed the Audi around until it blocked the lane. Once
he was satisfied she couldn't get out, he turned off the ignition,
shoved Daffy Duck out of his way, and tilted the seat all the
way back. But despite his exhaustion, he didn't immediately
drift off to sleep. Too many voices from the past. Too many re-
minders of all the ways love had kicked him in the teeth . . .
every damn time.

• • •

The cold awakened Annabelle even before her alarm, which she'd set for six. During the night, the temperature had dropped, and the blanket she'd pulled over herself couldn't ward off the morning chill. Molly had told her to stay in the Tuckers' private quarters at the B&B instead of an unheated cottage, but Annabelle had wanted the solitude of Lilies of the Field. Now she regretted it.

The hot water had been turned off last week, and she splashed cold on her face. After she helped serve breakfast to the guests, she'd treat herself to a long soak in Molly's tub. Yesterday, she'd volunteered to help with breakfast when the girl who usually worked the morning shift had fallen ill. A small but welcome distraction.

She gazed at the hollow-eyed face in the mirror. Pitiful. But every tear she shed here at the campground was a tear she wouldn't have to shed when she got back to the city. This was her time to mourn. She didn't intend to make a career out of being miserable, but she wouldn't beat herself up for hiding out, either. She'd fallen in love with a man who was incapable of loving her back. If a woman couldn't cry about that, she didn't have a heart.

Turning away, she snagged her hair into a ponytail, then slipped into jeans and sneakers, along with the warm sweater she'd borrowed from Molly's closet. She let herself out through the back door. The storm had finally blown off, and her breath made frosty clouds in the cold, clean air as she walked down the path to the lake. The soggy carpet of leaves sucked at her sneakers, and the trees dripped on her head, but seeing the lake in the early morning lifted her spirits, and she didn't care if she got wet.

Coming up here had been a good decision. Heath was a powerful salesman, and he saw every obstacle as a challenge. He'd be gunning for her when she got back, trying to convince her she should be satisfied with the place he wanted to relegate her to in his life—behind his clients and his meetings, his phone calls and his grueling ambition. She couldn't return until she had all her defenses firmly in place.

Fingers of mist rose from the water, and a pair of snow-white egrets fed near the bank. Through the weight of her sadness, she struggled to find a few moments of peace. Five months ago, she might have settled for Heath's emotional left-overs, but not now. Now, she knew she deserved better. For the first time in her life, she had a clear vision of who she was and what she wanted from her life. She was proud of everything she'd accomplished with Perfect for You, proud of building something good. But she was even more proud of herself for refusing to accept second best from Heath. She deserved to love openly and joyously—no holds barred—and to be loved the same way in return. With Heath, that wouldn't be possible. As she turned away from the lake, she knew she'd done the right thing. For now, that was her only comfort.

When she reached the B&B, she pitched in to help. As the guests began filling the dining room, she poured coffee, fetched baskets of warm muffins, replenished the serving dishes on the sideboard, and even managed to crack a joke. By nine o'clock, the dining room had emptied out, and she set off back toward the cottage. Before she took her bath, she'd make her business calls. A master executive had taught her the value of personal contact, and she had clients who depended on her.

Ironic how much she'd learned from Heath, including the importance of following her own vision instead of someone else's. Perfect for You would never make her rich, but bringing people together was what she'd been born to do. All kinds of people. Not just the beautiful and accomplished, but the awkward and insecure, the hapless and obtuse. And not only the young. Unprofitable or not, she could never abandon her seniors. Being a matchmaker was messy, unpredictable, and demanding, but she loved it.

She reached the deserted beach and paused for a moment.

Pulling her sweater closer, she walked out onto the dock. The lake was quiet without its summer visitors, and the memories of the night she and Heath had danced in the sand washed over her. She sat down at the end and drew her knees to her chest. Twice she'd fallen for damaged men. But not ever again.

Footsteps sounded on the dock behind her. One of the guests. She pressed her wet cheek to her knee, blotting her tears.

"Hello, sweetheart."

Her head came up, and her heart lurched. He'd found her. She should have known.

"I used your toothbrush," he said from behind her. "I was going to use your razor until I figured out there wasn't any hot water." His voice sounded rusty, as if he hadn't spoken for a while.

Slowly she turned. Her eyes widened in shock. He was mismatched, unkempt, and unshaven. Beneath a ratty red windbreaker, he wore a faded orange T-shirt and navy slacks that looked as though he'd slept in them. He held a bunch of Disney balloons in his hand. Goofy had deflated and hung against his leg, but he didn't seem to notice. Between the balloons and his dishevelment, he should have looked ridiculous. But with the polished veneer he'd worked so hard to obtain stripped away, she felt even more threatened.

"You shouldn't have come here," she heard herself say. "This is a waste of time."

He cocked his head and gave her his huckster's smile. "Hey, this is supposed to be like in *Jerry Maguire*. Remember? 'You had me at hello.'"

"Skinny women are pushovers."

His phony charm evaporated like the helium in the Goofy balloon. He shrugged, took a step closer. "My real name's Harley. Harley D. Campione. Take a guess what the *D* stands for?"

He'd mow her down if she didn't keep swinging. "Dumb ass?"

"It stands for Davidson. Harley Davidson Campione. How

do you like that? My old man loved a good joke, as long as it wasn't on him."

She wouldn't let him play on her sympathies. "Go away, Harley. We've both said everything we needed to."

He stuffed his free hand in the pocket of his windbreaker. "I used to fall in love with his girlfriends. He was a good-looking guy, and he knew how to turn on the charm when he felt like it, so there was a whole slew of them. Every time he brought a new one home, I let myself believe she'd be the one who'd stick, that finally he'd settle down and act like a father. There was this one woman . . . Carol. She made noodles from scratch. Rolled the dough out with a pop bottle and let me cut it into these little strips. Best thing I ever tasted in my life. Another—her name was Erin—she'd drive me wherever I wanted to go. She forged his name on a permission slip so I could play Pop Warner football. When she left, I lost my ride, and I had to walk four miles to practice if nobody picked me up on the highway. That turned out to be a good thing, though. I ended up with a lot more endurance than the other guys. I wasn't the strongest, and I wasn't the fastest, but I never gave up, and that was a powerful life lesson."

"Sometimes knowing when to give up is the real test of character."

She might as well not have spoken. "Joyce, she taught me how to smoke and a few other things she shouldn't have, but she had some problems, and I try not to hold it against her."

"It's too late for this."

"The thing is . . ." He looked at the dock, not at her, and studied the boards at his feet. "Sooner or later, every one of those women I loved left. I don't know. Maybe I wouldn't be where I am today if one of them had stuck." As he gazed back up at her, his old belligerence returned. "I learned early on that nobody was going to hand me anything. It made me tough."

But no tougher than she was. She steeled herself and rose to her feet. "You deserved a better childhood, but I can't change what happened. Those years shaped who you are. I can't fix that. And I can't fix you."

"I don't need to be fixed anymore. That job's already been done. I love you, Annabelle."

The pain was nearly more than she could bear. He was only saying what he knew she wanted to hear, and she didn't believe him, not for a second. His words were carefully calculated, chosen for the sole purpose of closing a deal. "No, you really don't," she managed. "You just hate not getting your way."

"It's not that."

"Winning is everything to you. The joy of the kill is your life's blood."

"Not when it comes to you."

"Don't do this! It's cruel. You know who you are." Her eyes filled with tears. "But I know who I am, too. I'm a woman who won't settle for second place. I want the best," she said softly. "And you're not it."

He looked as though she'd slapped him. Despite her own pain, she hadn't wanted to hurt him, but one of them needed to speak the truth. "I'm sorry," she whispered. "I won't spend my life waiting around for your leftovers. This time persistence isn't going to get the job done."

He didn't try to stop her as she left the dock. When she reached the sand, she crisscrossed her sweater over her chest and hurried toward the woods, ordering herself not to look back. But as she stepped onto the path, she couldn't help herself.

The dock stood empty. Everything still. The only movement came from a bunch of balloons drifting off into the bleak October sky.

It didn't take her long to pack. A tear dripped on her hand as she zipped the suitcase. She was so sick of crying. She picked up the bag and made her way numbly out the front door. With each step she took, she reminded herself that she'd never give up who she was for anyone. She came to a dead stop. Especially not for a man who'd blocked in her car with a sporty silver Audi . . .

He'd done a good job of it. A giant oak kept her from moving forward, and the Audi prevented her from going in reverse. The temporary Illinois tags left no doubt whose work this was. She couldn't bear another encounter with him, and she dragged her suitcase back inside the cottage, but she'd barely set it down before she heard tires on gravel. She went to the window, but it wasn't Heath. Instead, she glimpsed a dark blue sports car coming to a stop behind the Audi. The woods extended just far enough to block her view of whichever guest had decided to explore the campground.

It was all too much. She sank down on the couch and buried her face in her hands. Why did he have to make everything harder?

Light footsteps tapped on the porch, too light to be Heath's. She heard a knock. Dragging her feet, she rose, crossed the room, opened the door . . . and screamed. To her credit, it wasn't a horror movie scream, more of a yelpy kind of gaspy thing.

"I know," a familiar voice said. "I've had better days."

Annabelle took an involuntary step backward. "You're blue."

"A cosmetic procedure. It's beginning to peel. May I come in?"

Annabelle moved aside. Even without her blue face, which had begun to crack like a cheap alligator purse, Portia hardly looked her best. Her inky hair lay flat against her head, clean but not styled. Her white sweater had a fresh coffee stain on the front. She'd gained weight, and her jeans were a size too tight.

Portia took in the cottage. "Have you talked to Heath?"

"What are you doing here?"

Portia walked toward the kitchen and poked her head in and out. "Claiming my last introduction. You chose Delaney Lightfield. I choose you. Welcome to Power Matches. Let's see if we can find you some makeup? And a decent outfit wouldn't hurt, either."

"You're nuts."

She gave Annabelle a surprisingly cheerful smile. "Yes, but not as nutty as I used to be. It's interesting. Once you've terrified a restaurant full of people—a Burger King near Benton Harbor—you're basically liberated from ever again worrying about keeping up appearances."

"You went into a Burger King looking like this?"

"Potty stop. Plus Bodie dared me."

"Bodie?"

She smiled, her blue lips making her very nice teeth look a little yellow. "We're lovers. More than lovers. In love. Bizarre, I know, but I've never been happier. We're getting married. Well, he hasn't agreed yet, but he will." She studied Annabelle more closely and frowned. "From those red eyes, I can see you talked with Heath and that it didn't go well."

"It went very well. I told him no and walked away."

Portia threw up her hands. "Why am I not surprised? Well, as of now, playtime is over. You amateurs have had your fun, but it's time to step aside and let a professional handle this."

"You have clearly lost your mind, not to mention your looks."

Surprisingly, Portia didn't take offense. "My looks will be back in spades. Wait till you see what's underneath all this."

"I'll have to take your word for it."

"I told Heath not to talk to you without me, but he's pigheaded. And you . . . Of all people, you should have known to be more sensitive. Haven't you learned anything about this business? Two different men have ordered me not to call you a twit, but, honestly, Annabelle, if the shoe fits . . ."

She marched to the door. "Thanks for stopping by. Sorry you have to leave so soon."

Portia sat on the arm of the couch. "Do you have any idea how much courage it took for him to accept the fact that he's fallen in love with you, let alone to come here and lay his heart on the line? And what did you do? Tossed his feelings right back in his face, didn't you? Extremely unwise, Annabelle, especially with Heath. He's very emotionally insecure. From what Bodie's told me, I suspect that's exactly what his subconscious expected you to do, and I don't think he'll have the guts to ask you again."

"Insecure? He's the cockiest man in the universe." But Portia had shaken her confidence, and the floor no longer felt quite so steady. "He doesn't love me," Annabelle said more forcefully. "He just can't stand hearing anybody say no to him."

"You're so wrong." A voice spoke from behind her. She whipped around to see Bodie framed in the door. Unlike Portia, he was pulled together from head to toe in a gray sweater, great fitting jeans, and motorcycle boots.

Annabelle went on the attack. "Did Heath send you to talk to me? It would be just like him to delegate another one of those messy personal tasks he dislikes so much."

"She's a bit of a bitch," Portia said to Bodie, as if Annabelle weren't in the room.

He lifted an eyebrow. "Babe."

Portia held out her hand. "I know, I know . . . If she were a man, she'd be labeled aggressive. But honestly, Bodie, sometimes a bitch is just a bitch."

"Exactly."

Portia seemed amused. "Point taken."

He chuckled, and Annabelle began to feel like a tagalong at her own crisis. Bodie finally managed to drag his eyes away from Blue Girl. "Heath doesn't know either one of us is here. I only found out where he'd gone through an accidental telephone conversation I had with Kevin's kid." He slipped his arm around Portia's shoulders. "The thing is, Annabelle . . . What if Portia's right? And, let's face it, she has more experience with this kind of crap than you do. Just because she has a history of screwing up her own life—which I'm happy to say she's working through—doesn't mean she hasn't made a success out of other peoples' lives. Bottom line—there's a fairly simple way to settle this."

Fighting both of them had exhausted her already diminished resources, and Annabelle slumped into the sofa. "Nothing's simple when it comes to that man."

"This time it is," he said. "I caught a glimpse of him heading for that path that goes around the lake."

The same path she'd planned to walk this afternoon.

"Go after him," Bodie said, "and when you find him, ask him two questions. When you hear his answers, you'll know exactly what to do."

"Two questions?"

"That's right. And I'm going to tell you exactly what they are . . ."

Water from the soggy leaves seeped into Annabelle's sneakers, and her teeth had begun to chatter, more from nerves, she suspected, than the chill. She might be making the worst mistake of her life. She couldn't see anything special about the questions Bodie had posed, but he'd been adamant. As for Portia . . . The woman was scary. Annabelle wouldn't have been surprised to see her pull a handgun from her purse. Portia and Bodie were the weirdest couple she'd ever seen, and yet they seemed to understand each other perfectly. Apparently, Annabelle had a lot more to learn about being a matchmaker. She had to admit Portia was growing on her. How could you hate a woman who was so willing to put herself on the line?

The path grew steeper as it climbed toward the rocky bluff that jutted over the water. Molly said she and Kevin came here sometimes to dive. Annabelle paused as she rounded the bend to catch her breath. That was when she saw Heath. He stood on the rocky ledge gazing out at the lake, his jacket pushed back, his fingertips stuffed in his back pockets. Even unkempt and disheveled, he was magnificent, an alpha male at the top of every game he played, except the most important one.

He heard her footsteps and turned his head. Slowly, his hands dropped to his sides. In the distance, she saw a tiny speck in the sky. The balloons drifting away. It didn't seem like a comforting omen. "I need to ask you two questions," she said.

His stance, his shuttered expression, everything about him reminded her of the way the cottages had been closed up for the winter—no hot water, curtains drawn, doors locked. "All right," he said tonelessly.

Her heart hammered as she stepped around the NO DIVING sign. "First question. Where's your cell?"

"My cell? Why do you care?"

She wasn't sure. What difference could it make which pocket he'd stashed it in? Still, Bodie had insisted she ask.

"Last time I saw it," Heath said, "Pip had it."

"You let her steal another phone?"

"No, I gave it to her."

She swallowed and stared at him. This was getting serious. "You gave her your cell? Why?"

"Is this the second question?"

"No. Scratch that. The second question is . . . Why haven't you returned Dean's calls?"

"I returned one of them, but he didn't know where you were."

"So why did he call you in the first place?"

"What is this, Annabelle? Frankly, I'm getting tired of everybody acting like the world revolves around Dean Robillard. Just because he's developed this sudden need for an agent doesn't mean I have to jump to attention. I'll get to him when I get to him, and if that's not good enough, he has IMG's phone number."

Her legs gave out from under her, and she sank down on the nearest rock. "Oh, my God. You really do love me."

"I already told you that," he retorted.

"You did, didn't you?" She couldn't get her breath back.

Finally, he grew aware that something had changed. "Annabelle?"

She tried to answer, really she did, but he'd once again turned her world upside down, and her tongue wouldn't cooperate.

Hope battled against the wariness in his eyes. His lips barely moved. "You believe me?"

"Uh-huh." Her hammering heart created a ripple effect, and she had to clasp her hands to keep them from shaking.

"You do?"

She nodded.

"You're going to marry me?"

She nodded again, and that was all he needed. With a low moan, he pulled her to her feet and kissed her. Seconds . . . hours . . . she had no idea how long the kiss lasted, but he covered a lot of territory: lips, tongue, and teeth; her cheeks and eyelids; her neck. His hands reached under her sweater for her breasts; she fumbled beneath his jacket to touch his bare chest.

She barely remembered how they made it back to the empty cottage, only that her heart was singing and she couldn't move fast enough to keep up with him. Finally, he swept her into his arms and carried her. She threw back her head and laughed at the sky.

They undressed, their urgency making them awkward as they kicked away muddy shoes and wet jeans, hopped awkwardly to shake off clammy socks, bumped into furniture, into each other. She was shivering with cold by the time he pulled back the covers and drew her with him into the chilly bed. He offered the heat of his body to make the goose bumps disappear, rubbed her arms and the small of her back, suckled the warmth back into her puckered nipples. Eventually, his fevered fingers found the tight folds between her legs and opened them into summer-warmed petals plump with welcoming dew. He claimed every inch of her body with his touch. She gasped as he entered her.

"I love you so much, my sweet, sweet Annabelle," he whispered, everything he felt in his heart spilling into his words.

She laughed with the joy of his invasion and gazed into his eyes. "And I love you."

He groaned, kissed her again, and tilted her hips to take all of him. They abandoned themselves, not in beautifully choreographed lovemaking, but in a messy mating of spunk and juice, of sweet filth, luscious obscenities, of deep and total trust, as pure and sacred as altar vows.

Long afterward, with only cold water to wash themselves, they cursed and laughed and splashed each other, which led them back to bed. They made love for the rest of the afternoon.

As evening fell, a loud knock at the door intruded, followed by Portia's voice. "Room service!"

Heath took his time but eventually wrapped a towel around his hips and went to investigate. He returned with a brown paper grocery bag filled with food. Ravenous, they fed themselves and each other, gorging on roast beef sandwiches, juicy Michigan apples, and a gluey pumpkin pie that tasted like heaven. They washed it all down with lukewarm beer and then, groggy and sated, dozed in each other's arms.

It was dark when Annabelle awakened. Wrapping herself in a quilt, she went into the living room and retrieved her phone. Within seconds, she'd reached Dean's voice mail.

"I know Heath went a little nuts on you, pal, and I apologize for him. The man's in love, so he can't help himself." She smiled. "I promise he'll call first thing tomorrow and set everything straight, so don't you dare talk to IMG before then. I mean it, Dean, if you sign with anybody but Heath, I will never speak to you again. Plus, I'll tell everybody in Chicago that you sleep with a giant poster of yourself right next to your bed. Which you probably do."

She grinned, hung up, and retrieved a tattered pad of yellow lined paper from the drawer, along with a gnawed pencil stub. When she got back to the bedroom, she turned on a lamp and propped herself against the footboard with the quilt wrapped tightly around her. Her feet were freezing, so she slid them under the covers and up against Heath's warm thigh.

He yelped and heaved himself into the pillows. "You will definitely pay for that."

"Here's hoping." She propped the notepad on her quilt-draped knee and drank in the sight of him. He looked like a wicked pirate against the snowy pillowcases. Tan skin, disheveled dark hair, and the marauder's stubble that had chafed various sensitive parts of her body. "Okay, lover, it's time to deal."

He pushed himself higher onto the pillows and gazed at the notepad. "Do we really have to?"

"Are you nuts? You think I'm marrying the Python without an ironclad prenup?"

He fumbled under the covers for her cold foot. "Apparently not."

"First . . ." As he chafed the warmth back into her toes, she wrote on the pad. "There will be no cell phones, BlackBerries, minifaxes, or other as-yet-to-be-invented electronic devices at our dinner table ever."

He rubbed her toes. "What about if we're eating in a restaurant?"

"Especially if we're eating in a restaurant."

"Exempt fast food, and you've got a deal."

She thought it over. "Agreed."

"Now it's my turn." He draped her calf on top of his thigh.

"Selected electronic devices, excluding the aforementioned, will not only be allowed in the bedroom, but will be encouraged. And I get to choose what they are."

"If you don't forget about that catalog . . ."

He gestured toward the notepad. "Write it down."

"Fine." She wrote it down.

The blanket fell to the middle of his chest, momentarily distracting her as he spoke again. "Disagreements over money are the biggest cause of divorce."

She waved her hand. "Absolutely no problem. Your money is our money. My money is my money." She wrote away.

"I should make you negotiate with Phoebe."

She gestured toward his very fine chest with her pencil. "On the off chance I find out after we're married that your declaration of abiding love and devotion has been an elaborate con job perpetrated by you, Bodie, and Scary Spice . . ."

He massaged her arch. "I definitely wouldn't lose too much sleep over that."

"Just in case. You will give me all your worldly goods, shave your head, and leave the country."

"Deal."

"Plus, you have to hand over your Sox tickets so I can burn them in front of your eyes."

"Only if I get something in exchange."

"What?"

"Unlimited sex. How I want it, when I want it, where I want it. The backseat of your shiny new car, on top of my desk . . ."

"Definite deal."

"And kids."

Just like that, she choked up. "Yes. Oh, yes."

Her show of emotion left him unmoved as his eyes narrowed and he dived in for the kill. "We take at least six trips a year to see your family."

She slammed down the notepad. "That is so not going to happen."

"Five trips, and I'll beat up your brothers."

"One."

He dropped her foot. "Damn it, Annabelle, I'll compromise at four trips until the baby's born, then we see them every other month, and that's not negotiable." He grabbed the notepad and pencil and began to write.

"Fine," she retorted. "I'll go to a spa while all of you sit around and complain about the limitations of the sixty-hour workweek."

He laughed. "You are so full of it. You know you can't wait to dangle our firstborn in front of Candace's nose."

"Well, there's that." She paused, took back the notepad, but she couldn't see a word she'd written. As much as she hated letting reality intrude, it was time to get serious. "Heath, how do you plan to be a father to these children we want while you're working that sixty-hour week?" She spoke carefully, wanting to get this right. "With Perfect for You, my hours are flexible, but . . . I know how much you love what you do, and I'd never want you to give it up. On the other hand, I won't raise a family by myself."

"You won't have to," he said smugly. "I have a plan."

"Care to share?"

He reached for her arm, pulled her down next to him, and told her what he had in mind.

"I like your plan." She grinned and curled into his chest. "Bodie deserves to be a full partner."

"I couldn't agree more."

They were both so pleased they started kissing again, which led to a lovely—and very successful—testing of her powers as a dominatrix. As a result, it took a while to get back to their negotiations. They covered sleepwear (none), TV remote control (shared), children's names (no motor vehicles), and baseball (irreconcilable differences). When they finished, Heath remembered there was one question he'd forgotten to ask.

Gazing into her eyes, he drew her fingers to his lips. "I love you, Annabelle Granger. Will you marry me?"

"Harley Davidson Campione, you have got yourself a wife."

"The best deal I've ever made," he replied with a smile.

Epilogue

♥

Pippi lifted the tape recorder to her lips and shouted, "Testing! Testing! Testing!"

"It works," Heath exclaimed from the couch on the other side of his media room. "Do you think you could be a little quieter?"

"My name is Victoria Phoebe Tucker . . . ," she whispered. And then back to her normal volume. "I am five years old, and I live at the Plaza Hotel." She sneaked a look at Heath, but he'd watched the *Eloise* movie with her, and all he did was smile. "This is Prince's tape recorder that he says I *have to give back*."

"Darned right, you do." She was supposed to be watching the Sox game with him while the book club met upstairs, but she'd gotten bored.

"Prince is still mad 'bout all the phones I took when I was *only three*," she said into the tape recorder. "But I was just a baby, and Mommy found most of them and gave them back."

"Not all of them."

"Because I can't remember where I put them!" she exclaimed, shooting him her miniquarterback's glare. "I told you that about a million times." Dismissing him, she returned her attention to what she was doing. "These are the things I love.

I love Mommy and Daddy and Danny and Aunt Phoebe and Uncle Dan and all my cousins and Prince when he doesn't talk about phones and Belle and everybody in the book club except Portia, because she wouldn't let me be a flower girl when she married Bodie because they went to Vegas in an envelope."

Heath laughed. "They *eloped*."

"They eloped," she repeated. "And Belle didn't want Portia in the book club, but Aunt Phoebe *en*-sisted because she said Portia needed . . ." She couldn't remember, and she looked over at Heath.

"Noncompetitive female friendships," he said with a smile. "And, as usual, Aunt Phoebe was right. Which is why I, in my brilliance, convinced Aunt Phoebe to become Portia's mentor."

Pippi nodded and kept chatting. "Prince likes Portia. Portia used to be a matchmaker, but now she works for him, and Prince say she's the best dam' sports agent he's ever seed, and, because of her, their new ladies' sports dibision is getting bigger all the time."

"She's the third best sports agent," he said. "After Bodie and me. And don't say *damn*."

She sank deeper into the big recliner, crossing her ankles just like him. "Prince paid a lot of money to Portia for Belle's wedding present. Mommy said it was a dumb present, but Belle said Prince couldn't have gived her anything she liked more, and now Portia gives Belle advice on how to be a matchmaker." She scrunched her forehead. "What was that thing you gived Belle for her wedding present?"

"Portia's database from her old business."

"You should have gave her a puppy."

Heath laughed, then scowled at the television. "Don't swing at everything, you idiot!"

"I *don't* love the Sox," Pippi said emphatically. "But I love Dr. Adam and Delaney because *they* let me be a flower girl in their wedding, and Belle's mommy cried and said Belle is the best matchmaker in the world. And I love Rosemary 'cause she tells me stories and does makeup. Rosemary's in the book club now. Belle told Aunt Phoebe that if Portia got to be in the book club then Rosemary did, too, 'cause Rosemary needed friends just as much as Portia, and then Belle said she was too happy to hold on to old biddiness."

"Bitterness."

"Here's what I don't love." She shot another dark look at Heath. "I don't love Trevor Granger Champion. Who is a big poopy diaper."

"Here we go again." Heath shifted the bundle in his arms to his shoulder.

She set down the tape recorder, crawled out of the recliner, and climbed on the couch next to him, where she peered with displeasure at the sleeping baby. "Trevor told me he hates it when you carry him around all the time. He says he wants you to put . . . him . . . down!"

Since Trevor was only six months old, Heath doubted his language skills were that advanced, but he muted the volume and turned his attention to the jealous five-year-old. "I thought we talked about this."

She leaned against him. "Talk to me again."

He wrapped his free arm around her shoulders. Pip wasn't content unless she had every male in the free world at her beck and call, which she pretty much did. "Trev is just a baby. He's boring. He can't play with me like you do."

"And he's a big crybaby."

Heath felt a paternal need to defend his son's masculinity. "Only when he's hungry."

Pippi lifted her head. "I hear them moving around upstairs. I think it's time for dessert."

"You sure you don't want to watch the rest of the game with me?"

"Get real." It was her newest expression, and she used it whenever her parents weren't around.

Heath kissed Trevor Granger Champion on his fuzzy head and followed her upstairs.

Annabelle had put her stamp on his house right from the beginning. As he stepped into the living room, he took in the big, cozy furniture, the warm rugs and fresh flowers. A splashy abstract painting they'd bought in a Seattle gallery one rainy afternoon occupied the spot over the fireplace. Afterward, they'd celebrated the purchase with an afternoon of lovemaking they both believed had given them their son.

Beneath the painting, Portia and Phoebe stood with their heads together, probably plotting world domination. Molly bent down to listen to Pippi. The others had congregated around Rosemary. As Annabelle grew aware of his presence, she separated herself from the group and came toward him, that private smile he loved claiming her face. He took in Pip and the book club, then his beautiful red-haired wife. This was what he'd been searching for all his life. Women who'd stick.

"Any chance you can get your coven out of here in the next ten minutes?" he asked in a low voice as she reached his side.

She touched her son's cheek, and the baby instinctively turned toward her hand. "I doubt it. They haven't had dessert."

"Set it on the porch."

"Behave."

"That's what you're saying now," he whispered, "but you'll be singing a different tune later."

She laughed, pressed a quick kiss to the corner of his mouth, then the baby's head. Across the room, Phoebe Calebow caught his eye, and they exchanged a look of perfect understanding. Next week they'd be battling over Dean's new contract, but for now, peace reigned.

While Pip helped Annabelle serve dessert, he carried the baby upstairs to his expanded home office. He let the baby sleep in his lap while he made a few phone calls. With Bodie as a full partner, Heath's workload had lightened considerably. Instead of operating the biggest sports agency in the city, they were focusing on being the best, and they'd become highly selective in choosing their clients. Still, they could only control so much, and under Portia's direction, the new women's division had been growing by leaps and bounds, although she, too, had set limits. It had been a couple of years since he'd seen that pinched, frantic look on her face. Amazing what a good marriage and twenty extra pounds could do for a woman's disposition.

Perfect for You was also thriving. To the relief of Annabelle's seniors, Kate had given her daughter the Wicker Park house as a wedding gift. Acting on Portia's advice, Annabelle had hired both a secretary and an assistant. Ignoring Portia's advice, she continued to cater to a hodgepodge of clients. That was how she liked it.

Finally, he heard the book club beginning to depart. Trev was getting hungry, and the noise awakened him. As soon as the coast was clear, Heath carried him downstairs.

Annabelle stood by the wedge of windows, the afternoon sunlight pouring over her like liquid amber. As she heard him approach, she smiled as though she'd been waiting for this moment all day, which she probably had. He gave her the baby, then sat contentedly to watch his son feed. He and Annabelle talked a little. Not much. Upstairs, he heard his fax chime, and a few minutes later, his cell vibrated. He slipped his hand into his pocket and flicked it off.

Eventually, they bundled up their son, and the three of them went for a walk. A man and his family. A fine Chicago afternoon. The Sox on their way to a pennant.

"Why are you smiling?" his wife asked, with a smile of her own.

"Because you're perfect."

"No, I'm not," she laughed. "But I'm perfect for you."

The Python couldn't have agreed more.

AIN'T SHE SWEET?

In high school, Sugar Carey had reigned supreme. She had broken hearts,
ruined friendships, and destroyed reputations on a whim. But fifteen years
have passed, and life has taught Sugar its toughest lessons. Now she's
come home—broke, desperate, and too proud to show it.

Only the people of Parrish don't believe in forgive and forget.
Especially Colin Byrne. Fifteen years earlier, Sugar had tried to ruin his
career. Now he's rich, powerful, and the owner of her old home. But no
one has reckoned on the unexpected strength of a woman who's learned
survival the hard way. And while Sugar's battered heart struggles to
overcome old mistakes, Colin must choose between payback and love.
Does even the baddest girl in town deserve a second chance...?

978-0-7499-3508-5

DREAM A LITTLE DREAM

Rachel Stone's bad luck has taken a turn for the worse. With an empty
wallet, a car's that's spilling smoke, and a five-year-old son to support,
she's come home to a town that hates her. But this determined young
widow with a scandalous past has learned how to be a fighter.
And she'll do anything to keep her child safe...

Gabe Bonner has just about survived the loss of his wife and child.
Now all he wants is to be left alone, especially by the beautiful outcast
who's invaded his property. Rachel has a ton of attitude, a talent for
trouble, and a child who brings back painful memories. Yet this woman
with nothing left to lose might just be the one person strong enough to
teach a tough, stubborn man how to love again

978-0-7499-3638-9